BEYOND LIMITS

LAURA GRIFFIN

POCKET BOOKS
New York   London   Toronto   Sydney   New Delhi

Pocket Books
A Division of Simon & Schuster, Inc.
1230 Avenue of the Americas
New York, NY 10020

This book is a work of fiction. Any references to historical events, real people, or real places are used fictitiously. Other names, characters, places, and events are products of the author's imagination, and any resemblance to actual events or places or persons, living or dead, is entirely coincidental.

First Pocket Books paperback edition February 2015

POCKET and colophon are registered trademarks of Simon & Schuster, Inc.

For information about special discounts for bulk purchases, please contact Simon & Schuster Special Sales at 1-866-506-1949 or business@simonandschuster.com.

The Simon & Schuster Speakers Bureau can bring authors to your live event. For more information or to book an event, contact the Simon & Schuster Speakers Bureau at 1-866-248-3049 or visit our website at www.simonspeakers.com.

Cover design by Jae Song
Cover image by Maarten Wouters/Getty Images

Manufactured in the United States of America

10 9 8 7 6 5 4 3 2 1

ISBN 978-1-4516-8935-8
ISBN 978-1-4516-8938-9 (ebook)

"[A] perfectly gritty romantic thriller. . . . Griffin sprinkles on just enough jargon to give the reader the feel of being in the middle of an investigation, easily merging high-stakes action and spicy romance with rhythmic pacing and smartly economic prose."

—*Publishers Weekly* (starred review)

"Crisp storytelling, multifaceted characters, and excellent pacing. . . . A highly entertaining read."

—*RT Book Reviews* (4 stars)

"A first-rate addition to the Laura Griffin canon."

—*The Romance Dish* (5 stars)

"Be prepared for heart palpitations and a racing pulse as you read this fantastic novel. Fans of Lisa Gardner, Lisa Jackson, Nelson DeMille, and Michael Connelly will love [Griffin's] work."

—*The Reading Frenzy*

"*Far Gone* is riveting with never-ending action."

—*Single Titles*

Praise for Laura Griffin's Tracers series

"If you like *CSI* and well-crafted suspense, don't miss these books."

—*RT Book Reviews*

"With a taut story line, believable characters, and a strong grasp of current forensic practice, Griffin sucks readers into this drama and doesn't let go."

—*RT Book Reviews* (Top Pick)

UNFORGIVABLE

"The perfect mix of suspense and romance."

—*Booklist*

"The science is fascinating, the sex is sizzling, and the story is top-notch, making this clever, breakneck tale hard to put down."

—*Publishers Weekly*

UNSPEAKABLE

"A page-turner until the last page, it's a fabulous read!"

—*Fresh Fiction*

"Laura Griffin is a master at keeping the reader in complete suspense."

—*Single Titles*

UNTRACEABLE

"Evolves like a thunderstorm on an ominous cloud of evil. . . . Intense, wildly unpredictable, and sizzling with sensuality."

—*The Winter Haven News Chief*

"Taut drama and constant action. . . . Griffin keeps the suspense high and the pace quick."

—*Publishers Weekly* (starred review)

For Janet

Chapter One

The night was all wrong for an op, but they were going anyway, and not a man among them disputed the call.

Lieutenant Derek Vaughn sat wedged between his teammates in the Black Hawk helicopter listening to the thunder of the rotor blades as he pictured the city below. The rugged outpost was hemmed in on either side by mountains. Even by Afghan standards, the place was a hellhole, frequented by opium traders, arms smugglers, and Taliban fighters with Al Qaeda links, including a group that had recently hijacked a caravan of aid workers on their way back from a medical mission in Badakhshan Province.

The hijackers had killed the drivers and taken three hostages, all aid workers. Two were Swedish, and one was American, and both governments were scrambling to resolve the crisis while keeping it under wraps. But the situation had dragged on, which wasn't good. Derek had seen firsthand how TAQ fighters treated their prisoners, and the thought of what those people had likely been through made his blood boil. But he pushed away his anger and focused on his job.

"Five minutes," the crew chief said over the radio.

Derek closed his eyes. He regulated his breathing. He recalled the map of the compound that he and his teammates had memorized during the briefing. Drone photographs had shown two buildings separated by a narrow courtyard. The hostages were thought to be held in the basement of one or both of the houses.

Or so they hoped. Tonight's entire mission was based on a call traced to a phone believed to belong to one of the kidnappers.

One phone call. That was it.

Typically, deploying an entire platoon of SEALs required slightly more intel. But tonight wasn't typical, not by a long shot. Sixteen days ago, the kidnappers had demanded five million dollars in ransom from the international relief org MedAssist. Nine days ago, they'd upped the ante to ten mil. Two days ago, negotiations had broken down, and twenty-four hours ago, MedAssist had received an e-mail. The attached video clip showed twenty-six-year-old Ana Hansson blindfolded and kneeling before the camera, pleading for her life just seconds before her captors slit her throat.

"Four minutes," the crew chief said.

Derek pictured the two remaining hostages. Dr. Peter Lindh of Stockholm was forty-nine and had been in excellent health before his abduction.

Hailey Gardner of Boston had just graduated from nursing school before taking a job with MedAssist. Her passport photo showed a pretty blonde with a wry smile. The photo had immediately reminded Derek of a different woman, a woman he'd been trying to get out of his head for months now. It wasn't the blond hair or the smile but the determined gleam in her eyes that made Derek think of Elizabeth LeBlanc.

As if he needed a reason.

"Three minutes."

Derek snugged his assault gloves onto his hands. *Focus.* Thinking about Elizabeth or anything else besides the op right now was a good way to get his ass shot off. Or one of his teammates'.

The crew chief slid open the door, and the roar from outside cut off all communication. Derek got to his feet and edged closer to the opening, where he could see the valley below bathed in silver. They were infiltrating under a full moon into hostile territory with scant intel to guide their assault. The odds were stacked against them, but Derek knew that every last one of his teammates relished this mission. They'd trained together, fought together, lived, breathed, and bled together for six long months of deployment. On this tour alone, they'd racked up more successful tactical operations than anyone cared to count. But it wasn't every day they got the chance to rescue a civilian from the country they'd sworn their lives to protect and defend.

At the front of the helo, Derek's CO held up two fingers. Two minutes.

Derek pulled down his night-vision goggles, casting everything around him in a greenish hue. He checked his M-4, outfitted with a ten-inch barrel. The weapon was designed for close-quarters combat and had a suppressor to keep the noise down. He also had his Sig Sauer P226 in his thigh holster but didn't expect to use it. Tonight was a straight-up, take-no-prisoners rescue mission. Get in and get out, hopefully before anyone realized they were there.

That was the goal, but everyone knew it wasn't likely to become reality. And they were good with that. SEALs were trained to take whatever shit the mission threw at them and find a way to make a victory out of it.

The helo entered a hover, and the crew chief kicked out the rope attached to the fuselage. Both buildings had rooftop balconies. The pilot would drop off one group here, then the other on the neighboring roof, and each four-man element would assault down. Meanwhile, an armored Humvee would pull up to the compound and unload two more elements to clear from below.

Hit 'em from all directions, a classic SEAL tactic.

They stacked by size, with Derek first, followed by Mike Dietz, the team corpsman. Next was Cole McDermott, their best sharpshooter, who would man the roof. Luke Jones, another medic, would bring up the rear.

Derek grabbed the rope. Across the helo, Sean Harper grinned and shot him the bird.

Go time.

Derek's palms burned as he slid down and hit concrete. Fifty pounds of gear on his back, but he hardly felt the impact as he sprang to his feet and sprinted for the door. They'd expected it to be locked, but the heavy iron grillwork added a complication. Derek grabbed his kit and crouched down to prep a breaching charge. Having been shot at through doors on more than one occasion, he'd learned to do it kneeling.

Brakes screeched below as the Humvee arrived on target. Derek heard a string of pops, like firecrackers, as the other teams dealt with the doors. So much for quiet.

"Going explosive," Derek said, and everyone hunched down.

Pop!

The door burst open, and a barrage of machine-gun fire spewed through the gap. Derek rolled away, breathing hard. Even when you expected it, it was always a shock when bullets whizzed over your head. Luke laid down cover fire as Derek reached into the doorway and pulled away the ruined gate.

They darted through the opening, one, two, three, with perfect coordination born of years of training.

"Room one clear!" Luke shouted, tossing an infra-red chem light to the floor to signal his teammates.

Derek darted past him and cleared the next room. A staccato of bullets echoed in the stairwell.

"This is Alpha," Luke said over the radio. "Level two clear."

"This is Bravo. Level one clear."

Derek rushed down the stairs, stepping over a body as he joined his team. Two tangos lay dead in the middle of the floor, their AKs and chest racks beside them. Derek glanced around. Sleeping pallets, trash, empty food cans. The smell of cooking oil hung in the air.

Mike looked at him. "Notice anything funny?"

"No women, no kids."

Taken with everything else, it confirmed their intel. This was no typical family home.

"This is Delta. House two clear, and we need Dietz over here ASAP."

Mike rushed to answer the call, while across the kitchen, Luke kicked open a door.

"Basement!"

"Check for booby traps," Derek said, following him down a primitive staircase carved from the rock. At the bottom was a door with a heavy-duty lock.

"Need your sledge," Luke said.

Derek was already pulling it from his pack. They couldn't use a breaching charge in case a hostage was being held on the other side. Derek swung back the hammer and gave the door a sharp whack, sending splinters flying as it burst open.

Luke ducked in first. Derek covered him. The room was dark and cold and reeked of urine. In the corner was a shadowy lump with a mop of blond hair. She wasn't moving—not good news, considering all the noise.

"NVGs," Derek said, shoving his night-vision goggles up. Their goggles and greasepaint made them look like alien robots, and they didn't want to scare the hell out of her. Derek switched on the flashlight attached to his helmet as Luke reached to check her pulse. She flinched, then rolled over and suddenly started kicking and screaming like a banshee.

"It's okay, ma'am," Luke said. "Don't be afraid."

More shrieks and kicks.

"Hailey, it's okay."

She went still. Derek aimed the light at her as she cowered back. Dirt smudged her face, and the collar of her shirt was dark with blood. The nasty gash above her eye made Derek's stomach turn.

"I'm Petty Officer Luke Jones, U.S. Navy." He was already digging through his medical kit. "We're here to take you home."

Derek knelt down and looked the woman over. She held her wrist protectively against her body, and it was wrapped with a dirty scrap of cloth. Luke tore open a syringe as Derek peeled away the bandage to reveal an oozing green wound with bone jutting through the skin.

Derek glanced up at her. "We've got a helo coming to give you a ride."

"You're . . . American," she rasped.

"Yep." Derek got rid of the filthy-ass bandage as Luke prepped the shot. "Hey, your Bruins are doing pretty good. We plan to get you home in time for the Cup."

She made a wet, choking sound, and Luke darted him a look. He'd meant to distract her, not make her cry.

"Five minutes!" someone yelled from upstairs.

Derek's radio crackled, and he got to his feet. "Alpha, this is Delta. We need Vaughn or Jones over here."

Derek rushed back upstairs, checking his watch as he went. He'd known Sean since BUD/S training, and he could tell by the tone of his voice that something was very wrong. Probably the hostage. A cold feeling of dread gripped him at the thought of losing another one.

In the courtyard, one of his teammates was building a pile of guns and ammo. The heap of AKs, chest racks, and RPGs took up most of the space. Another pair of guys had already started SSE—sensitive site exploitation—which meant confiscating any potential intelligence, along with fingerprinting and photographing casualties and their weapons, not only for ID purposes but also so that if the mission came to light, the enemy couldn't claim they'd killed a bunch of innocent civilians.

Inside the second building, the SEAL pulling security directed Derek toward a stairwell leading to the basement. Someone had slapped a chem light on the wall with duct tape.

The cavern smelled as rank as the other one. Remnants of a wooden door lay on the floor. Mike emerged from a chamber with the doctor slung over his shoulder in a fireman's carry.

"He's alive," Mike said, answering the unspoken question.

Derek stepped out of his way. "We been on target too long, bro. Need to speed it up."

"Vaughn, get over here."

He followed a narrow corridor and almost stepped on a pair of legs jutting out from the wall. A young man was seated on the floor with his hands zip-cuffed behind him. He wore loose-fitting pants and high-top sneakers and was fifteen, max, but his eyes already had the flat, battle-hardened look of a warrior.

"Found him in the tunnel." Sean nodded toward

a passage that connected the house to who the hell knew what. The tunnel system here was like a rabbit warren.

Derek spotted a workbench littered with electrical wires, nails, several jars of black powder—all bomb components. He scanned the rest of the room, and his gaze came to rest on a large safe in the corner. It was a serious box, definitely imported, and would have been a major pain in the ass to get here.

Now Derek understood why he'd been called over. He glanced at the kid and tried to remember his rudimentary Pashto.

"What's the number?" Derek asked in Pashto, because he didn't know the word for "combination."

The kid didn't answer.

Derek pointed the stock of his gun at the safe. "Open it."

The kid looked away, sullen.

"Fuck this." Sean reached for his kit and got out some C-4.

Derek stepped over to check for booby traps. He didn't see any, but there was only one way to know for sure. Sean set a small charge, and they crossed to the other side of the room. The burst reverberated through the cavern, and they rushed back over.

"Shit, look at all this." Sean pulled out a stack of papers, singed around the edges and still smoking. He flung it to the ground and stomped the fire out as Derek reached in and pulled out a notebook computer.

"Two minutes," the CO said over the radio.

Derek cursed. Even with the extra minutes they'd built into the plan, they were running behind.

Sean was already pulling out his mesh bag, which they carried for this purpose. Some of the papers were in English, but Derek didn't take the time to read them as he jammed everything into the bag. He reached in and snatched a thumb drive as Sean grabbed another batch of papers. Loose pages fluttered to the ground.

His teammate held up a sheet. "Hey, look at this."

"No time to read. We need to move."

"It's a map."

Derek glanced at it. It was in English, with notes scrawled around the edges. Derek scanned the street names. His blood ran cold. He looked at Sean.

"Guys, move it!" someone yelled down the stairs.

Derek glanced at his watch. They'd been on target way too long. He glanced at the kid. In a matter of hours, this house would be looted and abandoned. In a matter of minutes, this guy would be in the wind.

"On your feet," Derek ordered.

Sean shouldered his pack. "They said no prisoners."

"On your feet!"

The kid stood grudgingly, proving he knew at least some English. Sean shot Derek a look before taking the prisoner by the arm and propelling him toward the stairs.

Derek's mind reeled as he looked at the papers strewn on the floor. He scooped up every scrap and checked the safe again to make sure he hadn't missed anything, then threw his bag over his shoulder and raced upstairs. All the windows rattled as a Black Hawk swooped overhead en route to the landing zone. He glanced into the courtyard just as their EOD guy ducked out. He'd been setting the charge on the ordnance, and the look on his face told Derek it was about to blow.

"Hey, what are you doing here? Haul ass!"

Boom!

Derek dropped to his knees as the house shook. Chunks of debris rained down from the ceiling.

"Come on!" Derek yelled.

They sprinted outside, where the last member of their team was holding security by the door. A few neighbors' lights had come on. People peered through windows and leaned out from doorways.

"Vaughn, where the hell are you?"

It was Luke's voice over the radio, probably already at the LZ, which was a vacant lot at the end of the street.

"We're half a click away."

They double-timed it toward the landing zone, pushing the prisoner ahead of them.

"We got company," Cole said over the radio as a truck screeched around the corner. It was a shit vehicle, but it was packed with armed men and had a .50-cal machine gun mounted to the roof.

Derek grabbed Sean's vest and yanked him out of the road. He pushed him down the alley leading to their alternate exfil route.

"Vaughn, report! Where are you?"

"Almost there."

The street smelled like sewer water. Trash swirled in the rotor wash as they neared the waiting helo.

Rat-tat-tat.

The gunner on the truck let loose with the .50-cal. His buddies with AKs were well out of range, but that didn't stop them from spraying bullets.

Derek rounded the building just in time to get a mouth full of dust. Mike was lifting the doctor into the chopper. Hailey had a SEAL on each arm, and they were practically carrying her, but she tore away from them and made a sprint for it. She flung herself onto the helo, and about a dozen hands reached out to pull her inside. Luke and Mike jumped in behind her.

Rat-tat-tat.

Derek and Sean ducked and sprinted while several teammates aimed over their heads and returned fire. The prisoner reached the helo first, and Mike pulled him aboard.

Rat-tat-tat-tat.

Sean crashed down behind him. Derek turned and hauled him to his feet. Noise drowned out the words, but Derek could read his friend's lips and the panicked look in his eyes: *I'm hit.* Derek heaved him over his shoulder and stumbled forward. Bullets peppered the helo's sides as Luke jumped down and helped lift Sean inside.

"Go, go, go!"

Derek grabbed the outstretched hands of his teammates as they seized his pack and yanked him aboard. His boots were barely inside when the Black Hawk lurched off the ground and lifted into the sky.

Texas Hill Country
Three weeks later

Elizabeth LeBlanc pulled over beside a sheriff's cruiser and surveyed the scene. Based on the number of emergency vehicles, it was worse than she'd thought, and she'd known it was bad the moment she picked up her cell. Nothing good ever came from a phone call at 4:11 A.M.

Humidity enveloped her as she stepped from her car. The air smelled like wet cedar, and the road was slick from a recent rain. An arc of yellow traffic flares marked off the right lane, where deputies and troopers milled around. Elizabeth studied the faces, looking for anyone familiar. Some of them were pulling the graveyard shift, while others looked as though they'd just rolled out of bed.

Elizabeth crossed the road and made her way past the crime-scene van to a young trooper manning a barricade. She held up her badge. He glanced at it, then gave her a nervous look before letting her through.

She made her way deeper into the whir of activity. The skeptical gazes of the uniforms followed her, but she ignored them as she analyzed the setup. They were on an isolated stretch of road between Del Rio and San Antonio. The landscape was hilly. Because of the speed limit and the narrow turns, most truckers opted for the highway, which meant traffic here was light during the daytime and practically nonexistent in the dead of night.

A bulky sheriff's deputy was eyeing her from across the crime-scene tape, and Elizabeth pegged him for her guy. He waved her over to the inner perimeter.

"Special Agent LeBlanc?"

"That's me." She held up her creds, but he didn't even look.

"Jim Perkins. Thanks for coming out." He gave

her charcoal pantsuit a quick once-over and lifted the yellow tape so she could duck under. "Watch your step there."

She followed him down a steep slope. The ground was muddy, and she chose her footing carefully, wishing she'd gone with boots instead of flats.

"Still no ID?"

"Only the cell," Perkins said. "He's got you on speed dial, so we figured he's one of yours."

He'd said the same thing over the phone, but Elizabeth had been too groggy to do more than jot down GPS coordinates. Did he mean one of her fellow agents? One of her confidential informants? As she'd rushed out the door, she'd thought about notifying her SAC. But her boss didn't like her, and she doubted he'd appreciate being called out of bed in the middle of the night over a CI.

"When you say 'speed dial,' you're talking about his call history?"

"Contact list," Perkins corrected. "Only two numbers listed, and yours was on top."

Elizabeth's chest tightened. "What about physical description?"

"Hispanic male, medium build, mid- to late thirties."

He'd just described half the men in her office. Her anxiety continued to build as they neared a white van nose-down in a ditch. The vehicle was illuminated by klieg lights and swarming with crime-scene techs.

Elizabeth halted in her tracks. A line of golf-ball-size holes perforated the van's side. What on earth kind of gun would it take to do that?

She knew a man who could tell her. Derek Vaughn

would know the make, caliber, and capacity of whatever heavy-duty weapon it was and no doubt how to use it, too. But Derek wasn't on hand to talk to her about guns or anything else, because he was across the world fighting terrorists. Her heart gave a little lurch at the thought.

They drew closer to the van, where the cargo doors stood open as a pair of CSIs dusted them for prints. Elizabeth recognized the forensic photographer crouched beside the driver's door snapping a picture of a body hunched over the steering wheel.

Perkins tromped past the van and led her into some scrub brush. Another set of klieg lights had been erected in the middle of the woods, casting eerie shadows over the rocky ground.

"Near as we can tell," Perkins said over his shoulder, "someone ran 'em off the road back at the S-curve. They Swiss-cheesed the vehicle, killed the driver, then went after the passenger when he tried to make a run for it."

They picked their way through oak and mesquite trees, staying away from the path designated by crime-scene tape. With every step, her sense of foreboding grew. This was no quickie drive-by. Someone had stalked this victim deep into the brush.

"'Bout a hundred yards, give or take," Perkins said. "Looks like they wanted to make sure he got dead."

The victim was sprawled facedown in a clearing. Bullet holes riddled his body, and his left arm was twisted behind him at an odd angle. An ME's assistant in white coveralls knelt nearby, jotting notes on a clipboard.

Perkins exchanged words with the sheriff as Elizabeth eased closer, trying to see the face. She dropped into a crouch.

The victim's eyelids were half-shut. Flies buzzed around his nose, and a line of ants had already established a trail up his neck and into his mouth.

She closed her eyes. Bile welled up in her throat.

"You know him?" Perkins asked her.

"Manuel Amato," she said.

Thirty-seven. Convenience store owner. Father of five.

She'd been so certain he was one of the good guys. How could she have been so wrong? Maybe her SAC was right. Maybe everything that had happened in recent months had taken a toll on her not just physically but mentally, too. Maybe she was losing her edge, losing her judgment. Losing everything that had earned her this job in the first place.

She lifted her gaze to the sky, where the first hint of dawn was peeking over the treetops. A half-moon glowed overhead, reminding her of summer mornings in Virginia, when she'd get up before sunrise to wait by the back door, hoping to intercept her dad as he left on one of his fishing trips. He'd take her along in the skiff and make her bait her own hook and show her how to cast the line so it wouldn't get tangled in the shallows.

Perkins pulled a notebook from his pocket and started writing. "So, I take it he's one of yours, then?"

She stood and looked down at the body, and a sudden wave of loneliness swamped her. There was no one to show her how to do anything this morning. And it was going to be a long day.

"Ma'am?"

She looked at him. "Yes, he was one of mine."

———

It was full-on rush hour by the time Elizabeth reached the city, so she crossed Starbucks off her list, although she sorely needed caffeine. Even without the call-out, she'd had a bad night. Most of it had been spent curled on her sofa, flipping channels and determinedly avoiding CNN as she downed chamomile tea, which was supposedly a natural sleep aid. After weeks of drinking the stuff, she'd discovered it worked great when accompanied by Ambien.

She pulled into the bunker-like parking garage and found a space. Flipping down the vanity mirror, she checked for any telltale signs of fogginess. Her eyes were bloodshot, her skin sallow. She smoothed her ponytail and fluffed her new bangs. She'd had them cut a few months ago in an effort to hide her scar, but she wasn't crazy about the look. A little too school-girl, which wasn't helpful. As a five-four blonde, she already had enough trouble getting people to take her seriously.

She flipped up the mirror, disgusted. She had more important things to worry about today than her appearance. Such as her boss's reaction when he heard about Amato.

Her stomach tightened with nerves as she rode up the elevator. Manuel Amato was just the latest in a string of mistakes she'd made since joining the task force investigating the Saledo cartel. The brutal crime ring was making inroads into Texas and had a hand in everything from drug smuggling to money laundering.

Amato owned a convenience store in Del Rio, across the street from a warehouse that was being used as a drop-off point by sex traffickers. He'd given Elizabeth's team a tip that had panned out, and since then she'd been cultivating a relationship with him and trying to persuade her SAC to let her use him as an informant. Her boss had resisted. She had persisted. Amato was a family man, a business owner, an upstanding citizen who was active in his church. Most important, he'd wanted to help.

After weeks of dogged efforts, Maxwell had finally given Elizabeth the green light, and she'd paid a visit to Amato to lay out the deal. Since then, she'd been awaiting his call. But that call would never come, because her promising new informant had been murdered while moving a load of coke for Saledo or one of his rivals.

The elevator slid open. Elizabeth made her way toward her cubicle and saw Maxwell talking to a pair of agents outside his office. He'd probably heard by now. Would he dress her down at the staff meeting or call her into his office beforehand?

He spotted her, and the grim look on his face told her he'd received the news. Elizabeth changed course, bracing herself for a blast of criticism as she approached.

"Sir, I need to talk to you about—"

"Save it. You've got a visitor." He tipped his head toward one of the men standing nearby.

"Hello, Elizabeth."

She blinked at him, taken aback. "Gordon. What—"

"Feel free to use my office," Maxwell told him, then gave her a sharp nod. "We'll talk later."

Gordon watched her, his look unreadable. He was based in Washington, but if he'd spent the morning on an airplane, you'd never know it from his immaculate suit and shiny wingtips. Agents who worked for him sometimes called him "Wall Street," and she hadn't figured out whether it was because of his clothes or because his all-business demeanor reminded them of Gordon Gecko.

He gestured toward the empty office. "After you."

Polite as always. She stepped inside and felt a chill down her spine as the door thudded shut. She glanced through the window into the bullpen and caught the baffled looks of her coworkers, who were obviously wondering why the Bureau's newly promoted assistant director of counterterrorism wanted to see her.

Gordon tucked his hands into his pockets and stepped past Maxwell's desk. He had an athletic build, good posture. His salt-and-pepper hair was trimmed short, as she remembered it. Despite the demands of his job, he took care of himself.

He turned to look at her. "How have you been?"

She started to say "Fine" but remembered something else she'd learned about him a year ago. He was a human lie detector.

"Busy," she said.

He lifted an eyebrow, then turned to study Maxwell's ego wall, which featured his Princeton diplomas, along with several framed photos of him rubbing elbows with VIPs: the FBI director, a few senators, the Texas governor.

"Have you been following the news out of Afghanistan?"

She cleared her throat. "You mean the hostages?"

"Yes."

"The newspaper said they were rescued by NATO forces."

The paper hadn't specified what type of forces. But since meeting a SEAL team last summer, Elizabeth had been paying close attention and had learned to read between the lines. A team of commandos storming a compound and plucking civilians from the hands of Taliban insurgents? The mission had SEAL written all over it.

"Many of the details weren't made public." Gordon turned to face her. "The team that conducted the raid recovered some interesting info during their SSE sweep."

SSE. She racked her brain.

"Sensitive site exploitation," he provided.

"You mean computers?"

"A laptop, a thumb drive. The information there was surprisingly minimal, but they also collected a cache of papers, including several detailed maps of Houston."

Houston. Not D.C., not New York, but Houston, Texas. Elizabeth's palms felt sweaty and she tucked them into her pockets. "What's in Houston?"

He smiled slightly. "You mean besides six million people? Three major sports venues, a world-renowned medical center, a Christian megachurch." He sat on the edge of Maxwell's desk. "Not to mention the corporate headquarters of some of the world's largest energy companies."

She clamped her mouth shut. Maybe she'd look less ignorant if she let him talk.

"It was a take-no-prisoners raid," he continued. "However, when the commandos saw this cache of intel, they grabbed a young man who'd been subdued, hoping some of our CIA guys could persuade him to talk."

"Did they?"

His mouth tightened. "He's no longer cooperating."

What did that mean, exactly?

"And unfortunately, after poring through all the intel, our analysts believe the terrorists planning the attack were not in the compound when the raid went down. As far as we know, they're still at large." He paused and watched her. "Homeland Security's staffed up a joint task force to investigate this potential plot and interrupt it."

Elizabeth's mind was reeling. She'd admired Gordon since the day she'd met him, both as an investigator and as a leader. The thought of working with him again made her giddy and nervous and terrified all at the same time.

He stepped closer and gazed down at her.

"Your SAC says you had a rough spring. He thinks you're not up for this assignment."

Anger welled in her chest.

"If you join my team, I need to know that you're one hundred percent. Are you?"

"One hundred and ten. Sir."

He held her gaze, the human lie detector. Her

heart thudded so loudly she could hear it. Time seemed to stretch out. He glanced at his watch. "Be at San Antonio International Airport in two hours. Pack light."

Relief flooded her. "We're going to Houston?"

"California. Naval Amphibious Base Coronado, to be precise." He crossed the room and reached for the door. "We need to interview some SEALs."

Chapter Two

It felt good to be back in the water after six long months in the mountains, where the air was so thin it made his lungs burn. Derek was trained to operate in all environments—sea, air, and land—but having grown up on the Texas coast, he'd always preferred the sea.

He glided through the water, moving mostly by instinct. It was just after sundown. The currents and boat traffic of San Diego Bay churned up sediment, and visibility was for shit. But Derek liked to work by feel. He was under the belly of the ship, skimming his hand along the hull in search of his objective.

He felt a tug on the line attaching him to his partner. Luke emerged from the shadows, holding the glowing attack board, which showed their depth and their precise location to within a meter. Luke signaled him. Twenty meters to go investigating the hull of this boat, and they still hadn't located the explosive. Derek checked his dive watch and kept swimming. He'd be damned if a crew of jarheads was going to beat him to the punch.

Tonight's training op came to them courtesy of an ongoing rivalry between Jeff Hallenback, Derek's CO, and a Marine commander who'd been one of his classmates at the Naval Academy. Each team was searching a guided-missile destroyer much like the USS *Cole*, which had been attacked by Al Qaeda terrorists while docked in Yemen. The objective was simple: find and disarm a timed explosive device hidden somewhere on the boat. May the best team win.

It was a classic SEAL mission and should have been no sweat, but Derek's team wasn't exactly operating on all cylinders. Sean's death was an open wound. Every last one of them had been hit hard, especially Luke, who'd been Sean's swim buddy during BUD/S training. The CO knew his men were hurting, so he'd arranged to squeeze in a few training ops before sending them on leave. To some it might seem cruel, but Hallenback understood his team, and they respected him for it. So despite tired bodies and flagging spirits, they were putting their full effort into tonight's exercise.

Not to mention that they were competitive. Tonight's winners would get a ride back to base aboard a motorized boat. The losers would get a rubber raft and a pair of oars.

Derek hated losing, whether it was a baseball game or a bet or a woman, and the idea of losing to a bunch of Marines was pretty much intolerable. It propelled him forward as he peered through the murky water and skimmed his fingers over the ship's skin.

He hit pay dirt.

His pulse spiked as his hands moved over the familiar shape. He tugged the line to signal Luke, who took one look at Derek's discovery and gave him a thumbs-up.

It was exactly what they'd expected: a basic limpet mine attached by magnet and rigged with a timer. As the designated EOD tech, Derek took the lead in disarming the mock explosive and detaching it from the ship. His teammates swam over, lured by some invisible force, like dolphins communicating underwater.

Mike tapped his watch. *Tick-tock*. Besides the Marines, they were up against their commander's stopwatch, and if the mission wasn't accomplished within the time limit, every one of them was rowing home.

Derek handed off the mine to Mike, their fastest swimmer. He took off like a torpedo.

Derek followed, feeling uneasy without knowing why. One limpet. He'd found it. Based on the size, it could tear a pretty good hole in the ship. But it couldn't bring her down, and that bothered him.

A sharp tug. Luke materialized in the shadows. Derek swam over and saw what had captured his attention: a second device illuminated in the glow of Luke's attack board. They traded looks. This was classic Hallenback.

One is none, and two is one. It was what their CO always said right before telling his EOD guys to back up their charges in case something went wrong, which had a tendency to happen in the heat of battle.

He and Luke made quick work of the second device. Derek checked his watch. Eighteen seconds.

Cradling the limpet like a football, Derek kicked

and swam for all he was worth, breaking the surface just in time to hear a cheer going up from the
Marines' boat. He glanced at his teammates bobbing
glumly in the water.

Hallenback stood on the dock, arms crossed. Derek
held up the second mine. A smile spread over the
CO's face, and he shot his rival a look.

Derek shoved his mask up and swam over to the
bulkhead, where Cole gleefully took the prize off his
hands and held it up like a trophy.

"Hey, girls, you missed one!"

A chorus of barks went up from the SEALs. They
leaped and cannonballed off the dock and converged
on the pontoon. Surrounded by jeers and insults,
the Marines unassed the boat. Derek heaved himself
aboard and pulled off his fins. One of the jarheads
had a few choice words about Derek's mom. Derek
grinned and threw him an oar.

It was a nice ride back, considering. There was a
moderate wind out of the west, a chop in the bay. He
glanced up at the night sky, still feeling a little strange
about being home after so many months away.

"Nice save." Mike sank onto the metal seat beside
him. "We owe you a beer. You going to O'Malley's?"

"I don't know."

"What don't you know? We haven't been there in
freaking forever." His gaze narrowed. "What're you,
sick?"

Always the medic.

"I'm pretty beat."

Mike smiled slyly. "So make it an early night."

They pulled up to the dock and briskly secured
the boat, everyone energized by the prospect of a

well-earned night off. Derek shouldered his gear and trekked back to the team building. He wanted a hot shower and a cold beer. And sex. That would probably help, too. But the thought of all the bullshit small talk it would take to get him there made his head pound.

"Yo, Vaughn." Luke walked over, still dripping in his dive suit. "Hallenback wants us at HQ."

Derek hung his fins in his locker. "What, now?"

"ASAP. As in eighty-six the shower. He said move."

Derek stashed his gear and traded his dive suit for BDUs. He was jamming his feet into boots when Luke rushed back, also in battle dress uniform. He was still buttoning his shirt.

"Know what it's about?" Luke asked.

"No idea."

They double-timed it across the grinder, where a line of recruits was struggling through night PT. Their backs sagged as they performed their umpteenth set of push-ups. One guy was dry-heaving in the grass, and the others looked ready to drop.

A Humvee zipped past them and pulled into a space beside a Lincoln Town Car. Hallenback climbed from the Humvee's passenger side as the team's chief petty officer hopped out from behind the wheel.

"We're in the SCIF room," the chief informed them.

The Lincoln's doors opened, and three men in suits piled out.

Make that three men and a woman.

Elizabeth LeBlanc slid from the car, and Derek's brain stalled. She wore a black suit and heels, and her straw-blond hair was pulled back in a ponytail. He watched her cross the pavement, dimly aware of introductions being made all around him. A second later, she was standing in front of him, watching him with those cool blue eyes.

". . . Petty Officer Luke Jones," Hallenback said. "And Lieutenant Derek Vaughn."

He tore his attention away from her and managed to shake a few hands. He remembered the tall FBI agent, Gordon Moore, from last summer.

Elizabeth offered a handshake. "Lieutenant."

"Ma'am."

Her skin was warm and soft. Jesus, how long since he'd touched her? He looked at those pink lips and remembered the honey-sweet taste of her mouth.

The cool expression faltered, and she tugged her hand away.

The chief pulled the door open, and Hallenback led the visitors inside. Elizabeth fell in line behind her boss, and Derek stared after her.

"It's about A-bad," Luke muttered.

Derek looked at him.

"Asadabad. He's with CT. Didn't you hear what they said?"

No, he hadn't. He hadn't heard a damn thing.

———

The Sensitive Compartmented Information Facility was a state-of-the-art briefing room with lead-lined walls to thwart electronic listening devices. Derek had been in it exactly once, and the conference table then had been packed with VIPs, meaning standing room only for a team of SEALs about to spin up on a top-secret mission.

This time everyone took a chair. Derek waited for Elizabeth to settle in and grabbed a seat directly across from her. Luke took the seat beside him, eyeing the suits around the table with a wary look.

Derek checked out the faces, sizing everyone up and trying to get his head around the situation. Twenty-five minutes ago he'd been underneath a destroyer. Now he was in one of the Navy's ultra-secure meeting rooms with a team of feebies that included Elizabeth LeBlanc.

Derek tried not to stare at her, but it was damn near impossible. Same eyes, same lips, same stubborn tilt to her chin. She was avoiding his gaze, which gave him a chance to get his thudding heart under control.

Derek hadn't seen her since last summer, when his best friend had found himself at the center of an FBI murder investigation. Elizabeth had been assigned to the case. Derek had spent nearly a week with her, and when he hadn't been dodging her questions and pissing her off, he'd been trying to get her to go to bed with him. No dice.

Had she thought about him at all since then?

"Let me start by saying the information we're about to discuss is highly sensitive."

Derek dragged his attention back to Elizabeth's boss.

"It's part of an ongoing investigation and must not leave this room."

"These men are familiar with the concept of a classified briefing," Hallenback said. "You can speak freely."

"Fine." Moore's attention locked on Derek. "Lieutenant Vaughn, I understand you offered to guard a prisoner directly following the rescue operation in Asadabad."

"Yes, sir."

"And I understand you know Pashto?"

Derek glanced at Hallenback. "I get by."

Moore looked at Luke. "Your CO tells me you're fluent?"

"That's correct, sir."

Luke had picked up the language while working alongside Afghan medical personnel. And now Derek understood where this conversation was going.

"So, you spoke to the prisoner." Moore's statement was directed at Derek.

"We had a few words."

"Why?" This from the suit beside Elizabeth. Potter. His introduction had included something about the CIA. "We had a trained interrogator en route to your location."

"Thought it wouldn't hurt to debrief him a little," Derek said. "Way things have been going with the CIA lately, you never know."

"You have a problem with our people, Lieutenant?" Potter leaned forward on his elbows, clearly affronted.

Derek glanced at Hallenback, whose expression told him he was clear to give his opinion. Not that Derek minded offending a few pencil pushers, but he didn't want to cause his CO any headaches.

"Not your people, your policies," Derek told him. "It's catch and release over there. We risk our necks taking down some Taliban stronghold, bag up a bunch of tangos, and two weeks later they're back in business making suicide vests and planting IEDs."

Derek glanced at Luke, whose teeth were clenched, probably as he remembered the raid. Sean had discovered a shit ton of intel and spent the last minutes of his life collecting it before taking a bullet. As soon as they'd touched down at base, the team had put him on a medevac plane to Germany, but he never made it.

"The A-bad raid netted a huge volume of information," Derek said now. "Plus a high-value prisoner. And yes, we were more than happy to guard him, case he had anything to say before the CIA showed up."

"Then I assume you noticed the maps," Moore said.

Derek had grown up in Texas, which this guy probably knew. Of course he'd noticed the maps. "They caught my eye, yeah."

"Did he say anything about the tactical objectives involved?"

"Well, as Agent Potter here pointed out, I'm not a trained interrogator. I knew that was a sensitive topic, and I didn't want to fuck it up." He glanced at Elizabeth. "'Scuse my language, ma'am."

Her expression didn't change, but Derek knew he'd annoyed her. She didn't like to be singled out for special treatment.

"So what *did* you talk to him about?" Potter asked.

"The houses, mostly. Who lived there. Who was in and out. We tried to get names."

"These guys operate in a network," Luke said. "We're always looking for the missing links. We needed names to plug into what we already had on the area."

"Did you get any?" Moore asked.

"He was pretty tight-lipped," Derek said. "Gave us a few names, but we were fairly sure they were bogus. And they never lined up with any preexisting info on our end. It's in the report, though, so the intel guys can follow up."

"How'd they do, anyway?" Luke asked. "Did the CIA drag anything out of him?"

Moore glanced at Hallenback. "The prisoner's no longer talking."

Derek shook his head, disgusted.

"We did, however, manage to develop some background on him," Potter said. "The Afghan police ID'd him as Khalid Rana. He's a known associate of Al Qaeda's chief recruiter in the area. Now that the war's winding down, they've been operating without much pushback."

Derek gritted his teeth. Did he think they didn't know this? With the troops leaving, the place was becoming a free-for-all, with native Taliban forces, foreign Al Qaeda fighters, and local militia groups coming out of their hidey holes and vying for power.

"In addition to that, he's obviously closely linked to the kidnappers, including Omar Rasheed, who masterminded the attack on the MedAssist convoy. Rasheed's been rising through the ranks of Al Qaeda for years, and this recent operation bumped up his status."

"What about the maps?" Luke asked. "Looked like they could be planning an attack on one of our cities."

"We're processing everything now," Moore said. "We've got our best people working on it."

Elizabeth looked at Moore, and something in her expression made Derek uneasy. Was it admiration? Respect?

Or something else?

Or maybe he was just wishing she'd look at him that way. She'd been across from him now for ten minutes, steadfastly ignoring him, as if just being in a room with him made her uncomfortable.

How many times had he thought about seeing her again? Countless. Only they hadn't been in a SCIF room, and they sure as hell hadn't been surrounded by other people. After all that dreaming, he couldn't believe she was *here,* in the flesh. And now he couldn't stop thinking about how he was going to get her alone.

She glanced at him for barely a second, but something sparked in her eyes, and he knew she'd read his mind.

"We received intel from Great Britain," Moore said. "They have word that Rasheed was in Bahrain last week meeting with a known Al Qaeda supporter."

"Supporter?" Derek asked.

"A financial backer. So we know he's on the move, and in the light of the maps your team recovered, that's an alarming piece of intelligence."

Alarming was an understatement.

"Are they sure they can't get Khalid to talk?" Luke asked. "Maybe they need a new team in there. Sounds like a little arm twisting's in order."

Potter scoffed. "Is that why he shut down on us? You tried a little SEAL arm twisting on a frightened kid?"

"Hey, we didn't touch him," Derek said.

"Don't let his age fool you," Luke added bitterly. "He's plenty old enough to hold an AK or plant an IED or rape a hostage."

Potter gave him a cool look that confirmed all Derek's suspicions. No way this guy had ever been in the field. He had analyst written all over him.

Moore stood up then, and that was it, meeting over. The feds packed up their legal pads, clearly disappointed with the outcome of their fact-finding mission. Yes, a couple of big bad SEALs had talked to the prisoner. No, they hadn't gleaned anything useful. And now the little shit had clammed up, leaving the CIA, the FBI, and about every other alphabet agency in Homeland Security standing around more worried about safeguarding a terrorist's civil rights than safeguarding an American city.

The suits filed out, and Derek watched Elizabeth, trying to catch her eye, but she managed to avoid him. Perfect. He had a few opinions for the investigators involved in this case. But something told him she didn't want to hear them.

Chapter Three

Elizabeth splashed water on her face and checked her reflection. She looked even worse than she felt.

Seeing him had been harder than she'd expected. People always said absence made the heart grow fonder, but she'd had a different experience. Derek's absence had made her heart grow smarter, and she'd thoroughly convinced herself that staying away from him was a wise decision.

Seeing him, though—even for a few minutes—had turned all of that logic on its head.

Nearly a year had gone by, and still the mere sight of him made her skin tingle. He had the power to make her forget every other thought in her head with just a look. She'd been surrounded by colleagues and matters of great importance, and *still* that warm, steady gaze of his had managed to completely distract her.

This trip was tougher than she'd imagined, because now she knew that he hadn't changed at all. He hadn't lost his touch, not one bit.

She looked at the mirror, studying her tired eyes and dull skin, the direct result of way too many weeks living with way too much stress and way too little sleep. *He* might not have changed, but she certainly had. So much had happened since she'd last seen him, and she didn't even think of herself as the same person now. She patted her face dry with a towel as her phone chimed.

She froze. Would it be him?

Of course it would. Derek was nothing if not persistent, and there was no way he'd let her sneak out of town without a conversation. She crossed the room to the dresser, where her phone was charging. Lauren's number on the screen brought an unsettling mix of disappointment and relief.

"Hi."

"Where *are* you?" Lauren asked.

"San Diego."

"What's in San Diego?"

She returned to the bathroom in search of an aspirin. "Long story."

"Hmm . . . and the plot thickens."

She pictured her friend flopping onto the sofa in her apartment and tipping back a glass of merlot. Lauren was one of only a handful of female agents in Elizabeth's office, and they'd bonded from the very first day.

"So how come you never told me you knew the legendary Gordon Moore?" Lauren asked.

"It's no big deal," Elizabeth said, rummaging through her purse. Over the past forty-eight hours, she'd managed to pop every aspirin in her vicinity.

"You're on a first-name basis with the assistant

director of counterterrorism," Lauren said. "That, my cupcake, is a big deal."

She remembered Lauren had been in the bullpen when Gordon summoned her into Maxwell's office. "It's a temporary assignment," Elizabeth told her. "It's not like a promotion or anything."

Lauren snorted. "You wait. I hear they're staffing up his whole department in D.C."

"Where'd you hear that?"

"Around. Just don't forget the little people, okay?"

Score. She found a chipped ibuprofen at the bottom of her makeup bag. She popped the pill and grabbed one of the cups beside the sink to guzzle some water.

"Don't forget the venti lattes, the swapped shifts—"

"Give me a break."

"—the cheeseburger Happy Meals hand-delivered to your car while you were on stakeout."

Elizabeth slipped off her heels and tossed them beside her suitcase near the window.

"Seriously, I'm happy for you," Lauren said. "Maxwell's been riding you. You needed a change."

"It's temporary."

"Well, do a kick-ass job, and maybe it won't be."

A knock at the door had Elizabeth spinning around. She crossed the room with a flutter in her stomach and peered through the peephole.

For a moment she just stared. Square jaw, erect posture, ridiculously muscled body. In her memories, she'd made him less impressive, more average-looking. But of course, that was wishful thinking. There was nothing average about this man, and he was standing outside her hotel room, refusing to go away.

He looked directly at the peephole, and her heart

skittered. He knew she was gawking. She pulled open the door, and her heart did another little dance. She'd forgotten his eyes, too—whiskey brown with gold flecks. The look in them now was pure determination.

God help her, he'd come here on a mission.

"Listen, Lauren, I have to go."

She opened the door wider, and Derek stepped inside.

"See? It's already happening," Lauren quipped. "Catch you later."

Elizabeth closed the door and tossed the phone onto the bed.

He wore a plain black T-shirt over faded jeans and scuffed brown cowboy boots that brought a fresh wave of memories. She lifted her gaze. His dark, longer-than-regulation-length hair curled at the nape of his neck, and his beard had to be going on day two.

"Hi," she said.

"Hi."

"How'd you know where I was?"

"Asked around." His gaze scanned the room and then settled back on her. He propped his shoulder against the wall. "What's it been, a year?"

"Almost."

"You don't call, you don't write." A smile curved at the corner of his mouth. "How the hell you been, Liz?" The smile was teasing, but his tone was serious. He was taking her to task for pointedly ignoring the messages he'd left for her back in December.

"It's been a busy year. I was assigned to a major case . . ." She let the thought trail off. He didn't really want to hear about it, and she definitely didn't want to tell him. "How are *you*?"

Dumb question—the man had just lost a close friend. But he shrugged it off. "Pretty hungry. We just finished a training op. Thought I'd stop by, see if you wanted to grab dinner."

"Actually, I just ate."

He eyed the PowerBar wrapper on the desk and lifted a brow. "Okay, how 'bout a drink, then?"

Temptation pulled at her. He probably thought she was being stuck-up, but that wasn't it at all.

The truth was, he terrified her.

Since meeting him, she'd devoured everything she could get her hands on about Navy SEALs. She'd learned about their dangerous missions in hot spots around the globe. She'd learned they spent ten months a year away from home, either deployed or training. She'd learned they had big egos, and rightfully so. She'd also learned that they had groupies, women who flocked to bars near the bases, desperately hoping to get picked up.

Elizabeth's stomach twisted as she looked up at him. Derek Vaughn was smart and confident and impossibly attractive to women who liked their men a little rough around the edges. But he knew it, too. And she couldn't stand the thought of becoming one of those forgettable women. It was high on her list of Reasons Not to Go There.

Another reason was that she had a case to work, possibly the most important case of her career. And a muscle-bound SEAL with a sexy gleam in his eye was sure to be a huge distraction. Elizabeth felt incredibly lucky to have been picked for this assignment, and the last thing she wanted to do was slip up.

"Come on. Lemme take you out." He stepped closer.

Her phone chimed, and she lunged for it. "Le-Blanc."

"You hear from Moore?" It was Jimmy Torres, who was staying in the room next door. Last time she'd seen him, he'd been on his way to dinner.

"I haven't talked to him. Why?"

Derek sauntered around the room, pretending not to eavesdrop.

"He wants a meeting."

"Now?"

"Five minutes, his suite," he said. "Bring your laptop. And I need Potter's number. I'm supposed to call him."

She glanced at Derek, who stood beside the desk, where she'd spread out her files. She ducked into the bathroom and fished through her purse for the business card Potter had given her when they'd met. She rattled off the number as she returned to the bedroom and slipped back into her shoes.

"Okay, see you in a few."

Derek was leaning over the desk now, unapologetically reading her files.

"This our guy?" He glanced up.

She eased closer to see the photo. He smelled like soap now instead of saltwater. He'd obviously cleaned up, and she felt a twinge of guilt for rejecting his dinner offer.

"Omar Rasheed. He's from a wealthy family in Dubai."

"He's in the deck." He tapped the photo and glanced at her. "The most-wanted terrorists. We call it the deck of cards. Who's this?"

"Ahmed Rasheed," she said, studying the picture.

"Omar's brother. He's dead, though. Killed in a drone strike two years ago in Kunar Province, where he'd been meeting with Al Qaeda leaders."

"Elizabeth."

She glanced up, and the flirty look was gone now, replaced by utter seriousness.

"You want to tell me what you're really doing here?"

"What do you mean?"

The way he held her gaze made her heart thud. She could tell by his expression that he already knew what she was going to say. So there was no use lying—not that she could get one past him, anyway.

She cleared her throat. "When Gordon told you Khalid had stopped talking, he was a little vague."

Derek's jaw tightened.

"He's not talking because he's no longer in custody."

"Whose custody?"

"Anyone's. We turned him over to the Afghans because he was wanted in connection with an attack in the capital. Two days later, he escaped."

He tipped his head back. "Jesus Christ."

"They've been searching for him, but no luck."

"Yeah, don't hold your breath on that. Those guys are so corrupt someone probably walked him right out the jail. What the fuck were they thinking turning him over?"

"I don't know."

"Did they at least question him first?"

"He wasn't talking."

Derek shook his head. "Unbelievable. The one living person we had in custody who could shed some light on this plot, and we let him go." He scrubbed his hand over his face. "We lost a man on that raid, Liz. He took a bullet loading out this intel."

"I know." She touched his arm. "And I'm so sorry. I—"

A rap at the door had her turning around. She glanced at Derek, then went to answer it.

It was Torres, wearing the rumpled remnants of his business suit and holding a McDonald's cup.

"You ready?" He glanced past her, and his expression darkened.

"I'm coming." She scooped up her computer bag, then gathered the files from under Derek's nose and slipped them in with her laptop.

Derek took his cue to leave.

"Sorry I can't talk more," she said, stepping out of the room. "We'll catch up later, maybe? After this case."

He eyed her computer bag, then looked at Torres. "Yeah, good luck with that. You guys have your work cut out for you."

Stepping into Gordon's suite, she caught a glimpse of herself in the mirror. Her cheeks were flushed. Big surprise. Whether it was anger or frustration or simple nerves, Derek always managed to stir up her emotions. Had Torres noticed? How could he not? And what did he think about finding her alone in her hotel room with one of the SEALs they'd come to interview?

Maybe she should strike up a conversation and mention that she'd met Derek the previous summer. But it was really none of his business. The main person whose opinion she cared about was Gordon, and he was well aware that she knew Derek, because he'd been in charge of the murder investigation in which Derek's SEAL teammate was a suspect.

Everyone was gathered around a table, and Elizabeth claimed a chair beside one of the Washington agents, Gordon's expert in all things technical. He had his laptop open and looked to be setting up a secure Internet connection. He glanced at Gordon.

"We're good to go, sir."

Gordon scooted his chair forward. "Okay, some new developments. First, you've all been sent an e-mail from our team at headquarters, which has been working on visuals of Rasheed."

Elizabeth booted up her computer. Her colleagues were doing the same. The group Gordon had picked to accompany him to California was a mere fraction of the group he had working on the case. Most of the others were back in Houston, the presumed site of the intended attack.

"They've created these pictures to show you how he might look with an altered appearance," Gordon said, "which we can assume he'd need to get through immigration."

She clicked open the attachment to find a clean-shaven, Americanized version of the missing terrorist. He was shown with various looks: bald, long-haired, with glasses, without glasses. One version even showed him with a false nose.

"This wouldn't really cut it, though, right?"

Elizabeth glanced at Torres, who was studying the pictures on his screen.

"You're right," Gordon told him. "Our facial-recognition software is designed to see past simple disguises and even plastic surgery. It's based on distance between pupils, earlobes, nostrils—physical characteristics that are nearly impossible to change. Which brings us to our next problem."

Elizabeth held her breath as Gordon scanned the faces around the room.

"Our techs have been busy analyzing the laptop recovered by the SEALs, and they discovered a fingerprint we can't identify. It doesn't belong to Rasheed, and it also doesn't match any of the kidnappers taken out during the raid."

"What about Khalid?" Elizabeth asked.

He shook his head. "Not a match."

"What about someone who could have handled the computer casually?" Torres asked. "Maybe when it was sitting around."

"This isn't just a casual fingerprint," Gordon said. "This laptop was equipped with a biometric fingerprint pad. It was programmed to recognize two separate prints: Rasheed's and this person we're calling Tango Two."

Tango, as in military slang for *terrorist*. Elizabeth glanced around the room, wondering if everyone else caught the ominous implication.

"So I assume we ran this print through all our databases?" she asked.

Gordon nodded. "We ran it everywhere. No hits, which means we're dealing with someone new. Which also means the odds of that person being in our faceprint database are much lower."

"And the odds that he could slip into the U.S. undetected are much higher," Elizabeth said.

"Exactly."

"What about the computer's previous owner?" Potter asked. "Didn't your lab say this laptop was stolen?"

"Before turning up in Afghanistan, the laptop was in the possession of a tailor in Dubai. Which leads us to believe maybe Rasheed swiped it last time he was in his home country. Our techs recovered the erased files, and they all have to do with what appears to be a legitimate clothing business. Besides the deleted business records, we also found detailed plans for three Al Qaeda attacks: the UN convoy and two bombings in Kabul. But that's it. All the information pertains to attacks that have already happened."

Elizabeth made a few notes on her pad. "What about e-mails?"

"No e-mails on the system," Gordon said. "Looks like it wasn't used for outside communication."

"Any prints on the thumb drive?" Torres asked.

"Only Rasheed's. It contains the video clip showing Ana Hansson's execution."

A sour taste rose in Elizabeth's throat. She'd seen the footage and hoped to God the girl's family never got a look at it.

"Maybe the surviving hostages know something," she suggested.

"The doctor doesn't. Hailey Gardner had more interaction with the kidnappers but insists she only saw four different people—Khalid, Omar Rasheed, and two of the guards who were killed during the raid."

Interaction. What a way to put it.

"Someone should talk to her again," Elizabeth said. "Wasn't she drugged part of the time? Maybe she's remembered more since her last interview."

Gordon tapped his pencil against the table, watching her. "She's in seclusion. She was being hounded by the press, so her parents sent her away somewhere and announced that all future interview requests must go through their family lawyer."

"Even us?"

"Even us."

That didn't mean they didn't know her whereabouts. Elizabeth had no doubt the Bureau knew precisely where she was. But it still might be tricky to talk to her.

"What about those names the SEALs had?" Torres asked.

"Dead ends," Potter said. "Just as they suspected. Looks like Khalid made up info to get them off his back."

"This whole trip has been a dead end." Torres folded his arms over his chest. "Five agents all the way out here, and what do we have to show for it?" He shook his head. "The SEALs don't know anything. The hostages aren't talking. This has been a waste of time."

Elizabeth looked at Gordon. As usual, his face gave nothing away. But he didn't look like a man who thought he'd wasted two days of his valuable time. He had a good reason for bringing them out here. Elizabeth just hadn't figured out what it was.

Chapter Four

Derek slid into the passenger seat and was greeted with a yelp.

"God, you scared me!"

"Look alive, LeBlanc. No sleeping on the job."

Not that she looked like she'd been sleeping—on the job or anywhere else. She looked exhausted, from her wilted suit and tired eyes to the little tendrils of hair that had slipped from her ponytail and clung to her damp neck.

Actually, the tendrils looked good. Sexy, even. Although it would have been a lot sexier if her skin had been damp from burning up the sheets with him and not from sitting in a rental car in the Arizona heat.

"What are you doing here?" she asked, obviously rattled.

"Oh, you know. Passing through town."

"How'd you get this address?"

"SEALs are a pretty smart bunch, Liz. Don't let anyone tell you different."

She looked through the windshield at the lush green golf course where Hailey Gardner's parents kept a condominium. "I thought you were going on leave this week."

"I am. Headed back to Texas to visit the famdamnly." He turned the key in the ignition and buzzed his window down. "As luck would have it, Scottsdale's on the way."

She shifted in her seat to face him, evidently coming around to the idea that he wasn't going anywhere. "What is it you want with Hailey?"

"Same thing you want. I think she knows something." He looked her over again, trying hard not to stare. She'd stashed her suit jacket in the backseat and undone the first few buttons of her shirt in a futile effort to cool off.

She looked amazingly tempting, like she'd stepped right out of one of the dreams he'd been having. During his last tour, he'd had some downtime and he'd spent a good bit of it fantasizing about getting Elizabeth LeBlanc out of those tailored suits.

"Have to say, I'm a little disappointed," he said. "Thought you'd be happier to see me."

She ignored that. "Hailey's in seclusion. All interviews go through the lawyer, and he's being an ass."

"There's a shocker."

She sighed and looked out at the perfectly manicured golf course.

Derek hadn't seen green like that in months, so bright it made his eyes hurt. He looked at Elizabeth instead. "If the lawyer's being an ass, then why are you here?"

"Gordon thought she might open up with me."

"Because you're a woman."

"I don't know, maybe." She folded her arms over her chest. "Probably."

"So what's the plan?"

"She left home a few hours ago. I'm hoping to catch her when she comes back."

"Five minutes."

"What?"

"She went to a yoga class that ended at seven. She should be back in five." He grabbed the water bottle from the console and twisted the top off. Elizabeth stared at him. "I did some recon earlier," he said.

"Derek, this is an official interview. I cannot allow you in there with me."

Cannot *allow*. He smiled and reached over to tuck a lock of hair behind her ear. "I ever tell you I love it when you get bossy?"

"You're not part of this case."

He chugged some water and glanced at the side mirror as a white Prius zipped past them. It swung into the driveway, and Hailey Gardner got out. She wore stretchy black pants and a matching top and had her hair pulled up in a ponytail. Dark sunglasses covered her face, probably in case some enterprising reporter managed to find out that her family had a second home in Scottsdale. Derek eyed the cast on her wrist and wondered how she managed the yoga with it. She dug some keys from her purse and disappeared inside the condo.

Derek shoved open the door and turned to Elizabeth. "You coming?"

"You're not going in there."

"Wanna bet?"

"Derek, please listen to me. This woman has been through a lot. She's traumatized, and you're . . . you. How do you know your presence won't intimidate her?"

He shrugged. "Call it a hunch."

She stared at him, and he tried to read her eyes. Ticked off, yes. Worried, yes. She thought his involvement in the raid was going to trigger a negative reaction, but Derek was betting on the opposite.

Elizabeth glanced at the condo, where her best shot at getting a new lead resided.

"You and I both know you're not leaving here without this interview," he said. "What would your boss think?"

"It's not about my boss. This is a high-priority investigation that's vital to national security. I want to contribute."

"I know. I also know you're competitive as hell, and you'll use every resource at your disposal, including me. So let's get this done."

He got out. She sat there stewing for another moment, and then she got out, too, grabbing her jacket from the backseat. He watched her slip into it and put on her agent face.

The evening air was oven-hot, like Afghanistan in July, only instead of smelling like rotting garbage, it smelled like fresh-cut Bermuda grass. The condo was sand-colored adobe with a tile roof and a two-story entranceway.

"I'll do the talking," Elizabeth whispered beside him.

Derek rapped on the carved wooden door. They waited a few beats. The door swung back, and Hailey looked up at him.

"Evening, ma'am. I'm Lieutenant—"

"I know who you are." She stepped out and threw her arms around his neck. She squeezed him tightly and held on so long he started to get embarrassed. Finally, she pulled back.

He cleared his throat. "Ma'am, this is Special Agent Elizabeth LeBlanc, with the FBI."

She eyed Elizabeth warily. "Any interview requests are supposed to go through my attorney."

"We'll keep this brief. We don't want to bother you."

She glanced at Derek, then back at Elizabeth.

"We wouldn't be here if it wasn't important," Elizabeth added.

Hailey stepped back to let them in. The house was a good thirty degrees cooler than outside, and Derek glanced around as she led them into a living room. A blanket was balled up at the end of the sofa. On the other end was a pillow with a flowered pillowcase that probably matched a bedspread somewhere upstairs. Mugs littered the coffee table, and a TV remote sat beside a pile of newspapers.

"You want anything to drink?" She looked at Derek, then Elizabeth. "I've got water, Gatorade . . ." She glanced toward the kitchen. "Chamomile tea."

"I'm fine, thanks." Elizabeth smiled. "We won't stay long."

"Okay, then . . . have a seat, I guess." She lowered herself onto the sofa. Elizabeth picked a leather ottoman, and Derek sat down in a striped armchair. Hailey was staring at him. He'd worn a T-shirt, jeans, and boots, thinking civilian clothes would make her more comfortable. But she seemed the opposite of comfortable as she pulled a pillow into her lap.

"How's the wrist?" He nodded at her cast.

"All right." She looked at Elizabeth. "What questions did you have? I'm not sure what I can tell you that you don't already know."

"Hailey, the SEALs who came to get you discovered some important information in the house where Dr. Lindh was being held."

She didn't move, didn't speak.

"That information's been analyzed," Elizabeth continued, "and it leads us to believe this group may be planning an attack. Something stateside."

Hailey flinched. "You mean here?"

"Somewhere in America, yes. We're not sure where, exactly. That's something we need to find out." Elizabeth paused. "Can you recall hearing anything during your captivity?"

She glanced at Derek and shook her head.

"Maybe a place name?" Elizabeth asked.

Hailey cleared her throat. "My Pashto's pretty minimal. I mean, it sucks, if you want to know the truth." She looked at Derek. "I really only know a few greetings and some medical terms."

"Mine's bad, too." Derek leaned forward and rested his elbows on his knees. "But you know, a lot of the place names—American place names—aren't all that different. Can you think of any words that sounded like something familiar? Maybe similar to English?"

She shook her head.

"Hailey, besides Khalid Rana," Elizabeth said, "you identified another one of your captors, Omar Rasheed."

Her shoulders tensed.

"You also recognized photos of two of the guards

killed by the SEALs. Can you think of anyone else who might have been there? Besides those we've identified?"

"Why?"

"We have fingerprint evidence that someone else may have been staying there in the house, too," Elizabeth said. "We're trying to figure out who."

Hailey shook her head. "Those are the ones I remember."

"There wasn't anyone else? Maybe you didn't see a face, but you heard a voice? Or heard another name being used?"

Another head shake.

Derek watched her, trying to read her body language. "Maybe Khalid mentioned someone?" he asked.

"He didn't." She was adamant. "None of them said much of anything to me. And what they did say— it's all such a blur." She squeezed her eyes shut. "I'm sorry."

"Take your time," Elizabeth said.

She set the pillow aside and stood up, folding her arms tightly against her. He thought she was going to ask them to leave. Instead, she laughed.

"You know, I used to have a good memory. That's the ironic thing. Now there're these . . . chunks missing."

Derek glanced at Elizabeth as Hailey walked to the window and looked out. The sun was sinking over the golf course, casting long shadows across the grass. But he doubted she was thinking about the scenery. More likely she was thinking of how it felt to be held captive by a bunch of filthy, stinking men who would have been happy to slit her throat. And Derek felt like shit for dredging all this up, but they needed to learn what she knew.

"Since I got back, I've become a total freak about everything." She glanced over her shoulder. "I'm so paranoid all the time, jumping at shadows. Everywhere I go, it's like there's people following me. Reporters, stalkers, people watching my house."

"You're not paranoid," Derek said. "People are watching your house."

She turned around. "What?"

"There's an unmarked FBI sedan at the end of your block," he said.

Elizabeth shot him a look as Hailey strode across the room and peered through the expensive blinds covering the windows.

"What the hell? Why are they there?"

"It's standard procedure whenever one of our citizens spends an extended time with terrorists," Elizabeth said. "We keep them under surveillance. As a safety precaution."

She snorted. "Don't you mean Stockholm syndrome? God, you think I'm joining forces with them now?"

"I don't think that at all, Hailey. It's just standard procedure."

She peered out the window again and returned to the couch. The nerves were gone now, replaced by a hefty dose of pissed-offedness.

"Khalid, Omar, and the guards. Those are the people I remember. But can I be sure? No. I was drugged some of the time, which I'm sure you know from reading my file. Probably some kind of opiate." She stared down at her cast. "So you think they might be coming here?" She looked up. "That's what you're saying, right? If they're planning an attack?"

"Rasheed's on the terrorist watch list," Elizabeth said. "We have his name, his photograph, his fingerprints. It's highly unlikely he could get in here."

"But you don't have this mystery person." She looked at Derek. "His name's not on the watch list if you don't know who he is."

"No, you're right," Elizabeth said. "We have his print, but that's all. That's why we needed to talk to you, see if you might remember something more."

Silence hung in the air. Derek watched Hailey, watched the tense set of her shoulders and the haunted look in her eyes. He felt a surge of anger over all the crap she was going to be dealing with, probably for the rest of her life.

She stood abruptly. "Sorry. I don't remember anything else. I'll let you know if I do."

And that was it. Interview over. Elizabeth managed to get her to take a business card in case she recalled anything. Thirty seconds later they were out on the sidewalk.

Chapter Five

They walked silently back to the gray rental car. Derek's pickup was parked around the corner. At the end of the block, a pair of bored-out-of-their-minds feds sat roasting in their vehicle.

Elizabeth's shoulders drooped and she seemed defeated, but Derek knew that was temporary. She wouldn't stay down for long.

"Why'd you tell her about the FBI tail?" She looked up at him.

"Girl thinks she's going crazy. Give her a break."

She sighed. "She doesn't look good."

"Better than last time I saw her."

"She's not sleeping."

Derek glanced at her. "She told you that?"

"Her house told me that." She stopped at the bumper and looked up at him. "You think she was being straight with us?"

"I don't know."

She looked back at the house. "I think she was holding something back." She pulled open the driver's-side door and tossed her purse inside.

"So where to?" He rested his arm on top of the door. "How about dinner?"

She gave him a quick half-smile that told him she'd been expecting the question. "I'd love to, but I've got a ton of work to do tonight."

"How 'bout you forget about work and have dinner with me?"

"I really need to report in."

He nodded. "Report in, and then have dinner with me."

She cracked a genuine smile now. Then she shook her head. "I thought you had family waiting for you in Texas."

"They'll keep."

She looked away. A breeze whipped up, picking up the loose wisps of hair.

He eased closer. "What are you scared of?"

"I'm not scared."

"You're afraid to go out with me."

"Don't be absurd."

He stroked his finger down her sleeve and caught her hand. She didn't pull back, just looked up at him with those clear blue eyes he'd been thinking about. "One dinner, Liz. Then I'll leave you alone, I promise." It was a flat-out lie, and she knew it. She looked away again, and a warm feeling spread through him because he knew he had her.

"I've got to make a phone call first." She met his gaze. "I'm staying at the—"

"Marriott by the airport, I know. I saw the tag on your dash." He smiled and dropped her hand. "I'll pick you up in thirty."

———————

She suggested the sports bar across from the hotel so he wouldn't have to drive and she could get back to her laptop at a moment's notice. Sitting in a booth, surrounded by wall-to-wall televisions and the spicy aroma of chicken wings, she felt guilty. The rest of the task force was back in Houston now, and she doubted they were getting much of a dinner break. Gordon was driving everyone hard. The potential threat to the nation's fourth-largest city had Homeland Security's full attention, and people across all agencies were doing everything possible to investigate without tipping off the media.

A voluptuous young waitress delivered their beers. She flashed a smile at Derek as she reached across the table to arrange his Shiner Bock just so on a little napkin.

"Your dinner will be right out."

Elizabeth's beer came with a curt nod.

She glanced around the restaurant, noticing all the women eyeing her table with interest.

"So," she said when the waitress was gone, "you were right about Hailey. She was glad to see you. Not sure I would have had the same reaction from her."

Derek tipped back his beer without comment. He'd seemed almost embarrassed by Hailey's response. It was a completely new look for him.

"I appreciate your help with the interview," Elizabeth continued. She was determined to use this time to touch on everything she needed to cover with him so he wouldn't have an excuse to call her. "It was very helpful, but I want you to know that the task force has a handle on it. We can take it from here."

The corner of his mouth curved, but he didn't look amused. "Why don't I believe that?"

"Okay, fair enough. Some mistakes have been made in this case. But Homeland Security—"

"Homeland Security fucked up, big time. They should never have let Khalid go."

He was right, but she tried to downplay it. "Khalid wasn't talking."

"He'd been in custody five minutes." He set his beer down. "Sometimes you have to sweat 'em out a little."

She glanced over his shoulder at the baseball game playing on one of the screens. She didn't want to talk about the mistakes of the CIA or the Bureau or anyone else. What was done was done. They had to focus on what they had.

"I get the feeling something's off with Hailey," she said. "That something's going on with her."

"What, you mean besides being kidnapped, raped, and beaten?"

"Yes."

Derek looked away and seemed to think about it.

He was very observant, and he'd talked to plenty of people under extreme duress. She wanted his impressions.

"She seemed protective of Khalid."

Elizabeth felt a wave of relief. She *hadn't* been imagining it. "I thought so, too." She paused. "Maybe he was nice to her."

"You're thinking Stockholm syndrome?"

"It happens," she said.

The waitress reappeared with two enormous platters of wings. She'd brought extra ranch dip, per Derek's request, and he thanked her with a wink. When she was gone, he looked serious again.

Elizabeth dipped a wing in sauce. "You think it's possible?"

"Possible." He chomped into a wing. "But I'd say not likely."

"Why?"

"I'm not getting that," he said simply. "Not based on what I saw."

She watched him, wishing he'd provide more to back up his opinion. But he would probably never reveal all the details of that or any other mission. He could be very evasive when it came to his work—yet another reason he was difficult to know. How could you really get to know a man who wouldn't discuss the very thing that was the focus of his life? It was one of the many issues she'd had stuck in her brain for the past year, especially in December, when he'd called her and tried to reconnect.

"Well, maybe I'm wrong," she said now. "Maybe it's just that Khalid was kind to her. In her debriefing, she mentioned him bringing her water and sometimes food."

"What a host."

She wiped her fingers on a napkin and leaned back against the booth. "You know, the Afghan police suspect him of stealing the uniforms used in a spate of suicide attacks, ones where the bombers walked into a secured area dressed as police officers. Khalid may be young, but that doesn't make him harmless."

"Hey, you're preaching to the choir." He nibbled his bone clean and added it to his growing pile. He'd ordered the jumbo platter and wasn't having any trouble putting it away. "I've seen kids younger than him planting IEDs. Not to mention it runs in the family. His older brother's been linked to several attacks in Kabul. And this guy Rasheed? Expert bomb maker. His handiwork's been identified in at least three roadside bombings along Khyber Pass."

She watched him uneasily. "You seem to know a lot about this network."

"Honey, SEALs know a lot about a lot of things. That's why they pay us the big bucks."

"I'm serious. Why do you know so much about this case?"

He added another bone to the pile. "It's my business to know."

"Because of Sean Harper."

"Because of Sean, yeah. And because I want to see that this gets handled right."

"Sean was in your BUD/S class?"

His brown eyes turned somber. "We were in the same boat crew."

Last summer he'd told her all about BUD/S training—the sleep deprivation, the never-ending beach runs, the night swims and log PT. He'd told her how it systematically broke men down, day by day, hour by hour, and then—for the few who withstood it—built them back up again. The training forged relationships, and the men who endured it together became a brotherhood.

She'd seen their unusual brand of loyalty up close when she'd tried to get Derek to turn on his teammate Gage Brewer, who was suspected of murder. She'd poured her heart and soul into the effort, but it had been a waste of time. The brotherhood these guys talked about wasn't just a slogan—it was something very real.

So the man sitting across from her now with the edgy, restless look in his eyes had lost a brother last week. It explained a lot.

"I'm sorry about Sean," Elizabeth said, feeling totally inadequate.

He nodded. "I appreciate that."

The waitress reappeared to clear their plates away, and Derek gave her a smile, but it seemed forced. He glanced around the bar. If he noticed all the women sneaking glimpses in his direction, he didn't let on.

He looked at her. "How about some darts?"

"What, now?"

"No, tomorrow." He smiled and stood up, obviously ready to change the subject.

Not to mention the mood.

He left several twenties on the table and then put his hand at the small of her back and steered her to the bar. Just that light touch of his fingers made her nerves flutter. He was treating her like his date, and she liked it.

A lot.

He peeled off another twenty and handed it to a bartender in exchange for darts and another round of beers. Elizabeth watched him, pulse thrumming. He had a confident way about him that she found way too attractive. His gaze settled on hers as he passed her another beer.

She'd known this would happen. He'd invited

her to dinner, but he wanted way more than dinner. He wanted the same thing he'd wanted last summer when she'd been investigating his best friend.

He wanted sex.

And he wanted information.

And he wanted sex.

Almost a year had gone by since then, and she'd spent many solitary moments thinking about him. And the situation hadn't changed. He was using her. Not in a malicious way, really. In fact, she understood it. He had an unshakable sense of mission. But he was using her just the same.

"You ever played cricket?" he asked, claiming an empty board.

"Think I remember it."

"Ladies first," he said, and handed her the darts.

She stepped up to the board and paused a moment to get her head in the game. Then she took a deep breath and made her first throw.

She smiled. "Triple twenty."

"Not bad." He tipped back his beer. "Looks like you spent some time on frat row when you were in Charlottesville."

She glanced at him.

She'd never mentioned she went to the University of Virginia. He'd been checking up on her, and he wanted her to know it.

"Not me." She sipped her beer and rested the bottle on a ledge beside him. "I was the geek always holed up in the library."

"Who taught you darts?"

"My dad." She threw another one. Outer bull's-eye this time.

"He must be good."

"He was. Darts, pool, fishing. He taught me all of it. I was the son he never had." She glanced over and saw by his expression that he'd noticed the past tense. "He died when I was twelve."

"It's a shame he never saw you graduate from the Academy," Derek said. "Bet he would have been proud."

Derek was right. As a public prosecutor, her dad probably would have been pleased to see his only child go into law enforcement.

"My mom was there," she told him. "And my stepdad." Which wasn't nearly the same, because she didn't even get along with her mother. She made her last throw. Triple twenty again. He watched her, obviously expecting her to say more. But she didn't like to talk about her family.

She wrote the score on the chalkboard, ignoring his expectant look.

Ever since her dad died, she'd had this feeling of being adrift. Her mother had felt it, too, and she'd run straight from her grief into the arms of an older husband. For years, Elizabeth had felt so much anger toward her for replacing her dad so quickly. And for giving into such blatant insecurity.

Elizabeth had tried to create her own security, using good grades and hard work. She'd set goals for herself and then stubbornly pursued them. She recognized the same trait in Derek—his relentless need to push. His tenacity. She doubted he'd be like that in a relationship, though. He was a SEAL. It defined him and dominated his life, and he couldn't truly commit to anything more.

But so what? Since when was she looking for commitment?

Derek watched her over his beer as she plucked the darts from the board. She knew the gleam in his eye, and it put a familiar tingle in her stomach. She'd never aspired to be one of his one-night stands. But there was something thrilling about the idea, too. She imagined spending an entire night with him and not letting herself regret a minute.

A cheer went up across the bar. She glanced at a TV as the Diamondbacks scored a home run.

She handed over the darts, and Derek stepped up to the board.

"So this task force you're on," he said. "You managed to narrow down the target yet?"

"You mean in Houston?"

"I grew up in Houston." He threw a sixteen. "It's a pretty target-rich environment. You've got the ship channel, the refineries, a former POTUS. And then there's about six million people who'd be affected if someone managed to get a dirty bomb into the country."

"You know, now that you're stateside, this isn't your job anymore. That's why we have this little thing called the Federal Bureau of Investigation?"

"So you haven't narrowed it down." He threw another dart.

"We're working on it. You don't have a lot of confidence in our people, do you?"

"People make mistakes," he said. "Even feds."

"Happens in the military, too."

"Absolutely. Thing is, in the military you make a mistake, maybe you get your foot blown off. People learn to pay attention. Err on the side of being cautious."

"You don't think we take this seriously?" She was getting annoyed now—not only by his attitude but by the fact that she'd allowed herself to be lured back into this conversation.

Once again, he was using her for information. And by being here with him, she was allowing it to happen.

"Your friend Potter—"

"He's not my friend," she said. "He's down from Langley. I met him yesterday, same as you did."

"Okay, that proves my point." He finished his turn. "He's not a field man."

She sighed. "How about we don't talk about work anymore?"

He shrugged, as if it didn't matter. "Fine by me." He retrieved the darts and updated the score. "What do you want to talk about?"

She had no idea.

He propped a shoulder against the wall, and his mouth curved as she stepped in front of the board again.

"What?"

"Nothin' at all." He said it with the low drawl that had bothered her when she first heard it. But she'd learned to like it, especially when it was accompanied by that slow half-smile.

She ignored his look as she focused on her throws.

Another cheer from the bar, and he glanced at the TV. "This is what I miss most," he said.

"Losing at darts?"

"People out, watching the ball game, having some brews." He lifted his bottle. "This stuff's not easy to come by in some of the places we go."

And women? Did he miss them, too? From the

moment they'd stepped in here, he'd been turning heads. Maybe he was used to it, and it didn't even faze him anymore.

She finished her turn and handed the darts over to him.

"Must be hard being away so much," she said. "I can't even imagine it."

"I can't imagine anything else."

She tipped her beer back and watched him as he threw a bull's-eye. Even playing darts, he looked athletic.

"So you ever gonna tell me about that scar?" He glanced at her.

"We said we weren't going to talk about work."

His gaze narrowed. "That happened at work?"

"It's a long story." She turned her attention to the ball game.

"I'm listening."

She looked at him, at the laser-sharp focus of his gaze. *I'm listening*. Just the thought made her chest tighten. He *was* listening. And she felt the urge to let her guard down, to let him in. But she knew where that would lead.

One kiss. That was all it had taken to get her in this much trouble. They hadn't even slept together, and somehow he'd managed to shake up her world for an entire year.

He'd wanted to sleep with her in San Francisco. He'd been very upfront about it, inviting her back to his hotel room after they'd gone drinking at a pub following what—at that point—had been the single worst day of her career.

Sometimes she wished they'd gone through with

it. She'd probably be embarrassed now, but at least she'd be able to place him solidly in the category of Drunken Mistakes. As it was, whenever she thought of him, she felt this burning curiosity.

What would it have been like?

She might never know, because instead of sleeping with her, he'd tucked her into bed and crashed on the sofa. In the morning he'd pulled on his cowboy boots and acted like it was no big deal.

He was still watching her, waiting. *I'm listening.*

He really was. And it felt so good to see him, to be near him. She felt more alive and awake in the last hour than she had in months, and she knew it was *him*. He had this effect on her. But if this was what it felt like just being near him, how would she feel if he ever really touched her?

Heat sparked in his eyes, and he stepped closer. "Liz . . ." He slipped his hand around her waist. "You're doing it again."

"What?"

"Looking at me like that."

Noise and people swirled around her as she gazed up at him, and they may as well have been the only people in here.

"When you look at me that way . . ." His hand trailed up and settled on her shoulder. He was going to kiss her, and she watched him, heart thudding.

Her phone chimed, and she stepped back. She looked around and spotted her purse under the table. Fishing the phone out, she found a text from Jimmy Torres.

"Shit."

Another message came in, this one from Gordon. Her stomach knotted as she read the words.

"Shit, shit, shit."

"What's wrong?"

She glanced up and started to tell him. Then she clamped her mouth shut.

"Nothing." She dropped the phone into her purse. "I'm really sorry, but I have to go."

Chapter Six

Elizabeth caught the first flight out before sunrise. By the time she landed and picked up her rental car, rush hour was dissipating, and so was her energy. She pulled into the office and did her hair and makeup in the parking lot before locking her suitcase in the trunk and rushing inside. After hurrying through security, she found the entire task force squeezed into a conference room.

Elizabeth slipped inside. Every seat was taken around the table, so she grabbed a bit of wall space beside Torres.

He did a double take.

"Who's this?" she mouthed, nodding toward the far end of the room, where a man stood talking.

He leaned over and whispered in her ear, "ICE."

Immigration and Customs Enforcement. So this lead had come from them.

"It's something we've been worried about for some

time," the ICE agent was saying. "It's a back door, and they've used it before."

Gordon was watching her from the head of the conference table. He'd wanted her here ASAP, so here she was. A little harried, yes, but she was present.

"The most serious attempt was several summers ago," the agent continued, "when a Mexico-based Al Qaeda cell tried to smuggle a truck bomb up through one of the border tunnels."

Elizabeth glanced behind the ICE agent, where a screen showed a black-and-white still shot of a dark minivan. It was parked beside a gas pump, and the image looked to have been taken by a surveillance camera.

"How far is this entry point from that location?" someone at the table asked.

"Not far at all. And the turf is controlled by the same cartel, the Saledos. They basically control all routes in and out of there and sell access to the highest bidder, which in this case might be foreign terrorists." The agent tapped on a laptop sitting open on the table, and a video filled the screen. The black-and-white footage showed the minivan pulling up to the gas pump. Elizabeth squinted at the grainy picture, not sure what to look for. Movement.

"There." The agent paused on an image of several people dashing away from the vehicle. "That's him."

"Any ID on the woman?" someone asked.

"No, but she's believed to be Nicaraguan. Same for a few others who were in this vehicle. The coyote transporting them works for the Saledo cartel. Another coyote"—he tapped the laptop, and a mug shot came up—"Manuel Villareal, works for a rival cartel that's horning in on this route. When Villareal got jammed up in San Antonio trying to offload his cargo, we pulled him in for questioning. He's got a long sheet, so it took him no time to lawyer up. But that's when he surprised us. Next thing we know, his lawyer's offering up a deal. Probation for his client in exchange for a tip about a rival coyote getting paid twenty grand to, quote, 'smuggle an Arab over the border.'"

"How good is this tip?" someone at the table asked. "I'd think this Villareal guy would say anything to avoid jail time."

"Holmes, you want to take this one?" The ICE agent gestured to his left, and Elizabeth was startled to see Lauren leaning against the wall.

"Special Agent Holmes has been investigating the Saledo organization for some time now," the agent said. "She interviewed the suspect."

Lauren made eye contact with Elizabeth. "Villareal's one of our frequent fliers." She glanced around the room. "And it comes as no surprise he's trying to wiggle out of some prison time by throwing one of his rivals under the bus. Villareal's boss finds out he got arrested making a delivery, he's going to want payback. He probably figures he'll get some leniency if he screws over a rival while he's in custody."

"You think he's reliable?" Gordon asked.

"Villareal? No. He'd sell out his grandmother to avoid prison," she said. "But it's hard to see how he could make this up. This tip about smuggling someone of Arab descent came out of nowhere, just hours

after our office got the memo about the missing terrorist who was thought to be targeting Texas. And so
far, his story's holding up."

"Villareal and this other coyote both pulled over at
the same truck stop in Del Rio, a place known to be
friendly to traffickers," the ICE agent said, pointing to
the screen. "You can see Villareal's pickup here, in the
background. He claims that while he was getting gas,
he actually saw this guy Rasheed getting out of the
other van. The surveillance footage you see here cor-
roborates that claim."

"How would Villareal know who it was?" Torres
asked.

"He didn't," Lauren said. "But when we put a
photo array in front of him, he picked him out right
away. Omar Rasheed."

The picture on the screen changed. Elizabeth
recognized the photo from yesterday's briefing.
It showed Rasheed as he'd appeared in one of the
recruiting videos, seated cross-legged on a carpet
against a backdrop of anti-American graffiti. He
wore traditional Afghan dress and had a dark beard.
Another picture appeared on the screen: Rasheed
standing behind a blindfolded Ana Hansson just seconds before he slit her throat.

The ICE agent sat down, and Gordon stood to take
over the meeting.

"This is what Rasheed looked like several weeks
ago. And this"—he tapped the laptop again, and
another picture appeared—"is what we believe he
looks like now."

Elizabeth recognized the doctored FBI photo
showing a clean-shaven man in a collared shirt.

"He's thirty-three. Comes from a large family in Dubai. He attended college in London, where he was radicalized. Then he moved to Afghanistan, where he's made a reputation for himself by recruiting and training for Al Qaeda."

"He's in the deck."

All eyes swung toward Elizabeth. She cleared her throat. "The deck of most-wanted terrorists, according to our military. We interviewed the SEAL team who raided his compound recently. They've been trying to take him out for years."

"Wish they'd succeeded," Potter muttered.

Another click, and they were looking at a close-up. Again, the surveillance footage was grainy, so it was hard to make out the details of the face.

"This may not look like much," Gordon said, "but our biometrics experts believe there's a ninety-percent probability it's Rasheed."

"He looks empty-handed," Torres said. "If he's armed, it's got to be something small."

"Where's he going?" someone asked.

"That's what we need to find out," Gordon said. "Could be meeting a ride. Could be hitchhiking. Or maybe he walked to the bus depot on the other side of town, where he could have picked up the four thirty to Houston."

"What time was this video taken?" Elizabeth asked.

"About four ten." Gordon let that hang in the air. "Is the timing a coincidence or part of a plan? We need to find out. We also need to find out his target, and we can't assume Houston just because of the maps recovered by our SEAL team. Keep an open mind, people. Maybe Houston is a staging area for an operation elsewhere. Or maybe it's the location of a sleeper cell that's now on the move. We can't let ourselves get tunnel vision, or we'll miss something important."

Gordon tapped his computer. The software-generated image of Rasheed reappeared on the screen.

"Study this picture. Memorize it. He's five-eight, one-forty. He speaks excellent English and is very familiar with Western culture. He does not look threatening, which is why he'll blend in. But let me assure you, he is very dangerous. He's become one of Al Qaeda's top operatives." His gaze met Elizabeth's. "As Agent LeBlanc pointed out, the military believes he's a formidable opponent, and so do we."

Gordon looked at his assembled team. "If Rasheed did, in fact, slip through a back door, then he's inside our borders. And you can be sure he's here for a reason."

———

After months of colorless desert, the brightness of the Texas hills seemed like a Disney movie. Derek let the summer air hum through his pickup as he steered up the tree-lined road.

His thoughts drifted to Elizabeth, as they had for most of the trip. Derek had a head for details, and when it came to Elizabeth, there wasn't anything too small to lodge itself in his brain and drive him crazy. He remembered her shivering on the sidewalk in San Francisco. He remembered the rain glistening in her hair. He remembered the warmth of her mouth and her curves under his hands and how willing she'd felt when they'd left the bar. He remembered touching her, tasting her, and knowing heaven was just a few blocks away.

But then the booze had hit, and it was game over. She'd puked her guts up outside his hotel, which—in her book, apparently—was an unforgivable party foul. Not that it mattered to him. He couldn't count the number of times one of his buddies had heaved up his liquor on the way home from a bar. But Elizabeth had been mortified.

It was his own fault. He'd suggested the pub. And he'd kept the drinks flowing, along with the teasing and conversation, because she'd finally seemed to relax around him. It was a side of her personality she didn't share much, but he'd seen it then, and he'd seen it again last night, and it wasn't just the alcohol. The chemistry was back. Yes, she was still wary, but he planned to get past that. Soon. He had ten days' leave remaining, and he didn't plan to waste a day of it *not* getting to know Elizabeth LeBlanc better, no matter what roadblocks she threw at him. He was a SEAL, for Christ's sake. He thrived on challenges.

His phone rattled in the cup holder, and he smiled as he picked it up.

"Hey."

"Hi, it's Elizabeth. Looks like I missed your call? I was in a meeting."

Her voice was all business. And she probably had no idea that he'd spent a good portion of the last twelve hours dreaming up ways to get her naked.

"So . . . did you make it home yet?" she asked.

"Almost. Decided to take a little detour first, drop in on a friend."

She got quiet, and he wondered if she'd take the bait. Male friend or female? Was she even the slightest bit curious? *Come on, Liz.*

"Listen, I'm glad you called," she said. "I wanted to apologize for rushing off last night. It was one of those things."

"No problem. What about you? You make it home yet?"

"Ha. Not unless Home Suites counts as home. But I made it to Houston okay."

"Any progress?"

Silence as she debated what to tell him. "With regard to the target, no. But there have been other developments."

He didn't respond. Sometimes the most convincing argument was none at all.

"I can't share the details," she added, "but it looks as though someone on the terrorist watch list may have managed to slip through the border and—"

"Who?"

"I can't—"

"*Who?*"

Another pause. "Omar Rasheed."

"There's an international manhunt on for the guy. How the hell'd he get in?"

"I can't discuss details," she said, "but it basically looks like he came through a back door."

"Meaning Mexico."

"He was spotted at a truck stop in Del Rio—that is, if it *is* him. The footage is a little blurry, so we're relying on facial-identification software."

"You check the surveillance cams? Get a look at his contact?"

Another pause. "I'm not even going to dignify that with an answer. And I can't go into all this with you."

"If he got out at a truck stop, he probably had a contact there waiting," Derek told her. "Or he used the stop to get a message out. 'I'm here, pick me up at the bus depot,' or whatever."

"We do this for a living, you know. We don't need you to—"

"Fine, all right. I don't want to fight with you. But Rasheed's in Texas? Jesus. That's not good."

Someone started talking in the background, and he heard her muffled response.

"I have to go," she told him. "Enjoy your leave. I hope you get a chance to relax. Take care, okay?"

And that was it.

He hung up, pissed. And not just because she'd managed to blow him off again.

Relax? Was she serious? One of the most-wanted terrorists in the world was in his own backyard, and the supposedly best law-enforcement agency on the planet didn't have a goddamn clue what he was doing there. Dread tightened Derek's gut as he continued up the drive.

He caught a glimpse of his destination through the trees. It sat high on a hill. The gleaming white building looked like a Greek monument that had been air-lifted into the heart of the Texas Hill Country.

The Delphi Center.

Besides being home to some of the country's brightest forensic scientists, the place was a decomposition research facility. Derek watched a buzzard swoop down into some trees and guessed he hadn't lucked into a squirrel. No, they studied people here. The very dead kind.

Derek pulled around to the back of the building as he'd been instructed. He turned into a service lot and spotted the woman he'd come to see, who happened to be his best friend's wife.

Derek parked his truck and got out. He barely had the door shut when Kelsey threw her arms around him in a tight hug.

"Hey, Kels."

"I'm glad you're home." She choked on the last word, and Derek got a lump in his throat as he stepped back to look at her.

"I'm so sorry about Sean," she said as her eyes filled with tears.

"Me, too." He glanced over her shoulder at the woman standing beside the service door. She had reddish-blond hair and wore a white lab coat. "You're Dr. Voss, I take it?"

"Mia." She stepped forward and smiled. "Kelsey and Gage have told me so much about you."

Derek shot Kelsey a look. "Uh-oh."

"So what'd you bring us?" Kelsey asked, recovering her composure.

Derek reached into the truck bed and unlocked the toolbox mounted behind the cab. He pulled out a smaller, portable black toolbox.

"A pair of beat-up, dirty-as-hell A.T.A.C. boots."

"All Terrain, All Conditions," Kelsey said. "Gage has some just like that. You want us to analyze them?"

"If you would." Derek had filled her in a little over the phone but hadn't gone into detail.

"What exactly are you searching for?"

"I don't know." He gave her a level look. "I been in some sketchy places recently. Think maybe I tracked something out."

" 'Sketchy' such as . . . a bomb factory?" She studied his face for clues. Being married to a former SEAL, she knew the score. He couldn't tell her the details of his mission, not even the location.

"What do you think we *might* find?" Mia asked. The woman was a microbiologist and probably needed to know which tests to run on the boots.

"Explosive residue, biological material, could be anything—which is why I've got them packed in an airtight metal container."

"Wow." Kelsey frowned. "Don't they have people on the base for this?"

"They do," Derek said. "But some new intel came through in the last few hours, and I started thinking about it while I was on the road. I know you guys work with weapons-grade materials here, so I figured you'd be set up to take a look, maybe run a few tests."

"We're happy to." Kelsey glanced at him. Her eyes welled up again, and she was looking at him the same way his mom did when he'd been away a long time, that look of *I thought I might never see you again.*

His job was hard on the people left behind, which was one reason he'd never been much on relationships. He'd seen too many of his friends try to make it work and get burned.

Derek shifted uncomfortably. "So . . . if you'll tell me where to take this?"

"Right this way." Mia swiped her ID badge over a panel. The service door opened, and he followed her inside.

———

Elizabeth had never been a runner. It was a weakness that almost did her in at the FBI Academy.

Sit-ups, yes. Push-ups, okay. She was surprisingly decent at chin-ups. But running? Nope.

She plodded along the sidewalk beside Lauren, sucking in oxygen mixed with car exhaust from Houston's early-morning commuters. Breathe in, breathe out. One step at a time. She focused on the scant patches of grass along the pavement, trying to imagine a more scenic route than the four-lane street lined with fast-food joints and strip centers.

She stopped at a corner and bent over to catch her breath as she waited for the light to change. She'd always hated those peppy, supercharged joggers who bobbed impatiently at intersections, refusing to break the pace.

"You got it?"

She glanced up at Lauren. She wasn't a bobber, either, but she looked much less winded.

"It's *hot*," Elizabeth wheezed.

"Humid." She stretched her arms over her head. "Ninety-percent humidity, which is worse than the heat."

The light changed, and they pushed onward. She could see the hotel. Four blocks left. Her skin was drenched, and her scalp was starting to tingle.

"Hurt, agony, pain—love it!" Lauren said, quoting the signs posted along the obstacle course at Quantico.

Elizabeth stifled an obscene gesture. She imagined Derek. She'd seen him running on the beach in San Diego once, and it was a sight to behold—shoulders back, skin glistening, muscles rippling as he ate up the sand with his powerful strides. He'd made it look easy. Fun. Beautiful, even.

She reached the hotel parking lot and stumbled to a halt.

"Good run," Lauren chirped.

Elizabeth slouched against a lamppost and scanned the lot for her boss's Taurus. At least he hadn't left for the office yet—a good sign.

A phone chimed, and she and Lauren reached for their fanny packs. They couldn't go anywhere without sidearms and electronic leashes.

"Mine," Elizabeth said, fishing out her cell. She sucked down a breath and tried to sound normal. "Hello?"

"How was your jog?"

Derek.

"How'd you know I was jogging?" She glanced around.

"IHOP across the street."

She pivoted again. Sun reflected off the windows, and she couldn't see him, but she spotted a gray F-150 parked in the lot.

"What are you doing here?" she asked.

"Taking you to breakfast."

Her stomach did a little somersault, and she glanced at Lauren.

"Your friend's invited, too."

"I don't have time for breakfast. I have a meeting soon. And I need to shower."

"And you need breakfast. Come on. Don't leave me hanging."

He clicked off, and Elizabeth stared down at her phone.

"Hot date?"

She glanced at Lauren. "A friend dropped by. He's from Houston," she added, as if that explained it.

"A breakfast booty call." Lauren grinned. "You go, girl."

"It's not a booty call, it's pancakes."

"Yeah, right." She started toward the hotel.

"You want to come?"

"No way." She gave her a wave over her shoulder.

Elizabeth glanced at the IHOP and then at her hotel room. She should shower first, but . . . what if he showed up at her door and wanted to wait? The idea of being in a steamy shower with him anywhere near her was impossible. She didn't trust herself.

She walked to the IHOP and ducked into the ladies' room to clean up before venturing into the dining area. It wasn't hard to spot him. All she had to do was follow the wistful looks of the waitresses milling near the kitchen.

She slid into the booth. "How'd you find me?"

He smiled. "You told me where you were staying."

"I said 'Home Suites.' There are probably half a dozen here."

"Yeah, and this one's by your office. I told you, Liz, don't underestimate us spec ops guys. We're not as dumb as we look."

She perused the menu, trying to get her heart rate under control. She was still winded. And maybe a little flustered from sitting across the table from a ridiculously hot guy wearing jeans and cowboy boots. He could have been a Levi's ad.

"Didn't know you were a runner," he said.

"I'm not."

"Looked pretty good to me."

"I nearly keeled over on mile two." She glanced up. "*Don't* laugh. Running's never been my thing."

But he was grinning at her as the waitress stopped by and flashed him a smile.

"What can I get y'all?"

He nodded at Elizabeth.

"I'll have the short stack with sausage links. And coffee."

"And you?" She looked at Derek.

"Coffee."

"That's it?" The waitress's overplucked eyebrows tipped up.

"That's it."

When she was gone, Elizabeth looked at him. "I thought you wanted breakfast?"

"That's for you. I already ate."

"It's seven thirty."

"SEALs are early risers." He leaned forward on his elbows. "We get up and hit it."

Her cheeks heated as she thought of Lauren's booty call comment. She looked away.

"Okay, now what?" she asked. "You've stalked me across four states. I assume there's a reason."

He smiled. "I'm not stalking you."

"No?"

"I'm trying to keep tabs on your case."

She shifted in her seat.

"Hey." His smile disappeared. "You know that, right? If I'm honestly making you uncomfortable, say the word."

She looked him over. He was serious. He didn't want her to think he was some pervert.

And he made her a lot of things but not uncomfortable. Nervous, maybe. Lustful, yes. Sometimes even a little stupid. But not uncomfortable.

"No, it's fine." She sighed. "I get it. You're interested in the investigation."

"That's right. And hey, if you decide to take me back to your hotel room to rock my world, that works, too."

She folded her arms over her chest as the waitress dropped off mugs.

"Relax, I'm kidding." He sipped his coffee. "I just wanted to check in, touch base. See how things are going."

"Things are going fine, but I can't discuss details with you."

"*Fine*, as in you located Rasheed? Identified his target? What?"

"You know, you have this exasperating way of not listening to what I say. I can't talk about it. It's like you with your missions."

"You know all about my mission," he countered. "You were in the meeting, back at Coronado."

"Sure, *one* mission. It's part of my case."

"Exactly. My team's part of this case. I'm just trying to get an update."

He made it sound logical, although she knew it wasn't. But she was tired of arguing with him. She glanced at her watch. She only had fifteen minutes left before she had to get back, so she couldn't give him more than an overview, anyway.

"We have not located Rasheed," she admitted. "We also have not identified the target."

"Have you narrowed it down?"

She paused. "Somewhat."

"What's that mean?"

"It means we have some possible leads we're investigating but nothing that's been substantiated."

"So basically, you have nothing."

She didn't answer, which she figured was answer enough.

Derek shook his head.

"We're working on it."

More head shaking.

"We've got some of our best people down here—"

"Straight answer, Liz. Have you even narrowed it down to Houston?"

The waitress was back with a heaping plate of food, and Elizabeth suddenly felt self-conscious. But then hunger overpowered her vanity, and she dug in.

He watched her intently as she swallowed a bite of sausage. "No."

His jaw twitched. He glanced out the window and then looked at her. "I'm here to make you an offer."

Her guard went up.

"You deliver me some intel, I deliver you your terrorist."

She stared at him. "Have you listened to a word I've said? You're not part of this investigation."

"You're wrong."

"Derek—"

"I became part of it the second my boots hit that rooftop in Asadabad."

No, the second his teammate got killed. This was about payback for Sean Harper, but he didn't want to admit it.

"Listen, I understand you want to help, but—"

"Hear me out, okay? And then you can lecture." He gave her a long look. "I graduated from BUD/S not long after 9/11. You know what I spent my first four tours of duty doing?"

She waited. But it became clear he wanted an answer. "I don't know," she said. "Looking for Osama bin Laden?"

"Every guy over there was looking for bin Laden. But do you know what I actually spent my time doing?"

"What?"

"Assaulting cave complexes. Afghanistan has more than a hundred fifty thousand square miles of mountains. That's miles of cave complexes and some of the most treacherous terrain in the world. We'd get a name and a scrap of intel, and it was like *go*." He snapped his fingers. "Over and over again, our mission was to find a needle in a haystack. And we did it."

He leaned closer. "I can find this guy in Houston. Hell, I can find him in Texas."

She didn't respond.

"Just give me what you have. A license plate, a phone number, an address. Give me some scrap of something about this tango or someone you even *think* might be helping him, and I'll turn it into a lead and track him down."

His confidence was mind-boggling. She would have laughed if he hadn't looked so stone-faced.

"You're serious."

He nodded.

"We've got an entire task force looking for this guy. What makes you think *you* can find him?"

"I'm better."

She shook her head. "Even if I wanted to involve you, which I don't, for about a dozen reasons, including that I could get fired—"

"What's more important? The lives of innocent people or your job?"

"Hey." She pointed her fork at him. "That's a cheap shot. Of course I care about innocent people, but I can't very well help them if I lose my job, can I?" She picked at her pancakes and tamped down her annoyance. "Even if I wanted to give you some magic bit of intel, the fact is, we don't have any."

"Not true."

"You're trying to tell me about my case?"

"You have more than you realize," he said. "Come on, think about it. Think about Del Rio."

"What about Del Rio?"

"Buck's Truck Stop."

She frowned. "How did you know that?"

"Common sense. It's the busiest place in the town. Best candidate as a hub of human trafficking. And ICE knows that, too. Am I right?"

"What are you saying?"

"I'm saying *look* at the place. Get out a Google map and study it. Better yet, go visit. The town has got to be wall-to-wall with security cams, a lot of them privately owned, some of them not. You've got fast-food restaurants, gas stations—"

"What's your point?"

He looked impatient. "Someone somewhere got a shot of this guy meeting his contact. He didn't vanish into thin air. He caught a ride. There's a scrap of information out there. It just needs to be found."

They had dozens of agents, in both Del Rio and Houston, searching for that very scrap.

"You want me to wave a wand and produce a lead? And then what?"

"I spent the better part of the last decade finding terrorists hiding in the Hindu Kush. I can do this, Liz. I promise you. You give me a lead on this guy, and I'll run him down."

———

Buck's Truck Stop occupied Del Rio's busiest juncture and did a brisk business twenty-four seven. Besides offering food, lodging, and a deluxe car wash, the place boasted no fewer than thirty-six gas pumps. *Thirty-six.* Elizabeth glanced at them now as she motored past the sprawling complex and followed her GPS instructions down a narrow side street. A few more turns, and she pulled into a parking lot, where she spotted a dusty blue Subaru that was doing a passable imitation of a civilian vehicle. The sparkling-clean Taurus she'd rented at the airport stood out, so she drove around back.

"Nice ride," Torres quipped as she pulled up alongside a banana-yellow Honda with gold rims. "How come we never get the pimp-mobiles?"

A garage door lifted, and a heavy man with long sideburns waved them in. Evidently, their rental car was too conspicuous, even in back.

Elizabeth slid into the service bay and looked around. Several cars were up on lifts, and the place actually resembled a brake repair shop. In reality, it was the headquarters for a multiagency surveillance operation.

They got out. The place smelled like old motor oil and new tires. They introduced themselves to the undercover ICE agent who was their liaison for the morning, and he looked less than delighted to meet them.

"I'm Brad Parker." He gave a brief nod. "Follow me."

Elizabeth followed, wondering about the name. It sounded like an alias, like a throwaway name you'd give people from a rival agency you didn't really trust. He led them down a dingy hallway and into an even dingier room filled with computers. Agents sat at all of the monitors, tapping away or staring at surveillance footage.

"We've had two people on this since yesterday,"

Parker informed them. "No sign of your guy." He led them to the far side of the room. "This is Juan Garza, by the way. He just took over."

Garza—if that was really *his* name—glanced up from his computer and traded nods with his colleague.

"Special Agents LeBlanc and Torres, out of Houston," Parker said.

They weren't actually out of Houston, but she didn't bother to correct him.

"We're here to take a look at the surveillance footage," Elizabeth said. "Hoping you have some new leads for us."

Garza lifted a brow. "Not since I got here. Still no sign of him."

"We have him leaving the minivan, but that's it," Parker said. "No sign of him entering the store or of him walking off the premises. We've been through the truck stop footage twice already."

"Yours or theirs?" Elizabeth asked.

"Both. This spot has become a way station for traffickers. We've had surveillance on the place for fifteen months."

"We've expanded our search to surrounding businesses." Garza nodded at his screen. "Restaurants, ATMs . . . This right here is from the bank across the street."

Elizabeth watched the grainy black-and-white image for a few moments. Cars pulled in and out of the parking lot and the drive-through teller windows, business as usual, nothing sinister happening at the truck stop across the street. She glanced at the time stamp at the bottom of the screen. A full sixty-six minutes after Rasheed was filmed fleeing the coyote's vehicle.

"You want my guess?"

She looked at Parker.

"He had a ride waiting," he said. "Slipped around the corner of the building, hopped right in."

"Why don't we have that on camera, then?" Torres asked.

A shrug. "It's not like we have every angle. There are blind spots."

"Hey, hey." Garza straightened in his chair. "Check this out."

Everyone inched closer to look at the screen.

"What?" Parker asked.

Garza tapped the keyboard, rewinding the footage. "Upper left corner. Dark sedan."

Elizabeth watched, holding her breath, as a dark-colored four-door car moved into view. It rolled to a stop, and a shadow moved toward it.

"That's him! Pause it!" She leaned closer as he stopped the tape.

Torres looked at her. "Looks like we found his ride."

Derek had been right. The lead they needed was right in front of them, caught on camera. She felt the sudden urge to call him, but of course, she couldn't.

She studied the footage. Unfortunately, the car was angled, so no plates were visible. And the driver was nothing more than a dark silhouette. But still, they'd found a vehicle. Even without a plate, it could provide a wealth of information.

"Can you zoom in on that?" she asked.

"Not much." Garza clicked on the corner of the screen and managed to zoom a little but not enough to see anything of the driver besides the outline of a baseball cap.

"Our technicians can enlarge it, clean it up," Torres said.

"So can ours."

Turf wars. Perfect.

"Why don't you make us a copy, and we'll both take a crack at it?" Elizabeth looked at Parker. "We're going to need footage from every other security cam anywhere near this corner at"—she glanced at the time stamp—"five fifteen."

She leaned closer and studied the car's chassis. "That's a Chevy Cavalier," she said. "Cobalt blue, it looks like. Those tires aren't standard. Should be fourteen-inch, not eighteen."

Garza gave her a startled look. Men were always shocked that she knew anything about cars.

She glanced at the time stamp again. "That's sixty-eight minutes after he slipped from the truck. What was he doing all that time?"

"Sure you don't have him inside the truck stop?" Torres asked.

"We've been through it all," Parker said. "Repeatedly. Nothing of him entering the convenience store or the bathrooms. No cams in the restaurant, unfortunately, but—"

"There's a restaurant?" She looked at Torres. "We need to interview the wait staff."

"*Two* restaurants," Parker corrected. "This place has everything—a deli counter, showers, an Internet lounge, an arcade."

"An Internet lounge?" Her heart lurched.

"Yeah, right by the car wash. There're no cameras in there, though. We already checked."

But she wasn't thinking about cameras anymore. "Show me the Internet lounge."

Chapter Seven

Derek wasn't good at being on leave. He always felt restless. Twitchy. About three days in, he was usually bored out of his skull.

He'd woken up this morning at his parents' house, staring at a shelf full of swim trophies and auto-graphed baseballs. He'd pounded out ten miles and spent the remainder of the morning hauling boxes to the attic and changing lightbulbs for his mom. When he was all out of chores and errands, he'd loaded up his .300 and decided to hit the range.

Now he lay in the dirt with the steady pop of gunfire all around him. The smell of grass and CLP oil filled his nostrils as he peered through the rifle scope. He took a deep breath. Let it out some. Squeezed the trigger.

"Nice," murmured Cole, lowering the binoculars.

Cole had the same problem as Derek, the same problem a lot of SEALs had. They'd forgotten how to be home. When Derek had called, his teammate had been more than happy to make the hour-long drive from his family's place in Clear Lake to send a few rounds downrange.

Now Derek picked up the binocs as Cole adjusted his rifle and lined up his shot. He was using a .300 Win Mag, too, but his was brand-new, outfitted with an Accuracy International folding stock and a Night-force scope. The gun kicked ass. As one of the top marksmen in the teams, Cole took pride in having the best equipment available.

Derek glanced at the range flag. "Moderate wind, full value," he said.

Cole waited. Guys on either side of them fired, but Cole held back. Patience was a sniper's secret weapon.

Derek watched through the glass and mentally ticked off the seconds until his friend squeezed the trigger. The bullet found its target, a fifteen-inch gong ten football fields away.

"Perfect."

Cole smiled. "Yeah, not bad."

They'd gone through the ammo, so they stood and collected their gear. Derek shook out his stiff legs and glanced around. It was after five, and the range was filling up with potbellied sportsmen and weekend warriors.

"So you want to get a beer?" Cole asked.

"Sure." Derek grabbed the binocs.

"Hey, hold up. Maybe we should stay awhile."

Derek followed his friend's gaze to the front office, where a hot-looking blonde stood talking to the range master. Derek's heart gave a kick. Elizabeth was in one of those tailored gray suits that didn't quite hide her Glock 17 or the handcuffs she kept tucked under her jacket.

Cole whistled. "Man, I'd like to see her handle a gun."

The range master pointed in their direction, and she strode toward them with a determined gleam in her eyes.

"You know this girl?" Cole looked at him.

"Yep."

"Shit, I shoulda known. So much for that beer."

She stopped in front of them, and she had that set to her chin that got Derek's blood going.

"Sorry to interrupt. Do you have a minute, Lieutenant?"

Lieutenant. Derek smiled.

"Cole, meet Special Agent Elizabeth LeBlanc. She's with the FBI. Liz, Petty Officer Cole McDermott."

She offered him a hand. "Good to meet you."

"Likewise." He smiled at Derek. "Catch you later, bro." He slapped him on the back and headed off.

"Impressive setup." Elizabeth looked out at the range. "What is that, eight hundred yards?"

"A thousand. How'd you find me?"

"Talked to your mom," she said. "Very nice lady. A little shorter than I expected. Your dad must be huge."

The breeze played with her hair, and he noticed her scar again, the scar she'd somehow gotten at work. She didn't want to talk about it, which told him he wasn't going to like the story—if he ever managed to coax it out of her.

He couldn't *make* her tell him. It wasn't like they were in a relationship. No, if they'd been in a relationship, he'd still be spending months at a time away from her, but at least when he came home, he'd get some relief from the relentless yearning that wouldn't stop dogging him. As it was, he couldn't get anything from her, not even a phone call. He'd called her up after his last deployment, and she hadn't even bothered to return his messages.

But she was here now. And although he was ninety-nine-percent sure this little visit was about work, he'd take whatever advantage he could get and exploit the hell out of it.

"Want to do some shooting?" he asked. "I can grab us some ammo."

"No, thanks. I'm here on business. Is there somewhere we can talk?"

He led her around to the front, where he slipped some quarters into a drink machine. He pounded out a Coke and offered it to her, but she shook her head. He took her to a low brick wall that divided the range from the gravel parking lot. Her generic white rental car looked like a toy in the sea of pickups.

She sat down on the wall. "I've been thinking about your offer."

He smiled as he popped open the can. "Which offer is that?"

She pretended not to understand. "You said you might be able to help locate Rasheed."

"Not 'might.' I said I would." He swigged his drink. "Provided you give me some intel."

She glanced around, clearly uncomfortable, which told him she was doing this on the down-low. She pulled a folded slip of paper from her purse. "You were right." She handed him the paper. "About the surveillance cams. We have Rasheed getting into a 2005 Chevrolet Cavalier."

Derek sat down beside her and studied the pic-

ture, which had obviously been enlarged. Rasheed
was fairly clear, but the driver was little more than a
shadow wearing a baseball hat.

"No plate?" He looked at her.

"Unfortunately, no. We've checked stoplight cams,
ATMs, all the gas stations in town."

"Where'd this come from?"

"A bank several blocks from the truck stop," she
said. "It's the only camera footage we've been able to
find. The driver navigated to and from the truck stop
on side streets, avoiding all major intersections—
which suggests to us that they know the area is under
surveillance and scoped it out ahead of time."

"These guys are smart. They plan operations years
in advance. You can't underestimate them."

"I know." She leaned closer, and he could smell
her perfume or her shampoo or whatever it was. She
pointed at the picture. "See this back panel here?
There's a slight dent in it. Another distinguishing
characteristic is the oversized tires. Factory tires for
this car are fourteen inches, not eighteen. But aside
from that—"

"It'd be better to have a license plate."

"I know." She looked up at him. "But right now,
this is it. Sixty-eight minutes after Rasheed is first seen
arriving at the truck stop, he catches a ride with a blue
Chevy Cavalier. I'm working one more lead, though:
the registration sticker on the windshield. I sent the
image to our lab techs to see if they can enlarge it."

He looked at her. "Not a bad idea."

"Thank you."

Derek stared down at the picture, examining the
time stamp. "Come on." He swung his legs over the

wall and led her to the parking lot. He dug a map from the glove box in his truck and spread it out on the dusty hood.

"What are you looking for?" she asked.

"He slipped through our back door into Texas. He knows Del Rio's a hub for trafficking. He knows it's under surveillance by the feds. Which means his contact knows better than to circle around town, attracting attention. I'm thinking the driver was waiting somewhere else and made the trip straight in, which gives us a seventy-mile radius . . ." He scanned the towns around Del Rio.

"*If* he drove the speed limit."

"Safe bet. If they're avoiding surveillance cams, they're avoiding traffic cops, too. Bingo." He tapped the map. "Uvalde. You should check out this town."

"We're already on it. But you're assuming someone drove straight there. The driver could have waited after getting the call, then come from someplace only a few miles away."

"I'm not seeing it," Derek said. "Why risk exposure longer than necessary? And how about communication? Was he using a cell phone?"

"We're checking electronic surveillance in the area," she said, "but no leads so far. I think he may have had another way of communicating."

"Like what?"

"There's an Internet lounge at Buck's."

"There you go."

"We sifted through everything that day, the browsing history on ten separate computers. It's all your basic stuff—people checking e-mail, Facebook, some thinly disguised porn sites. But there was something unusual." She leaned against his truck. "One user—who used a prepaid credit card, by the way—visited a home-improvement blog."

"Home improvement," Derek repeated.

"Yeah, sounds odd, right? I wrote the site address on the other side of the page I gave you. It looks like Rasheed posted a comment. Our analysts believe it was a coded message to his contact about when and where to pick him up."

"Interesting tactic."

"I know." She met his gaze and seemed to realize she was standing close enough for him to see down her blouse. She eased back. "Here's how this is going to work."

He lifted an eyebrow.

"You dig up anything—and I mean anything—about Rasheed's whereabouts, I need you to call me immediately."

"How about I tell you in person?" He reached over and tucked a wisp of hair behind her ear. "That way you'll have a chance to thank me."

"Do you ever think about anything besides sex?"

"Yeah, but I have to be honest, Liz. I've been thinking about it a lot lately."

"I'm not joking here." She looked frustrated, which was even more of a turn-on than when she looked businesslike. "If you find anything at all, I need you to call. Don't go all cowboy on me and try to take him down yourself."

"Cowboy?"

"You know what I mean. I'm sticking my neck out for you here, and I need your word."

"If I find anything, I'll let you know." *Eventually*.

She looked up at him, and the little line between her brows told him she didn't fully trust him. The woman had good instincts. She broke eye contact and pushed off of the truck. "So that's it."

"Where are you going?"

"I'm late for a briefing." She checked her watch. "I drove all the way out here, and now I have to fight traffic back to my office."

"So why'd you come?" He stepped closer.

"I agreed I'd try to get you something. I honor my agreements."

"Yeah, but you could have done it over the phone."

She looked up at him, and her cheeks flushed, because they both knew he was right.

He smiled. "Thanks for the tip."

"Sorry it's not much to go on."

"Don't be sorry. It's more than you think."

————

Luke was being followed.

He wasn't sure how he knew, exactly, but his frog sense had been going crazy the last few hours, starting before his beach run and continuing when he swung by the grocery for pizza and beer. He'd shaken it on the way home, but as he pulled into his parking lot it was back again, that jangly feeling that told him someone was on his tail.

Luke checked his rearview. Nothing. He grabbed his groceries and got out, subtly scanning the area as he neared the building.

Gotcha.

Dark blue sedan, end of the block. He'd seen the

same vehicle parked at the beach, but there had been a couple of patrol cars there, too, responding to a call, so he'd chalked it up to San Diego PD.

Luke headed for the mailboxes, which gave him a few extra seconds to scope out the car. Dark blue Taurus, late-model, antenna on the back. Two silhouettes inside, both tall. He took out his phone, tried to remember who was around. Derek and Cole were in Texas. Owen had gone to L.A. with some cocktail waitress, and Greg was with his fiancée. He called Ric Gonzales.

"Gonzo, it's Jones. What's your twenty?" He could tell from the noise that he was somewhere crowded, most likely a bar.

"I'm at O'Malley's. You coming?"

No way. Luke was still feeling the effects of last night and the night before that. He'd spent the past four days getting wasted and hooking up with women whose names he barely remembered, in a pathetic attempt to forget their last mission. But it was still stuck on replay in his brain.

"Think I'm in for the night." Luke rested the phone on his shoulder as he shifted his bags and unlocked his mailbox.

"Dude, you're killing me. Come play pool with us. I just won fifty bucks off some jarheads. Easy money tonight."

Luke grabbed a pile of junk mail. "I'll think about it. Hey, I got a question for you. You noticed anyone on your six today?"

"No. Why?"

"I've got someone following me."

"Who?"

"Feebies, I think. You haven't noticed anyone?"

"No, man. Why would feds be tailing you?"

It was a good question. And he was beginning to think it had something to do with the meeting he'd had with all the suits the other day. In which case, they might only be tailing him and Derek. Or maybe just him. Luke glanced around and spotted a second familiar vehicle, a white Toyota he could have sworn had been in his rearview mirror when he stopped at the store. So two cars following him. No silhouette in this one.

"Jones?"

"Yeah, forget it," he told him. "It's probably nothing."

"What the fuck do they want?"

"Who knows?"

"Bring 'em on down to O'Malley's, and we'll ask 'em."

"Yeah, maybe I will. Catch you later."

"Later."

Luke dropped his phone into his grocery bag and glanced at the car one last time as he headed back toward the stairs. Gonzo had a good idea. Maybe he'd screw with these guys a little before giving them the slip.

Luke's apartment building was a two-story square. All four sides looked out over a central courtyard that was basically a patch of asphalt ever since the el cheapo management company decided to fill in the pool that used to be there. The place had two staircases and a walkway that surrounded the second floor. His unit was closest to the west staircase. Luke took the steps at a deliberately slow pace, unlocked his door, and paused to listen.

Footsteps on the other staircase. He set his stuff inside the door and loudly pulled it shut. Then he crept soundlessly around the corner and waited.

More footsteps.

He slipped past the north-facing units and around the other side. He reached the south units just as a dark form disappeared around the corner.

Rookie. Luke would have loved to tackle him right there, but he'd probably piss his pants or maybe fire off a shot. He'd settle for letting him know he'd been made. A few more steps. He listened. Nothing.

Luke rounded the corner and smacked into the guy, sending him sprawling on his ass.

Only it wasn't a guy. Luke's heart damn near stopped.

"Holy shit, *Hailey*?" He dropped to a crouch beside her. "Are you okay?" He noticed the cast peeking from the sleeve of her windbreaker. "Shit, did I hurt your arm?"

She rolled to her knees. "It's okay."

He wanted to help her to her feet, but he was scared to touch her. She got up on her own, and then they were standing there, and she was gazing up at him with those blue eyes that had been haunting him for weeks.

"Hi." She smiled. Sort of. It was more like a grimace.

"Really, did I hurt you?"

"I'm fine." She glanced around. "I didn't mean to crash into you."

She met his gaze again. *Hailey Gardner*. It was freaking bizarre. At first he'd thought he was hallucinating, but she was right there, staring up at him from beneath the brim of a Boston Red Sox cap. What the hell was she doing here?

"You're probably wondering why I'm here."

"Yeah, I am."

"Is there a place we can talk?" She glanced over her shoulder. "There's something I need to tell you."

Chapter Eight

Luke was hyperaware of the fact that he hadn't shaved in three days and he smelled like ass from his six-mile run. But Hailey didn't seem to notice as she took a seat at the graffiti-covered picnic table in the middle of the courtyard. He'd considered taking her to his apartment . . . for about a nanosecond. But the place was a mess, and he was pretty sure he'd left a condom wrapper on the table by the couch.

He sat downwind of her on the bench. She wore a black windbreaker that swallowed her and probably belonged to her dad or maybe her boyfriend, and she'd flipped the cuffs up. Under the jacket, she had on one of those clingy black yoga outfits. She also wore Adidas running shoes, no socks, and she had her hair pulled back in a ponytail. The sporty look had always done it for him, and her stretchy top showed off a very nice rack. And he was probably going straight to hell for thinking about her breasts right now, but they were right there in front of him, and he couldn't help it.

"You look surprised to see me," she said.

"You could say that."

Last time he'd seen her, she'd been sitting on a gurney in the base infirmary waiting to have her arm set. Her face had been tear-stained and filthy, and Luke had been trying for weeks to forget the shattered look in her eyes.

"One of my college roommates lives here," she said. "She thought maybe I could use a break, so . . . she invited me out for a visit."

He just looked at her.

"She lives up in La Jolla," she added, because he was sitting there like a moron, not making this any easier for her.

"So you're staying up there, or . . . ?"

"I'm at the Del."

The Del. As in the Hotel Del Coronado. He remembered that she came from money—at the time of the raid, her family had actually been trying to help MedAssist come up with the ransom money. Ten million dollars. They had to be seriously loaded to think they could even get near an amount like that.

She glanced around the courtyard, probably second-guessing her decision to come here.

He still couldn't believe she was *here*. The feds on his street were starting to make sense now. Derek had told him that when he'd dropped in on Hailey at her parents' condo, she had her own private security detail. So the feds hadn't been tailing him. They'd been tailing Hailey, who'd been tailing him. He'd bet the white Toyota down the street was her rental car.

Damn, it was weird to see her.

"How's your arm?" he asked.

"Fine." Her smile was tight this time. Maybe she didn't want to be reminded about her ordeal. Although he doubted a minute went by that she didn't think about it.

"How are *you*?" she asked.

The look of concern on her face made his chest tighten. She was worried about him? He wasn't the one who'd come home in a cast. Or a pine box.

"I'm doing all right." He thought of his alcohol-fueled sex binge. "Most days, anyway."

"That's good to hear." She looked down at her lap. "So there's something I need to tell you. Two things, really." She touched her hand to her neck and cleared her throat. "Sorry. This is harder than I thought."

Luke waited. Dread pooled in his gut as he thought about what on earth she could have traveled hundreds of miles to tell him. Even if she'd come out here to see a girlfriend, she'd still gone to the effort of finding him at home.

She met his gaze. "First, I want you to know how sorry I am. About Sean Harper."

His throat burned. "Thank you."

"You two were close, I take it?"

He nodded.

She looked down again. "I could tell. Everything you did in the helicopter . . . the way you talked to him. I'm sure it was comforting to him to hear your voice right then."

As he bled out, she meant. Luke had been elbow-deep in Sean's blood, and by the time they'd loaded him onto the medevac plane, he'd barely had a pulse.

She looked across the courtyard at a pair of abandoned scooters. "I keep thinking about that day—the first day—about how if we'd taken another route, or left earlier, or had one more car in our convoy, none of this would have happened."

"Don't." He put his hand on her knee, then quickly pulled it away. "You can't think like that. Take it from me. You can't think like that, or you'll go crazy."

For a moment, she just stared at him. Then she said, "The other thing I wanted to say is thank you."

He didn't respond.

"What you guys did for me . . . what *you* did—"

"It's my job," he said, and it came out too harshly, because she looked stung. "I mean, you don't have to thank me. It was—" *My pleasure to rescue you?* If he said something that stupid, he should be strung up from the nearest tree. "It was my privilege to be able to help."

Which sounded only slightly less idiotic. She was staring at him now, no doubt thinking he was a total asshole, and he didn't blame her.

"So . . . how long are you in town?" he asked.

She bit her lip as she looked at him, and he prayed she was going to get off the serious stuff. He wasn't good at shit like this. It was no secret that his bedside manner sucked. It was even a joke in the teams—his bedside manner consisted of bedding as many women as possible in any manner he could.

And if she'd been able to read his mind right now, she'd probably run straight back to La Jolla.

"My plans are kind of up in the air," she said, looking away. "I was thinking a long weekend."

"Well, I hope you enjoy your stay."

The silence stretched out, and the only sound was

the faint noise of a TV in one of the nearby apartments. She stood up, taking her cue, and he felt a mix of relief and disappointment as he stood, too.

She was leaving. This was it. He'd probably never see her again. Something clawed at his stomach, but for the life of him, he couldn't think of what to say or how to keep her in the courtyard of his slummy apartment for even a minute longer.

"Well . . . 'bye, then." She held out her hand, cast and everything. "It was good to see you."

———

Elizabeth sat on the floor of her hotel room amid case files and cartons of Thai noodles. After a marathon team meeting, they'd downshifted into sweatpants and carryout food.

"I still can't believe I'm here."

Elizabeth glanced over at Lauren as she picked at her noodles. "Why?"

"Do you realize we're working for Gordon Moore? I can't understand why he put me on this team."

Elizabeth set her carton aside. "He works in mysterious ways."

"You, I get," Lauren said. "You've worked for him before. But why me?"

"Because you're an expert on the Saledo cartel, and they play an important role in this. And because you're a great agent."

She snorted.

"What?"

"I won't argue," Lauren said, "but really, come on. Let's get real. I'm a good agent, yeah, but this task force already has a token female." She reached for Elizabeth's carton. "You finished with that?"

"Help yourself."

Elizabeth had thought long and hard about why she'd been picked for this task force, and she doubted it was because she was a token female. She had the sneaking suspicion that Gordon had put her on the team specifically to keep tabs on Derek. Gordon was manipulating her, and by getting closer to Derek, she was playing right into his hands.

"Anyway," Lauren said, "I don't want to look a gift assignment in the mouth, so . . . done worrying about it. How'd breakfast with your friend go?"

"It got cut short." Elizabeth slurped her drink. "I had a meeting."

Her mind flashed to today's encounter with Derek on the firing range. And even more unexpected, her encounter with his mother. SEALs often seemed like superheroes, capable of death-defying feats of strength and bravery. Sometimes it seemed like they came from another planet, so it was almost surprising to discover that Derek came from a tree-lined street in suburbia.

His mom had seemed so normal. So friendly. And clearly bursting with curiosity about why an FBI agent would want to talk to her son.

"That's it?" Lauren stared at her. "That's not much of a review."

"It wasn't much of an event."

Elizabeth watched Lauren finish off the noodles and thought about whether to tell her about Derek. She felt awkward. Opening up about her personal life didn't come naturally.

"There's more, isn't there?" Lauren asked. "Are you hung up on this guy?"

"What? No."

She was saved from further explanation by a knock at the door and jumped up to answer it. "That'll be Potter."

Lauren sighed. "So much for girl talk."

It was standing room only the next morning in the briefing room.

"Something's up," Torres muttered as he grabbed a patch of wall space next to Elizabeth.

Torres was right. There was a definite tension buzzing in the air. The entire team was here, and the only hint that it was Saturday morning was that several agents wore workout gear instead of their usual suits, as if they'd been called in on their way to the gym. Elizabeth had a feeling their morning plans were about to get disrupted.

Gordon strode through the door, closely followed by his tech expert from Washington. He looked over the assembled troops and motioned for everyone to sit. He sank into a chair as his assistant flashed some slides onto a screen.

"Several updates," he said briskly. "As you all know, Interpol uses one of the most advanced facial-recognition programs on the planet at border checkpoints. What you may *not* know is that that system was recently upgraded. They just implemented a state-of-the-art software package that allows them to identify, match, and cross-check literally millions of faces a day with unbelievable accuracy. Today it identified these two men."

Two separate pictures appeared of men standing at immigration checkpoints. Elizabeth recognized Rasheed.

"Both of these images were captured ten days ago," Gordon said. "The man on the left is traveling under the name Martin Delgado, but you'll recognize him as Omar Rasheed."

"Who's the man on the right?" Torres asked.

"As of now, he is our biggest problem." Gordon paused and looked around. "His name is Zahid Ameen. He's on the terrorist watch list for numerous bombings and was most recently implicated in an attack on a bus in Kabul."

The image of a charred bus carcass flashed onto the screen.

"Sixteen schoolchildren died in this bombing, all girls, along with twelve adults. The bus was on its way to a newly opened school."

Silence fell over the room.

"Ten days ago, Ameen boarded a flight from Athens to Caracas, Venezuela, that landed just hours before Rasheed's flight. One week ago, Rasheed entered the U.S. with a Mexican coyote, most likely through border tunnels controlled by the Saledo cartel. We believe Ameen did the same."

"What do the Venezuelans have on them?" The question came from Lauren, who was seated across the room.

"Nothing," Gordon said. "Or at least, nothing they're willing to share. Our relations with them haven't exactly been cozy lately."

Elizabeth's stomach tensed as she looked at the mangled bus. Sixteen schoolgirls. There had to be a special place in hell for someone who would do that.

"If he's on a watch list, why didn't they pick him up in Athens?" Lauren asked.

"His passport worked," Gordon said. "And he's had some plastic surgery recently. Looking at our previous photos of him, there isn't much resemblance, so it's no surprise they missed him. But this new biometric security software they've got—it's beyond anything anyone's ever seen before. Its matches are amazingly accurate. Based on this intelligence, we are now operating under the assumption that both Rasheed and Ameen are within our borders, and they're working in tandem. We believe they have contacts here. And we believe they're planning an attack."

Gordon turned to face the screen displaying the charred bus. "With Ameen involved, we know that no target is too soft—schools, shopping malls, subway stations. Heavy civilian casualties are his trademark, and he's completely without conscience. We are pulling out all the stops to find him. Every agency in Homeland Security is engaged in this manhunt."

"How about enlisting outside help?" Elizabeth suggested.

"We have," Gordon said. "Interpol has been cooperative, and they're working on the Venezuelans."

"I meant American help. Special ops people, like SEALs. Hunting terrorists is what they do."

Gordon's jaw tightened. "That's right. But what they *don't* do is conduct operations on U.S. soil. That's our job."

"What about the DEA down in Del Rio?" Lauren asked. "Are we still working on that license plate?"

"No new leads on the plate, but we're pursuing another angle. Our lab techs have enlarged the surveillance image and are trying to get a number off the vehicle registration sticker affixed to the windshield. If they're successful, it could lead to a name and address of this mystery accomplice." He looked at Elizabeth, whose idea it had been, and she felt both proud and relieved to have come up with a fresh lead.

"You think it's the same person whose print is on the laptop?" Lauren asked.

"Could be," Gordon said, "but we won't know unless we get our hands on that Chevy and have a chance to recover prints. Personally, I'd rather get my hands on the terrorists.

"Meanwhile, our cyber-crimes team is focused on the chat-room angle. Torres and LeBlanc are working with the Del Rio agents, in case they come up with something new."

A young admin stepped into the room and whispered something in Gordon's ear. He listened a moment, nodded, and then sat forward in his chair, clearly ready to wrap up the meeting.

"Each one of you has a job to do. But I need you to be ready to move the second we get word on that car registration. SWAT is on standby if and when we get an address." He stood up. "That's it."

Everyone filed out as Gordon reached for the phone in the middle of the table.

"LeBlanc, wait." He muted the call. "You've been in touch with our SEAL friends, I take it."

She glanced at the phone, wondering who was on the other end—someone important enough to adjourn the meeting. She looked Gordon in the eye. "They're eager to help, sir. They've seen this sort of carnage up close, so they're in a unique position to understand the threat we're facing. Plus, they're skilled at tracking terrorists."

"They're also skilled at killing terrorists. Your friends in particular have a personal vendetta, as one of their teammates died in the operation that started all this. Make no mistake. If those SEALs find Rasheed, they will take him out, and we'll never even know they were there. The FBI's objective is to apprehend these men, interrogate them, and put a stop to their attack."

His look was intense, and she glanced over his shoulder at the burned-out school bus.

"But—"

"You have a job to do, LeBlanc, and we don't have time to waste."

Chapter Nine

Kelsey greeted Derek in the Delphi Center lobby with a wary smile.

"You're back," she said, giving him a hug. She wore jeans with dirt patches on the knees, which told him she'd probably spent her morning outside digging up bones. "Mia's not in this morning. And I don't think she's done with your analysis yet."

"I know," Derek said. "Gage told me I'd find you here. These are for you."

"Hmm . . ." She took the brown paper bag and peeked inside. "Peach kolaches, wow. I feel another favor coming."

"Word is you guys have one of the best cyber-crime units in the country."

"*The* best. It's headed up by Mark Wolfe. He's a legend in law-enforcement circles."

"He around?"

"No."

"Any of his people around?"

Kelsey tipped her head to the side. "I could probably scare someone up for you. You'll need to sign in, though."

Kelsey got him a visitor's badge from the security guard, and Derek followed her to a bank of elevators.

"You always work Saturdays?" he asked.

"I taught a class this morning on postmortem interval and insect activity."

"Sounds like a class I'd be tempted to ditch," Derek said.

"Actually, there's a waiting list." She watched him as they stepped onto the elevator and were whisked up to the top floor. "You know, a lot of guys spend their leave drinking beer and picking up women."

"So I hear."

The doors slid open, and they stepped out.

"This is about that mission that went sideways, isn't it?" she asked.

"'Fraid so."

She led him down a long glass corridor. It had a view of the Hill Country on one side and a computer lab on the other.

A tall, lanky man stepped into the hallway. Scruffy, goatee. He wore a Sublime T-shirt and had a computer bag slung over his shoulder.

"Damn, you're leaving," Kelsey said.

"What's up?" His gaze shifted from Kelsey to Derek.

"Ben Lawson, this is Derek Vaughn, a friend of Gage's. He's hoping to get your input on something."

"I've got an Ultimate game at ten."

"This'll take five minutes," Derek said.

"Let's grab a conference room," Kelsey added,

not giving him a chance to resist. She led them into a room across the hall, and Ben sank into a chair. Derek took the seat across from him.

"I've got a Web address," Derek said, "and I need the physical locations of the computers that have posted comments on the site. That something you can do?"

Ben looked Derek over a moment, then put his computer bag on the table and pulled out a Mac. Derek rattled off the address.

"Lot of comments here," Ben said as he scrolled through the site. "It'll take some time."

"But you can get the locations?"

"Sure, provided they didn't use anonymizers. Even if they did, I can still get them, but it's more work."

Derek slid a slip of paper across the table. "I need everything starting with this comment. Especially anything posted from a Houston-area location."

Kelsey leaned over Ben's shoulder and read the screen, frowning. "Bathroom tile? What is this?"

"Reads like a coded message," Ben said.

Derek nodded. "It was posted from a truck stop, possibly by a terrorist who'd just slipped through the border. I think he's using this home-improvement blog to communicate with his cell."

Ben leaned back in his chair. "A terrorist."

"That's right."

"Why isn't the FBI involved?"

"They are. I'm hoping you're faster."

"Um, hello?" Kelsey looked at Derek. "Terrorists who tile? What the hell is this?"

"The cyber-jihad," Ben told her. "The Internet's become a town square for terrorist orgs. They use it for clandestine communication, recruiting, reconnaissance, even psychological warfare—like when they executed that aid worker and posted the video."

Derek clenched his teeth as he thought of Ana Hansson kneeling in the dirt. Hailey Gardner would have been next in line.

"You think this is some kind of initiation code?" Ben asked.

"Could be."

Ben glanced at his watch. "Looks like my game just got canceled."

Kelsey leaned closer and read the words aloud. "'Interesting Advice Here on Bathroom Tile/Shower. Ready to start Five by Fifteen room.'" She looked at Derek. "Sounds awkward, but how is it a code?"

"Look at the caps," Derek said. "Maybe it really means, 'I Am Here at Buck's Truck Stop. Ready at Five Fifteen,' which is the exact time our tango was picked up by someone at that location. I want to know who that someone was."

"Mohamed Atta used something similar," Ben said. "He sent a coded e-mail to Al Qaeda right before the 9/11 attacks. But this could be one-way communication. So I can run this down for you, but there's no guarantee anyone answered back."

"I know," Derek said. "Just do the best you can. Any comment that looks like a reply to the truck stop comment, or anything at all from the Houston area, could be from an accomplice. What I need is a location. Oh, and heads-up, you need to be stealth about it. Don't leave any footprints on the site unless you want trouble with the feds."

Ben smiled. "Stealth is my specialty."

Derek glanced at Kelsey, who was giving him a worried look. It stayed on her face all the way down to the lobby, and he knew what she was going to say as she ushered him out the door.

"Thanks for the help," he told her, trying to distract her. "Gage speaks highly of your people here."

"This isn't your problem anymore, Derek. If they're in our borders, the FBI has jurisdiction."

"I'm aware."

"Then why are you involved?"

"I'm not."

She looked at him.

"Just doing a little recon, that's all," he said. "If I get anything useful, I'll pass it along."

———————

"Hey, it's me." Derek's low drawl sent a rush of warmth through her.

"What are you doing?" she asked.

"Working. How 'bout you?"

"Same."

"How's it going today?"

Crappy, she wanted to say. She'd spent the past six hours sitting in a sweltering car, sans air-conditioning, staking out an Internet café in Montrose. "Fine," she said instead.

"Any sightings?"

"No."

"Me, neither."

The passenger door opened, and two-hundred-plus pounds of muscled man slid in beside her. Elizabeth's heart lurched.

"How did you get here?" she blurted.

"Drove."

"No, I mean how'd you find this place?"

He smiled. "That's top secret."

She waited, watching him, and he leaned closer.

"How bad do you want to know? 'Cause I'm willing to give it up."

"Derek, I'm serious."

He sighed and grabbed the water bottle from the cup holder. "I know you are." He took a swig. "I found this place the same way you did, I'm guessing. Traced a blog comment to an ISP. Any new leads?"

She looked out the window, trying to get her heart rate back to normal. Not possible with him in the car. He was in jeans and cowboy boots again, but now he had a leather jacket on, too, probably to conceal the loaded pistol he was no doubt carrying.

"Elizabeth?"

She cleared her throat. "As a matter of fact, yes. We managed to trace the registration sticker."

"You don't sound excited."

"The Chevy's registered to a student at Rice University," she said. "He sold his car three weeks ago, presumably to one of our tangos."

"And?"

She looked at him. "And a week later, he was killed in a mugging."

"A mugging."

"Someone accosted him outside a bar here in Montrose. Shot him at point-blank range, took his phone, his wallet. We're investigating the case now, obviously. There's an evidence response team at the victim's apartment, turning the place inside out, looking for anything on this car buyer he met up with right before his death."

Derek shook his head.

"What do you think?"

"I think they're cleaning up loose ends," he said, "eliminating anyone who can identify them."

She sighed. "That's what I think, too."

"Also sounds to me like the car's important. Maybe part of the plot somehow."

She thought back to the mangled school bus and stifled a shudder. In the right location, a car bomb could wreak havoc. Should she tell Derek about Zahid Ameen? She'd thought about it. It was something he'd definitely want to know, but he was already too involved.

She looked across the street at the Galaxy Café. It had a giant moon for a logo and offered coffee and free Wi-Fi to a steady stream of starving artists and college students.

"It's a good strategy," Derek said.

"What?"

"Staking out the neighborhood. People are creatures of habit, even terrorists. We know one of them used the Internet here. We know one of them bought a car from a kid in school less than a mile away. This feels like their comfort zone."

"You think? Because to me, it feels like a dead end." She couldn't hide the frustration in her voice. "If these guys are so smart, they won't use the same Internet café more than once."

She glanced at Derek, whose attention was trained on the door. She thought of his petite mother, who'd been so friendly to her when she stopped by the house yesterday. *I'm sorry you missed Derek. Come back anytime.* Was it just typical Texas hospitality, or did she really mean it? Elizabeth wasn't sure why it should matter to her, but it did.

"How's your family?" she asked.

He sent her a sideways look.

"Your parents? Your sisters? Have you had a chance to see them all?"

"They're fine." His tone was cautious, as though he was surprised she'd asked a personal question.

Because why would she? For days, he'd made no secret of wanting to jump into bed with her. But heaven forbid she might ask about his personal life.

She took the bottle of water from him. "They don't mind you coming home, then immediately going AWOL on them?"

"I don't stick around the house much when I'm in town. Makes me stir-crazy."

She guzzled some water. She pictured him at a bar, drinking and picking up women. He probably didn't even have to put much effort into it. From what she'd seen, women threw themselves at him wherever he went.

The thought put a sour taste in her mouth. Looking out the window again, she wiped the sweat from her brow with the back of her hand. God, she probably looked terrible. Not that it mattered. But she'd been sitting in this car so long every inch of her felt sticky.

"You ever going to tell me about that scar?"

She looked at him, then back at the café. "It's a long story."

He shifted in his seat, settling in. "Good thing we've got time to kill."

He wasn't going to let it go. She'd known he wouldn't, but she'd been stalling. She should just tell him and get it over with before he realized how much she hated talking about it.

"It was one of our biggest cases this spring," she said. "You might have missed it because you were deployed. There was a bombing at a university—"

"Philadelphia. I saw the story. You were involved in that?"

"You sound surprised."

"I am. Would have thought the Philly office would be all over it."

"They were, but we got pulled in because of a Texas connection. Anyway, we traced one of the suspects to San Antonio. I was following up on a lead, and one of them found me." She fixed her gaze on the café and let the words flow out without thinking about them. "He disarmed me. Pistol-whipped me. Took me hostage. Would have killed me if someone hadn't discovered where I was in time."

"Name?" His voice was neutral, but his look was sharp as a blade.

"What, you want to go after him?"

His silence told her that was exactly what he wanted.

A chill snaked down her spine, and she glanced away. "Doesn't matter. He's locked up, and he's never getting out."

Quiet settled over them, and the only sound was the grumble of traffic outside. She slid a look at him. Would he really hurt someone for her? In her heart, she knew he would. The thought was disturbingly comforting.

"That wasn't that long a story," he pointed out.

She gazed out the window. She'd omitted a few parts. The icy terror of feeling the muzzle against her neck. The burning humiliation of being disarmed and smacked down and at the mercy of a man's fists. The raw panic of trying to look people in the eye afterward, especially people at work.

Some details she still couldn't talk about, couldn't even think about, until Demon Insomnia bitch-slapped her awake in the middle of the night.

Derek reached across the console and squeezed her hand. "Thanks for telling me."

"Sure." Like it was no big deal.

She stared at his hand, big as a baseball mitt, and felt a warm pull. He'd always seemed so brave. So strong. And she had the urge to fall into him and let everything out, all the pain and fear and anxiety of the past three months. Maybe if she curled up on a giant bed with him, she could just *sleep* and not lie awake all night, listening to the sound of her own pulse racing.

Yeah, right. If she got anywhere near a bed with him, sleep would be the last thing on her mind.

She tugged her hand away and checked her phone. Nothing. Gordon hadn't pinged her all afternoon, demonstrating exactly how much importance had been placed on this stakeout: none. No one believed their suspects would use the same Internet café twice.

"Hey."

She glanced at Derek.

"You look tapped," he said. "How long you been sitting here?"

"Six hours."

"Let's get some food. Torres can cover for you."

She frowned. "How did—"

"Black Ford at the end of the block. You guys need to get some better cars."

She stared at him for a long moment, and she knew that he was right. She'd skipped lunch, and she was completely fried.

She picked up the radio and called Torres.

"You have eyes on the door?" she asked.

"Yeah."

"If you can cover this, I'm going to take a quick dinner break."

"How long?" His tone was clipped, meaning he'd seen Derek slip into the car with her.

"Thirty minutes? I'll let you know when I'm back."

She started up the car, cringing at the blast of hot air that shot from the vents. She cranked the AC to high and glanced at Derek.

"Where to? Somewhere close," she said.

"There's a Dillo Burger two blocks over."

She winced. "Sounds like roadkill."

"Finnegan's is on Sunset."

She'd been to Finnegan's. It was a popular sports bar lined with dark, cozy booths.

"Dillo is closer," she said, pulling out of the space. She squeezed her way into traffic and glanced at Derek. "Any other leads you want to tell us about?"

He looked at her and raised an eyebrow. "Nope."

She wasn't sure whether to believe him. She'd known when she passed along the car info that there was a strong chance he might shut her out and go off on his own. But after all the recent setbacks, it was a chance she was willing to take. SEALs were experts at escape and evasion, and she could use a fresh perspective.

She eased into a turn lane and swung into Dillo Burger's parking lot. A giant aluminum armadillo sat atop the sign, and she couldn't believe she was about to buy meat here. She pulled into a space.

"They'd better not have a wait," she said. "I'm starving."

Derek clamped a hand over her wrist. "Hold on."

"What?"

He was staring at the side mirror. Elizabeth turned to see what he was looking at, and her breath caught.

"Oh, my God. It's him."

Chapter Ten

Her brain registered details as she shoved the car back into gear: five-eight, one-forty. Omar Rasheed was clean-shaven, neatly dressed, and sliding behind the wheel of a blue Chevy Cavalier. He pulled out of the gas station.

"Move over."

She glanced at Derek. "What?"

"I'm a better driver than you."

She snatched up the radio and shot backward from the space. "Torres, it's me. You copy?"

Static filled the car as she swung out of the parking lot.

"Liz, really, you're going to get us burned."

She let a BMW cut in front of her, creating space between her and the Chevy.

"Torres, you copy?"

"Yo."

"We've sighted Rasheed at the Exxon—" She looked around, gripping the radio. "Montrose and

Filmore. He's headed south in a blue Chevy Cavalier."

"Copy that." His voice vibrated with excitement. "You're sure it's him?"

"I'm sure."

"Ease back, Liz, you're too close."

She shot Derek a glare, then tapped the brakes. The Chevy was now three cars ahead. She followed, trying to stay inconspicuous.

"Crap, he's turning," she said.

"Take it slow."

"Torres, he's on Richmond, proceeding west," she reported. "I repeat, *west* toward the Galleria."

Elizabeth watched the car, hardly able to believe it. But it was real. It was Omar Rasheed, and she wasn't mistaken about it. She hung back now, watching with panic as the Chevy sailed through an intersection and the light turned yellow.

"Shit!" She slapped the steering wheel.

"Relax. He'll catch the next one." But Derek's tone wasn't relaxed at all as the Chevy became a distant dot amid a river of taillights.

The light changed. Elizabeth gunned it.

"Don't get burned," Derek warned as she veered around a delivery truck. The car ahead hit the brakes, and she swerved, cutting off a pickup and earning an angry honk.

She navigated through traffic, trying to keep her nerves under control while her mind raced. Where was he going? Whatever happened, she couldn't lose him. But she couldn't get burned, either.

She felt Derek's tension beside her as she sped through the next intersection, trying to keep him in sight.

"He's heading for the Galleria," she said tightly. The largest mall in Houston, in the entire *state*. And it was Saturday.

"Light's about to change," Derek said.

It turned yellow, and she stomped on the gas. They sailed through the intersection. She fought traffic for several minutes, gripping the wheel and trying to keep the blue Chevy in view.

"Elizabeth? You copy?"

"Torres, he's nearing the mall—"

"Turning north," Derek cut in.

"He just turned *north*—"

"What street?" Torres asked.

"No idea. Southeast of the mall." She shot a look at Derek and knew he was thinking the same thing. *What's he doing at a shopping mall?*

Horns blared as she swerved around a minivan and made a sharp right. She glanced around.

"Where'd he go?" She scanned the cars, the parking lots. No sign of the Chevy. She slowed, looking from left to right as her heart galloped inside her chest. Beside her, Derek muttered a curse.

"I'll circle the block," she told him. "He didn't just disappear." But even as she said it, she felt a sharp pang of disappointment. The streets around the shopping center were clogged with traffic, including SUVs and delivery trucks. He could easily have gotten lost in the shuffle.

"LeBlanc?" Torres sounded impatient.

"Now I don't see him."

"There." Derek braced a hand on the dash.

"What? Where?" She tapped the brakes.

"Two o'clock. He's on foot. Pull over."

"I'll park."

"No time."

He shoved his door open. She jabbed the brakes, and he jumped out.

"Wait! Where are you going?"

"I'll take Rasheed. You find the Chevy."

"But—"

"Get your bomb squad on that car, Liz. It could be rigged."

———

The mall was crowded with teens and tourists and stroller-pushing moms seeking shelter from the heat. Thousands of unsuspecting civilians during peak hours.

Derek spotted the subject riding an escalator to the second floor, which looked out over an ice rink. Rasheed had his phone pressed to his ear. Keeping to the shadows, Derek watched him. Rasheed cast a furtive look over his shoulder, and Derek ducked into a shop. It sold men's shoes, fortunately, and he pretended to be looking at some Nikes as Rasheed ascended out of sight.

Derek slipped out. Using the crowd for cover, he caught the escalator and got the man in his sights again. He was off the phone now. He made his way through the mall slowly, constantly checking over his shoulder, and everything about him was a red flag. Derek didn't like his body language or his paranoia, and he definitely didn't like his leather jacket in July.

Derek watched, taking in every detail, from his slow gait to the shift of his head. Was he looking for someone? Casing the place? Was this a dry run?

Or was the mission here and now?

Rasheed glanced over his shoulder again as he approached the railing. He leaned his arms against it and looked out over the rink, where kids and adults were slip-sliding across the ice. He reached into his jacket.

Derek reached for his gun.

———

Elizabeth rushed through the door and was hit by a wall of cold air. She cut through Neiman Marcus, weaving through makeup counters and perfume-wielding models as she hurried for the main mall.

She whipped out her phone just as it chimed.

"Where are you?" she demanded.

"East end of the skating rink," Derek told her. "Where's the car?"

"Torres spotted it in the southeast parking lot. HPD has a bomb dog there, but it hasn't alerted on anything. We've got SWAT on the way." Elizabeth cut through a mob of teen girls chattering and texting on their phones. "Damn it, this place is packed. Do you have him?"

"He's hanging out by the ice rink, second level. Just put on a red baseball cap." His tone sounded ominous.

"What, you mean he bought it in a store?" She was race-walking now, scanning the crowd for the red cap while trying not to draw attention to herself.

"Pulled it out of his jacket."

"You think it's a signal? Like maybe he's launching an attack?"

He didn't say anything, and Elizabeth's stomach plummeted.

"Derek?"

"I get the feeling he's waiting for someone. Maybe someone who doesn't know him. Could be what the hat's about."

She reached the ice rink, which was jammed with kids. She cut through a group of little girls dressed in tutus and tiaras. She skimmed her gaze over the railing, but clusters of birthday balloons blocked her view.

"I don't see him," Elizabeth told him. "You said a *red* ball cap?"

"Yeah. I think he's meeting someone."

And then she saw it. A red cap. The man leaned casually against the railing, but he was scanning the crowd. Derek was right—he was waiting for something or someone.

"I've got him," she said.

"Hang up, okay? And don't attract attention to yourself."

Eye contact.

She turned around. "Oh, damn."

"What? What is it?"

She stepped behind an information board. "He saw me."

"Fuck."

"What happened? What's he doing?" she asked.

"He's taking off."

————

Elizabeth cut through the crowd, scanning the heads for the red cap. It was nowhere. He'd probably tossed it by now.

A commotion ahead. A yelp. A woman yelled

something over her shoulder and stooped to pick up a spilled Starbucks cup.

Elizabeth spotted him. No cap now as he darted through groups of people. He threw a look over his shoulder as she ducked behind a cluster of teens.

Had he seen her? She rushed after him again. He was heading for another section of the mall, and she had no idea whether the agents Torres had called were in place at the exits yet. This mall had dozens of exits. Maybe hundreds. Elizabeth plunged through the crowd, desperately trying to keep sight of the black leather jacket and dark head. Her phone chimed, but she ignored it. Then the radio crackled, and she remembered it in her pocket.

Rasheed jumped onto an escalator. A chorus of protests went up as he pushed through people in his sprint for the bottom. Where was he going?

She grabbed the radio. "Torres! He's on the run. Where is everyone?"

Static. "—your location—" More static.

"Near Macy's. First floor."

She hit the escalator just as Rasheed tossed a look over his shoulder. Their gazes locked, and then he lunged into a corridor.

She hurried down the escalator, squeezing between people with shopping bags. She couldn't lose him. Where was Derek? He had to be close.

She jumped the last two steps. Pain zinged up her ankle. Ignoring it, she took off toward the corridor and noticed a gold placard. A hotel.

Panic shot through her as she remembered the high-rise building attached to the mall. It had to be ten floors, maybe twelve. And it was a traffic hub. He could catch a taxi, hijack a car, grab a hostage. She yanked open a glass door and entered a carpeted lobby with yet another set of escalators. Glancing up, she saw a soaring atrium and realized she was now below street level.

Her pulse roared in her ears, drowning out the classical music, the *ding* of elevators. A loud metallic clatter had her spinning around as shouts erupted behind a gray door.

She pushed through the door marked EMPLOYEES ONLY and found herself in an industrial kitchen. Steam enveloped her. The smell of overcooked vegetables hung in the air. Across pots and pans and cooktops, she saw the blur of a movement as Rasheed shoved a waiter aside and dashed through a door.

She shot after him, darting past kitchen workers. She plowed through another door and into an enormous ballroom that was being prepped for an event. Dozens of tables, hundreds of place settings. Waiters were busy dropping off water glasses. She caught someone's eye, and he pointed toward a pair of double doors.

"Thanks!" she said, sprinting across the room and pulling her phone from her pocket. Another carpeted lobby.

"Where are you?" she asked Derek.

"First-floor lobby. Where's Rasheed?"

A high-pitched shriek had her spinning around.

Elevator.

She rushed for the bank of elevators as the doors whisked shut. A woman stood in the lobby, clutching her hand to her chest.

"He . . . he *attacked* me! Did you see that? He just *yanked* me right out—"

"Something wrong, ma'am?"

A security guard walked up, and Elizabeth whipped out her ID.

"FBI. Where's your security room?"

"Where's . . . what?" His befuddled gaze jumped from her ID to the distraught woman and back to her ID again.

"The room that houses your security cameras. I'm in pursuit of a suspect."

Another glance at her ID. "Uh, this way."

He led her to another gray door and used a code to gain access.

"You say you're after a *suspect*?" He glanced over his shoulder as he led her down a cinder-block corridor.

"We have to hurry." She started jogging, checking the placards on all the doors. "I need to know which floor he gets off on."

"Up ahead on the left," he said, lumbering after her.

The door was ajar, and Elizabeth rushed inside to find a bank of computer monitors.

A uniformed woman with frizzy brown hair glanced up at her, frowning. "Hey—"

"She's FBI," the guard cut in. "She needs to see the elevator cams."

Elizabeth scanned the row of monitors, all black-and-white. Lobby, lobby, lobby, fitness room, pool. And elevators.

"There he is." She tapped the screen as Rasheed glanced up and looked directly into the camera. "He's going up. How tall is this place?"

Both guards looked blank.

"How many floors?"

"Twelve," the man said.

"What's on top?"

"Uh . . . twelve's our helipad, our rooftop fitness center."

The elevator doors parted. Rasheed got off.

Elizabeth leaned closer. "What floor is that? Where's he going?"

"Uh . . ." The woman glanced at the monitor. "Looks like . . . six."

She lifted the phone to her ear. "You hear that, Derek? Sixth floor. He just got off. But he might try to go down again."

"He will. He's got no exfil route up there. You need agents on street level."

"I know. Where are you?"

"Stairwell."

"Don't let him past you," she ordered. And then to the security guards, "I need these elevators shut down now."

———

Elizabeth took a service elevator to the sixth floor and got off. She was now juggling a phone and a walkie-talkie on loan from the guard, who was still monitoring cameras. Her FBI radio was tucked into the pocket of her blazer.

"He just entered a stairwell," the guard reported.

She turned and ran for the door.

"South stairwell," he corrected. "End of the hallway."

She halted and reversed direction. She hadn't realized there were two stairwells. Which one was Derek in?

"Where's he going?" she asked.

"I don't know. We don't have security cameras in the stairwells, so—"

"Derek, you getting this?" She lifted the phone to her ear. "He's in a stairwell."

"Not this one. It's silent as a tomb."

"I don't know whether he's going up or down."

"My guess is down," Derek said. "I'll cut over and try to head him off."

She pressed her ear against the door to the stairs and forced herself to stand still and listen, but the only sound was the pounding of her own heart. She dropped the walkie-talkie and the phone into her pocket and pulled out her Glock. She took a deep breath as she opened the door and stepped onto the landing.

A dark shape sprang from the corner, smacking into her. She fell back against the door and saw a flash of metal. Knife! White-hot pain seared her arm as the blade came down. Her hand spasmed, and her gun clattered to the floor.

Thunder from below. Rasheed lunged for the door. She leaped to block it and spun at him with a side kick, missing his groin, connecting with his thigh.

"Elizabeth!" Derek's voice boomed from below.

Rasheed shoved past her and dashed up the stairs. She swooped down for her gun but discovered her arm wasn't working. She grabbed the weapon with her left hand and scrambled upstairs. Footsteps reverberated above and below. She took the steps as fast as she could, ignoring the noise and the pain as she tried to think.

Backup.

The instant the thought formed, her phone chimed. She transferred her gun to her injured hand and used her left to dig the phone from her pocket. Gordon.

"I need backup, ASAP! I'm in the hotel stairwell, seventh floor, maybe eighth."

"Where's Rasheed?" Gordon demanded.

"Headed for the roof."

"Torres is in the lobby, but the elevators are down. Which stairwell, north or south?"

"South." She glanced at the red numbers painted beside each door. "I'm on nine."

Her heart hammered. Two stairwells meant two escape routes, even with the elevators shut down.

"SWAT's on the way," Gordon told her. "ETA three minutes. Stall him any way you can, but take him alive. Is that clear? We *must* interrogate him and get to the rest of this sleeper cell. You got that?"

"Got it," she said, and tucked the phone away.

Take him alive . . . even if he slits your throat. He hadn't said the last part, but his meaning was clear.

Derek's boots echoed below. He had to be four, maybe five floors down, but he was pounding closer. Maybe she should wait.

Twelve's our helipad, our rooftop fitness center.

A fitness center meant potential hostages. Rasheed was desperate—she'd seen it in his eyes.

She rounded another corner. Above her, a door burst open.

He'd reached the roof.

———

Derek took the stairs three at a time, leaping around
the landings like a madman as he followed the trail of
blood.

Eight.

He bounded up the steps, spurred by the image of
her alone on that rooftop with Rasheed.

Nine.

Blood smears on the railing. He didn't want to
think about what that meant.

Ten.

He focused on his battle plan. Two stairwells. Two
exfil routes.

Eleven.

Derek yanked open the door and rocketed down
the hall.

———

Wind howled against the building, whipping her hair
into her eyes and flattening her flush against the wall.
She tipped her head back against the concrete and
clutched her gun in the two-handed grip she'd learned
at the Academy.

She strained to listen. When the gusts subsided, she
heard the bleats of traffic below. But no footsteps. Not
a sound or a shadow to betray Rasheed's location.

She stepped sideways, staying as close to the wall
as possible. She'd never been afraid of heights, but
twelve floors up with only a four-foot concrete wall
separating her from certain death, it was hard to
remember that. She trained her attention on the space
immediately to her right, the helicopter-size parking
spot that right now was empty. A wall of windows

looked out over the helipad, and the late-day sun illuminated a trio of women on treadmills.

A scuff of footsteps, and her nerves jumped. She held her breath. Every instinct told her he was around the corner, lying in wait, planning his escape. He'd make a run for the other side, break his way into the building, and grab a hostage if needed on his way to the other stairwell.

Take him alive.

She adjusted her grip on her gun. Her hand was crimson with blood, and her forearm was on fire. Heat radiated up from the roof, and she felt the sun-baked concrete through the soles of her shoes.

Another scuff of footsteps. He was nearing the corner, getting ready to make a dash for the far door. She glanced at the women behind the glass. With their ears stuffed with plastic and their gazes glued to the TV, they were oblivious to the danger only a few feet away.

Elizabeth took a deep breath. She gripped her gun, whispered a prayer, and swung around the corner.

"FBI! Drop the weapon!"

He crouched beside the building like a panther waiting to spring.

"Drop it!"

He rose slowly to his feet. Sun glinted off the blade in his hand. His dark gaze narrowed, and he moved toward her.

"Drop the weapon." Her voice shook. "Hands above your head."

"LeBlanc, you copy?"

Torres. She ignored him.

"LeBlanc?"

She pointed her gun at his center body mass, as she'd been trained. *Take him alive.* Her heart beat uncontrollably as she stepped closer, just out of his reach.

"On the ground. Now."

His gaze darted across the helipad. She felt him analyzing, weighing his options. Would she have the courage to pull the trigger?

To her left, a flash of movement. Derek shot across the rooftop like a missile. Bodies smacked to the ground. The knife skittered across the pavement as Elizabeth rushed forward with her handcuffs.

"Check for weapons!" she shouted as Derek flipped him onto his stomach and wrestled his arms behind his back.

Elizabeth snapped the cuffs on as Rasheed squirmed and cursed. Derek roughly searched him for weapons.

Elizabeth's radio squawked. She ignored it.

"He's clear." Derek yanked him to his feet. He eyed Elizabeth, taking in her torn jacket and bloodied arm. He grabbed Rasheed by the shirtfront and shoved him backward, cursing. Rasheed attempted a head butt. Derek popped him in the jaw, and his head snapped back.

The radio continued to squawk, and then came the steady thrum of an approaching helicopter. Swirls of dust kicked up around her, stinging her eyes.

She glanced at the chopper. "Is that ours?" she yelled over the noise.

"News!" Derek shouted.

Panic shot through her. "We have to interrogate this man! We can't have his face on TV. Wave them off!"

The helo swooped closer, creating a mini-tornado of dirt and debris.

Derek grabbed Rasheed and hauled him to the nearest door. Elizabeth tried to open it, but it was locked. She cast a frantic look across the helipad. The treadmill users were standing at the window now, staring slack-jawed at the unfolding scene. The chopper dipped lower, kicking up more and more dust, and she realized it was trying to land practically on top of them.

Derek stepped onto the helipad and waved them off.

Elizabeth glanced at Rasheed, who was inching back from her. Their gazes locked. She stared into his eyes, and an icy fist closed around her heart as realization dawned.

Time slowed down.

"No!" she screamed, lunging after him, grasping for his arm, his jacket, anything.

But she was too late, and he hurled himself over the wall.

Chapter Eleven

Gordon took over the hotel's security headquarters as a makeshift command center. Agents in plain clothes and SWAT gear crowded into the space, sucking up all the air.

Elizabeth spotted Derek on the far side of the room watching a row of video monitors. He stood rigid, arms crossed over his chest, and he looked to be narrating events for an agent who was furiously taking notes.

His gaze homed in on her. After a trip to the nearest urgent-care center, she'd spent two hours being debriefed and then another hour at the morgue. She hadn't stopped to take a breath, and the events of the last four hours tumbled through her head.

"LeBlanc, Torres."

Her attention snapped to Gordon.

"Come with me." He crossed the room. "Lieutenant Vaughn?"

He led the three of them down a narrow corridor

and into a windowless room. From the ancient coffee-pot parked on the counter, she took it to be the break room. Potter sat at the end of a faux-wood table, talking on his phone and jotting notes on a legal pad. He ended his call as Gordon pulled out the chair beside him and everyone sat down.

Everyone except Derek. He leaned his shoulder against the wall and gave Elizabeth a look she couldn't read. Glancing at the faces around the table she realized it was the group from Coronado, except this time Derek was the only SEAL.

Gordon looked at Elizabeth. "Tell me about the morgue."

She took a breath and tried to collect her thoughts. "The assistant ME was called in to do the autopsy."

"He had to be *called*?"

She looked at Potter, then glanced at the clock on the wall. "Well, it was already nine, so yeah, it's after hours. Normally they'd wait until morning, but given the circumstances, they're getting started right away. Agents Holmes and Chen are standing in to observe."

"And you collected the personal effects?"

That had been her purpose in going there. "Got everything sealed up and delivered to our lab guys," she reported. "Some of the analysis can be done here, but for DNA, I think they'll send it to Quantico."

"What'd you find?" Gordon asked.

She stifled a shudder as she pictured the bloodied clothing that had been cut from the body, the clumps of brain matter stuck to the jacket.

"Your basic clothes, shoes, belt, all domestic brands."

"Pockets?"

She glanced at Derek and remembered him checking Rasheed for weapons. "Not a lot," she said. "Lieutenant Vaughn took the knife off him during the
takedown. He had some pocket litter—loose change,
Marlboro Reds, eighty-three dollars in cash."

"Wallet?" Torres asked.

"No. And no driver's license. So no tentative ID, at
least not from the ME's office."

Although the story of the suicide jumper had made
the local news, without an ID, there was no hint of
connection to something bigger, so it hadn't garnered
much attention. But that could change.

Gordon watched her, his look intent. "So what do
you think happened?"

She stared at him. She'd spent two hours recount-
ing what had happened to no fewer than four senior
agents, including him.

"You want me to rehash—"

"I mean on the roof," Gordon said. "I've been
going over the video footage. I want to know what
happened up there. What prompted him to jump?"

"I—" She glanced at Derek. "I can only guess. He
knew he was about to be arrested. Interrogated."

"Tortured."

At the sound of his voice, she shot Potter a look.

"If the 'takedown,' as you call it, was any indication
of how he was going to be treated," Potter said, "then
he knew he was going to be subjected to extreme measures."

"Extreme?" Derek's voice was ice. "What the fuck's
that mean?"

"It means—let's be honest here—the apprehension
was a little rough." Potter glanced at Gordon. "She

should have waited for backup so the suspect could be secured properly, and this whole situation could have been avoided."

"The *suspect*?" Derek didn't move a muscle, but his face was taut. "Barely three weeks ago, this piece of shit walked in front of a video camera and slit a woman's throat." Derek looked at Gordon. "A few hours ago, he went after your agent with a combat knife. And by the way, where the fuck was her backup *then*?"

"We were on our way," Torres said, and Elizabeth could feel the tension ratcheting up.

"Too bad they didn't get there sooner," Potter said. "Our key suspect wouldn't have had a chance to kill himself before he told us anything valuable."

"What, are you blind?" Derek stepped away from the wall. "He told us plenty. This man covertly entered this country for the sole purpose of carrying out a major attack."

"A major attack?" Potter folded his arms. "We haven't confirmed that, Lieutenant. In fact, we know very little about his plans, and now we may never know, because he's dead."

"Let's look at the facts," Derek said, clearly struggling for patience. "U.S. forces raid an Al Qaeda safe house and recover intel pointing to a terrorist attack in Texas. Soon after, a top Al Qaeda operative is smuggled into Texas through a narco tunnel controlled by one of Mexico's most powerful cartels."

"Two operatives," Gordon said.

"What?"

"Rasheed had a traveling companion. Zahid Ameen." Derek shot Elizabeth a look that told her he knew exactly who Ameen was—and he was not happy to have been left out of the loop.

"That just proves my point," Derek said. "Another person provided transportation in Del Rio, and today yet another person Rasheed had never met before was meeting him at the mall."

"How do we know he'd never met him?" Torres asked.

"The red hat," Elizabeth said. "It seemed to be a signal."

"We're up to four people at a minimum," Derek said. "This sleeper cell probably contains three times that. Everything about the logistics involved tells us they're planning a major strike."

"But on what? That's the question." Potter slid a look at Gordon. "And now we can't answer that question, because the suspect is dead."

Suspect. Elizabeth wanted to reach across the table and slap him.

"He was already dead. Don't you get it?" Derek shook his head. "He'd decided to die for his cause before he ever showed up here. He just did it early to protect the mission."

Gordon shifted in his seat. "Lieutenant—"

"Do you people even understand what this is?" Derek demanded. "I don't think you do. We have a cell of suicidal jihadists operating inside our borders. They don't care about the rule of law or the Geneva Conventions or anything else. These guys specifically go after innocent civilians, women and children—the softer the target, the better. And you're worried about a rough *apprehension*? This fight is no holds barred, the more barbaric, the better, because they want to amplify their message. I've seen these guys up close." He jabbed a finger at Potter. "Have you?" He jabbed at Gordon. "Have you?"

Tense silence.

"These men are without rules, without conscience, and there is nothing they won't do." He pointed at the ceiling. "Including take a header off a twelve-story building. And it's not because they're crazy. It's because they're committed." He started to say more but cut himself off. He shook his head and moved for the door.

"We're not finished here," Gordon said.

Derek halted and turned around. "Let's get something straight. I don't work for you. I work for the American taxpayers, who have spent years training me to protect and defend this country." He looked from Gordon to Potter and reached for the door. "I don't know who you work for."

———

Luke stood in the lobby of the Hotel del Coronado, feeling more than a little out of place. SEALs, like the name said, were trained to operate in all conditions— SEa, Air, Land. But Stuffy Victorian Hotel Lobby hadn't made the list.

The looks from the staffers behind the desk were at least a six on the hostility scale, and he knew he probably should have shown up here in dress whites instead of his current nondressy, nonwhite attire. But after his conversation with Derek, he'd pretty much jumped into his truck and zipped over. Totally spur of the moment. Impromptu. *Vamanos, muchachos*, he was headed to the Del on a matter of national security.

Right. As if getting one more chance to sit next to Hailey Gardner and look into her perfect blue eyes before she went back to Boston was a national emergency.

He crossed the lobby to the elevator bank to wait, because—big surprise—this visit wasn't actually unplanned. No, he hadn't woken up this morning knowing the shitbag terrorist who'd murdered Ana Hansson was going to throw himself off a roof today. But Luke *had* thought about coming here a time or ten. He'd planned it, in fact, down to the tiniest detail. Only his plan had been a little different.

In his fantasy version, he'd walk into the lobby dressed in jeans and his A.T.A.C. boots that women seemed to go for. He'd pick up the lobby phone and call Hailey. *So, if you're not busy with your friend in La Jolla, I'd be happy to show you some of the sights this afternoon.* Afternoon would turn into evening, which would turn into dinner, which would turn into after-dinner drinks in her room overlooking the ocean . . .

At which point, his little fantasy tale would cease to be G-rated. Which was why it remained a fantasy.

The reality was slightly less exciting and involved him standing in the lobby of an insanely expensive hotel, once again in his sweat-soaked running clothes, as he waited to see a woman who made his heart stutter. It was, without a doubt, one of his stupider plans, and there was no going back now, because she was on her way down.

Elevator doors slid open with a polite *ding*, and

Hailey stepped out. She had on another form-fitting yoga outfit but with a sea-green top today instead of black. Adidas again, no baseball cap this time. Still, she had the sporty look going, with her shiny blond hair pulled up in a ponytail.

"Hi." There was a question in her eyes as she stopped beside him. And something else, too. Did she actually look happy to see him?

"Hi."

God, she was pretty. And maybe he should have planned some dialogue to go with his choreography. "Something's come up," he said. "Do you have time to talk?"

"Sure." She glanced at the hotel staffers. "Let's go out on the deck."

He followed her past an old-fashioned candy shop and into the cool night air. The Del's deck occupied a huge-ass strip of prime California beachfront. The smell of fried seafood wafted over from one of the restaurants as she led him past some picnic tables and found an empty bench overlooking the shore. Waves crashed against the sand, the moon shimmered off the water, and it was a damn nice view he was about to ruin.

Luke sat down beside her on the bench. "My teammate told me he stopped by to see you a couple days ago."

"Lieutenant Vaughn, yes."

"He mentioned you were upset to hear that the group that kidnapped you and your friends might be trying to enter the U.S."

Her body stiffened. "Are they here?"

"Omar Rasheed entered a few days ago."

She stared at him.

"Now he's dead."

She didn't move, didn't even blink. "How?" she asked.

He considered lying, or at least sugarcoating it. *He died while being apprehended by Homeland Security.* But the man had raped her and slit her friend's throat. Maybe it would help her to know he'd met a heinous end.

"The FBI located him," Luke told her. "They cornered him on the rooftop of a building, and he jumped."

She just looked at him.

"From twelve floors up," he added.

Yes, he's really dead. One less mofo for you to have nightmares about.

Because that was the reason he'd come here. Not the only reason but the only remotely noble one.

"Wow, that's—I don't know what to say." She rested her elbows on her knees and rubbed her forehead. "I should probably call Ana's parents."

"It's been done."

Relief washed over her face. "Really?"

"Yeah, someone from the FBI notified them tonight."

"Oh, thank God." She shook her head. "They've been calling me to talk about everything. But I can't talk to them. I hate lying, but I can't tell them the truth about everything. It's too . . . God. There isn't even a word for it."

"I know."

She leaned closer, and the look in her eyes made his chest ache. The breeze picked up her ponytail and played with it. "*You* understand," she said. "You're one of the only ones who can. You've been there, and you *know*. It's one of the reasons I knew I had to come out here and talk to you."

Like he was a therapist or something. And she needed a therapist—no question about it, after all the shit she'd been through.

But this was surreal. She wanted him to help her? He was one of the most fucked-up people he knew.

Her gaze locked on his, and there was so much hope in it, so much expectation. She was really lost. And he was about the last person on earth who was qualified to help her. The mere idea terrified him.

You've been there, and you know.

He did know. He'd seen some horrific shit over the years. Guys who'd been turned into a pink mist before his eyes. He'd seen men with limbs blown off and head wounds—men he knew—and he'd spent count-less hours crouching in the dirt, frantically trying to stanch the bleeding and stave off death.

But rape? He looked down into her haunted eyes, and he knew it didn't matter where he'd been or what he'd seen—he was totally out of his league here.

He cleared his throat. "The thing is, Hailey, I'm not really a doctor. I mean, I'm a medic, yeah, but it's totally different. I didn't go to medical school, and I'm not really qualified—"

"I've got a doctor," she said sharply. "He has white hair and a potbelly, and he went to Harvard. And I know he's never set foot in a war zone."

Tension snapped between them. She looked pissed off, and he didn't blame her.

But then she gazed out at the water, and her face

softened. "I can't talk to my doctor right now. Or my parents. Or Ana's parents. I need to talk to someone who understands." She looked up at him, and he knew he had to get away from her before he did something truly stupid. "Please?"

Jesus. What could he possibly say to that?

He didn't say anything, just turned to look at the surf. And then he said the only thing he could think of, the same thing he said whenever Derek or Mike or Cole called him up after a mission and needed to get his head right.

"You want to go get a drink?"

Chapter Twelve

By the time Elizabeth threw in the towel on her train wreck of a day, it was already tomorrow. The night air was heavy with humidity as she crossed the mall parking lot and started searching for her car. A pickup rolled to a stop beside her, and the passenger window slid down.

"Get in," Derek said.

She stared at him. He was in the same clothes he'd had on three hours ago, and his face looked just as grim. Those brown eyes drilled into her, and she knew it was pointless to argue.

She climbed into the truck. It had a king cab and plenty of legroom. Glancing around, she realized it was the first time she'd actually been in a space that belonged to him. How many hours had she spent thinking about this man, and yet she knew so little about him?

He exited the lot onto a street that was nearly deserted. He didn't seem to want to talk or tell her where they were going, and she didn't feel like asking.

She stared out the window, watching the parking lots and storefronts whisk by. The area seemed eerily calm compared with a few hours ago, when it had been swarming with emergency vehicles. Even the news vans had gone home, because they still hadn't figured out that tonight's suicide jumper was an international terrorist. It was a stroke of luck that would run out at some point, probably by morning. ME offices were known for leaks, and the Bureau's interest in the autopsy had surely attracted attention.

Derek drove a few blocks and pulled into Finnegan's. The place wasn't crowded, and he had no trouble finding a space for his big pickup.

Elizabeth sat in silence for a moment, gazing at the neon beer signs, feeling numb. She flipped down the visor and checked the mirror, but her appearance was beyond help. Her makeup was smudged. Her shredded blazer was in a trash bin at the urgent-care center, and she was down to a bloodstained white blouse that did nothing to conceal her bandage, not to mention her gun.

Derek opened her door and held out his leather jacket, obviously reading her mind. She slid from the truck and slipped into it. It was warm and heavy and smelled so much like him it was like being wrapped in his arms.

What was she doing here?

He led her to the door and held it open. The place was busy but not packed. She'd expected him to want one of the cozy dark booths, but he took her to the bar instead. Her mind flashed back to a pub in San Francisco.

"This feels familiar," she said, trying to lighten the mood. "You planning to get me drunk again?"

"Maybe."

She cut him a look as she slid onto a stool. A curvy blond bartender walked up and beamed a smile in his direction.

"Hi. What can I get y'all?" The smile was for Derek, but she aimed the question at Elizabeth.

Her mind went blank. She couldn't think of a single thing she wanted to drink.

"Martini?" Derek prompted.

"God, no." She shuddered. "I'll have a bourbon and Coke."

Derek ordered bourbon on ice, and for a while they simply sat there, not talking, staring at the TV above the bar. Tension radiated from his body. He was still ticked off about Ameen, but she wouldn't apologize for that. She'd offered to give him a tip, not a daily briefing.

"How's your arm?"

She glanced at him, startled. "Fine."

"How many stitches?"

"Twelve."

His jaw twitched, and he glanced up at the TV. "Does it hurt?"

"They numbed it at the clinic."

He looked at her. "That's not what I asked."

"It's fine."

But he watched her steadily, and she could see he knew she was lying.

The bartender slid their drinks in front of them.

Elizabeth took a sip. It felt cool going down but immediately warmed her stomach.

"You never told me about Ameen." Derek tipped his glass back.

"That's right."

He watched her, waiting for an explanation.

"There are a lot of things I never told you about. You're not on the task force. I'm surprised Gordon even let you into the room tonight. What were you doing there?"

"Looking for the phone."

The phone. Gordon was obsessed with it. When Derek had first entered the mall, he'd seen Rasheed talking on a cell phone. But when he did the pat-down on the rooftop, no phone. Nothing had turned up at the morgue, either, which meant Rasheed had ditched it somewhere.

Derek was watching her now, clearly wanting an update.

"We still haven't recovered it," she told him. "We've got an evidence response team at the mall, searching trash cans. In the meantime, we're combing through security footage. Whoever he was meeting is probably on there. Possibly Ameen."

"You have a recent picture of him?"

"In my files."

"I'd like to see it," he said, "although I doubt it was him today."

She sipped her drink. "You mean because of the red cap?"

"I think it's someone Rasheed doesn't know," Derek said. "But whoever it was, he was in disguise, believe me. These guys know all about facial-ID software."

"It's worth a shot. Interpol's got a new software system that's much more advanced. It can match people based on only a profile. Potter's trying to get someone over there to analyze some footage for us."

His expression hardened at the mention of Potter.

"Don't look like that." She stirred her drink with the slender red straw. "He's not all bad, you know. You guys are just different."

She could tell he didn't like even being mentioned in the same sentence with Potter. As Derek had pointed out earlier, the man wasn't a field agent. He wasn't a man of action. To Potter, gathering intelligence was something you did at a desk.

Derek was action personified. He was constantly moving, maneuvering, seeking out a tactical advantage.

Elizabeth checked her watch and felt a pang of guilt. It was well after midnight, and the evidence team was probably still scouring that mall—all for the sake of a phone, which was now their most promising lead, even though it was most likely a burner that wouldn't yield any useful clues. Only hours ago, they'd had Rasheed in custody—an actual person who could have revealed an entire terrorist plot targeting hundreds, if not thousands, of people. Rasheed had been their best hope of heading off the attack, and now he was dead.

Pain pounded behind her eyes. She rested her elbow on the bar and rubbed her forehead. "What a screw-up."

"What is?"

"Today." She looked at him. "We could have all of them under surveillance right now, do you realize that? We could have agents surrounding some apartment somewhere, preparing to take down the entire cell. And what do we have? Nothing. God, why did I let him see me? It was the weirdest thing. I wasn't anywhere near him, and he turned and looked right at me."

"It happens."

"It didn't happen to you."

"I'm a frogman. I've had slightly more training at being invisible."

She watched him, picturing him creeping down some dark alley, armed to the teeth and wearing night-vision goggles. She didn't like to picture him working, because she hated to think about the dangers of what he did.

"It goes back to biology," he told her. "Predator versus prey. Animals in the wild know when they're being hunted. They have a sixth sense about it. They get itchy."

"You're saying I walked into the mall and made him *itchy*?"

"No, you walked into the mall and you looked right at him. Never do that. They teach you that in sniper school. When you're pursuing a target, don't stare at it, don't arouse that sixth sense, especially someone like Rasheed. People spend years in a war zone, their instincts get honed. They sense when they're in the crosshairs."

"Predator and prey. That's good. Think I missed

that at the Academy. Maybe we spent a little too much time on check fraud."

"Hey, honey, stick with me." He gave her shoulder a squeeze. "I can teach you a lot."

She ignored the innuendo and picked up her drink. She swilled the rest and plunked the glass onto the counter.

"The day wasn't a total loss," Derek said. "One's been eliminated, at least. Rasheed's been on the watch list for years."

"What do you think the chances are they'll decide to abort the mission, whatever it is, and go home?"

His silence answered her question. The chances were nonexistent. They'd gone to a great deal of time and effort to get their people in place, which meant they'd prepared for contingencies. Rasheed had chosen to die rather than reveal his mission, so it was safe to assume the mission was still a go.

And—in Rasheed's mind, at least—it was a mission worth dying for.

The bartender was back with a smile, and Elizabeth could have sworn she'd undone another button on her blouse. Derek ordered another round.

Elizabeth turned away, distracting herself by scanning the faces around the room. It was mostly couples tonight, people drinking and flirting and probably planning to go home together. She shouldn't be here. She knew that. She couldn't sit in a bar with this man and *not* think about going home with him. And where would that leave her? She'd spent almost a year tied up in knots over him, and they hadn't even had sex. What was she doing to herself? He was going back to San Diego in a matter of days and then off to some violent hot spot.

From the moment he'd burst into her life last summer, she'd been mesmerized by him—his looks, his voice, the relentless way he pursued everything he wanted, including her. But when she took a step back and looked at it objectively, she knew nothing could ever work. He was a SEAL through and through and didn't have room in his life for anything else.

She felt his gaze on her and turned to face him. He had that simmering look in his eyes, that look she'd seen before, the look that made her nervous and hopeful at the same time. For so long, she'd resisted him, because she didn't want to get her heart pulverized. But maybe she should leave her heart out of it. Maybe for one night, she should let herself go and let herself feel things without any inhibitions, and it didn't matter where he jetted off to tomorrow. It could just be what it was, nothing more and nothing less.

She brushed her bangs from her forehead, and his attention drifted to her scar. He reached out and traced his finger over her sleeve. His eyes locked onto hers.

"Can I ask you something personal?"

———

She looked surprised by his question. Then she looked wary.

"What?" she asked.

"What'd your family say? About what happened to you in the spring?"

She scoffed. "What family?" She stirred her drink, and Derek could tell she wanted to take the words back.

"It's just my mom now," she elaborated. "I mean, there's my stepdad, yeah. But I don't have any brothers or sisters." She looked at him. "I always wanted a brother."

So she didn't want to talk about her parents. He sensed there was a story there, but he let her change the subject.

"I grew up surrounded by women," he told her. "Nail polish, hair spray, curling irons. They like to say I ran off and joined the Navy just to have some male companionship." He rattled the ice cubes in his glass. "Could be some truth to that. The guys in the teams, they're like brothers to me."

He drank his bourbon. What a shit day it had been. He thought about Potter and Rasheed and the clusterfuck on that rooftop. He wasn't sorry the guy was dead. Not at all. Anyone who had seen that execution video wouldn't be sorry Rasheed had jumped off that roof. Derek would have gladly pushed him off and not lost a wink of sleep over it.

Still, he recognized the lost opportunity. But SEALs were adaptable. They looked for new opportunities, and there were plenty left, such as the missing phone, or the contact who'd probably been captured on film entering the mall, or the Chevy Cavalier that was now at some crime lab somewhere being scoured top to bottom for evidence.

Yes, it had been a shit day, but at least it was improving. He glanced at the woman beside him, the woman he'd been thinking about for months, the woman who had been the star of so many lust-soaked fantasies he couldn't even count. She was on her second drink now, and instead of looking all crisp and buttoned-up like she usually did, she had that messy, disheveled thing happening that made him want to eat her alive.

She was watching him now. She reached out and put her hand over his.

"You're thinking about Sean, aren't you?"

Sean. She thought he was thinking about his lost brother.

No, I'm thinking about how badly I want to get you out of those clothes.

"I'm thinking about you," he said, only partly lying. "You ever considered getting a desk job?"

She looked startled. "No."

He eyed her scar again. "You know, when I was thinking about you back here at home, I never pictured you getting pistol-whipped. It's a tough image to get out of my head."

Tough was an understatement. It was impossible. And he knew she hadn't told him the full story. She'd told him she'd been beaten and taken hostage. Had she been sexually assaulted, too? The thought of it made him want to kill someone, the same way he'd felt when he'd sprinted up that stairwell and seen the blood trail.

She tipped her head to the side and looked at him. "You know, the FBI Academy—it's really hard to get into. And the training itself is very rigorous. Not like BUD/S or anything, but it was challenging for *me*. It was the toughest thing I've ever done." She sipped her drink and rested it on the bar. "So, no, I wouldn't consider a desk job. What about you?"

"No," he said without hesitation.

"Don't want to stop chasing bad guys and jumping out of airplanes?"

"Not in this lifetime."

"That's what I thought."

The bartender reappeared, which seemed to annoy Elizabeth. "Last call," the woman chirped.

Elizabeth looked at him. "I should get back."

Derek paid for the drinks and refused the money she tried to give him. Back in the parking lot, the air was like a sauna, but she kept his leather jacket on as she slid into the truck. She stared out the window as he pulled out. Obviously, his attempt at career advice had pissed her off. She'd shifted to defensive mode, and now it was going to be an uphill battle getting her to loosen up again.

She kept her attention directed out the window as he navigated the after-hours traffic.

"So where's this file you have?"

She looked at him. "Which file?"

"Ameen's picture."

"Back at my hotel." She paused. "You can drop me off there if you need it tonight."

"I do."

It was something. He wasn't sure what it meant, but he planned to find out. He got onto the freeway and buzzed the windows down as they drove, thinking maybe some fresh air would relax her.

Because, yes, she'd been right before—he had a one-track mind. And even though it had been a

shit day and she was injured and tired and probably
emotionally wasted, he was still dying to take her to
bed.

While he was overseas, especially after she'd
ignored his phone calls, the prospect of sleeping
with her had seemed like a fantasy. She lived and
worked in San Antonio. He lived and worked wherever Spec War Command sent him. But now she was
here, right beside him, and he'd be damned if he was
going to let her slip away again, not if there was even
a chance in hell she'd say yes. He had no desire to
spend another eleven months burning up with frustration.

The Home Suites parking lot was full, and he
counted half a dozen dark sedans that had to belong
to feds. He found a space not far from her room and
noticed her glance around cautiously before she got
out.

She slid a keycard from her purse and briskly
opened the door. As she stepped inside, she shrugged
out of his jacket and held it out to him.

"Thanks," she said.

"Sure."

He pulled the door shut behind him. The room
smelled like her, probably her lotion or her perfume
or something she'd put in her hair that morning.
A rolling suitcase was parked beside the closet. A
dark suit hung inside, along with several crisp white
blouses. His gaze drifted to the white lace bra dangling from the door handle.

"It's in here somewhere." She rummaged through
her computer bag. "Here."

She crossed the room and handed him an eight-by-ten photograph. It was black-and-white, but at least it was recent compared with the last photo he'd seen. Derek studied the narrow nose, the strong chin, the prominent cheekbones. He took out his cell phone and snapped a picture of the picture.

"Plastic surgery?" He glanced up.

"We think so."

He tucked his phone away and put the picture on the dresser. "Thanks."

"You're welcome."

They stood there staring at each other, and the moment stretched out. He slid his hand around hers and pulled her closer. She tensed.

"Why are you gun-shy with me?"

She tipped her chin up. "I'm not."

He kissed her, pulling her against him, and she resisted. For maybe a second. Then he felt her loosen and let go, and she was finally, finally, *finally* kissing him the way he'd wanted her to for months. Her arms came up around his neck, and he pulled her hips against him. She tasted better than he remembered, hot and sweet, and he hoped to hell she meant what she'd said, because he couldn't stop right now if he wanted to. He slid his hands over her blouse and felt those soft curves he'd been dying to touch, and her fingers were in his hair now. He filled his palms with her breasts and rubbed his thumbs over her nipples, and she moaned into his mouth and pressed closer.

She tasted so fucking good and felt so perfect he couldn't believe he'd waited so long to do this. He should have come during his last leave. He should have just shown up at her door and forced her to look him in the eye and tell him she wasn't interested. Because the way she was kissing him now told him the opposite. She was hot and willing and felt like maybe, just maybe, she'd been thinking about this as much as he had.

She jumped back like she'd been scalded.

"What?" he asked.

She stared at him wide-eyed as his heart pounded in his chest, and he couldn't believe she was putting the brakes on.

More pounding, but this was behind him. He turned around as she crossed to the door. If it was Jimmy Torres, he might have to punch the guy.

But it was a woman in jeans and a T-shirt. Her jogging buddy, the FBI agent.

"Hi." She shot a glance over Elizabeth's shoulder and lowered her voice. "*Very* sorry to bug you, but we have a meeting."

"Now?" Elizabeth sounded frustrated but not nearly as frustrated as he was.

"Gordon's suite, five minutes. It's important."

She ran her hand through her hair. "What is it, do you know?"

"We recovered the phone."

———

Luke pulled open the lobby door, and they swept inside with a gust of air. Hailey was laughing. *Laughing.* Over some dumb joke he'd made as they'd come in off the beach. And he tried not to think along his normal lines—that a woman laughing at his jokes was a good sign he might be getting laid tonight. Because he wasn't. No way, no how. Not tonight or any night ever as far as Hailey Gardner was concerned.

She unzipped her jacket as they crossed the lobby. "Wow." She glanced back at him over her shoulder. "It's chilly out there. Is it always like this in the summer?"

"Not usually. Lows are typically in the sixties," he said. Holy shit, were they actually talking about the weather? Maybe she was trying to distract him from the fact that they were once again standing near the elevators. Her hotel room was just a short ride away. And his frog sense was going haywire now, because every instinct told him she was going to invite him upstairs.

She tipped her head to the side. "You want to come up?"

God help him. Only it wasn't the sexy, come-hither *You want to come up, sailor?* but more of an innocent *You want to come up and hang out and, I don't know, watch* Glee *reruns?* It sounded totally innocent, and the look on her face seemed innocent enough, too. But there was nothing innocent about what was going through his head right now. In fact, if she knew, she'd probably be out of here in no time. He had to remind himself that this was a woman who'd been through a severe trauma recently. As in *recently*. As in her arm was still in a freaking cast. She had PTSD and all kinds of psychological problems to recover from. Luke wasn't superstitious, but there wasn't a doubt in his mind that if he went up to that hotel room right now, he'd get struck by lightning within twenty-four hours.

But damn, she was beautiful. Her cheeks were

flushed from the chill, and her hair was all wind-blown, and little strands of it had fallen out of her ponytail. And a minute ago, she'd been laughing. That was the most amazing part.

He'd mustered the *cojones* to take her out to talk, like she'd wanted, only when they'd gotten to the bar, she hadn't talked about A-bad at all. She hadn't even talked about the job that sent her over there. Instead, they'd talked about growing up in Boston and Nash-ville. They'd talked about siblings and parents. They'd talked about hockey and baseball and pretty much everything in the world except what was really on her mind.

It had been surprisingly easy. The hard part was now, looking down at her, wanting to take her upstairs so badly his skin burned, but knowing that was the very last place on earth he should be. When it came to women, he had an extremely crappy track record for resisting temptation. Typically, he not only didn't resist it, but he went after it full-throttle.

He thought about lying to her. He could make something up about early-morning PT or a visiting relative or some other lame excuse. But something about the way she looked at him made it impossible for him to lie.

"I should get home," he said. It was the God's hon-est truth.

"You sure?"

"Yeah."

She smiled slightly, but her eyes looked sad. "Well, good night, then."

She reached up and hugged him, gently squeezing his neck, and by the time he reacted, she'd stepped away.

"Thanks for the beer," she said.

"Sure."

She moved toward the elevators, and he forced himself to walk away.

"Luke?"

He turned around, and she smiled.

"Thank you for talking."

———————

Lauren was waiting near the vending-machine alcove on the way to Gordon's suite.

"Where'd we recover the phone?" Elizabeth asked.

"Oh, no, no, no, no." She caught her arm. "Not so fast. Is *that* the friend from Houston? Breakfast Booty Call?"

"It wasn't a booty call," Elizabeth said. "I told you—"

"He's that SEAL you've been talking about in the meetings."

"How'd you know he's a SEAL?"

"Are you kidding? Look at the man! He's completely ripped." Lauren grinned. "And he's packing heat, too, in case you didn't notice. You didn't tell me you knew him *personally*."

Elizabeth stepped up to the vending machine. The last thing she wanted to do was show up for the meeting talking about this. "I don't. It's not like that."

"It's not?"

"No." She fed in a bill and pounded out a Coke, which she hoped would cancel out the alcohol on her breath.

Lauren's gaze narrowed. "Then why do you have beard burn?"

"Shit! I do?"

"Oh, my God, you *are* doing him!" Lauren smacked her arm. "Why didn't you tell me? I want details!"

"There's nothing to tell."

"You're sleeping with a SEAL, and there's nothing to tell. Right. Obviously, you have no concept of the Mojave Desert that is my current love life. Give me something juicy. Pretty, pretty please?"

Elizabeth popped open her drink and took a sip to cool her throat. She pressed the can to her chin. Beard burn? Good Lord.

Lauren was still watching her.

"What do you want me to say? There's nothing really going on, except . . ." She trailed off, not sure how to describe it.

Lauren beamed. "I'm so happy for you. God, what's it been, eighteen months? Two *years* since you had a boyfriend?"

"He's not my boyfriend. It's not like that at all." She guzzled more Coke.

"What's it like, then?"

"I don't know. Casual."

"Casual."

"As in we barely even know each other."

"Hey, listen, I'm thrilled for you," Lauren said, not buying a word of it. "Just be careful."

"How do you mean?"

"I mean he's a SEAL. From what I hear, those guys are pretty busy these days, right?"

She was right. And a sour ball formed in Elizabeth's stomach just thinking about it.

"I'd hate to see you get hung up on some spec ops warrior who's gone all the time," Lauren continued. "I mean, don't get me wrong—*indulge* and everything. Get with the man. I sure as hell would. Just don't for fall for him."

"I'm not."

"Not unless you have an emotional death wish."

Chapter Thirteen

"Where are you?"

The sound of Derek's voice sent a jolt through her, and for an instant she was back in her hotel room with his hands all over her and her bed just inches away.

But then she snapped back to reality, which consisted of the windowless cubbyhole where she'd spent the past four hours watching blurry footage of the shopping center's thirty-two entrances. And those were only the public ones.

She sighed. "I'm back at the mall."

"Got a pen handy? I have a lead for you."

"Where are you calling from?"

"Doesn't matter. You ready?"

"Wait, hold on." She grabbed a pen and paper as Lauren mouthed, *Who is it?*

Derek, she mouthed back, and Lauren's eyebrows tipped up.

"A maroon Nissan Sentra, four-door, dented front bumper," he said.

"What is that?"

"Ameen's vehicle."

"*What?* Where'd you get this?"

"That's not important. But it's good as of yesterday."

Elizabeth's pulse skittered. She looked at Lauren, who was obviously wondering what he'd said to get her all worked up.

She hit pause on her surveillance footage and stood up. After a quick glance around, she took the call into the break room, which was empty at the moment.

"Okay, back up." She leaned her hip against the counter. "Where are you?"

"I'll keep you posted."

"Wait! Don't go. Where did you get this? Have you actually seen him?"

"Not yet."

"What does that mean?"

"I talked to someone who recognized him," he said.

"Oh, my God, where?" She glanced out the door. Where was Gordon? She should put him directly on the phone.

"I'm not there anymore. And anyway, I'm tied up with something else now."

"But we need to know your source."

"Keep your phone on. I'll be in touch."

"Hold on! Derek?"

But he'd already hung up.

———

Derek could see Elizabeth's ambush coming a mile away, but he walked right into it, partly out of curiosity and partly because her mouth was so fresh in his mind he could practically taste it.

He pulled into the narrow parking lot and found an empty space facing a row of pine trees. Elizabeth's rental car was parked near the trailhead, and she stood beside a wooden post, stretching her hamstrings. She wore short black running shorts and a tight pink shirt that could have inspired an entire BUD/S class to tackle a twenty-mile beach run.

She eyed him coolly as he walked over.

"I figured you'd stand me up," she said.

"Not a chance."

She stretched her arms behind her head, and he noticed her bandage. "You're running in those?" she asked.

He glanced down at his hiking boots. He'd had some shorts stashed in his truck but no running shoes. "Sure, why not?"

"Suit yourself. You ready?"

"Always."

She set off down the trail, and he fell into step beside her. Ninety-nine degrees, ninety-five-percent humidity. The towering longleaf pines blocked the late-day sun, but in Houston during July, nothing could cut the heat.

"I'm surprised you wanted me to meet you," he said. "Thought you didn't like running."

"I don't. But it's a necessary evil when I'm away from my gym."

He picked up the pace just to needle her and for a while, they ran without talking. He wondered how long it would take her to bring it up. He guessed half a mile, but by the one-mile marker, she'd proven him wrong.

"So." She gave him a sideways glance and caught him looking at her breasts. "You had a busy morning."

"Yep."

"You go home to sleep at all?" Fishing, as he'd expected. She wanted his time accounted for so she could figure out where he'd gotten his intel.

"I caught a few hours," he said vaguely.

She didn't talk for a while, so he picked up the speed again, passing a couple with a Weimaraner.

"You know—" Her breathing was more labored now. "Your tip earlier wasn't exactly helpful."

"No?"

"You have any idea how many maroon Nissan Sentras there are in Houston?"

"No, but I bet you do."

"Eight hundred and three," she said. "And that's in Harris County alone. Add the surrounding counties, and it's twice that. Where'd you get this lead?"

"I'll tell you later, maybe over beers."

Her cheeks flushed, but she pounded along, not letting her temper show. She set a decent pace, and she was in good shape. The main problem was her stride, but she made a solid effort to keep up with him as they veered around walkers and joggers and people pushing strollers. She didn't talk. He waited. When another mile marker whisked past, he sensed she was ready to take another stab at it.

"I know you think you're helping," she said, "but you're really not."

He picked up the pace again, and they passed a trio of joggers.

"Derek, I'm going to have to insist that you be more forthcoming."

He smiled. "Didn't I tell you what it does to me when you get bossy?"

"I'm not joking." She shot him a glare. "Gordon is threatening to charge you with obstruction of justice."

"For sharing intel?"

"For meddling in a federal investigation." She glanced at him. "Why on earth are you smiling? You could get arrested, do you realize that?"

He shook his head. "Now, that's something I wouldn't recommend, Liz. How are you going to find Ameen with me in custody?"

"*We* are going to find him. As in the FBI, not you. How many times do I have to tell you, you are not—"

"—part of this investigation. Yeah. Got it. I came up with a vehicle today. What have you guys come up with?" He glanced at her. "Come on, let's hear it. Last I checked, you had four new leads: the autopsy, the Chevy, the cell phone, and the mall cams. So tell me, what have you guys managed to make of all that?"

No response.

"What's that? Nothing? Out of that mountain of evidence?"

She surged ahead of him, leaving him in the dust. He quickly caught up to her, and then it was an impromptu race to the end of the three-mile loop. Not that it was any contest, really. He didn't have the heart to pour on the speed like he would if he was with

Luke or Gonzo. He sailed past the last signpost and glanced over his shoulder at her.

She was bent at the waist, gulping down air. He circled back, and she straightened when he reached her. Wet strands of hair clung to her neck. She was flushed, panting, and pissed off at him. The Holy Trinity of turn-ons, and he couldn't resist grabbing her hand and pulling her in for a kiss, but before his mouth connected, he got a sharp shove to the solar plexus.

"I'm trying to help you!" she snapped. Heads swiveled in their direction, and she lowered her voice. "Do you even realize how serious this is?"

"Matter of fact, I do, yeah."

"If you don't cooperate with this investigation—"

"I told you I'd be in touch, and I will. You just have to trust me."

"Gordon wants to talk to you *now*. We need to know where you're getting your information. What sources do you have that we don't know about?"

He looked down at her and almost felt sorry for her. As ambushes went, it wasn't exactly a victory. "Be patient. Let me work, okay? And then I'll let you know."

"Derek—"

"Good run, Liz." He squeezed her shoulder. "Thanks for the invite. Anytime you want to work up a sweat, just give me a call."

"You're making a mistake here."

"Oh, and don't bother tailing me." He smiled over his shoulder as he headed to his truck. "I'd lose you in a heartbeat."

"He just turned left," Elizabeth told Lauren over the phone. "Now it looks like he's parking."

"You want me to wait?"

"Yeah, somewhere close but out of sight." Elizabeth glanced around as she pulled into a parking lot that had potholes the size of bathtubs. "Be sure to lock your doors."

She parked her rental sedan at the end of a row of pickups. The neighborhood would have been sketchy even during daytime, but late at night it looked downright dangerous. To her west was a boarded-up strip center tagged with gang graffiti. To her east was a vacant lot overtaken by weeds and littered with rusted shipping containers.

Elizabeth slid from the car. Practically every pickup in the parking lot looked like it was on steroids. Derek's fit right in. He was inside it talking on the phone, and she felt a surge of satisfaction at goosing *him* for a change.

Only he didn't get goosed. His gaze narrowed when she yanked open the door, but he didn't even flinch.

"Okay, thanks," he said as she slid inside. "I owe you a beer." He ended the call and frowned at her.

"What?"

"I know for a fact you didn't shadow me from my folks' place," he said.

"You're right, I didn't."

He looked at her. He wouldn't acknowledge that she'd one-upped him by asking how she'd found him, but it didn't matter. She knew she'd done it, and she also knew it irked him that he'd missed something.

She turned her attention to the glowing red sign

above the Pussycat Lounge. "Channelview's Premier Gentleman's Club," she recited. "Nice hangout."

"Ameen thinks so."

Her heart lurched. "He's here?"

"*Was* here," Derek said. "Three nights in a row. Showed up at ten and stayed till closing."

She checked her watch. It was after eleven.

"No sightings tonight," Derek said. "And he wasn't in yesterday."

"How do you know?"

"The bartender's my new best bud. She filled me in over lunch today at the bar. Four-ninety-nine steak platter, by the way, 'case you're interested."

"She's sure about this?"

"ID'd the picture. Not by name, but she definitely remembers him. Said he pays for everything in cash and he's a good tipper."

Elizabeth glanced around the parking lot, her mind spinning. Ameen had been here. But was this witness reliable? She looked at Derek. "How'd this bartender see his car?"

"She didn't—one of the dancers did," Derek said. "Apparently, he offered her a ride home when she was leaving work, but she declined. Said he seemed skeevy."

"Skeevy?"

"Her word, not mine."

They needed to get a team here, pronto. "How'd you find this place?"

He looked at her. "You really don't know?"

"If I knew, we'd be here."

He watched her for a moment, probably debating whether to share, as she waited, biting her tongue.

She'd gotten over her frustration from earlier. She'd talked herself out of it because he so obviously got a perverse thrill out of pushing her buttons, and she was done letting him do it. Or at least letting him know he was doing it.

"The pat-down," he told her.

"You mean Rasheed?" She tried to remember it, but everything on the rooftop had happened so fast. "What—"

"I turned his pockets inside out. He had a matchbook with the Pussycat's logo."

"You *stole* crime-scene evidence?"

"I didn't steal anything. I noticed it."

"Then why didn't we recover this matchbook?"

"Beats me. Your CSIs must have missed something. Or maybe it blew off the roof."

She took a deep breath and glanced around. A tall man in a cowboy hat emerged from the club and crossed the lot to his vehicle. He was followed by a shorter man in an Astros cap. "Hey, isn't that your friend?"

"Cole offered to cover for me so I could go jogging." He looked at her. "And no, he didn't see him inside tonight."

"I'm sure he's sorry you wasted his evening."

Derek's phone rattled in the cup holder, and he picked it up. "Vaughn." He smiled. "Hey, how's it going? Seen my guy around?" He shot Elizabeth a look, and she knew he had news. "Gimme a description."

She looked around for the maroon Sentra, but it was all trucks and SUVs.

"You happen to see his ride?" Derek turned the key in the ignition and thrust the truck into gear.

"No, don't worry about it. I think I saw him. Thanks, babe. Appreciate it." He shot backward out of the space.

"Someone saw Ameen?"

"No, but the guy he was hanging out with all three nights just left. Tall build, cowboy hat."

"The Avalanche," Elizabeth said. "He just pulled out of here. Where are we going?"

"Don't you want to know who he is?"

"Yeah, but what about Ameen?"

"He's not here. This guy is." He jammed to a stop at the edge of the parking lot. "Make up your mind, Liz."

"Follow him." She took out her phone and called Lauren. "Are you nearby?"

"Yeah."

"Can you pull into the Pussycat and stake out the lot? Keep an eye out for the maroon Sentra while I follow up on something else."

"Got it."

Derek was speeding down the road now, and traffic was light, which was both good and bad. He neared an intersection.

"There he is, three cars up," Elizabeth said. "Can you get closer?"

"Not without getting burned."

"I need the license plate."

"I've got some binoculars in back."

She twisted in her seat and scrounged around in the back of the cab, where he'd stashed cowboy boots, a duffel bag, boxes of ammo. She grabbed the binoculars as he turned the corner.

Derek cursed.

"What?" She straightened in the seat and looked for the Avalanche. It was a distant pair of taillights getting farther and farther away. "Can you close the gap?"

He didn't answer, just kept a steady thirty-mile-per-hour pace. They bumped over a set of railroad tracks. She glanced around. The area was industrial—chain-link fences and warehouses and grassy lots filled with heavy machinery.

"We're near the ship channel," she said.

"I noticed."

His tone was clipped, and she understood why. The Houston Ship Channel was one of the country's busiest waterways and served as headquarters for America's booming petrochemical industry. It was on the FBI's short list of targets for a terrorist attack.

The Avalanche hung a left. Derek hit the gas. He neared the corner, then switched his lights off as he swung into the turn.

They were on a dark dead-end street, no traffic whatsoever, only a few signs glowing in the distance.

Derek smacked the steering wheel.

"Keep going," she said. "He turned in somewhere."

They passed the first sign, which was spotlighted from the ground. EastTX Shipping, it read. Up the road she spied another sign for Amfreight. She couldn't read the third sign, so she lifted the binoculars.

"Oil Trans." She looked at him. "Okay, we have three options. What do you want to do?"

He swung into the first driveway. A security guard

stepped from a gatehouse, clipboard in hand, as Derek pulled over.

"Now would be a good time to flash your badge," he told her, but she was already getting out of the truck.

"Special Agent Elizabeth LeBlanc, FBI." She approached the guard. "We're in pursuit of a suspect. Black Chevy Avalanche. Anyone pull in here in the last few minutes?"

No one had. Same verdict at Amfreight. They neared Oil Trans, which had not only a guardhouse but also a ten-foot security fence topped with razor wire.

"Gotta be door number three," Derek said, pulling over again.

Elizabeth slid out and gave her spiel to yet another security guard.

"He pulled in a few minutes ago," he said, frowning. "You say he's wanted for something?"

"We just have some questions."

The guard trudged back over to the gatehouse, and Elizabeth followed, aware of Derek's footsteps close behind her.

The building was a closet-sized space barely big enough for a vinyl stool and a computer terminal. Mounted above the window was a pair of monitors showing views of traffic coming and going.

The guard tapped his keyboard.

"Matt Palicek." He glanced up from the screen. "That's who you're looking for?"

"He was in the Avalanche?"

"That's right. ID badge checked out and everything. Looks like he's on our tank maintenance crew."

"Y'all do a lot of tank maintenance this time of night?" Derek asked.

The guard looked him over and seemed to assume he was law enforcement, too. The bulge under his leather jacket probably had something to do with it. "Not usually, no."

"Could you rewind that tape, see which way he went?" Elizabeth nodded at the monitor.

The guard hesitated only a moment before tapping a few more keys. The screen blurred.

"Like I say, it was just a few minutes ago." Another tap. The Avalanche appeared on the monitor as it passed through the security gate. About fifty yards inside the perimeter, the taillights glowed, and the vehicle made a right.

"Hmm." Another frown from the guard.

"What?"

"He turned west. His crew uses the east parking lot."

"What's on the west side?" Derek asked.

"Some storage buildings. The three-nineties, the docks."

"What's a three-ninety?" Elizabeth asked.

"Our biggest tanks. Three-hundred-ninety-thousand-barrel capacity."

Derek looked at Elizabeth, and she knew what he was thinking.

"We need to take a look," she told the guard, holding her badge up again to drive the point home.

"I can't leave my post—"

"Don't worry, we'll find it." They hurried back to the pickup and zipped through the gate as soon as the metal arm went up. Derek followed the Avalanche's route and took a right.

No other vehicles in sight. Enormous cylindrical tanks lined the roadside. A row of lights to their left drew their attention to a long pier.

"Damn, that's huge," Elizabeth said, looking at the oil tanker moored at the dock.

"This channel's about forty-five feet deep, so it can handle some of the biggest tankers."

A pair of headlights swung into their path and zoomed toward them.

"It's not him," Elizabeth said as the vehicle closed in. It was a pickup, and as it pulled up alongside them, she saw the logo of a private security firm emblazoned on the door.

"Evenin'." This guard was older, and his friendly greeting didn't match the look in his eyes. "Hear you folks are looking for someone."

Elizabeth slid out so she wouldn't have to do the badge-flashing thing across the driver's seat. The guard pulled over and cut the engine. In the relative quiet that followed, she listened but didn't hear any other vehicles, only the high-pitched whine of some distant equipment.

The guard pulled out a Maglite and studied her ID.

"We're looking for the driver of a black Avalanche that just pulled in here," she said, "possibly driven by Matt Palicek."

"What's he wanted for?" he asked, casting a look in Derek's direction.

"At the moment, just a few questions." Elizabeth glanced around. "You see the vehicle anywhere?"

"Not tonight."

"Any other exits besides the front?" Derek asked.

"There's the two west."

"I need you to call them," Elizabeth said. "That vehicle needs to be detained if it tries to leave."

The guard shifted a lump of chaw in his mouth and watched them skeptically. He ducked back inside his truck and got on his radio.

"Something's wrong here," Derek said.

Elizabeth looked around. The air smelled of saltwater and diesel. The dock was well lighted but not busy. Across the channel was a row of container ships. Giant steel cranes lined the shore behind them.

The guard slammed shut his door and trudged back over. "He already left. Southwest gate, ten minutes ago."

Derek muttered a curse.

"Any idea what he was doing here?" She checked her watch. "At almost midnight on a Sunday?"

"One way to find out." He crossed the road and led them to a low cinder-block building with a satellite dish mounted on the roof. It was a larger version of the gatehouse, with multiple computer terminals and about a half dozen video monitors. The sports section of a newspaper sat open on the counter beside a Dairy Queen cup that had been converted to a spittoon.

The guard jabbed a few keys, and several of the screens went black.

"You have a view of the docks?" Elizabeth asked.

A picture appeared on the monitor. It showed the entrance to the dock where the tanker was moored but not the road nearby. Another screen came to life and this one showed a wider angle, including not only the dock but also the road and the swampy area east of the pier.

"Here we go," Derek said as the Avalanche moved into view on-screen and rolled to a stop.

"What's he doing?" Elizabeth asked.

They watched. The Avalanche didn't move. The driver with the cowboy hat craned his neck around and seemed to be looking for something.

"When did that tanker come in?" Elizabeth tapped the screen.

"Yesterday. It's a domestic boat—Baltimore, I think. Scheduled to pull out in the morning."

"She full?" Derek asked.

"To the top. Light sweet crude."

"There!" Elizabeth pointed at the monitor. "What's that?"

The guard hit a few keys and rewound the video.

Once again, she saw a shadow move toward the passenger side of the truck. Everyone leaned closer to the screen.

"He's picking someone up," Derek said.

The interior light flashed on briefly before the Avalanche moved out of view.

"Run it again," Derek said.

"Wait." Elizabeth pointed to the screen. "What's that on the ground?"

The guard rewound the footage. Again, they watched a dark form move into camera range and approach the truck. The light went on for an instant, then the truck pulled away.

"That shadow on the ground there." Elizabeth pointed. "That wasn't there before. Is that . . . a puddle?"

"I'll be damned." The guard stared at the screen. "Is it blood?"

"Water." Derek looked at Elizabeth. "Whoever he picked up, he came in from the drink."

————

Derek strode out the door, and Elizabeth rushed after him. He crossed the gravel road and walked onto the pier.

"What are you thinking?" she asked.

"I'm thinking someone linked to an Al Qaeda sleeper cell's poking around this tanker in the middle of the night."

The tanker stretched the length of two football fields and was tethered to the dock by thick lines secured to enormous steel cleats. Derek stopped and planted his hands on his hips as he studied the boat. Only minutes ago, someone had been in that water.

Elizabeth's stomach clenched. She listened to the water lapping against the dock. "You think he planted a bomb?"

"This whole place is a bomb. Look around you."

She did. Warning signs were posted everywhere: FLAMMABLE LIQUIDS, DANGER, FIRE HAZARD, ABSOLUTELY NO SMOKING.

"Where's your maintenance building?" Derek asked as the guard approached them.

"Across the street there," he said. "Why?"

"I need to check something."

Elizabeth whipped out her phone as Derek tromped off with the guard. She should have called this in before now, but she hadn't known what to say. *Hey, Gordon, this bartender at this strip club saw this guy who* might *be friends with someone who* might *be Zahid*

*Ameen, and we followed him out to this shipping termi-
nal where he works and watched him* . . . what? Pick up
a suspicious person? For all she knew, Matt Palicek
was giving a coworker a ride home. And maybe the
bartender was mistaken and Palicek didn't even *know*
Ameen. And maybe this was nothing more than a
wild-goose chase.

Except that they happened to be standing beside
the Houston Ship Channel, which was on their short
list of terrorist targets. And it was the middle of the
night. And Derek was right—something was very
wrong here.

She got Gordon's voice mail and left an urgent
message. Then she called Lauren.

"Where are you?" she asked.

"At the Pussycat. Why?"

"I can't explain it all now, but keep your eyes
peeled for anything unusual, and add a vehicle to your
list: a black Avalanche. If you see one anywhere near
there, get the plate and . . ." Her voice trailed off as
Derek emerged from the maintenance building, followed by the guard.

"Elizabeth? You there?"

"Lemme call you back." She disconnected. "What
are you doing?"

Derek set a scuba tank on the dock beside her and
dropped a coil of rope at her feet. "Going in."

"Going in the *water*?"

He crouched down and started unlacing his boots.
"That hull could be rigged."

"But—" Her heart skittered. "You can't just jump
in there."

"Why not?"

She shot a look at the guard, who was now on his cell phone, no doubt calling his supervisor's supervisor's supervisor. This situation was spinning out of control, and she hadn't even reached Gordon.

Derek hefted the tank onto his back, then clamped a buckle around his waist and jerked it tight.

"But what if you find something?" she asked.

"Like an IED?"

"Yes, like an IED! What if it's rigged?"

"I'll unrig it. That's what we do with IEDs on boats. 'Specially boats filled with flammable liquids, 'specially when they're moored near giant tanks of crude oil. You want to see this place fireball?"

"But—"

"Relax." He squeezed her arm. "It might be nothing."

———

For the second time in a week, he found himself in pitch-black water, feeling his way around the hull of a ship. He worked bow to stern, moving with less speed than usual, because the only fins in the maintenance closet had been about six sizes too small. The water was like a bathtub. Given the sediment in the water, visibility was nonexistent, so he moved by feel, hyperalert for any debris that might be lurking beneath him, waiting to slice up his feet. He knew that while the main channel was definitely kept dredged and clear, the inlets weren't nearly as high a priority. Without water, this whole place would be a barnacle-covered junkyard.

Derek felt the curve of the ship's skin. He was nearing the propeller. The prop was a high-probability area to plant a device, so he slowed his search.

Nothing.

He adjusted his regulator and continued searching. His gut was churning, and his sixth sense was gnawing at him, and he knew without a doubt that the man who'd caught a ride in that Avalanche had been up to something. Had he planted a bomb in the channel? But why target a channel when there was a perfectly good explosive right here? One that would make a hell of a fire show on the six o'clock news, too. The media's motto was "If it bleeds, it leads," but if it freaking *exploded*, get ready. It would not only lead, it would be on continuous replay for the next two weeks.

Derek did one last pass, and still nothing. He kicked to the surface and spied Elizabeth pacing the dock as she talked on her phone. She rushed over.

"What'd you find?"

He shoved his mask up. "Nothing so far. Throw me that line, would you?"

She glanced down at the coil of rope and pulled the end to a free cleat. He watched her secure the line as he swam over.

"Their chief of operations is on his way," she said, "along with the fire chief." She tossed him the line as he reached the dock.

"Someone needs to find the Avalanche," he said.

"We're working on it."

The bulkhead was covered with razor-sharp barnacles, so he climbed the rope hand over hand to avoid trashing his feet. Water gushed from his jeans as he stood on the dock.

"Gordon's en route."

He looked around. "What's he doing?" He nodded at the security guard, who was dragging a wooden barricade over to a marshy area beside the road.

"I found some footprints in the mud, while you were under."

"Fresh ones?"

"Looked fresh to me," she said. "Our crime-scene techs can take a look, maybe get something useful."

Derek surveyed the swamp grass. He looked from the water to the spot on the gravel road where the Avalanche had picked up the passenger.

"Shit," he muttered.

"What?"

He crossed the dock. He followed the road a few paces and stepped off the gravel into the marsh. Mud oozed between his toes as he looked out at the water.

"Fuckin' A."

"Derek, what is it?"

He waded back in.

Elizabeth scanned the surface, searching for any sign of him.

"He still down there?"

She turned to look at the guard and nodded.

Another truck sped up to the dock and skidded to a stop. There were four now, all with the same private security company logo on the door. They'd also been joined by the chief operations officer for Oil Trans, who'd pulled up in a fancy white Suburban and was now standing on the dock talking on his cell phone.

No one seemed happy with the fact that an FBI agent and a diver from an as-yet-unnamed law-enforcement agency had suddenly started snooping around their boat dock.

Elizabeth squinted at the water. She checked her watch. Her heart pounded as she stared out at the shimmery surface. He'd been under almost half an hour. What could possibly be taking so long? With every minute that ticked by, her dread increased.

A dark shape on the rippled surface. Was it . . . ?

She squished her way through the grass as he rose out of the water like some sort of swamp monster.

"What'd you find?" Water swirled around her ankles as she trudged out to meet him.

He raked his hair out of his face, and the look in his eyes made her stomach clench.

"What is it? What's wrong?"

He glanced over her shoulder. "Your guys here yet?"

"They're on their way."

"Tell them to double-time it."

"Is it a bomb?"

"It's a sub."

She stared at him. "A what?"

"Like an SDV, only smaller. Given the size and shape, I'm guessing it's from Mexico or maybe Central America. Could be Colombian."

She waded closer until she was knee-deep in water as she tried to get her brain to process the words. "What are you talking about? What's an SDV?"

"It's *like* an SDV. A SEAL delivery vehicle used to insert covertly into enemy territory. But this boat's actually bigger."

"Are you telling me you found a *submarine* out there?"

Water glistened on his face as he looked down at her. "A narco sub, yes. Probably big enough for a three-man crew and a shit ton of cargo, all of it long gone at this point. Damn thing's been scuttled."

Her mind reeled. "But . . . how the hell would someone get a submarine up the Houston Ship Channel?"

"Wrong question, Liz." He clamped a wet hand on her shoulder. "What you need to worry about is why."

Chapter Fourteen

Torres picked up on the first ring.

"I need an update on Palicek," Elizabeth told him.

"This place is dead. Nothing happening, and it's been almost an hour."

"Not even a drive-by?"

"Zip," Torres reported. "And we've got four unmarked units staked out around his apartment complex. If anyone did a drive-by, we'd have seen it."

So where had Palicek taken his mystery passenger?

Elizabeth glanced around the waterfront, bustling with emergency workers. Firefighters and Coast Guard personnel stood in knee-deep water, watching as the narco sub was slowly pulled ashore by a huge winch attached to an industrial-sized tow truck. The vessel was black, bullet-shaped, and about forty feet long. Made of fiberglass, it would be practically invisible to both radar and sonar.

Gordon stood beside the submarine now, talking

to the Coast Guard captain. He caught her eye and broke away from his conversation.

"If you ask me, we're wasting our time here," Torres said. "I don't think this guy's coming home tonight."

"Okay, call me if you get anything," she said.

"You, too."

Gordon trekked through the marsh toward her. He wore the suit from earlier, but his wingtips had been replaced by heavy rubber boots on loan from the security chief.

"Where's Lieutenant Vaughn?" he wanted to know.

"I—" She glanced over her shoulder. "He was just here." She skimmed the roadside, and her gaze landed on a shiny red ladder truck.

Parked right where Derek's pickup had been a few minutes ago.

She looked at Gordon. "I don't know. I think he went to get changed."

Gordon's phone buzzed, and he pulled it from his pocket to check the screen. "Tell him we need him over here." He glanced up at her. "He hasn't been debriefed yet, and the Coast Guard captain needs to talk to him."

He headed off to take the call, and Elizabeth's dread mounted as she dialed Derek. She'd bet money that while she'd been distracted with all the chaos, he'd pulled one of his ninja tricks.

"Where are you?" she demanded when he picked up.

"On my way to see Lexi."

"Who?"

"The dancer from the Pussycat who spent time with our boy Zahid."

"We need you here at the dock. You haven't even given a statement yet."

"This is more important, Liz. This woman spent time with Ameen. She might have picked up some info about him while she was giving him a lap dance."

"She probably did, and this is exactly why we need to debrief you. If you'd bothered to give us a statement, we could have interviewed her already."

"Yeah? And who's she more likely to talk to, me or some suit with a stick up his ass?"

"You are not an investigator."

"Hey, if you really want to get her talking, why don't you send Potter over with his legal pad? I'm sure she'll loosen up real quick."

"Derek—"

"Tell you what, lemme take a shot at it first. I'll let you know how it goes."

And that was it. Gone.

Elizabeth glanced over at Gordon, who was still on his phone, but from the look on his face, he'd figured out the problem. He ended his call as she walked over.

"I just spoke to Lieutenant Vaughn," she said. "He's following up with the dancer at the nightclub, the one who spent time with Zahid Ameen."

"He's interviewing our witnesses now? What else is he doing?"

"I don't know," she said, and Gordon's gaze narrowed.

"Does he know where Ameen is? Let me tell you something, LeBlanc. If Vaughn knows his where-

abouts and withholds that information from the task
force so he can go out on his own—"

"That's not what he's doing, sir."

"—he'll be charged with obstruction so fast his
head will spin. And his SEAL days will be over."

"I can assure you—"

"Don't waste your breath assuring me anything.
Get him the hell back here, or get him in custody.
Tonight."

———

Elizabeth navigated the streets of northwest Houston,
where a surprising number of people were still out enjoying the airless July night. Her phone chimed from
the cup holder.

"You find him yet?" Lauren asked.

"No."

"I thought you traced him to Palicek's apartment?"

She switched to speaker so she could use the
tracking app on her phone. "I did, but he didn't stay
long enough for me to get there. Now he's on the
move again." She glanced at the screen and watched
the glowing green dot that represented Derek's
pickup. Lauren had installed a tracking device on
Derek's truck while Elizabeth distracted him at the
jogging trail. As she watched now, the dot exited the
freeway.

"Any idea where he's going?"

"Not really," she told Lauren, although that wasn't
true. She had a very good guess where Derek was
going, and with every second that ticked by, he was
proving her right.

She got off the phone, fuming. What did he think? That he could blow her off for hours and then just come knocking on her door? *Hey, babe, sorry I left you in the lurch back there. Want to go grab a drink?* Or since the bars were closed, maybe he'd show up with a bottle of Jack Daniel's and some crude suggestions.

The green dot came to a stop at her hotel. Elizabeth's temper festered. She exited the freeway and wended her way there. It was after three A.M., and the hotel parking lot was full, but she didn't see his truck. Cars, SUVs, pickups, but no gray F-150. She touched her phone, zeroing in on the green dot as she combed the parking lot. Finally, she slid into an empty space and walked up to a gray Ford Taurus bristling with antennas.

"Son of a bitch," she muttered.

Potter walked out from the vending-machine alcove. He carried a computer case in one hand and a bag of Doritos in the other.

"You find Lieutenant Vaughn yet?" he asked.

"Were you just at Palicek's apartment?"

"I did a drive-by," he said. "No luck. Why?"

She stalked back toward her car.

"LeBlanc?"

"Forget it. Good night."

She jerked open the car door and grabbed her purse and cell phone. Derek's number appeared on the screen. Somehow in the thirty seconds she'd been out of her car, she'd managed to miss his call. She listened to the message as she crossed the lot.

"Hey, I caught up with Lexi," he drawled. "No new leads, and she doesn't know where Ameen's staying. But sounds like he may know where *she* is. She's worried he followed her home from work the other night, so you need to get some agents over there, ASAP. She's staying someplace else for now, but the girl's spooked."

Elizabeth reached her door and jabbed her keycard into the lock.

"Oh, and one more thing," he said. "Tell Lauren next time she plants a Snitch on a vehicle, she needs to slide it *under* the chassis. Wheel well's a little too obvious."

Elizabeth shoved open the door and flipped on the light. She wanted to hurl her phone across the room, but instead, she took a deep breath and closed her eyes. Staking out the dancer's apartment was a good idea, and she should have thought of it hours ago. She sent Lauren a text message and asked her to talk to Gordon.

Elizabeth rubbed the bridge of her nose. She was tired, ticked off, and lightheaded with hunger. She jammed her phone into the charger, and it chimed before she even put it down.

"LeBlanc," she snapped.

"Whoa," Lauren said. "Somebody's pissed. What happened?"

She dropped her keys and purse onto the table. "Derek's being an ass."

"Hmm. Guess that means you didn't find him?"

"No."

"You think he found the Snitch?"

"Yes." She didn't mention that he'd not only found it but also attached it to Potter's vehicle just to piss her off. She took off her jacket and tossed it onto the chair. "Did you get my text?"

"That's why I'm calling. I'll fill Gordon in about the stripper. I'm guessing you're avoiding him since our SEAL friend is still at large?"

"You guessed right." She went into the bathroom and turned on the water. "And thanks. I owe you one."

"Get some sleep," Lauren said. "You sound stressed."

Stressed didn't cover it. She was so worked up she wanted to hit something, and the thing she most wanted to hit wasn't available. She splashed water on her cheeks and tried to cool off. She glanced at her reflection. She looked frazzled and cranky, and the humidity had done a number on her hair. She was tired to the bone, and what she needed was a hot shower and a pizza, but she would have given a week's pay for an ice-cold beer.

She turned the shower to scalding and thought about the crushed granola bar at the bottom of her computer bag. She'd ignored it for weeks, but right now she was famished enough to eat it. She walked into the bedroom and gave a startled yelp at the sight of Derek leaning casually against the wall.

How'd you get in here? was on the tip of her tongue, but she bit back the words, refusing to give him the satisfaction. She glanced at the drapes. He'd gotten past the sliding glass door somehow. Or maybe not. He could just as easily have gotten past the front door, or sweet-talked the desk clerk, or shimmied through a damn *vent* if he wanted to. In his world, there wasn't a place or a person that was off-limits.

"Looking a little tired, Liz. Rough night?"

"You shouldn't be here." She crossed the room and checked the peephole. The sidewalk was empty, so she hoped no one had seen him.

"You get an agent over to Lexi's?"

"Yes."

"Thank you."

She snatched her jacket off the chair and hung it in the closet. She pulled off her mud-caked shoes and chucked them beside her suitcase.

She returned to the bathroom, and he had the nerve to follow her right in as she turned off the shower. She fumed at him through the cloud of steam.

"Gordon wants you in custody," she said. "I'm supposed to arrest you on sight."

He smiled. "What's stopping you?"

She whisked past him, but he shot an arm across the doorway, blocking her.

"I promise not to resist." He slid his free hand around her and tugged the handcuffs from her waistband. He held them up in front of her.

She ducked under his arm and crossed the bedroom, swiftly unbuckling the belt that held her holster. He had a thing about women with guns. She knew that. And she wasn't going to stand here feeding his little fantasy while he laughed at her.

He sauntered over. "You're ticked off."

"You're observant." She set her Glock and holster on the dresser.

"You think I'm being an ass."

Damn him. *When* had he slipped in here?

He stepped closer. "I got you in trouble with your boss, didn't I?"

She folded her arms. He took another step until he

was inches away, the handcuffs still dangling from his fingers. He held them up.

"Go ahead. Cuff me."

She calmly took the handcuffs and just as calmly placed them on the dresser beside her firearm, but she couldn't keep her cheeks from flushing as she glared up at him.

He moved closer. She flinched as he rested his hand at her hip where her gun had been, and his thumb seemed to burn right through the fabric as he traced her hip bone.

"Come on." His voice was low. "What are you afraid of?"

"I know what you're doing. You're egging me on, and I'm *not* afraid of you, so get that through your thick head."

He eased closer, close enough that his thighs brushed hers, close enough that the solid mass of his chest was right in front of her.

"Know what, Liz?" He dipped his head down, and his breath tickled her temple. "I think you're lying."

Chapter Fifteen

His mouth crushed against hers, hot and demanding. He tasted like the other night—like bourbon—and she knew he'd been out drinking with a stripper while she'd been driving around the city searching for him. Knowing it should have made her want to smack him, but her hands were too busy sliding over his shoulders and tangling in his hair. This was a bad idea. She knew it, but she couldn't push him away. In fact, she was pulling him closer.

After hours of chaos and frustration, he was actually *here*. She should follow orders and take him into the office for paperwork and interviews, but she wasn't taking him anywhere. She wanted him alone. She wanted him in her bed, under her, with his mouth all over her and his hands everywhere and his three-day beard scraping her skin. He changed the angle of his kiss and went after her with a fierceness that shocked her and thrilled her all at once.

God, he could *kiss*. He kissed with the same power

and confidence that had attracted her from the beginning. No hesitation, just a brutal onslaught against all of her senses.

She tugged his T-shirt from his jeans and slid her hands under the cotton to feel the warm hardness of his skin. His tongue tangled with hers, challenging her on yet another level as his body pinned her against the dresser.

She couldn't believe she was kissing him like this after so many months of yearning and wondering. After so many months of telling herself she was going to steer clear, stay away, protect herself from the heartache that would inevitably follow this stupid, stupid decision.

But it didn't feel stupid right now—in fact, it felt unbelievably good to have his wide shoulders under her hands and his body pressed against her. She combed her fingers up into his hair and rocked her hips against him, and the groan deep in his chest gave her a rush of adrenaline. Was she really doing this? Right in this room, barely a stone's throw away from all the people she worked with? She dug her nails into his scalp and kissed him with a vengeance that pushed the doubts and logic out of her mind.

His knuckles brushed against her stomach as he worked the button of her pants free, and she heard the soft hiss of the zipper. She pulled back, and their gazes locked as her slacks slid to the floor. Her legs felt bare and exposed. The hot intensity in his eyes made her stomach flutter and made her think again about what she was doing, but before she could voice any objections, his hands closed around her waist, and he lifted her onto the dresser as if she weighed nothing. He clutched the back of her knee and hitched her thigh up to his waist, and she wrapped her legs around him and pulled him close.

"You are so fucking sexy." His mouth burned a trail over her jaw, her neck, her collarbone. She tipped her head back and closed her eyes and stroked her hands over his shoulders. They were so big—*he* was so big, everything about him.

They kissed and kissed until she felt like she was going to combust, and then he unhooked her ankles behind him. He dropped to a crouch to untie his boots, still watching her, desire burning in his eyes as he jerked the laces.

He was here. They were doing this. The determined look on his face made her ears ring and her pulse race. He stood up, then toed off his boots and kicked them away.

She reached for the waistband of his jeans and pulled him closer as he yanked the shirt over his head. And then they were fighting with his belt, his button, his zipper.

"Hurry, or I'll lose my nerve."

"No, you won't," he growled, nipping her neck. He shoved his jeans down, and she squeezed her legs around him as hard as she could. He lifted her right up off of the dresser and carried her to the bed and laid her back on it with surprising gentleness. His movements were careful, but the fierce look in his eyes made her heart skitter.

And then her gaze slid down his body, and her heart nearly stopped altogether.

Oh, my God. She sat up on her elbows to look. She traced a hand over his shoulder, his chest, his perfectly sculpted abs. He rested his knee between her thighs, and he stretched out over her, supporting himself with his arms as she looked at him in awe. She knew he kept in peak physical condition. She knew he spent hours and hours a week running and swimming and lifting and God only knew what else. But actually seeing the evidence of it . . .

"Wow," she said, and her cheeks warmed, because it sounded so childish.

He smiled and kissed her, and she ran her hands over his shoulders, unable to get enough of him, so blown away it was almost embarrassing. No, it definitely was embarrassing. She'd never been with a man who was so completely *male* in every conceivable way. She squirmed out from under him, and he gave her a confused look as she nudged him onto his back. Heat flared in his eyes, and she felt the shift in equilibrium as she shoved him back against the bed and straddled him.

"I need to just—" She settled herself against his erection, and he closed his eyes and groaned.

"Sorry." She brushed her hair from her eyes. "I need to look at you."

"Don't be sorry. Jesus." He gazed up at her, and his jaw was tight, and he looked like he was almost in pain as she sat back on him and stared. "Look all you want."

He'd asked about *her* scar, but he had so many more. She traced her finger over the welt on the side of his shoulder and the one under his collarbone. She traced over his chest to the trail of dark hair that started at his navel, then ran her finger back up to his ribs, where there was a jagged mark. Shrapnel? Her heart jumped into her throat, but she forced a smile.

He slid his hands over her thighs and up under her blouse, and she closed her eyes and tipped her head back as he cupped her breasts with his huge palms. His thumbs rasped her nipples, sending little shivers down her spine as she undid her buttons one by one.

He watched her intently as she shrugged off her shirt and reached back to unhook her bra. She slid it from her arms, and he sat up and dragged her against him, and the hot pull of his mouth made her go dizzy. He felt so good. Everywhere. Everything. His lips, his hands, the big, hard ridge of him pressed between her legs.

She rocked against him, again and again, until the tension started to build and their movements and kisses became more and more urgent. He shifted her and held her at the edge of the bed with one arm as he pulled her panties down her legs and tossed them away, and then she was back astride him, fusing herself against him and kissing him until she could hardly breathe. She noticed the condom sitting on the nightstand and had no idea when it had come to be there, only that she needed it desperately. She reached across him, and he went after her breast, and she fell against the table with a yelp. His mouth was hot and greedy against her skin. She pressed the condom into his hand and then distracted herself by kissing him as he shifted and pulled it on. And then he moved under her.

"Liz."

"Hurry."

"I don't want to hurt—"

She cut him off with a kiss and moved her hips and—

Pain and pleasure speared through her. She gasped and gripped his shoulders.

"Oh, God." She closed her eyes and surged against him, loving the pressure and the pain and the hot, hard friction of him.

He clutched her hips. The stubble of his beard scraped her tender breasts as he kissed her and nipped at her and she set a rhythm.

"Derek," she gasped. "Oh, my God."

"Tell me when." He said it through gritted teeth, but she couldn't respond.

She couldn't do anything but urge him to keep going and going and—

"Tell me."

She squeezed her eyes shut, rocking her hips against him again and again. "*Yes.*"

He bucked under her, and there was a white-hot burst, and her body shuddered and convulsed as she crashed against him. And then it was like the earth rose up beneath her, and he flipped her onto her back, and he was driving her up, up, up, all over again. She couldn't see, couldn't breathe. She could only cling to him and dig her nails into his back as he plunged into her over and over and the tremors started again. They took over her body, and just as she couldn't take another moment, another instant, he pulled back and gave a final, powerful thrust and fell against her.

She lay beneath him, too stunned to speak or even move. Not that she could have with his weight pinning her against the mattress. She shifted her hips, and he pushed up on his arms and then flopped onto his back with a groan.

She watched him, her pulse still roaring in her ears and her body throbbing.

"Holy Christ, Liz." He turned to look at her.

She didn't say anything, and he got up and disappeared into the bathroom briefly. When he rejoined her in bed, she scooted close, resting her head on his biceps. Because it felt natural. It seemed like the thing to do. She flattened her hand on his chest and felt his heart pounding against her palm.

Her mind reeled. For nearly a year, she'd talked herself out of this, she'd stayed away, she'd resisted. And then he'd shown up tonight, and she'd attached herself to him like a limpet. She'd practically jumped his bones, and now he surely knew how pathetically long it had been since she'd had sex with someone.

She looked at the sheen of sweat on his skin. At least, he'd exerted himself, too. He pulled her closer, and she felt a swell of emotion as she traced her finger over his muscular arm.

"Is that . . . glitter?"

He slid a look at her. "Huh?" He glanced at his arm. "Oh, yeah. From Lexi. She had it on when I saw her."

"And she just . . . happened to shed it on you?"

"It probably rubbed off accidentally." He squinted at her, then propped himself up on his elbow and gazed down at her. "You're pissed."

"Not at all." She hated the snark in her voice, but she couldn't help it. She was lying here naked, and now all she could picture was some dancer with her double-D cups rubbing glitter on him. She glanced down at her own chest—perfectly average Bs, thank you very much—and suddenly realized every light in the room was blazing.

"Hey." Derek smiled down at her, clearly enjoying her petty jealousy. "I didn't touch her. Not like that."

"It's fine. Could you turn off the light please?"

"Why?"

"Because it's almost four in the morning."

"You're not planning to sleep, are you?" His smile widened, and she felt a maddening rush of heat.

She sat up and reached for the lamp herself, bumping her head against his chin.

"Ouch!"

"Sorry," she said, not sorry at all as she plunged the room into darkness.

He hauled her on top of him and shifted her hips until she was straddling his lap, and she felt his hot mouth close over her nipple.

"It's okay," he murmured, making his way down her body. "I can work in the dark."

Chapter Sixteen

Elizabeth awoke disoriented. Her eyes felt swollen, her limbs heavy. She squinted at the man sprawled beside her, and everything came back in a flood of erotic images.

She glanced at the clock. The room was gray. Light seeped through the gap in the curtains, and she looked at Derek again. He lay on his stomach with his head turned away, but the slow rise and fall of his torso told her he was sound asleep.

She watched him breathing, still dazed by what had happened. He'd woken her up again and again, as if he couldn't get enough of her. Four times in three hours. She hadn't known men were capable of that. At least, not with her.

In the privacy of the dim light, she sat up and allowed herself to really look at him unguarded for the first time. She studied his muscled arms, his wide shoulders, the deep valley of his spine, where she saw the faint scratches she'd made with her fingernails. He had a scar on his back that she hadn't noticed before, a diagonal slash beneath his left shoulder blade that had to have been made by a knife.

Her blood chilled. Had he gotten it in training? Or in hand-to-hand combat with someone who actually wanted him dead? The thought of it made her heart squeeze. She silently slipped out of bed and reached for her crumpled blouse on the floor.

He moved and she froze, holding her breath as he turned onto his back with a heavy sigh. His eyelids didn't even flutter—he was still out cold. She picked up her blouse and took a moment to stare at his strong jaw, his perfect mouth, his scruffy beard, which she now knew could send shivers over her most sensitive skin.

She crept into the bathroom, eased the door shut, and switched on the light. Whoa. She cringed at her reflection. She looked as though she'd been up way too late having way too much fun—which she had.

The last time she'd shared a hotel room with Derek, she'd woken up horribly hungover—parched throat, headache, dizziness, the whole thing. She felt the same way now, even though she hadn't had a drop of alcohol. So, a sex hangover. Another first for her.

Four times. Maybe for him it was normal, but for her it was . . . unexpected. Surprising.

Maybe even life-altering.

She turned on the shower and climbed under the steaming-hot spray, careful to keep her bandage from getting wet. She hoped the shower would revitalize her, since ten minutes of sleep hadn't done the trick. Her legs were sore. And her mouth. As she slathered soap on herself, she discovered a hickey on the swell of her right breast. God, when was the last time that had happened? Derek didn't just have sex, he had *sex*, with the same relentless intensity he did everything else.

As the water sluiced over her, she realized she was ravenous. He had to be hungry, too, and she thought about inviting him to breakfast. But maybe that was too relationship-y.

'Morning, sweetie. How about an omelet? She imagined him sitting across the table from her, his big hand curved around a coffee cup. She imagined watching him eat pancakes while she remembered him kissing her and licking her and . . . there was no way she could sit across from him ever again and not think about all the ways he'd touched her.

Suddenly, her brain snapped awake. She couldn't take him to breakfast. What was she thinking? She couldn't take him anywhere. Gordon's orders last night had been to get him in or get him in custody. As in arrest him if needed. As in do not stop for sex or pancakes or Starbucks lattes. She needed to get him up and out of her hotel room so he could deliver himself to the office, pronto, to provide the statement he should have provided last night. He needed to document his evening from start to finish, from his underwater discovery to his interview with the dancer. And please, God, omitting the part where he sneaked into an FBI agent's hotel room and set her off like a firework.

Four times.

She jumped out of the shower and wrapped herself in a towel. She cracked the door to the bedroom to let the steam escape as she hurriedly dragged a brush through her hair. She could dry it later, after she got

Derek up and moving. She stepped from the bathroom and looked at the bed.

Empty.

Her stomach dropped as she glanced around. His boots were gone. His jeans were gone, his T-shirt, his belt, his socks. Every sign of him had vanished, even the condom wrappers that had littered the nightstand, and she stood there, stunned, in her too-small bath towel.

He'd gone without a word. Without a kiss. She scanned the room. He hadn't even left a note on the dresser.

Tears stung her eyes. But she refused to go to the window, refused to allow him to catch a glimpse of her peering through the curtains looking for him.

She went back into the bathroom and brushed her hair again, more slowly this time. She should have seen this coming. Escape and evasion. One of his specialties. He probably did this with all the women he slept with. Why would she be any different?

Her phone *ding*ed, and she felt a pitiful burst of hope as she rushed to pick it up. She saw a slew of messages from Lauren and Torres and even Potter—who'd texted her three times. Nothing from Derek, though. And nothing from Gordon, either.

A sharp rap on the door had her looking up. For a moment, she didn't move. More rapping, and she could tell it was a man, although she knew it wasn't Derek. The SEAL who'd slipped into her hotel room like smoke wouldn't come pounding on her door in broad daylight, loud enough to wake the dead. She threw on some workout clothes as her phone *ding*ed again with yet another message. She ignored it and answered the door.

"Where's your phone?" Potter demanded. "I've been texting you."

He stood there in his perfect pinstripes, a Starbucks cup already in hand, and she fought the urge to slam the door in his face.

"I don't usually text from the shower. What's up?"

"We found Matt Palicek," he informed her.

"Great. Where was he?"

"*Not* great. He's in the morgue."

———

Matt Palicek's apartment was swarming with law enforcement—Houston PD, FBI, there was even a sheriff's cruiser. Derek spotted Elizabeth's white rental car at the far corner of the parking lot beside Potter's Taurus.

After cleaning up at his folks' place and wolfing down some breakfast, Derek had finally made it to the FBI field office to recount the previous day's events ad nauseam. He'd also filled out paperwork and answered questions from a bunch of suits, including Elizabeth's friend Lauren, who'd relayed the not-so-surprising news that Matt Palicek had turned up dead last night. His Avalanche still hadn't been found.

Derek pulled his pickup into a space and watched the crowd of cops in his rearview mirror. His mission here was twofold. One, glean some useful intel about Ameen's dead accomplice. And two, talk to Elizabeth. As he got out and scanned the scene, he knew the second part of his mission was going to be tougher than the first.

He spotted Jimmy Torres eyeing him from beside a stairwell leading to what he assumed was the victim's apartment. Derek walked over.

"How's it going?" he asked amiably, although he knew for a fact that Torres didn't like him. Some of that was just the usual territorial bullshit, but he was protective of Elizabeth in a way Derek didn't much like.

"It's going."

"Lauren said I'd find Elizabeth around here. You seen her?"

"She's inside." He jerked his head toward the stairwell, where two agents were tromping up. They wore dark blue windbreakers with yellow letters on the back: FBI.

"Where'd they find the body?" Derek asked.

Torres watched him silently, probably deciding whether to tell him anything. Derek returned his stare and waited for him to realize that if it weren't for Derek's legwork, they wouldn't even have this guy, not to mention any new leads on Ameen.

"In a ditch off the Southwest Freeway," Torres told him. "HPD got the call about five. He had his wallet on him, ID inside."

"Murder weapon?"

"Something high-caliber, maybe a forty-five. We'll know more after the autopsy."

"Any sign of the gun?"

"Nope." Torres glanced up as a pair of agents came down the stairs. Still no Elizabeth. "Could have belonged to the vic, though. He has a big cache up there, all the serial numbers filed off."

"I'd like to have a look."

"It's all tagged and bagged." Torres pulled out his phone and brought up a digital picture.

The photo showed a row of guns lined up on the carpet, presumably in Palicek's living room. He had an array of pistols, some short-barrel shotguns, half a dozen machine guns.

Derek looked at Torres. "That a Honey Badger?"

"Yep. Fully automatic," Torres said, reading Derek's mind.

"You got a picture of this guy?"

Torres flipped to another photo, and this one looked like a mug shot. "This is Palicek. He got popped for drunk driving a couple years ago."

"Mind sending it to me?"

"Yeah, no problem."

More footsteps on the stairs, and Derek glanced up to see Elizabeth. She looked quite a bit different from when he'd last seen her, starting with the fact that she wasn't naked. She wore a crisp white blouse, and her look today was all business. Her gaze landed on him as she reached the sidewalk.

"Are you here to give a statement?" she asked.

"Already gave it back at your office." He studied her face, trying to read her expression. "You have a minute?"

"Sure."

He followed her across the lot to her car. She tossed her purse inside and turned to face him. Her hair was pulled back in a smooth ponytail, not a strand out of place.

"What are you doing here?" she asked coolly.

"Information gathering."

She cast a look over his shoulder. Clearly, she didn't want her boss to see him here.

"I hear he has a pretty good stash up there," he said. "Any idea who his gun connection is?"

"We're working on it. I can't really talk right now, though. I have to go."

"Where?"

"The office. I may have a lead on where Ameen's been staying, but I need to run down the details."

Derek held her gaze. Silence stretched out until he could tell she wasn't thinking about the case anymore. "Sorry about earlier," he said.

"Forget it." She looked away.

"Your phone was going crazy on the table, and I figured someone was going to show up looking for you. I didn't want to get you in trouble."

"It's fine."

Still no eye contact, and he knew it definitely *wasn't* fine. The hot, eager sex goddess from last night was long gone, replaced by this buttoned-up federal agent who wouldn't even look at him.

He eased closer so she had no choice but to lift her gaze or stare straight at his chest. "I want to see you tonight."

"I'll probably have to work late."

"After work. Whenever you're done. I'll take you to dinner."

"Tonight's going to be really busy."

"Tomorrow, then."

Something sparked in her eyes, but then they went cold again. "Tomorrow's busy, too."

"So what, then? That's it?"

"Derek—" She blew out a sigh. "Aren't you leaving in a few days?"

"Yeah. In the meantime, I want to see you."

"I'm busy."

"I want to see you when you're not busy. It can be late. After your work wraps."

She shook her head and glanced away.

"Liz, look at me."

She did.

"Last night was incredible."

She turned away.

"We were off the charts together," he said, and she still wouldn't look at him. "If you tell me you don't want that again, you're flat-out lying."

"Derek—"

"*Look* at me."

"Fine. God." She looked up at him now, eyes blazing, and he saw a glimpse of the woman he'd had sex with all night.

He still couldn't believe it. It was like she just ignited right there in his arms, and he had to keep putting the fire out, again and again.

"Let me ask you something," she said now. "How do you see this playing out?"

Okay. Clearly, she wasn't feeling so fiery at the moment. She was in analysis mode.

"I've got six days left," he said patiently. "I plan to spend them working on this case, same as you. But when we're not working, I want to spend time with you. Alone."

"And then?"

"And then I've got an eight-week training cycle." And after that, he was going to come straight back to Texas to see her again.

She was gazing up at him now, but he couldn't read her expression. She shook her head and glanced across the parking lot. "Derek—"

"Derek *what*? Spit it out."

"You don't understand."

"What don't I understand?"

"Forget it."

"No. Tell me."

"I'm not like you." She glared at him. "I can't have sex with someone over and over without getting attached. I'm not wired that way. And I know you're not looking for . . . attachments. So I don't see the point."

"Attachments as in a relationship?"

"Yes."

The R-word should have been a big red stop sign, but he kept going. "Are *you* looking for a relationship?"

"I don't know—maybe. Certainly not with you!"

He drew back, stung. "Well, shit. Tell me what you really think."

She glanced away, shaking her head again, and anger welled in his chest. The rational part of his brain told him to let it go. Now wasn't the time to argue with her. They were both sleep-deprived and stressed and surrounded by other people, and he knew he shouldn't get offended, but God damn it, he couldn't help it.

"I'm not relationship material. Is that what you're saying?"

She rolled her eyes. "You're not *here*. That's what I'm saying. You're gone all the time—off on training missions or overseas. And when you are here, you slip into my hotel room at three in the morning and then sneak out at sunrise, and that's not a relationship."

"I knew you were pissed about that."

"Fine! Yes, I'm pissed. You made me feel sleazy and . . . forgettable."

Forgettable. The hurt look in her eyes was like a knife in his gut. She had no idea how amazingly *un*forgettable she was to him.

He'd left early, yes. But if she'd been some random woman, he wouldn't even have stayed that long. Clearly, she wasn't up on standard operating procedure for a meaningless hookup. Usually, he completely dodged the whole morning-after scene filled with needy looks and awkward conversation. But with Elizabeth, he would have liked to have been there. He'd definitely wanted to see her sex-mussed hair and her sleepy smile, but her phone had been blowing up, and he'd known without a doubt that someone on her team was about to come banging on her door, so he'd hightailed it out of there.

And landed himself on her shit list.

Although he might have landed there anyway, because if there was one thing he was learning from this conversation, it was that despite her hot and completely eager attitude toward him last night, she now had regrets, big time. She'd finally let her guard down with him—not just once but four times—and she was using his stealth exit as a reason to blow him off.

She was uncomfortable. And if he ever wanted to see the sex goddess side of her again, he had some work to do. And he had to do it fast, because, as she'd correctly pointed out, he didn't have much time left. And the thought of going back to base without touching her again was pretty much unbearable.

Forgettable. She had no freaking idea.

"I never meant to make you feel like that," he said now.

"Drop it. I'm done talking about this."

"I'm going to make it up to you."

"I don't want you to make it up to me. I want you to drop it."

He took her hand. "Liz—"

"I mean it. Just forget it, okay?" She pulled her hand away. "I need you to just leave me alone and let me do my job."

———

Elizabeth was still rattled an hour later when she left the office. Some of it was from lack of sleep—she was going on day eight without a solid night, and her nerves were frayed—and part of it was the pressure of working a high-stakes case.

But part of it was Derek, a big part. She couldn't get him out of her mind, and whenever she tried to focus on work, all she could think about was the intent look on his face when he'd come to her room last night.

Torres held the door open as they stepped into the midday sunshine. Another blazing-hot day that had already hit triple digits. Heat radiated up from the asphalt, and her clothes felt glued to her skin.

"I'll drive," Torres said. "You're a mess today."

She glanced at him as they crossed the parking lot. She hadn't realized she looked quite as awful as she felt.

"Sorry," she said, sliding into the passenger seat. She was doing something she never did, letting her personal life interfere with her work. She needed to focus. She checked her notes and programmed their destination into the GPS.

"Looks like we're taking the Southwest Freeway," she said.

Torres glanced at her as he pulled out of the lot. "You've got a thing going with that guy, don't you?"

She looked up. "Who, Derek?"

"Yeah, Derek." He smiled. "The guy you've been drooling over ever since California."

She glanced out the window, embarrassed. "Is it that obvious?"

"Maybe, maybe not."

She looked at him.

"Relax, it's not *that* obvious," he said. "But I've known you longer than most of these people."

They picked up the freeway, and he veered into the left-hand lane. She was glad he was driving so she had a chance to get her thoughts under control.

The timing of all this couldn't have been worse. She'd been handpicked for the most important case of her career, and she'd decided to become infatuated with one of the men involved.

She was now convinced, though, that the timing wasn't accidental. At least, not on Gordon's part. He'd selected her for this case. Her, a relative newbie compared with the other agents on the task force. And he'd done so knowing full well that she had a personal connection to one of the SEALs involved in the raid. There was an underlying plan there. Gordon didn't do anything without a reason. And he didn't miss much, either, which meant that he, like Torres, probably knew she now had a "thing" going with Derek.

Elizabeth sighed. "What am I doing?"

"I don't know."

Torres looked completely relaxed behind the wheel. He was so low-key about everything that sometimes she had to remind herself she wasn't talking to Lauren.

He glanced at her. "Are you asking my advice?"

"I don't know. Do you have any?"

"Yeah."

"Let's hear it."

He swerved around a minivan. "You want my advice as your friend or as someone who'd like to take you out sometime?"

"As my friend." Whoa, talk about awkward. But he was grinning now, so she hoped he wasn't taking any of this too seriously. She should have waited to talk to Lauren.

"As your friend, my advice is to look at his rap sheet," he said.

"He doesn't have a rap sheet."

"His personal rap sheet. You know, with girls. *Women*," he corrected himself, cutting a glance at her. "Is he a love-'em-and-leave-'em type, or is he going to stick around? That's what I tell my sisters to think about. If he's the kind of guy who's going to stick around and you like him . . ." He shrugged. "Then what the hell? Give him a shot."

She turned to look out the window. It sounded logical and not that far removed from what they'd been taught about human behavior at the Academy. People were predictable. And the best predictor of future criminal behavior was past criminal behavior.

So what did Derek's personal rap sheet tell her?

She didn't know. She didn't know him well at all, which was one of the problems. But as for sticking around? That wasn't happening. He wasn't sticking anywhere—the SEALs were his life.

She looked at Torres again, hoping to dispel any awkwardness by being direct with him. "So what's your other advice?"

He smiled. "That's easy. Don't waste your time with him. He's a loser who's going to break your heart and leave you in the dust."

She choked out a laugh. "Great. Something to look forward to."

"Hey, you asked."

"You need to exit up here."

Torres cut across two lanes of traffic and took the exit that would lead them to the Happy Trails Motel.

Situated between a Smoke 'n Toke and an adult video store, the place was high-class all the way. Elizabeth had found the phone number for it scrawled on a takeout menu in Matt Palicek's apartment, which had prompted her to wonder if there was a chance they'd get lucky and learn that Ameen had been staying here at some point.

Torres slid into a space beside a souped-up black Cadillac with gold rims.

He straightened his tie. "I'm feeling a little underdressed," he joked as they got out.

They approached the front office. The window beside the door sported a spiderweb crack and a hole clearly made by a bullet.

"Nice." Torres pulled open the door. "Think they have a restaurant here? I'm craving crab cakes for lunch, maybe a little chardonnay."

They stepped inside.

"Sixty a night, twenty an hour," droned the man at the desk. He didn't look up from his crossword puzzle as they approached him.

"Are you the manager?" Elizabeth asked.

He frowned at her over his reading glasses. "Who's asking?"

She pulled out her ID, and he muttered something under his breath. His gaze slid to Torres.

"Your people were here yesterday. I told them I didn't see the guy."

"Which guy?" Torres leaned a palm on the counter.

"Are you here about the drug bust?"

"Nope."

The manager frowned at Elizabeth again as she pulled a photo from the pocket of her blazer. "We're looking for this man." She slid the picture of Ameen across the counter.

"Never seen him."

"What about this man?" She pulled out a second photo, this one of Rasheed. He gave it a glance.

"Nope."

"You sure?" Torres asked. "Take a good look."

The man stared at him stonily.

"They may have been driving a blue Chevy Cavalier or possibly a maroon Nissan Sentra."

Elizabeth caught a flash of movement in the office behind the manager. A woman rolled back in a desk chair.

"A blue Cavalier?" she asked through the doorway.

"That's right."

Elizabeth's nerves fluttered as the woman heaved herself out of her chair and waddled over. The manager glared at her as she picked up the picture, but she either didn't notice or didn't care.

"We had a blue Cavalier in last week." She tucked a frizzy gray curl behind her ear. "I don't recognize either of them, though."

"It had a dinged back quarter-panel," Elizabeth added.

"And big tires. I remember it."

Torres shot a look at her. *Score*.

"You know the guest's name?" Elizabeth asked.

"No," the manager said, adamant now as he glowered at the woman beside him, presumably his wife.

"You don't keep names of your guests?" Torres asked, heavy on the disbelief.

"The guests, not the cars," the manager said.

"But it definitely wasn't these guys." The woman handed back the picture. "I've got a memory for faces."

"You notice who was driving the car?" Torres asked her.

"No, but Jamie probably did. She was on nights last week, wasn't she? So she might've checked them in." She looked at her husband, who grunted a confirmation.

"If it's not too much trouble," Torres said, "we'd like to see a list of your guests last week." Instead of a warrant, he offered her one of his friendly smiles, which Elizabeth hoped would work, because she didn't want to face any more red tape today.

"No trouble at all."

Hallelujah. The day was looking up.

Fifteen minutes later, they stood before room 112. The motel was running at sixty-percent capacity, and the room hadn't been occupied since the previous guest had left Friday. That was the good news. The bad news was that the guest had paid in cash and checked in under the name John Smith, a name that no doubt appeared frequently on the motel's register. And the clerk who had checked him in had conveniently neglected to take a driver's license number.

"Think she'll remember them?" Torres asked as he opened the door with a keycard.

Elizabeth donned a pair of paper booties before following him inside. An evidence response team would be over soon to comb through the place, but until then, they wanted to have a quick look around.

"Depends," Elizabeth said, scanning the room. Gray walls, faded bedspreads. She glanced up. Brown water stain on the ceiling that she really didn't want to think about. "If they slipped her a fifty for a quickie, no-hassle check-in, then she probably remembers them."

"Fifty? I'd think she'd remember for twenty." Torres walked over to the nightstand and opened the drawer with a gloved hand. "Girl makes minimum wage."

"The dancer at the Pussycat said these guys are big tippers."

Elizabeth glanced at the channel guide propped on top of the TV alongside the remote control—which happened to be number one of the top five locations to look for fingerprints in a hotel room.

She sighed. "The crime-scene techs are going to hate this place."

Hotel rooms, particularly those that weren't cleaned well or often, yielded a mountain of forensic evidence. Fingerprints, hair, DNA—the sheer volume made it difficult to process.

Torres crouched down and looked under the bed. "I can already hear the bitching and moaning. This place hasn't been vacuumed since 1985."

Elizabeth peered into a trash can. Empty, but that didn't mean the techs wouldn't find something there. An alternative light source would probably reveal trace biological evidence.

She carefully opened the closet using only the tip of her gloved finger. A familiar scent hung in the air, and she tried to place it.

"You smell something?" she asked.

"Mildew."

"Besides that."

"Cheap-ass piña colada air freshener."

"Besides that." She stepped into the bathroom, home to the remaining four on the top five list for prints: faucet handle, shower handle, toilet flusher, and toilet seat, a high-probability area for male prints.

The bathroom had one of those one-piece shower stalls. This one had rust stains near the drain and was surrounded by chipping caulk where it didn't quite meet the wall. Nothing had been left behind on the shelf, not even a microscopic bar of soap for the next Happy Trails guest.

Elizabeth stepped back into the sink area and glanced around. On the linoleum floor, she noticed a row of copper-colored droplets. She crouched down for a closer look. Then she stood and examined the sink again, where she spotted a copper-colored smear on the faucet handle.

A memory hit her, and she was inside a cramped

apartment in Fairfax, Virginia, two years after her father died, during what her mother called "the lean years." She could see her mother primping in front of the bathroom mirror, getting ready for a date as Elizabeth looked on, brimming with resentment.

Why do you have to wear all that pancake stuff?

Her mother had bristled. *You think you're always gonna look like that, Miss Priss? Just wait till you hit forty.*

Those had been the days before Richard. Before Glenn. The days of coupons, and ramen noodles, and home dye jobs in the bathroom sink. Her mother's color had been Clairol Light Ash Blonde, and it smelled faintly of ammonia—just like this motel room.

Elizabeth's stomach suddenly felt squishy. She crouched down and studied the droplets, along with the strand of long hair caught against the baseboard.

Her throat went dry.

"What's wrong?"

She looked up at Torres. "I can't believe I missed it. We all did."

"Missed what?"

She stood up and glanced around, panicking. How had she, of all people, been so blind? How many clues, how many possible leads, had she overlooked?

"The mystery accomplice," she said. "The driver. The one who bought the Chevy and murdered the college student and picked up Rasheed in Del Rio. The one who's been here, laying all the groundwork for all this."

"What about him?"

"I think it's a woman."

Chapter Seventeen

Derek left another message for Cole as he sped out toward the firing range. If anyone could help him out right now, it was the team's best sharpshooter. But he wasn't picking up. Odds were, he was already on a plane.

In another shit development, Derek's entire team had been called back early. They'd been ordered to report for duty at 0800 Thursday, less than two days away. They were going OCONUS—out of the continental United States—and although the CO hadn't given details, Derek knew this was no training mission. If everyone's leave was being cut short, it meant something bad was heating up in some terrorist haven.

The timing sucked. Something was already heating up here in Houston, one of the country's largest cities, which also happened to be home to damn near every member of Derek's family. The body count was rising, and Derek was a thousand-percent certain the Houston sleeper cell was gearing up for something big. And while Elizabeth seemed confident that her task force could handle it, Derek wasn't so optimistic.

The feds had world-class investigative resources—he'd give them that—but the problem was their tactics in the field, where it mattered most. Even if they managed to make a few arrests, Derek had no confidence whatsoever that they'd conduct the kind of intensive interrogation needed to uncover a plot in time to put a stop to it. The way things had been going lately in Washington, some pencil pusher would probably make sure anyone the task force did arrest had a goddamn lawyer at his side before they asked him a single question. So unless the task force managed to bag up every last member of the terror cell or figure out their selected target, then the attack was on.

And from what Derek could tell, the feds didn't have a clue what that target was. Which was a slight problem. A little gap that needed to be filled. Right along with the names and locations of the four known tangos, who might only make up a small portion of this cell.

As for reporting back to base in forty-two hours, Derek wasn't happy about it.

The other reason he wasn't happy was Elizabeth. His sudden departure would only prove what she'd been saying earlier—that he was never here, that he was always jetting off on some training mission or some top-secret op.

And she was right about that. He was gone a lot. But he saw no reason why that meant he couldn't see her *tonight*. If anything, his abbreviated time made spending tonight with her even more urgent.

He thought of all those months he'd spent away from her. He'd wanted her for so damn long that after she'd blown him off last winter—and she'd hate this—he'd made getting her to sleep with him a personal conquest. He'd been determined, and his determination had gotten him what he wanted.

Only it wasn't what he wanted now. Not completely. Not after last night.

He pictured her pushing him onto his back and taking control. He pictured the look on her face as she let go of all those tightly held inhibitions. She'd blown away his wildest fantasies. It was amazing. But it was a problem, too, because now instead of some fantasy, he had the real thing to think about, and he couldn't do what she claimed she wanted, which was leave her alone.

Just forget it. Yeah, right. He wasn't forgetting anything. And as soon as this next op ended, he was hauling his ass straight back to Texas. Or maybe he'd even fly. He'd do whatever he needed to do to see her again.

But that was getting into relationship territory, which she'd said she didn't want, at least not with him. She'd made that clear. He wasn't relationship material, probably because he wore greasepaint and boots to work and jumped out of planes for a living. Maybe she wanted a relationship with some doctor or lawyer or some suit from her office. Someone who was around consistently and didn't go wheels-up at a moment's notice. Maybe someone like Jimmy Torres or even Gordon.

Would she sleep with Gordon Moore? He had no idea, but just the thought was enough to make him crazy. The idea of her sleeping with *anyone* while he was gone made him completely batshit.

But did he really want a long-distance relationship? He honestly didn't know. He knew he wanted Elizabeth alone tonight, so much it was burning a hole in his gut. Seeing her again was his objective, and he planned to clear any obstacle she tried to throw in his path.

Derek slammed on the brakes as he nearly flew past the turnoff to the firing range. He hooked a sharp turn onto the gravel road as his phone rattled in the cup holder. It was Cole.

"You get the callback?" Derek asked without preamble.

"I'm headed out tomorrow."

"Driving?"

"Flying," Cole said.

"Listen, any chance you're at the range right now? I just pulled in."

"I'm at my sister's place. Why?"

Derek turned into the parking lot and found a space. The crowd was sparse, with it being a Monday—just some guys who looked like off-duty cops, maybe getting in a few mags before the swing shift.

"I've got a question for you," Derek said. "If I needed to get my hands on a Krinkov, a Super-Shorty twelve-gauge, and an AAC Honey Badger, who would I talk to?"

Silence on the other end.

"That's some serious hardware," Cole finally said. "A Honey Badger fully *automatic*?"

"Yeah. You know anyone around here?"

"I know a few guys, but you'd be looking at some coin. That's quite a list."

"I don't want to buy it. I need to know who might have sold it recently."

"How recently?"

"Last few weeks," Derek said. "I have a feeling the buyer came into a nice payday."

Cole got quiet. Then he asked, "Is this about the tango who took a dive off that roof?" There was a touch of jealousy in his voice, and Derek knew that if there was something going down, Cole wanted to be a part of it.

"I need the name of someone local," Derek said, answering the question indirectly.

"Shit, I don't like the sound of that, but lemme ask around, see what I can get."

"I appreciate it."

"Hey, you want to come out tonight? Grab some beers before we head back?"

"Thanks, but I've got plans."

"Yeah, I bet you do." Cole sounded like he was smiling now. "Be sure to tell her hi for me."

Another call came in as Derek hung up. The Delphi Center.

"Hey there."

"Derek, it's Mia Voss."

"I figured."

"I completed those tests on your boots," she said, and something in her voice set off a warning bell.

"Yeah, I was going to swing by there tomorrow on my way back through."

"This won't wait till tomorrow," she told him. "I'm coming to you."

"Our facial-recognition software is cutting-edge," Elizabeth said. "It's good against disguises, even plastic surgery. But the best countermeasure out there is a burka."

Gordon watched her skeptically from across the conference table. He and everyone else in the room clearly weren't sold on her female accomplice theory.

"All this is based on a smell?" Gordon asked.

"It was prompted by that, yes, and then an eighteen-inch-long hair recovered from the motel room," she said. "I believe we should seriously consider the idea that the elusive accomplice we've been searching for could be female. I mean, why shouldn't it be a woman?"

"How about a couple thousand years of tradition?" Torres said. "How about strict religious beliefs? Their whole motive for this thing is their anti-Western ideology."

"Their strict religious beliefs didn't keep them away from the Pussycat three nights running," Lauren countered. "Looks to me like they're willing to bend the rules when it suits them."

"Let's get back to the facts," Gordon said. "Did anyone at the motel actually see a woman coming or going from this room we're looking at?"

"Not that we've been able to locate," Elizabeth said. "But one of the maids told us she heard what she thought was a female voice coming from the room one morning when she walked by."

"Maybe they had one of the Pussycats over," Torres said.

Elizabeth glanced around, frustrated. "Let's just assume for a minute that Tango Two *is* a woman. It makes their plot so much easier, especially in terms of facial-recognition software." She focused her attention on Gordon. "The vast majority of the faceprints in the terrorist database are male. If she had a decent passport, a good forgery, she could have walked right through immigration posing as a British national or a Canadian or someone from any of our other non-visa countries. We don't have her prints or her photo on file, so how would we know?"

"It would be in keeping with their MO," Lauren said, throwing her a lifeline. "We know two of these guys posed as Latin American businessmen so they could get over here and then sneak through a border tunnel. With the right passport in hand, a woman wouldn't even have to sneak."

"What do we know about these guys' wives and sisters?" Torres asked Gordon.

He was leaning back in his chair, contemplating the whiteboard where investigators had taped photos and biographical info about the two known terrorists. The two unknowns—the driver of the Chevy Cavalier and now the passenger from the narco sub—had no pictures on the board yet, only big red question marks.

"Neither of them is married," Gordon said. "As for sisters, we're running that down now. What we do know is that Rasheed and Ameen lived in London at the same time and attended the same mosque."

"So lots of connection points, and maybe that extends to others in the family," Elizabeth said.

"Yeah, but isn't the whole family on a watch list?" Torres asked.

"Yes," Elizabeth said, "but even if they are, what do

we really know about the women? That's my point. We don't have their images or prints on file. And while we've been busy combing the globe looking for the *men*, one of the women in either of these families could have slipped into this country months or even years ago to start laying the groundwork for an attack."

The door opened, and Potter entered the room, juggling an armload of files.

"Hi." He glanced around, then dumped the folders at an empty place at the table. "Updates on the families." He opened a file. "Neither Ameen nor Rasheed is married, which we already knew. As for sisters, between Ameen and Rasheed, there are four. Add the sisters-in-law, and we're up to eight." He glanced around the room. "Ameen's brother has three wives, and Rasheed's brother Ahmed *had* a wife."

"The brother who was killed in the drone strike?" Elizabeth asked. "Maybe it's the widow."

"Doubtful," Potter said. "She's actually in the system, because she attended college in England, which was where they met. The Brits have a jacket on her from when she applied for a student visa."

"What about pictures?" Gordon asked.

"Those are much harder to come by," Potter said. "We have Rasheed's sister-in-law, like I mentioned. But other than that . . ." He thumbed through the papers. "It's thin. We have a couple of surveillance pictures from public venues. Of course, the women are covered. The only shots we have that show any facial details are from years ago." He pulled a picture from one of the files. "Here's Rasheed with his family at a soccer match. He's nineteen in this picture, and the only reason it was taken was that his father is standing next to the Saudi Ambassador to the U.S., which attracted the Agency's attention, so they caught the shot." Potter stepped over and pinned the photo to the board with a magnet.

"We should focus on Rasheed's family," Elizabeth said. "Maybe losing a brother to a drone strike caused one of the sisters to shirk gender traditions and join the jihad."

"If her parents would allow it," Potter said. "These two families are very conservative."

Elizabeth glanced at Potter's mountain of files, then at Gordon. He and Torres still looked doubtful, which was probably a good indicator of how the rest of the team would react when they heard this theory.

"We need to confirm this one way or another," Torres said, "so we don't waste everyone's time. What do the CSIs have from the submarine?"

"Still working on it," Gordon said. "But we have a new lead on who might have been the passenger in the submarine, assuming he's the one who murdered the ship channel worker, Palicek. The victim's Avalanche was discovered in a vacant lot a few miles from the scene where the body was dumped. Someone had doused the front seat with gasoline and set it on fire."

"Probably to destroy prints," Lauren said. "Which makes me think they know we have them on file. Any chance we can get anything useful?"

"From the truck, it doesn't look good," Gordon said. "But police recovered a discarded gas can not far from the vehicle, and the prints on *that* might give us our best lead yet about who killed Palicek."

"What about evidence from the motel?" Torres asked.

"We're waiting on DNA from the motel room and also the Chevy Cavalier," Gordon said. "Preliminary tests can tell us whether we're dealing with any female subjects, but that may not mean anything. Just because a woman was in the motel room at some point or in the car—even if her DNA's all over the steering wheel—that doesn't mean she's a terrorist. It's not like we have DNA on file to compare it to, and it could have been left by someone not involved."

"What about familial DNA?" Elizabeth suggested. "I've seen it used to solve cases before. We have Rasheed's from the autopsy. We can find out if the DNA at any of these crime scenes is from the same family line. And if so, if there's a Y chromosome."

Gordon nodded. "Good idea, but that technique works best with people who share the same mother. As Potter pointed out, a lot of the men in these families have multiple wives. How many wives does Rasheed's father have?"

Potter shuffled through one of his folders. "That would be . . . three. Rasheed's mother was the first, which is sort of an honor position."

Lauren rolled her eyes. "Gimme a break."

"We should talk to the lab," Potter said. "See what they can come up with comparing the profiles."

Elizabeth glanced at the clock. "That could take days or weeks. What about now? We need to talk to that motel clerk."

"Agreed," Torres said. "If she checked them in or even saw them coming or going, she probably noticed whether they had a woman with them."

"We sent a pair of agents over to her home earlier, but she wasn't there," Gordon said.

"Did they stay?" Elizabeth asked, thinking about Palicek and the murdered college student and the stripper who was now in hiding. "If she saw anything at all, she's going to need protection."

The door opened again, and Gordon's assistant ducked in to give him a message. Gordon read it and shot a look at Elizabeth.

"Send them in," he told the assistant.

A moment later, a beautiful young woman stepped into the conference room, followed closely by Derek.

Chapter Eighteen

Elizabeth's first thought was that this was Lexi, the dancer from the Pussycat, but Derek introduced her as Dr. Mia Voss from the Delphi Center crime lab. Mia was dressed casually in jeans and sandals. She declined Gordon's offer of a chair, preferring to stand beside the whiteboard.

"I dropped by Delphi a few days ago," Derek said, also standing. "I asked Dr. Voss here to run some tests for me, see if we could learn something about what our friends in Asadabad were up to when we raided their compound."

"What kind of tests?" Gordon asked.

"She looked at the boots I wore during the op. I spent some time in the basement of the compound, where they'd set up their own little bomb-making factory."

"And?" Gordon looked at the doctor.

"I tested for a range of substances: explosive residue, ricin, sarin, anthrax—"

"Anthrax?" Torres cut in.

"Al Qaeda's been working on it for years," she said. "It's difficult to weaponize, but that hasn't stopped them from trying. But that isn't what I found. Extensive testing revealed trace amounts of white phosphorus."

Silence settled over the room as eyes shifted to Derek for clarification.

"An explosive packed with a white phosphorus payload—that's guaranteed to ruin your day," he said. "In the military, it's known as Willie Pete, and it's very bad news. It eats through clothing, skin, even metal."

"The chemical sticks to skin and burns," Mia explained. "Absorption in the body causes multiple organ failure. It also produces a hot, dense smoke called phosphorus pentoxide that can cause illness or even death if inhaled."

Elizabeth sat speechless, trying to visualize a chemical like that being used against a civilian target, such as a mall or a movie theater. Or, heaven forbid, a school.

"Plus, it ignites on contact with air," Derek added. "Did I mention that? This stuff's highly flammable."

"Because of its extreme flammability," the doctor said, "it's transported in molten form as a semiliquid."

"So you're saying they were working with this material at the compound the SEALs raided in Afghanistan?" Lauren asked Derek.

He nodded. "Yes, ma'am, that's exactly what I'm saying."

"Is this stuff hard to come by?" Torres asked the doctor.

"Here in the U.S.? Yes, it's a controlled substance," she said. "It's used in some pesticides and fertilizers.

The DEA has it listed as a precursor chemical for a number of illegal drugs, including methamphetamine."

"Which means it's around," Gordon stated.

"I'm guessing it's easier to come by outside the U.S." Torres looked at Gordon. "Like maybe in Mexico. If our guys wanted to get their hands on it, I bet they could buy it off the same cartel they hired to smuggle them through the border tunnel."

Elizabeth looked at Derek. "How hard would it be to make it into a weapon?"

"It would take some legwork," Derek said, "but an expert bomb maker could handle it. Ameen definitely qualifies."

"We should test the narco submarine specifically for this material," Lauren said. "Maybe they smuggled in not just a person but a chemical weapon."

"I'm betting it's both," Derek said. "And this person, whoever he is, is a key player. Someone on our watch list."

Potter turned to Elizabeth. "We need to find out if your theory is accurate. If we could get a description or an alias, that could be the break we need."

"What theory?" Derek was watching her.

"Agent LeBlanc found some evidence suggesting that Tango Two might be female," Gordon said.

"So you're thinking what?" Derek asked. "She seduced Palicek into helping with the attack?"

"It's a theory at this point." She tried to sound low-key, but she was pretty charged up about the idea, because it opened up a whole new set of leads. "If it turns out she *was* involved with Palicek, he might not have fully understood what she was up to, just that she needed a favor."

"We should interview that motel clerk," Lauren said. "Maybe we can even get a composite sketch."

Elizabeth glanced at her watch. "She's due at work by six."

"What about this chemical?" Torres asked. "Should we assume they smuggled it in, or should we start looking for local angles on that?"

"Don't assume anything," Gordon said. "For now, we don't know what they were smuggling. We need to get the CSIs back out to run more tests on the sub."

"Test all you want," Derek said, "but don't waste time getting a bead on these tangos. Whatever their mission is, we're getting to the zero hour."

———

Lauren pulled into the convenience store a block down from the Happy Trails Motel. They'd spent the past two hours combing southwest Houston in a fruitless search for the motel clerk.

"I'm getting a bad feeling about this girl," Lauren said, rolling up to a gas pump. "Any more updates from Torres?"

"I'll check. You want anything inside? I'm getting coffee."

"Cherry Icee."

Elizabeth made a face.

"What? I skipped lunch."

"One Cherry Icee coming up."

She called Torres as she entered the store and made a beeline for the drink section. "What's the word on Jamie?"

"I talked to her landlady," he reported. "She rents

a garage apartment over here on Cottonwood Drive, but she hasn't been by in a few days."

"That's not good."

"Maybe not as bad as it sounds. This woman's the busybody type. Says her tenant keeps weird hours and is in and out a lot with her boyfriend, spends the night at his place a lot."

"Let's hope so." Elizabeth put a lid on her coffee and then filled a cup with red slush. "We know the boyfriend's name?"

"Just that he's 'Negro' and drives a pickup."

"'Negro'? How old is this landlady?"

"About a hundred and fifty," he said. "But she seems pretty sharp, and she basically camps out in her recliner near the window watching her street. She's got a clear view of the driveway, so she probably would have seen if Jamie came home today."

Elizabeth waited in line as the checkout clerk carded a kid for beer. His fake ID was so bad Elizabeth could spot it from five feet away. The woman turned him down on the beer, so he settled for a pack of cigarettes.

"Are you at the motel yet?" Torres asked.

"Almost. Jamie's shift starts in ten minutes."

"Hope you find her, because we're striking out on this end."

"I'll keep you posted."

Lauren was on the phone when Elizabeth slid back into the car and tucked their drinks into the cup holders.

"We're just getting there," Lauren was saying. "Her shift starts at six." She shot Elizabeth a look. "All right, I'll tell her." She got off the phone and pulled out of the parking lot.

"Gordon?"

"Nope. Your SEAL. And he's not happy that we're staking out the motel. He says this is a crappy neighborhood."

"How'd he get your number?"

"I gave it to him." She smiled. "And before you freak out, no, I'm not hitting on him. He wanted it in case he needed to reach you. He said you were screening his calls this morning."

Elizabeth couldn't believe he'd told her that.

"Was it that bad?" Lauren asked, and Elizabeth didn't pretend not to understand what she was talking about.

"It wasn't bad at all. It was—" Amazing. Thorough. Exhilarating. "It was fine, right up to the point when he disappeared."

Lauren looked at her. "Really?"

"It's my fault. I don't know what I was thinking, and I *really* don't want to talk about this now, so—"

"So at least tell me what you think of his theory. That we might be dealing with a chemical weapon."

"You're taking a left up here."

Lauren shifted lanes. "Well?"

"I think it's a serious possibility," Elizabeth said. "Based on what I know about Ameen, he has the expertise to pull it off, and if he's planning something, it's probably against civilians. Gordon said civilian targets are his specialty. Here, this is it."

Lauren pulled into the lot, but they saw no sign of Jamie's white Honda. She circled the building, bumping over potholes behind the motel as they squeezed past a Dumpster. Elizabeth noted a pair of black pickups in the Smoke 'n Toke parking lot and called Torres.

"The boyfriend's pickup truck," she said. "You know what color that is?"

"Sorry—yeah, it's white. And there's a logo on the side. I think he has a lawn-mowing business."

Lauren parked in one of the motel's front-row spaces facing the office. "I'll check inside," she said. "Maybe she got dropped off."

"Doubtful. We're early." Elizabeth glanced around, but she didn't see any white pickups. "We're not seeing her," she told Torres, "but we have a few minutes—wait, hang on."

Elizabeth twisted around in her seat as a white pickup truck pulled out of the lot's east exit. There was some lettering on the side, but she couldn't read it.

A woman rounded the corner of the building, and Elizabeth's pulse quickened.

"Think I see her," she told Torres. "Let me call you back."

She pushed the door open and tucked her phone into her pocket. The woman was five-two, plump, wearing cutoff shorts and flip-flops. Her jet-black hair was at odds with her fair skin, and her eyes looked wary as Elizabeth approached.

She attempted to relax her with a smile. "Are you Jamie?"

Rat-tat-tat.

Elizabeth hit the ground, smacking her chin against the pavement. *Gun!* The word rocketed through her brain as she jerked her weapon from the holster.

Her heart jackhammered as she looked for the shooter, trying to keep her head down. She saw tires and bumpers and asphalt. She spied a pair of purple flip-flops and scrambled toward them.

"Jamie!"

The girl was flat on her back, motionless, in a rapidly expanding pool of blood. Elizabeth frantically dug for the phone in her pocket as she tried to stay low.

Rat-tat-tat-tat.

She sprawled over Jamie's body, covering their heads with her arms as she tried to flatten them both into the pavement.

Tires squealed. Horns blared. She hazarded a glance up, then grabbed Jamie's arm and pulled her behind the shelter of the nearest car. Blood was everywhere—streaming down the girl's face and neck, soaking her hair.

"Call nine-one-one!" she shouted, hoping Lauren or anybody could hear. She darted a look at the motel office, where shards of glass glistened like ice crystals at the base of the shattered door. She pictured Lauren and the office manager crouched behind the desk, and she prayed they were already calling, because *where the hell was her phone?*

She put her gun down and stripped off her blazer to press it against Jamie's neck.

"Hang on, okay?" Her voice trembled. "Help's coming."

She tried to remember her location, tried to recall the type of gun used, the car. The weapon was definitely automatic.

Blood gushed from Jamie's neck, and Elizabeth felt a surge of panic as she glanced around.

She spotted her phone. It was on the sidewalk near the front bumper of the Taurus, but between here and there was an empty car space. She grabbed her gun and made a dash for it, immediately ducking behind the engine block as she snatched up the phone. *Thank God.*

A faint wheezing noise sent an icy jolt of fear through her. On the asphalt beside the Taurus, a black shoe.

Elizabeth darted around the car and found Lauren slumped against the wheel well, her head against the tire.

"Lauren!"

Blood seeped through Lauren's fingers as she clutched her side with one hand and tried to work her phone with the other. Elizabeth grabbed it from her and hit the emergency button. Lauren's lips moved, but Elizabeth couldn't hear over the roaring in her ears.

"Oh, God. *Lauren!*"

Lauren's eyelids fluttered shut, and she made a rasping sound. Elizabeth's heart clenched.

"Hang on, okay?"

She was bleeding from her abdomen. Elizabeth pressed her hands against the wound as a soft, tinny voice emanated from the phone.

"Nine-one-one operator. Please state your emergency."

"Shots fired! We have an agent down!"

Chapter Nineteen

Derek struck out at the gun shop. After talking to the third of three people on Cole's list, he'd gotten nowhere. None of them had had any dealings with Matt Palicek or had even heard of him.

Or so they said. Gun guys tended to be tight-lipped, but it wasn't like Derek was walking around with the letters *ATF* tattooed on his forehead. Derek had made sure to mention that he was teammates with Cole, but still he'd netted nothing useful.

He jumped onto the freeway and pointed his truck toward the FBI office. He needed an update from Elizabeth or someone on her team. Hell, even Potter might be able to help him. He wanted a physical description of this female jihadist, preferably a picture. He was beginning to think she was playing a much bigger role in this than they'd given her credit for.

All Derek knew was that she was likely related to one of the terrorists, either by blood or by marriage. If she was a wife or a sibling, that put her in her twenties or early thirties. She'd likely have dark brown hair, which Elizabeth believed she'd dyed auburn. And if she spoke English—which seemed logical if she was laying the groundwork for a plot in America—she probably spoke with an accent. No doubt she'd be wearing Western-style clothes to fit in.

It sounded like a lot to go on, but it wasn't, and Derek needed a photo or at least a composite sketch to flash around, along with the photo of Palicek that Torres had given him.

He trained his gaze on the bloodred horizon. The sun was setting on his last day in Texas, and his tension was mounting. He couldn't stay, but he damn sure couldn't leave with so much unfinished. He had less than twenty-four hours to get a break in this thing, or he would face the choice of leaving the task force high and dry or going UA. An unauthorized absence was no small offense, especially in the teams, and especially when they were going wheels-up on an honest-to-God mission, not some training bullshit out in the desert. If Derek failed to report Thursday morning, Hallenback would have his ass in a sling, and possibly even his job.

He tried Elizabeth again, and again it went straight to voice mail. He scrolled through his phone and called Lauren. Three rings, and then Elizabeth answered.

"Hey, I've been calling you all night."

"My phone's dead." she said, and her voice sounded strange.

"What's wrong? Where are you?"

Silence on the other end, and a wave of fear hit him.

"Elizabeth?"

"I'm at the hospital."

———

Elizabeth paced the room, compulsively darting glances at the double doors. Nothing. She passed by the wall of windows that looked out over the medical center. She swung by the coffeepot, then back to the chairs. It was a well-worn path in the carpet where hundreds or maybe thousands of anxious people had walked before.

The doors opened, and she whirled around, hoping to see the doctor. Instead, it was Gordon. His face was a hard mask, and she struggled to read the look in his eyes as he walked toward her.

"No change," he said. "She's still in recovery."

Her throat tightened. "It's been over an hour."

"When she stabilizes, they'll move her. Until then . . ."

He didn't need to finish. Until then, they'd wait. Lauren had pulled through the surgery, but the doctor had described the procedure as "complicated." The bullet had ripped through her right kidney. They'd had to remove the kidney and repair several organs.

Elizabeth glanced at the door as Lauren's sister walked through and went straight to the coffeepot. She looked like an older version of Lauren—straight dark hair, willowy build. She'd been glued to her phone since she showed up at the hospital.

"I understand her parents are driving down from Dallas?"

Elizabeth looked at Gordon. "That's right."

"We need someone here when they show up," he

said, "but I have to go by the crime scene. They're wrapping up there."

"I'll stay."

"Torres is on his way in, so you can leave when he gets here."

"What's happening with Jamie?" she asked, changing the subject so she wouldn't have to argue.

"No updates."

The motel clerk had been hit by a bullet that grazed her neck. The wound had bled profusely but done little damage. The more serious injury had occurred when she dropped to the pavement and hit her head. She had cerebral swelling and was currently in a drug-induced coma.

"We've got an agent stationed at her door," Gordon said. "When she comes out of this, we'll need to interview her."

If she came out of it.

The working theory was that the clerk had seen something important—otherwise, why bother to eliminate her?

Gordon's phone buzzed, and he pulled it out to check the screen.

"I have to go." He gave her a sharp look. "When Torres shows, I want you to go home, get some sleep."

"Sir—"

"No arguments. You've been here for hours, and you worked late last night, too. I need you rested for tomorrow. We're short-handed now."

His words shut her up. They were short-handed because Lauren was in a hospital bed, fighting for her life. Elizabeth's stomach churned, and she glanced at the doors again.

"Go home and rest, LeBlanc. You can't help us if you're dead on your feet."

He walked away, leaving her alone once again in the maddeningly quiet waiting room.

She paced over to the chairs, where the television was tuned to CNN. The volume was muted, but she could read the headline crawling across the screen: TERROR SUSPECT DEAD IN APPARENT SUICIDE.

A reporter with a local TV station had finally broken the news that the roof jumper from Saturday had been on the terrorist watch list. The story had taken off, and although the media had gotten many of the details wrong, the upshot was accurate: the man had committed suicide as federal agents apprehended him. Now conjecture was running wild about what he'd been doing inside the United States at the time of his death.

Elizabeth watched the taped footage of an FBI spokeswoman standing at a podium. Her canned statement that she couldn't share details "due to national security" had only fueled speculation.

An elevator opened, and Elizabeth turned to see Derek stepping off. Her heart lodged in her throat. He quickly spotted her and strode across the room.

"Any news?"

The look in his eyes made her chest hurt. She wanted to throw her arms around him, but she kept them firmly at her sides. "She's out of surgery. That's all I know."

He nodded. "Hang tight. This is one of the best hospitals in the world. They'll pull her through."

She turned away.

"I've been working the gun angle."

She looked at him, trying to process the words.

"Did you get a look at the weapon?" he asked.

The weapon. Used in the shooting. "I barely even saw the car," she told him, as she had told investigators back at the crime scene. "Something white, maybe an SUV," she added. "The motel manager got a better look at it. The gun was an automatic."

"Probably a submachine gun, based on the range."

"How do you know the range?"

"I went by the motel on my way here," he said. "Saw the skid marks. Looks like they approached from the northwest corner, unloaded from the passenger side, then took off south—probably jumping right on the freeway."

She tried to envision it. Everything he'd said fit with what she'd experienced. She'd been facing Jamie, not the street, when the shots erupted. She'd never seen it coming.

"Typical setup for a drive-by," he said. "Which is probably intentional."

"The motel was hit recently in some sort of drug thing," Elizabeth said. She pictured the bullet hole in the office window. Their tangos had probably noticed the same thing when they were considering ways to eliminate yet another eyewitness without attracting undue attention.

Derek was gazing down at her, his brow furrowed. "How long you been here?"

"I'm fine."

"You need a break."

The elevator opened again, and Torres stepped off. He glanced at Derek, then Elizabeth, as he walked over.

"Passed the boss in the lobby," he told her. "You have orders to go home, get some rest."

"I can stay."

Torres squeezed her shoulder. "I'm on. You go. I'll call you if anything happens."

"My phone's dead."

"We've got mine," Derek said.

"Go," Torres repeated. "I'll let you know if anything changes."

She cast a glance at Lauren's sister, who was still on her cell phone. Then she followed Derek to the elevator. The doors swept shut, and she stared down at her feet, at the black leather flats that she'd rinsed off in the hospital bathroom because they'd been smeared with blood. She still wore her bloodied slacks, too, but the jacket she'd used as a bandage was back at the crime scene. Or maybe in a trash can. Or maybe it had been bagged up by the evidence team.

She looked up to find Derek watching her in the mirrored doors.

"Thanks for coming," she said.

He didn't respond.

The doors slid open, and they stepped out into the same lobby she'd rushed through only a few hours ago. Another set of doors, and then they were standing together in the muggy night air. The streets were dark and deserted. All was quiet except for the distant wail of an approaching ambulance.

"What's the theory?" Derek asked, leading her across the street.

"What do you mean?"

"You're bound to have one. What is it?"

He led her away from the parking garage, and she

spotted his truck on the street beside a fire hydrant. They climbed in.

"We believe they're eliminating eyewitnesses," she said. "What I don't get is why. Why not just stage the attack and get it over with?"

He gave her a grim look.

"You think they're biding their time," she stated.

"I think they're waiting for something. Something specific." He pulled into the street and stopped at an intersection. It was nearly midnight, and traffic was light. "Where to?" he asked.

"I don't know."

He hung a left. "You hungry?"

"No."

"Thirsty?"

"No." The last place she wanted to be right now was a noisy bar. "I guess just take me back to the hotel."

"You got it." He took a right and headed for the freeway.

She looked at him. "I'm sorry if this sounds bitchy, but please don't get the wrong idea about this."

"And what would that be?"

"I don't think we should sleep together again." Somehow everything that had happened made it easier to say it, to just get it out in the open. "I don't think it's a good idea."

"I happen to think it's a great idea, but it's your call."

She turned to look out the window, bracing herself for the guilt. But it didn't come. She actually felt relieved that she'd taken it off the table.

They drove without talking as the lights of Houston rushed by. Her stomach clenched as she thought of Lauren being loaded onto the gurney and whisked away in the ambulance. She'd felt so helpless, so utterly useless, staying behind to answer questions. She'd felt even more useless pacing the hospital waiting room.

She rested her forehead against the window and let the truck's vibrations numb her as she closed her eyes. Her eyelids burned. She combed through the events in her mind. She went through them systematically, looking for any detail she'd missed, anything she'd omitted when she gave her report.

The truck slowed, and she opened her eyes as Derek pulled into the familiar parking lot.

Elizabeth zeroed in on her room. She pictured Lauren sitting cross-legged on her floor, surrounded by case files and cartons of Thai food. Derek whipped into a space, and she felt a wave of nausea.

"I can't go in there."

He looked at her.

"I'm sorry," she said. "I just can't. I—"

"No problem." He thrust the truck back into gear.

"I'm sorry."

"I get it. Stop apologizing."

He pulled out of the parking lot, then headed back toward the freeway.

She eyed his phone in the cup holder and felt sick again. Who was she kidding? She couldn't rest tonight. She should go straight back to the hospital and wait for news.

"There's nothing you can do there," Derek said, clearly reading her mind. "Your boss is right. You need a break."

She turned to look out the window as he got back onto the freeway. "So where are we going?"

"You trust me?"

She hesitated. "Yes."

"Then relax." He glanced at her. "Close your eyes, clear your head. I'll let you know when we get there."

———————

Luke stepped away from the throng of people surrounding the bar and pressed his phone to his ear.

"What's that?"

"I said, it's Hailey."

Holy shit. He looked at his phone again. He hadn't recognized the Boston area code.

"Hang on." He squeezed through the crowd to the hallway outside the men's head. It smelled like beer and puke, but at least it was quieter.

"Sorry to call so late."

"No, it's fine." He checked his watch. He hadn't expected her to call at all, and definitely not at 2200 on a Monday night.

"Are you in Boston?" he asked.

"I'm still in town. I leave tomorrow." She paused. "Where are *you*? It sounds really loud."

"O'Malley's." He pushed open the back door and stepped into the alley off the parking lot, where it reeked even worse.

"Guess that means you're with friends, huh? I was going to see if you wanted to come over."

He blinked out at the parking lot. "To your hotel room?"

"I was thinking the bar downstairs. I can't sleep

again, and I thought we could get a drink and talk or whatever."

His mind whirled. He'd had a few too many beers for this conversation. She wanted to get a drink and *talk or whatever*—which in his experience was girl-speak for sex. He shook his head, trying to shake off the beer buzz and the crazy-ass idea that Hailey Gardner wanted to sleep with him.

"What, you mean now?" he asked.

Silence.

"Sorry," he said. "My bad. I'm—"

"Sounds like you're busy."

"I'm not, I just—" Shit, *now* what was he doing? He couldn't actually go over there. He definitely wanted to see her, but he was half loaded. If he got anywhere near her right now, his dick would take over, and he'd waste no time talking her upstairs.

"Luke?"

"I'm here."

"I can tell I'm freaking you out, and I don't mean to. It's not what you're thinking." She was talking fast, like she was nervous. "It's just that I can't sleep, and it really sucks. And I thought maybe we could, you know, just hang out and talk."

He tipped his head back and squeezed his eyes shut. "That's probably not a good idea."

Was he really turning her down? Hailey Gardner, who couldn't sleep and wanted to *just hang out and talk?* And then it was back—the image of her cowering in the corner of that rathole back in A-bad, her face dirty and her hair tangled and her eyes . . . God damn it, of course she had trouble sleeping. But he couldn't be around her.

"Listen, Hailey—"

"You don't have to explain."

"I wish I could come, but—"

"Forget it."

"Hailey, wait. Hailey?"

She'd already hung up.

He stared down at his phone, feeling like crap. He'd made the right call, though. He knew it. He had no business going anywhere near her or her hotel room in his current state of semi-inebriation.

"Fuck."

He turned and looked at the door behind him. The thought of going back inside suddenly had zero appeal. What he should do was go find one of his buddies who'd had less to drink than he had and catch a ride home. But he didn't want to do that, either.

I can't sleep, and it really sucks.

God damn it. Luke shoved his phone into his pocket and headed for the beach.

Chapter Twenty

Derek drove west, leaving the skyscrapers and the hospitals and the shopping malls behind. He drove through the suburbs until he reached the fringes of the city, and then he exited the freeway and drove some more. Finally, he turned off the highway onto a narrow asphalt road that not so long ago had been nothing but caliche.

Elizabeth stared out the window, not talking. But her body language said a lot. She was clutching the door handle in a white-knuckle grip and glancing at his phone in the cup holder every ten seconds.

Pine trees rose on either side of them. The road curved, and his headlights swept over the sign for the trailhead. The landscape looked different from what he remembered, and he nearly missed his turn.

He rolled to a stop and looked at Elizabeth across the console.

"Where are we?" she asked.

"Sugarberry Dam Park." He pushed his door open

and went around back, where he unlocked the tool-box and rummaged around until he found what he was looking for.

Elizabeth slid out and glanced around. She climbed the steep incline to the ridge and stopped cold when she reached the top.

"Whoa." She stood there, staring out over the reservoir. They were in a dry spell, and what was often a full-blown lake in springtime was now an empty field surrounded by trees. A full moon cast a silver glow over everything.

"Here." He tossed his jacket onto the ground. "Don't dirty up your clothes."

"These clothes are history." But she sat down on the edge of his jacket, looking out over the view.

He sank down beside her, and she glanced back at the truck.

"You left the radio on."

"I know." He unscrewed the top of his flask and offered it to her. She eyed it suspiciously before taking it.

"This is quite the setup." She sniffed, then took a sip. "How come I feel like I'm not the first woman you've taken out here?"

The whiskey made her voice hoarse, and he smiled. "Woman? Yes. Girl? No." He looked out over the meadow. "I brought Ashley Ferrell out here on her first car date." She passed the flask back, and he took a swig.

"Do I want to know more?"

"Nah, the rest is top secret."

She slipped her shoes off and tucked them beside her, then rested her arms on her knees. She leaned her head back and looked up at the sky.

"We don't get stars like this in San Antonio."

"Light pollution." He glanced up. The stars looked nice, but it was nothing compared with the dead of night on the open ocean. Or in the Hindu Kush. On top of the world like that, the sky looked like a big dome of glitter directly over his head.

"I would have figured you for country," she said.

He glanced over his shoulder, straining to hear the soft, soulful music drifting from his pickup.

"Yeah, well, I like a lot of stuff. Country, blues, jazz."

"You're full of surprises."

He looked at her. "Maybe you need to get to know me better."

She knew some of his preferences but not nearly enough. And he was learning hers—including the mind-blowing fact that she liked to take control during sex.

And maybe she could read his mind, because she looked away.

He took another sip from his flask and tried not to think about sex, because it wasn't going to get him what he wanted, which was to get back into her bed not only tonight but the next time he had leave, too. And the time after that.

It would have to be her call, like he'd said, so he was playing it cool, trying to make her comfortable.

She gazed up at the stars again. "It's nice here."

"Yep."

He handed her the flask, and she took another sip. Sometime in the last hour, she'd lost the anguished look that had been eating away at him since he'd first seen her standing in that hospital. But still she looked edgy.

A warm breeze stirred the trees as they sat there,

not talking. It felt good to be home, surrounded by the familiar scent of dirt and pinesap. It seemed unreal that seventy-two hours from now, he'd probably be strapped into a C-17 over the ocean.

He should tell her. At least mention it. But she had enough to worry about right now, and he didn't want to add to it.

"Alison Krauss, 'Killing the Blues.'" She looked at him. "My dad liked to listen to her when she played with Union Station. They're from the same town in Illinois."

"Illinois, huh? How'd you guys end up in Virginia?"

"He went to law school there. UVA."

"Your alma mater," he said, hoping she'd keep going. She never talked about her family, and he knew it was a nut he needed to crack if he wanted to understand her. "So he practiced law there?"

"He was an assistant commonwealth's attorney in Fairfax." She cleared her throat. "I guess I never really told you how he died."

"No, you didn't."

She paused and seemed to be collecting her thoughts. "It was a convenience-store holdup. He had this concealed-carry permit because of some of the people he'd helped prosecute. He always had his Beretta on him, and he tried to intervene in the holdup. The perp was roughing up this clerk, but there were two of them—one in the back, which my dad didn't realize, so . . . it all went sideways."

Derek reached over and squeezed her hand. "You and your dad were close?"

She nodded.

"And your mom?"

Wrong question. He could tell by the way her shoulders tensed. She slid her hand out from under his and rested her arms on her knees. "She remarried a few times. The latest guy's okay, but I don't know." She shrugged. "There's still a lot of resentment there."

"You should patch that up," he said, venturing an opinion she probably didn't want to hear. "I used to have shit like that, too, with my dad. He rode us pretty hard growing up. For years, I thought I hated him."

He looked out at the meadow bathed in moonlight, not so different from the conditions they'd had during the raid in A-bad.

He looked at Elizabeth, and she was listening. "But then a couple years ago, we lost our CO. He was killed in a helo accident." It hadn't really been an accident, but he didn't want to go into all the details. "He was tough as hell, and he'd always reminded me of my dad. Then one day, he was just gone, no warning. And I realized you can't take people for granted. Life's too short."

She held his gaze for a long moment, and then she looked away. Evidently, she didn't like his advice.

The silence lengthened, and they stared out over the reservoir. A distant pair of headlights bumped over a road on the other side. It was so quiet, with just the wind and the music drifting over them, the low hum of the cicadas. He'd always loved this spot. When he came here, it was hard to believe the sprawling city of Houston was only a few miles away.

She glanced back at his truck again. "I have this album on my iPod."

"Yeah?"

"I couldn't sleep, like, the entire month of May. So I'd sit on my balcony at night and listen to this."

She looked so pretty sitting there, and he reached out to stroke her hair away from her face. "Because of what happened?"

She shrugged. "I had trouble sleeping before that. Getting the shit beat out me didn't really help, though."

He gritted his teeth at the reminder and glanced at her scar.

She looked at him. "I thought about you a lot, you know."

———

She held her breath, waiting for what he'd say. Her own words surprised her. They were the first truly honest words she'd said to him about the time when he'd been gone. She didn't know why she was telling him this now, but it seemed to want to come out.

"I thought about you, too." He covered her hand with his in the dirt.

"I thought about you getting shot down in a helicopter, or driving over some roadside bomb, or jumping in front of a bullet for one of your teammates."

"We generally try to avoid bullets." The corner of his mouth lifted in a smile. "IEDs, too. First thing they teach you in SEAL school."

"I'm serious," she said.

"I am, too."

She looked out at the meadow, and the tension was back again, bunching up her muscles, making her neck tight. He always wanted to defuse any tension with a joke, but she was trying to be honest with him. Honest about why things would never work. Why she felt adamant about not sleeping together again when she knew he wanted to, and she wanted to, too.

"I ever tell you about my first tour?"

She turned to look at him. He'd never told her about any of his tours. When he talked about his work, it was usually about the training.

"This was up in the mountains," he said, and she took that to mean Afghanistan. "End of the fighting season, so it was getting cold at night. Your breath would turn to frost in the air, and you'd have to stomp your feet to keep from freezing. We'd spent the whole summer assaulting cave complexes—which is hot, filthy work—and we were glad to finally get some cold, even though we knew we were going to be hating it in only a few weeks.

"Anyway, we get this intel from one of the terps at base camp in the valley. And this isn't just any valley, it was a snake pit—that's what we called it. The whole place was crawling with TAQ—Taliban/Al Qaeda fighters."

"What's a terp?"

"Sorry—interpreter. This one was working with the Army guys at the base. He brings us this intel that an HVT—that's a high-value target—is hiding out in a cave complex in the neighboring valley. This target was tops on our list. We knew he'd been recruiting kids in the villages for suicide missions in Kabul— marketplaces, security checkpoints, that kind of thing."

"He was getting kids to do this?"

"Yeah, this guy was a real scumbag, no moral code whatsoever. That was something I learned on my first tour: some of the top TAQ guys were the biggest cowards. So this guy's high-priority, and we get this tip about him, but of course, we're wary. Single-source intel tends to be unreliable. But the commanders get together and decide to send some guys in, see if we can get the dope on this cave complex. It wasn't on any of our maps."

"Sounds like a red flag."

"Yeah, but you never know. Especially back then. This was early days in the war, and we didn't have all the intel we have now. In some of the more remote places, we were still using Soviet maps, if you can believe it."

"So I'm guessing you were on this team they sent in?"

"Me, Gage, Luke, and this guy Kevin Bunker. You haven't met him, but he's big. He was in the BUD/S class ahead of me, aced all the PT. He could bench-press three-fifty, but he was fast, too—always smoked everyone in the timed runs. He got the nickname 'Hill' because of his size."

"As in Bunker Hill?"

"You got it."

He offered her the flask again, and she shook her head. She wanted him to keep talking freely. He'd never shared so much about his job before, and she was lapping it up.

"So there's a village located near this supposed cave complex, but it's on a steep hillside, and I mean steep. We're talking accessible by goats and locals, not outsiders. So they get out the maps and determine that the best way to get to this area is to hike down to it, and that's what we did. Our four-man element dropped in high about 0400 hours. It was a straight SR mission, search and recon. Depending on what we found in terms of forces and weapons, we were planning to bring a bigger team in to finish the job.

"We start making our way down, and like I said, it's steep. So we're traveling combat light, which means we've left a lot of our armor on base. Even without it, each of us is carrying forty to fifty pounds of gear—water, radios, ammo. It's only a twenty-four-hour op, but you never go anywhere without at least five pounds of water and an MRE in case things go off the rails."

She watched him talk, deeply disturbed by the image of him behind enemy lines, moving around without body armor.

"We spend the better part of the day getting down through this forest, making sure to stay invisible among the spruce. By the time we near the destination the sun's getting low, which is what we want, and we check our coordinates, and there's the village out to our east. And then we start looking around and spot this cave right where the terp said it would be. It's on the side of a cliff, this big, dark mouth, with some goat trails leading up to it. So we huddle together and go over the plan. After nightfall we're going to slip up there, check it out, see what's what. But then I start looking around. I'm on glass—binoculars—looking down at the village, and I start getting antsy. Something's off with the setup, and I can feel it."

She watched him, waiting.

"And that's when it hits me. It's too quiet. The village is too calm, too empty. Not nearly the kind of activity you'd expect in the evening when people are preparing meals and everything. And I turn to Gage to tell him, and that's when all hell breaks loose. Bullets start smacking into the trees right above our heads, branches snapping off, bark spitting everywhere."

"An ambush," she said.

"Yeah, we were getting pummeled from all directions. Except down, so that's where we went—we just started running down this mountain. And I'm talking ten- and twenty-foot drops, sheer cliffs, but there was nowhere else to go. We're running full speed, sliding, jumping, trying to take cover behind rocks whenever we could, and the bullets are slapping around everywhere, and I hear one of my teammates scream, and I know he's been hit. And I start running in that direction, but the bullets are flying, and it's hard to stay oriented. Basically, I knew up and down, but every other direction didn't exist in the chaos of it all. I end up behind this boulder with Luke, and his weapon's jammed, and he's trying to clear it, and I'm damn near out of ammo, so I'm starting to get worried, and then suddenly, that was it. Nothing."

She stared at him. He's under attack with no armor and scarce ammo, and he's *starting* to get worried? "What do you mean, nothing?"

"Silence." He sliced the air with his hand. "Zilch. No more shooting. For a while, Luke and I just wait. We don't know whether they've run out of bullets, which had been known to happen, or whether they're trying to wait us out. Finally, after a while, our daylight's totally gone, and we figure it's real, the shooting's actually stopped. So we start maneuvering around the mountain in NVGs looking for Gage and Hill. We find Gage pretty quick, but Hill isn't anywhere. At last, I pick up a heat signature and manage to spot him under this holly bush behind some rocks, and he's injured. His whole foot is twisted around, about a hundred eighty degrees off."

She cringed.

"It was ironic, really. We'd had all this parachute training, where they teach you how to land, but he's injured from a fall, not a bullet. Meanwhile, Gage is on the radio, trying to get us some air support, but the timing's bad, and all our Apaches are in a neighboring valley involved in a firefight. Our guys over there are really getting rocked, and there're no spare choppers. Our CO manages to track down a Pave Hawk that can help us. We just have to get up to the top of this mountain where there's a plateau. It's the only viable landing zone for miles."

"But Hill can't walk."

"His leg is broken in three places, so we carry him. Fireman's carry, taking turns. And I'm not gonna lie to you—he was heavy. Luke had managed to get a needle in him and give him some morphine, which helped his pain but made him more like dead weight. We're carrying him, and he keeps telling us to put him down, leave him there, come back later, but that wasn't going to happen, so we take turns. At one point, we get to this very steep part, and Luke—you remember him?"

"From the meeting, yes."

"He grew up kind of backwoods Tennessee, but he's smart as hell. Innovative, too. He gets out his Ka-Bar knife and starts sawing branches off these trees, and we rig up this thing that's kind of a sled. We strap Hill to it with some bungee cords and drag him up that rock face. We get to the top of the LZ, and then it's a waiting game. Our helo's on the way, but we're jumpy, because there's only one place to land for miles around, one extraction point, so everyone on the mountain knows where we'd go, and we're feeling like sitting ducks. We're stuck there waiting and wondering, were they really out of ammo, or was that just a mindfuck to get us into another ambush?"

Elizabeth held her breath, waiting.

"And then I hear it. The helo's coming, and we've got our infrared lights there to guide her down, and I still can't believe we're getting out of there. We load Hill into the bird, and I glance into the trees, and I see this green figure—that's what it looks like through my goggles. It's a TAQ fighter, and he's got an RPG on his shoulder. Gage starts yelling and pushing me, and the three of us jump in and get the hell out of there."

"What about the RPG?"

"He missed. Firing at night from a distance, it was literally a shot in the dark, but it rattled our cage anyway."

She tried to digest the words. He never talked about his missions, not in any detail. She looked out over the landscape. Just listening to his story left her feeling dizzy. She looked at him. "Why did you tell me that?"

"I want you to know what it's like." His face was deadly serious. "We have each other's backs. That's ironclad. We move mountains for each other."

The brotherhood thing again.

"Will you miss it when it's over?" she asked quietly.

"When what's over?"

"The war. Everything's winding down."

"Yeah, well. It's never really over for us."

She'd known that, but she wanted to hear it from him. What he did was too important to ever actually stop. The war on terror would continue in the shadows, and spec ops forces would continue to fight it.

He wouldn't quit, anyway. He believed in the fight, and he didn't want to leave his brothers.

And she wouldn't ask him to.

Which brought them right back to the same dilemma she'd predicted when she'd first met him, when he'd burst into her life and turned everything upside-down. She looked at his strong profile now, at his muscular arm resting on his knee. She couldn't remember ever being so drawn to a man, so hopelessly attracted. She respected him, and he made her laugh, and he made her pulse pound whenever she got near him, but that was chemistry, and it didn't get rid of the very real obstacles. He was gone all the time, putting his life on the line. And he was so committed to his team she didn't believe he had room for anything else. She looked at him, and he was watching her with that steady gaze that made her nerves hum. Slowly, carefully, he was dismantling all the fences she'd built around her emotions. And she was letting him.

A distant buzz of a phone, and Elizabeth scrambled to her feet. They rushed to the truck, and Derek reached through the open window and plucked his cell from the console.

"Vaughn." He listened for a moment and held the phone out. "It's Torres."

She snatched it up. "What is it?"

Chapter Twenty-one

"She's stable," he told her. "They've upgraded her condition, and they're moving her into a room."

Elizabeth's heart clenched. "Is she awake? Can I see her?"

"No and no. Doc says a few more hours. Her parents just arrived, though, so they'll be here when she wakes up." There was a tremor of emotion in his voice. "So that's the news. Sounds like she's going to make it through."

She squeezed her eyes shut. *Thank you, God.* "What about Jamie?" she asked.

"Still the same. They're watching her. I'll call you if we get anything new."

"Please. No matter how late."

She got off the phone, and Derek was staring at her in the dimness.

"Doctors say she's stabilized."

"She awake?"

"Not yet." She handed him the phone, then walked

around to the passenger side to climb in. She stared numbly at the dashboard.

Derek climbed in, too, and pulled shut the door. He looked at her. "You all right?"

"Yeah." But she sat there, motionless, replaying the news. *She's going to make it through.* Suddenly, her lungs constricted, and she couldn't breathe. She clasped her hand to her chest and realized she was shaking.

"Liz?"

"I was so sure she was going to die." She covered her face with her hands, but that didn't stop the hot flood of tears.

"She's going to be okay."

She turned away.

"Hey." He leaned across the console and pulled her into his arms.

"I was so *sure*," she said against his shoulder. "People die. It happens. They die in the line of duty or doing something careless or stupid or for no reason at all." Her voice hitched. "I can't believe I wasn't paying enough attention, and it's my fault."

"It's not your fault."

Her arms tightened, because she wanted so much for the words to be true. She rested her head against his neck, and at the first scent of him, it was over. The tears just came. His chest was hard and solid, and his arms felt so strong wrapped around her. How many times had she dreamed of him holding her like this?

She wished things were different. She wished they could be like other people, normal people. But they couldn't. They weren't.

"Sorry." She pulled back, but he wouldn't let her go.

"Look at me."

She wiped the tears away.

"You weren't responsible," he said. "They were. Get that straight."

She nodded. But the look of tenderness on his face made her eyes well again. He reached up and gently brushed her cheek with his thumb, and his eyes were intent in the dimness. And then he leaned over and kissed her forehead, and she just . . . lost it. There was no other way to describe it. Whatever hold she'd thought she had on her feelings disappeared, and she reached up and dragged his head down to kiss him. It was wet and sloppy, and she would have been embarrassed, but he pulled her right across the console, practically into his lap.

And then everything went into overdrive. His hands were everywhere. Hers, too. She tried to get her balance as he shifted her on his lap. When she looked up, his eyes were dark with desire, and a shiver of anticipation moved through her as all the memories rushed back. She wanted him so much she couldn't breathe, couldn't think—with the exception of one persistent thought that wouldn't go away.

Why does he have to leave?

His hand slid under her shirt and found her breast, and heat speared through her as every thought left her except that she wanted him. She twisted closer. He gripped her hips and pulled her firmly onto his lap until she was straddling him and her knees were wedged against the console and the door. It might have been painful, but she was too distracted by the warmth of his hands and his thumbs rasping over her nipples. She kissed him and kissed him and arched her body against him, and then he pushed her shirt up and went for her breast.

She combed her fingers into his hair and tipped her head back. She loved his mouth, his hands, the roughness of his beard against her skin. He'd been growing it out for days now, and the friction of his face against her sent a shot of lust through her.

She pulled off his T-shirt and tossed it away and pressed closer to kiss the hell out of him. She loved the sharp taste of him and the way every time he kissed her, it was a battle of wills.

His hands slid down her back and dipped beneath her clothes. He pulled her against the rock-hard bulge in his jeans, and she was so turned on her skin felt tight, like she was about to burst.

She broke the kiss and pulled back. "Where's the hotel?" she gasped.

He looked dazed.

"The hotel? How far?"

"I don't know. Fifteen minutes?" A look of dread filled his eyes.

Fifteen minutes. It may as well have been fifteen hours.

She reached for his belt, and his look of relief was so intense she felt giddy. She fumbled with his buckle and his zipper as he pulled her against him and wrestled her shirt over her head. Then he flung it to the floor, and they were skin-to-skin, their mouths fused, as she slipped her hand inside his jeans.

"I have to touch you," he said, doing it through her clothes as he kissed her until she was dizzy.

She squirmed away from him, then leaned back against the other seat as she kicked her shoes away and struggled to get her pants off. He helped, jerking them down her legs along with her panties and tossing everything away. In one swift motion, he levered his seat back and pulled her on top of him.

"Condom," she squeaked, but he was a step ahead of her, digging one from his pocket and tearing it open with his teeth. She darted her gaze around, amazed that they were doing this here, in public, in the front seat of his truck, where anyone might come along—

"Hold on." He gripped her hips and pulled her down, and she gasped at the pure, shocking pleasure of it.

She braced her hand against his shoulder as he moved under her. The denim of his jeans rubbed against her thighs. His hands were on her breasts, shoving the lace of her bra aside, and then his mouth was on her.

Everything was happening together, all at once, and it felt so good, so perfect, so right. But it was going way too fast.

"Derek."

He pulled her closer, pressing deep inside her, again and again, and the friction was mesmerizing. She rode the wave of it, higher and higher and higher, until she couldn't stand it, couldn't go another second. And then everything broke, and she felt the powerful thrust of his body as they crashed together.

She slumped against him. Her pulse pounded. She rested her cheek against the dampness of his skin until the pounding subsided. Their breathing slowed, and she could hear the cicadas again.

He sighed deeply.

She smiled and looked up at him in the darkness. His eyes were closed, his head tipped back against the seat.

A faint humming noise reached her. Not insects but—

He sat up. "Car."

Lights flashed across the dashboard, illuminating everything in blinding white as she dived into the passenger seat.

Derek swiveled and cursed.

"What are they doing?" she asked, scrambling for her shirt. She found it on the floor and dragged it over her head. The lights grew brighter and brighter, then dimmed.

"Turning around, looks like."

The inside of the truck glowed red. She darted a glance in the mirror and saw the taillights receding down the road. A punch of relief hit her.

He levered his seat up, and she heard the rasp of his zipper. She felt around in the dark, searching for her clothes.

"Sit tight," he said, and shoved open the door.

———

When he returned from the trash cans, she was dressed again but still groping around.

"They're gone," he said, pulling the door shut. He started the engine and buzzed the windows up, but it was too late to keep the mosquitoes out.

He glanced at Elizabeth. She was still looking for something. He felt around on the floor until he found her shoe and handed it to her.

"Thank you."

Polite. Not a good sign.

He paused a moment, watching her, then followed his instincts and put the truck into gear. She didn't seem like she wanted to hang out and enjoy the view anymore.

He made a three-point turn—just like the car that had rolled up on them—and headed back down the road.

She kept squirming in the seat.

He glanced over. "What's wrong?"

"I can't find my underwear."

He braked and switched on the light. He checked the back, and there they were: Elizabeth's white lace panties draped over his hiking boots. He handed them to her, and her cheeks flushed an even deeper shade of pink as she shoved them into her pocket.

He switched off the light and drove on. Silence settled over them as he neared the highway.

He felt the regrets coming, fast and furious. Not only had they had sex after she'd announced her intention not to, but they'd done it in his truck in a public place.

"It was probably just a couple of teenagers," he said. They'd probably chosen that road for the same reason he had.

She looked out the window. "I can't believe that just happened."

"Why?"

"Why? Because my friend's in the hospital, and I'm getting off in some car."

He turned onto the highway. His brain was still a little scrambled, but he knew better than to argue with her right now.

She shook her head. "I don't know what I'm doing."

"How about having some fun?"

She snorted.

"What? What's so bad? If I didn't know any better, I'd think you actually liked it."

"Of course I liked it! That doesn't matter. If that had been a cop back there, he would have asked for your ID and mine, too. And then it would have been a mess. I can see the headline: 'FBI Agent Arrested for Public Lewdness.'" She grabbed her shoes off the floor and shoved them onto her feet. "I told you, I'm not cut out for this."

"Cut out for what?"

"*This.*" She waved her hand at his truck as if it were a rolling brothel.

"You're trying to make it into something shallow so you can push me away." He looked at her. "We both know what's really happening here."

"Oh, yeah? Tell me, Dr. Phil, what's really happening here?"

"Forget it." He trained his gaze on the road.

"No. Please enlighten me. What would you call this?"

He took a deep breath and swallowed down his temper. He didn't want to fight with her. Not tonight. Not on his last night home, probably for months.

Shit.

He definitely should have told her he'd been called back early, but now it was too late. If he told her now, she'd think he'd kept it from her on purpose.

Which, truth be told, he had.

Fuck.

"I'm going back tomorrow."

No response. He glanced over, and she looked as though he'd reached out and slapped her.

"They called us back early. Everyone. I have orders to report at 0800 Thursday."

She cleared her throat. "Is it training or—"

"I can't talk about it."

She looked away. Her cheeks flushed again, but this time it looked like frustration. She'd asked him a simple question, and he couldn't answer it.

There was nothing good to say, so for the rest of the drive, he didn't say anything. He just drove, feeling more and more miserable the closer they got to her hotel.

He didn't know what to do about this relationship. Because no matter what she said, it *was* a relationship. Granted, they'd gotten off to a rocky start, because she'd been investigating his teammate. And yes, it had been punctuated by months and months where they hadn't even spoken to each other, much less been intimate. But that part was over now. They'd crossed a line. There was no going back, and her stripping her clothes off in the front seat of his truck was proof. She'd probably think it was crude and even egotistical, but the fact that she couldn't keep her hands off of him after telling him in no uncertain terms that she wanted to call a halt to the sex *proved* he had a chance with her. She didn't think he was relationship material? He'd show her she was wrong.

Starting now. Tonight.

He pulled into the parking lot of her hotel and found a space near her door. No sneaking around anymore, and if that got her in trouble, too bad.

"Elizabeth."

She looked at him, and he saw the hurt in her eyes. He didn't know what to say. He'd done a shitty job handling this up to now, but he could do better. He had a chance with her, and he was determined not to blow it.

He reached over and took her hand. "I went about this all wrong tonight. I should have insisted on taking you to dinner."

She looked down at their hands together. "I don't know what I'm doing," she whispered.

"I do." He leaned over and gently kissed her mouth. "You're inviting me in."

———

Still awake?

Luke pressed send and stared down at his phone, half wanting, half dreading an answer. Finally, it came.

Yes.

And two seconds later: *Where R U?*

He took a deep breath and typed: *Downstairs.*

He watched his phone. Piano music wafted over from the bar behind him as hotel guests drifted in and out. He shifted on his feet as he waited for Hailey's response.

I'm in 623.

He waited for the fear to hit him, and *smack*, there it was, a quick pop in the gut. He gripped his phone in his hand and tapped a reply with his thumb: *Meet me in the bar.*

As countermoves went, it was pretty good. Direct

but not rude. Simple and to the point. It would have been the perfect response if he'd bothered to send it, but instead he got on the elevator.

The sixth floor was at the top, and it was every bit as pretentious as he'd expected. He made his way down the too-quiet hallway. He stopped in front of the door, and as he stood there staring at it, it hit him.

Holy, holy, *holy* shit. What was he doing? Before he could come with an answer, the door swung open.

Instead of a yoga outfit, she wore cutoff shorts and a flannel shirt. She was freaking barefoot, and he forced himself not to stare at her legs.

"Hi," she said.

"Hey."

Her makeup was smudged and her eyes looked pink from crying, and that right there should have been his first cue to leave, but his feet stayed planted.

"You want to come in?"

She pulled the door back, and his feet unplanted themselves and stepped into her room.

"I'm surprised you came," she said, closing the door.

"Me, too."

She looked up at him, and his heart did a little tap dance. Even with her eyes puffy and her makeup smeared, she was beautiful. "Want something to drink?"

"What do you have?"

"I think everything."

She turned and led him across the room, and he glanced around. The suite was deep and spacious, and he could have parked about three of his closet-sized apartment right there in the living room. He followed her past an overstuffed sofa to a tall wooden cabinet that held the minibar.

Great. Just what he needed. He'd sobered up some on the way over, so why the hell not?

"Let's see." She opened the fridge. "Heineken, Guinness, Corona—"

"I'll take a Corona."

She handed it to him. "No limes, sorry."

"I'm good."

He glanced around, suddenly noticing the blanket piled at the end of the sofa. He caught a glimpse of a huge-ass bed in the adjacent room.

"Nice balcony," he said, stepping over to take a look. The slider was already open, and he stepped outside, as far away as he could get from that unmade bed.

The balcony had an ocean view, and a full moon shone down on the Silver Strand. A pair of lounge chairs faced out, and on the table between them was a room-service tray and one of those insulated coffee pots. Hailey reached down and poured a cup.

Luke stepped to the railing and squinted in the direction of the base. No nighttime PT happening, but it was still early.

She came to stand beside him and rested her cup on the railing.

"No wonder you can't sleep," he said.

"It's decaffeinated." She smiled slightly. "I was never much of a coffee drinker, but it was the first thing they gave me back at Bagram. It tasted like heaven."

He shifted his gaze out over the water, the exact location where he'd spent countless hours doing boat drills and night swims. Down the beach was the pile of rocks that had nearly knocked him unconscious during BUD/S.

He turned to look at her and forced himself to man up.

"So you can't get to sleep?"

"I get to sleep okay," she said. "It's the staying asleep that's hard." Ignoring the lounge chairs, she sat down on the concrete and leaned back against the wall. "You ever get that?"

He didn't want to tower over her, so he sat down beside her and rested his beer on the concrete. "It's been a while."

The breeze picked up, and she wrapped her hands around the coffee cup. "I keep having these dreams." She paused. "Or maybe *flashbacks* would be a better word."

He watched her profile. The yellow glow from inside spilled onto the balcony, and he realized every light in the suite was blazing.

"It's always the same." She looked at him, maybe giving him a chance to change the subject. "A burst of gunfire. The SUV skids to a stop." She looked down at her coffee. "I never knew, before that moment, that fear has a taste. And all I can think is that this *can't* be happening, but it is."

He watched her, feeling sicker by the moment.

"Then they throw a hood over my head and stuff me into a truck. All around me, I can hear them shouting and cursing. And then we're moving again, and I can't see anything, but the fear is suffocating, and I realize my whole life— all of it—has been reduced to two things: I'm American and I'm female. And the terror's so thick it's like I'm drowning in it."

He took her hand and held it. His touch seemed to steady her, and she took a deep breath.

"That's the flashback I keep having. The moment it started. I think the worst of it's still blotted out. I don't know." She pulled her hand away and curled her fingers around her coffee mug. "New pieces are coming back, though. Voices. Faces."

He cleared his throat. "Any names?"

She looked away and seemed to think about it. "Rasasa. I remember Khalid saying it. I don't know if it's a person or a thing." She put her coffee aside and pulled her knees to her chest. "I don't know anything, really. It's all so fuzzy. Maybe the opium was a good thing."

He watched her, wanting her to keep going and also wanting her to stop.

She turned to look at him. "Do you know what happened to him? Khalid?"

The question surprised him. "There's a lot of people looking for him, last I heard."

She shook her head. "You wouldn't think I'd care, but . . . he was the only one who showed any spark of humanity. It's ironic, really. The whole reason I went there was to help children. Kids not much younger than him. Looking at it now, it seems so naive. So much has changed. I feel . . . warped, in a way. Because of fear. And I *hate* that. I don't want to be a slave to fear the whole rest of my life."

Luke tried to just listen, tried to dial down the anger inside him. He hated the pain she was feeling—and the men who had caused it, he hated them more. "In BUD/S training," he said, trying to sound calm, "they use fear to make you better. They throw it at you every way they can, physically and mentally.

Whatever you're afraid of—drowning, diving, jumping out of a plane—they figure out what it is, and they hit you with it. They do everything they can to bring your darkest fears to light, because that's when you tap into your deepest survival instincts."

She looked at him, and he knew he had her complete attention.

"They push you to your breaking point. Then push you some more. Starting out it sucked, and I kept thinking, 'Focus on tomorrow. Just make it to tomorrow.' And then it got worse, and I thought, 'Just make it to the next hour.' And by the end I just wanted to make it to the next minute. One minute at a time, you survive. That's how I did it, at least."

She gazed up at him, and he wondered where she'd gone in her head all those days she'd lived in that hole. "So what was yours?" she asked. "Your fear when you started?"

"I don't know." He paused. "No, that's not true. I do know. It was HALO jumps—high altitude, low opening. I've never been a big fan of heights, and the first time I got up there, my heart damn near stopped."

"What about now?"

"Now?"

"Yeah. What keeps you up at night now?"

A lump rose in his throat, and he looked out over the water. He wanted to say something glib and lighten things up, but he couldn't think of anything. "I'm afraid of letting people down." He looked at her. "Not being there when one of my brothers needs me, maybe because I'm injured or out of the op for some reason."

She stared up at him for a long moment. A tear slid down her cheek, and she brushed it away. "God, you must hate me," she whispered.

"Why would I hate you?"

"Your friend died because of me."

"Whoa. Back up. Not because of you. Because of some Taliban fuckhead with an AK."

She flinched at the words.

"Sorry." *Shit.* "I'm just—"

"You're angry. It's okay."

He clenched and unclenched his teeth. "I'm angry, but it's not because of you." He looked at her and tried to explain. "I'm angry because the last few years, it's like we've been fighting the enemy with one hand tied behind our backs. I'm angry because some people seem to think the war's over, we won. Let's pack it in and go home. Meanwhile, the enemy is out there flourishing, and the people trained to fight are being held in check. And all the spin doctors create this illusion that it's safe for aid workers and relief orgs, and it's a fucking lie." He shook his head. "Sorry. I'm pissed off at things I can't control."

She choked out a laugh. "Yeah. I think I'm in touch with that emotion." She wiped her cheeks and took a deep breath.

"Didn't mean to rant."

"No, it's good," she said. "You should say what you believe. I think you've earned the right to have an opinion."

She rested her head on his arm, and his heart did a little flip. He looked through the bars of the balcony and tried to focus on the waves.

"Were you really afraid of heights?" she asked.

"I was. Nearly booted my guts up on that plane."

The wind picked up. She shivered, and he resisted the urge to put his arm around her.

He stared at the surf and wondered again what the hell he was doing here.

"I'm afraid of the dark," she said softly.

"Do you sleep with the lights on?"

"Yeah."

Her head felt warm against his arm. He looked down at the pale wisps of her hair, and his pulse started to thrum.

"I don't want to do that forever, though. It feels, I don't know, irrational. Like I'm giving into fear."

"Give yourself a break," he said. "You just got home. You need time to get your life back."

She pulled her head away and looked up at him, and the expression in her eyes made his chest hurt. "Thank you," she said.

"For what?"

"For talking."

He leaned down and dropped a kiss on her forehead. It was a friendly kiss, barely a kiss at all. Any other girl, any other moment, it would have been no big deal, but the second he did it he knew it was a mistake. She slid her arms around him and nestled her head against his chest, and panic spurted through him.

He couldn't do this. He could *not* stay out here another minute with her, not without doing something truly dumb.

"It's late," he said. "I should get going."

She nodded against him. "Can I ask you something?"

No. No, she could not. "Sure."

"Will you stay here tonight?" She tipped her head back and looked at him. "Please?"

————

Elizabeth lay beside Derek, tracing a pattern on his chest. She ran her finger over the scar there and then trailed lower, to the one along his rib cage.

Her throat tightened, and she stopped tracing. Instead, she slid her thigh over his and nestled closer. His body felt warm and solid, and she tried to keep her mind in the present. If she could focus on his arms around her, she might actually get some sleep tonight.

"People do it, you know."

She turned her head. "What?"

"The long-distance thing." He eased his arm out from under her and propped himself on his elbow to look at her. "It's tough, but it works. Not always but sometimes."

She slid her leg away and rolled onto her back to look at the ceiling. The bathroom door was ajar, letting a wedge of light into the room. "I don't want a relationship like that."

"With me, you mean."

"With anyone." She sat up against the headboard and pulled the sheet up.

"What's so bad about it?"

She stared at him. "We'd never see each other, for one thing."

"We would when I have leave."

"That's what? A few weeks a year?" Frustration

welled up in her chest. Why did he want to talk about this right now?

"That's a cop-out, and you know it. You just don't want to try."

She looked at him there in the dim light. He was propped on his elbow, staring at her, all muscular and perfect and scarred and determined.

Her heart felt sore. He thought she was weak. And she wasn't. But she knew herself a lot better than he did, and she wished he'd at least try to understand.

She reached out and brushed her finger over his knuckles. "Have you ever been to a place, and it's so different from what you're used to—you're not there that long, but it's so different that you notice every detail?" She watched him. "Maybe somewhere exotic, like the Himalayas or the rain forest or, I don't know, somewhere underwater?"

He nodded slightly.

"That's what it was like with you. I memorized every detail. And then you were gone, and it was really hard." She met his eyes, and her nerves fluttered as she let the words come out. "I missed you so much. It took me a long time to deal with that and accept that we were too different. The circumstances were too impossible. It was hard to face up to, but I did it. And I don't want to have to go through that again."

She saw the frustration in his eyes, and she could tell he still didn't get it. He'd always been the one to leave, not the one left behind.

"There was so much waiting and worrying," she said. "I would have these moments of panic every time I watched the news. And I'd read in the paper about some suicide bomb or some helicopter crash, and I'd look for some hidden clue that it was or wasn't you involved."

His brow furrowed, but she kept going.

"I know how you are, how when there's trouble you run to it, not away. I knew you guys were in on that raid before Gordon even told me. I knew it in my bones, Derek. It was so dangerous—who else would they send?"

"This isn't really about me, is it?" His voice had an edge. "This is about your dad."

She looked at him for a long moment. "Maybe in a way. I know what it's like to lose someone important. The hurt is so deep I can't even explain it. And I know how hard it is after. I don't want that kind of fear in my life again. It's taken me years to get away from it, and I know that's not what I want. Can't you try to understand that?"

He held her gaze for a long moment. "I understand fear better than anybody. Part I don't understand is giving in without a fight."

Chapter Twenty-two

A faint buzzing noise jarred Derek awake. He stared up at the ceiling and felt a heavy weight on his chest. Snagging his jeans off the floor, he dug his phone from the pocket.

"Vaughn."

"You up?" It was Luke.

Derek sat up and glanced over his shoulder at Elizabeth. She was out cold, her arms tucked snugly under the pillow. She didn't move a muscle as he got up and pulled on his jeans.

She'd been so wrung out that she'd completely crashed. He knew from experience that she didn't like emotional drama, but last night had been pretty maxed out.

"You there?"

"One sec." He opened the glass slider and stepped onto the balcony. Although *balcony* was being generous. It was barely big enough to stand on—maybe if you were a hobbit sneaking a cigarette, but that was about it. He slid the door shut behind him and blinked up at the sun.

"What's up?" he asked.

"I just talked to Hailey, and I've got some intel."

"You *just* talked to her?" He checked his watch. It was 0600 in California.

"This was last night. She was going through some shit, and she asked me to come to her hotel to talk."

"And you went."

"Hey, fuck you, Mr. Self-Righteous. I didn't touch her."

Derek hoped for Hailey's sake that Luke was telling the truth. He raked a hand through his hair and sighed. "I hope you know what you're doing."

"Do you want this or not?"

"I do."

Derek definitely wanted it. He looked out over the kudzu-covered bayou that separated Elizabeth's hotel from a freeway packed with morning commuters. This thing, whatever it was, was ramping up, and the feds were still chasing their tails.

"Rasasa," Luke said. "I don't know if it's a name or a place or what, but Hailey said it's something Khalid was talking about during her captivity."

"Rasasa."

"Yeah, you roll the *R*. I think it's a person, but it could be anything. I figured you could pass it along to the FBI. Can you reach Elizabeth?"

Derek glanced over his shoulder. The bed was empty now. "Yeah," he said, stepping back into the room.

So much for the naked send-off he'd been hoping for. But the bathroom door stood ajar, and the shower was running, so maybe he had a chance.

"She mention anything else?" Derek asked.

"Not really."

Derek scrubbed his hand over his face. "Okay, well, let me know if she comes up with something more."

"I will. So are you back yet?"

"Nah, I'm still in Houston."

"I thought you were driving."

"I am."

The water went off, and Derek watched Elizabeth's perfectly wet and perfectly naked body step out of the tub.

"Listen, I gotta go."

"Right. Got it." Luke laughed, and Derek knew he'd figured out exactly why he was still in Houston. "Hey, don't stick around too long. We're wheels-up Thursday."

"I know."

Derek shoved his phone into his pocket and stepped into the bathroom as she was wrapping herself in a towel. She looked wary, maybe a little uneasy around him in the cold light of morning. She was typically so restrained all the time, and last night's maelstrom of tears and emotion and lust had caught them both off-guard.

She moved to step past him, and he caught her arm.

"'Morning."

"'Morning." She stood on tiptoes and kissed him. Not exactly the full-frontal assault he would have liked, but it was friendly.

"How's the arm?" he asked, looking down at her bandage.

"Fine."

Uh-huh. He'd bet it hurt like a bitch.

"Who was on the phone?" she asked, slipping out of his grasp to walk to the closet.

"Luke. Hey, does the name Rasasa mean anything to you?"

"No. Should it?"

"I don't know." His phone vibrated, and he tore his gaze away from Elizabeth to read a text from Cole. The message was long and rambling, and reading it prompted him to shuffle his plans for the morning. He texted back a response.

"Where'd that come from?"

He looked up. "Hailey Gardner." He tucked the phone away. "Luke talked to her last night."

Her eyebrows tipped up as she slipped past him again—fully dressed now, unfortunately—into the bathroom. She wore another one of those crisp white shirts with charcoal slacks. She ran a brush through her hair, eyeing him in the mirror. "I didn't know he'd been in contact with her."

The implication was that Derek *had* known and hadn't told her. He didn't want to get into it. "Mind if I use your shower?" he asked, changing the subject.

"Of course not." She leaned close to the mirror and swiped mascara on her eyelashes. "I have to go, though. Gordon called from the hospital."

"How's Lauren?"

"Good." She applied lipstick. Then she stuffed all her makeup into a zipper bag. "They moved her to a private room. Also, the motel clerk is awake now. Gordon's bringing in a forensic artist, hoping she'll be up for an interview. He wants me to sit in, see what develops." She paused. "Are you getting on the road today?"

"That's the plan."

Her gaze dropped to his chest, and she looked like she wanted to say something. He waited, but nothing came.

"I've got to check something out first," he said. "Cole sent me a new lead on a gun dealer, so I'm going to follow up."

"You should let us do it." She lifted her gaze, and her voice was businesslike. "You don't want to be late reporting for duty."

"I'd just as soon handle it. Where are you going to be later?"

Someone knocked on the door, and she glanced across the room. "That's Torres." She pulled her still-damp hair into a ponytail, then squeezed past him again and went to the dresser.

"Where will you be later?" he asked again.

"After the hospital? Probably the office."

She put on her belt, threading it through her holster as he eased closer to watch. When he'd first met her, the gun had been a major turn-on. Now it was mostly a reminder of what he didn't like about her job. She thought his job was dangerous? He'd been with her a week, and she'd been knifed and shot at.

She finished buckling and looked up. "Why?"

"I'll catch up with you before I go. Keep your phone on."

More knocking. She grabbed her jacket off the chair and shrugged into it, watching him. "If you can't, I understand," she said.

He pulled her to him and kissed her hard. When he let her go, she blinked up at him. "Keep your phone on."

———

It would have been a tricky interview anyway, but with Jamie still groggy, communication was difficult. Gordon seemed determined, though, and by mid-morning, he'd cut through all the hospital's red tape and had one of the nation's top forensic artists on-site and ready to get to work.

Fiona Glass had a stellar reputation in law-enforcement circles, and Elizabeth had felt a wave of relief upon hearing she was on the case. Her relief disappeared, though, when the artist announced that she didn't want any investigators sitting in on the session. The witness's comfort was of paramount importance, especially when that witness had been the victim of a violent crime.

So Elizabeth spent the better part of the morning pacing between the waiting room and Lauren's hospital room, where her family was gathered around waiting for her to emerge from the fog of pain meds.

Elizabeth had just poured her third cup of too-weak coffee when the sound of heels on linoleum had her turning around.

"You're finished?" She hurried up to the artist.

"We are."

Elizabeth had expected Fiona Glass to be an artsy, earth-mother type, but instead, she looked more like an attorney. She pulled a legal-size file folder from her leather attaché case and handed over a drawing.

Elizabeth took one look at the color portrait, and her breath caught. "It's Rasheed."

"You know him?"

She looked up, then down at the drawing again. Done in colored pastel on buff-colored paper, the picture was a nearly photographic likeness of Omar

Rasheed, right down to the dark mole on his nose that Elizabeth hadn't even realized she'd noticed before.

She studied the flinty look in his eye, and her stomach tightened. She remembered the same defiant expression when they'd faced off on that rooftop.

Elizabeth cleared her throat. "This is—it's incredible. I can't believe you got this much detail with the witness as injured as she is. And medicated, too. Didn't she have trouble communicating?"

"Communication barriers of one form or another are the rule, not the exception," she said. "Try interviewing a traumatized three-year-old whose first language isn't English."

Elizabeth nodded, still taken aback.

"As witnesses go, she was slow to respond and definitely tired but very clear about what she saw."

"It's an impressive drawing," Elizabeth said, "but it doesn't help us much from an investigative perspective. We already have this subject ID'd. And unfortunately, he's dead."

The artist tipped her head to the side. "Jamie tells me there was another man she remembers entering the motel room, but she only saw him from the back, so I wasn't able to get a sketch. I got the other subject, though." She slipped the first drawing back into her folder and tugged out another. The sharp scent of fixative wafted up as she handed it over. "This one we just completed."

Elizabeth's pulse jumped. "You got the woman." She studied the drawing. Auburn hair, as she'd suspected. Dark eyes, olive skin, strong cheekbones. She was beautiful, and it was no surprise she'd managed to seduce Matt Palicek into helping her.

If, in fact, she had.

"This person's new," Elizabeth said. "So this is definitely a lead."

"But . . . what? You seem unsure."

"Not about the drawing. It's just—we've put together a list of potential subjects. Females. And unfortunately, the only photos we have of them are from childhood."

She nodded. "Well, obviously, recent is better, but we get IDs based on age-progression drawings all the time. A huge part of what I do involves missing children. In many cases, I've been able to age the picture ten, twenty, even thirty years and get something that bears an uncanny resemblance to the adult."

"Really?"

"Certain features of the human face remain the same from infancy all the way into adulthood. You'd be surprised."

"I am." And Elizabeth knew she sounded skeptical, but she wanted to be convinced.

"Take the shape of the nostrils, for instance, and the shape of the eyes. The eyebrows, too—although some women alter that cosmetically." She stepped closer and pointed at the portrait. "Look at the contour of the mouth here. See the seam where the lips meet? Very hard to change that. Also, the way the tops of the ears line up with the eyes and where the earlobes line up with the nose. Even with orthodontics or plastic surgery, those features are nearly impossible to alter."

"You make it sound like an exact science."

"Well, I don't want to oversell it," she said. "We *are* dealing with a drawing based on someone's recollection. If we were comparing two photographs, it would be exact. However, I should point out that you have something going for you in this case."

Elizabeth stared at the picture, trying to guess.

"The hair," the artist said. "Cowlicks, widow's peaks, those features don't change over someone's lifetime and are easy to notice." She traced her finger over the woman's hairline. "See? She has a widow's peak. It was one of the first things Jamie mentioned."

Elizabeth studied the drawing, fascinated. Her pulse was racing now, and she wanted to rush back to the office and look at the photos they'd compiled of the female relatives of the terrorists.

A shadow fell over the paper, and she glanced up to see Potter.

"That's her?" he asked, frowning.

"What do you think?"

"I think we need a name to go with the face." He looked at her. "Where's Gordon?"

"At the office. Why?"

"I just got a call from Interpol. You know the name you passed along this morning? They've got 'Rasasa' on file as a nickname for Ahmed Rasheed."

"Ahmed," she repeated. "The brother who was killed in the drone strike?"

"Reportedly killed. Turns out they had visual confirmation on the ground but no DNA. That particular detail got left out of the file on our end."

Elizabeth's stomach twisted. "You're saying it's possible he's alive?"

"Very much so," Potter told her. "It's also possible he's here."

Elizabeth clicked open the e-mail attachment, and the image appeared on the screen.

"Fatima Rasheed," she said. "She's seven years younger than her brother Omar, which makes her twenty-four."

Gordon's brow furrowed as he studied the photograph, which showed eight members of the Rasheed family standing inside an upscale shopping mall in Dubai.

"How old is she there?" Torres asked.

"Ten." Elizabeth glanced up at the picture. "So she's not fully veiled, only the head scarf."

"And where'd you get the photo?" Gordon asked.

"NSA. They've been watching this family since 9/11."

Torres sighed heavily, and Elizabeth looked at him across the table.

"What?"

"I'm not seeing it." He nodded at the second image, the forensic drawing, which was displayed on-screen alongside the family snapshot. "I mean, yeah, there's a resemblance, but so what?" he said. "Same could be said about a lot of women. What about Zahid Ameen's female relatives?"

"We don't have photos," Potter said.

"Ameen's from Saudi Arabia," Elizabeth pointed out. "Women are much more limited there. Many wear the niqab, which covers the face except for the eyes. They're not supposed to mix with men socially. They aren't allowed to drive, and they're required to have a male guardian to go anywhere, even the doctor's office."

"Because of the strict rules," Potter said, "we know next to nothing about the women of Ameen's family."

"Put Ahmed Rasheed's wife back up there," Gordon said.

Elizabeth clicked the mouse and changed the image. Yes, some of the basic features were similar, but the resemblance wasn't nearly as strong.

"I think it's the sister, Fatima." She clicked the girl's picture back up. "I know it is."

"You can't be sure," Torres argued. "Not if we're basing this on a drawing."

"But look at the hairline, the way it points down in the middle. It's right there. Even if she changed her name, she can't totally disguise her appearance. I'm telling you, the woman we're looking for is Fatima Rasheed."

"Why are you so sure?" Gordon leaned back in his chair, frowning.

"She has motive, means, and opportunity."

"Motive being her brother was killed in a drone strike," he said. "But we now know he probably *wasn't* killed."

"Even if he wasn't killed, he was still targeted by an American drone," Elizabeth said. "That's enough to inspire hate."

"What's the last concrete info we have on her?" Torres asked.

"She entered Turkey four years ago. Her father has relatives in Istanbul, and we assume she was staying with them."

"That's before the drone strike," Gordon pointed out.

"Yes, but it's what she did after that we need to be concerned about. What if she joined the cause? What if someone helped her put a new identity together, and she got on a plane to Canada or Mexico or maybe even New York City? I'm telling you, Fatima Rasheed is the face of this operation." She waved a hand at the screen. "If you think about it, it's perfect. Look at all we have on her. A snapshot of a little girl. She's a face we'd never expect. But I believe she *did* do this. I believe she got herself over here and started laying the groundwork, finding a safe house and buying a car and coordinating all the meetings, gathering everyone together."

"What about eliminating witnesses?" Torres asked. "That college kid who sold his car to them—he was murdered before Rasheed and Ameen got over here. You're saying she did that?"

"Why's that so impossible?" Elizabeth asked, getting annoyed. "A woman can hold a pistol, same as anybody. This kind of thinking is playing right into their hands, you guys. They know we're resistant to the idea of a female terrorist. And they're using that to their advantage."

Elizabeth looked at the faces around the room—all of them male and most of them skeptical. Why was this so difficult to believe? Maybe they didn't like the idea of hunting down a woman.

She wished Lauren were here to back her up.

"Okay, so what about Ahmed Rasheed?" Torres asked. "Do we have confirmation he was aboard that submarine?"

"We're still waiting on the print from that gas can," Gordon said.

"But it's looking likely," Potter added. "Hailey Gardner remembers Khalid talking about someone named Rasasa. That's Ahmed's nickname, and it means *bullet*. He's got a reputation as an expert marksman, and we've got video footage of him teaching shooting at an Al Qaeda training camp."

Gordon tapped his pen on the table. "If Ahmed Rasheed is alive—which hasn't been confirmed, by the way—it would make for an interesting scenario. It puts the idea of an assassination back into play. But the discovery of the narco sub had led us to believe they were trying to smuggle in a chemical weapon."

"Do we know this for sure?" Torres asked. "That there was a bomb aboard that sub?"

"Word from the lab is the submarine tests positive for explosives residue," Gordon said. "Despite water washing away much of the evidence, they were still able to detect trace amounts."

"What about white phosphorus?" Elizabeth asked, cringing inwardly at the thought.

"Inconclusive. However, with Zahid Ameen involved, we have to assume chemical weapons are a strong possibility."

Her stomach clenched. This was sounding more and more like her worst nightmare: a chemical attack on innocent civilians. She studied the sketch posted on the screen, then looked at the smiling schoolgirl in the photo.

"Where's Lieutenant Vaughn?"

She looked at Gordon. "On his way back to base."

I'll catch up with you before I go. It was nearly four o'clock. Obviously, he hadn't had time for a big goodbye with her or even a phone call.

She dragged her attention back to the matter at hand. "I can see you're not all convinced, but please listen." She focused on Gordon. "If Fatima is the front man for this operation, then that is a strategic advantage that this terror cell will want to maximize. The

motel clerk told the artist she saw this woman getting
into her car in the late afternoons but not the mornings. The woman kept a regular schedule, which
makes me think she has a job. Whatever it is, she
probably got it in order to gain access to something or
someone. That job could tell us what their target is."

Silence fell over the room.

"Let's run down the list again." Gordon nodded
at his assistant, and a long list of targets appeared on
the screen. "The NSA's reporting an increase in over-
all chatter, so the theory is that whatever they're planning, it's probably happening soon."

Elizabeth's phone vibrated in her pocket. She
slipped it out and saw a text from Derek.

Come outside.

Her pulse skipped. *I'm at the office*, she replied.

A few seconds later, *I know*.

She subtly excused herself and slipped out of the
room, ignoring Gordon's look. She made her way
through the bullpen and downstairs to the lobby. She
passed through the security checkpoint and spied Derek's
truck sitting in the visitors lot. Her pulse skipped again.

She strode over as he lowered the driver's-side window. "Did they cancel your callback?"

"No," he said. "Come on, get in."

"What are you still doing here?"

"Get in, Liz. We don't have time to waste."

She stood for a moment, debating. Then she
rounded the front of the truck and climbed inside.
"This better be important. I—"

"What's the word on the target?" he interrupted,
shoving the truck into gear.

"We're working on it."

He shook his head as he pulled out of the lot. She looked him over. He wore the same jeans and T-shirt he'd had on yesterday. And he still hadn't shaved. But what really caught her attention was the tense expression on his face. Clearly, he was amped up about something.

"Why aren't you on your way back to San Diego?" she asked. "And where have you been all day?"

He laughed, but he didn't look amused. "Places you never want to go. Talking to people you never want to meet."

"Who?"

"Doesn't matter." He pulled into traffic and floored the accelerator. "What matters is I got a hit on that name from Cole."

"What do you mean, a hit?"

"I tracked the guy down. He's a slippery son of a bitch, but I finally found him."

"Who is he, and why does he matter?"

"Name's Vincent Planter. Works at a pawn shop over on Richmond."

She braced her hand on the dashboard as he took a sharp right.

"I have good reason to believe he sold Matt Palicek all his hardware recently."

"Okay."

"And he might have sold stuff to Matt's girlfriend, too."

"So where are we going?"

"To talk to him."

She looked at her watch.

"Planter's background raises red flags," he said. "For one thing, he's former Army. Fort Hood. Dishonorably discharged five years ago."

"Why?"

"Don't know what his file says, but this guy was a unit supply specialist. Rumor is some supplies went missing under his watch."

She got a sinking feeling in her stomach. "What kind of supplies?"

"You know, MREs, boots." He cut a glance at her. "Guns, ammo, hand grenades."

"If that really happened, why isn't he serving time?"

"They didn't have enough evidence, from what I hear." Derek picked up the freeway and quickly merged into the left lane. "I *also* hear he's still got connections in uniform, which helps his business. Guy's popular with the local preppers. People who are busy stocking up for Armageddon."

Elizabeth looked out her window, absorbing everything. Should she call Gordon or not? She wanted to keep him updated but not if this lead turned out to be nothing. She looked over at Derek. It didn't feel like nothing. He seemed worried—not exactly his usual state.

They sped down the freeway, weaving in and out of traffic. He was in a hurry, and he hadn't really explained why.

"What aren't you telling me?"

He glanced at her. "What do you mean?"

"There's more to this lead. What is it?"

He didn't say anything, and her anxiety ratcheted up a notch.

"*Derek.*"

"Let's just see what we see, okay? You have any luck with the witness this morning?"

Nice change of subject. "We got a drawing," she

told him. "Actually, we got two. Omar and a woman who I now believe is Fatima Rasheed."

"His sister."

"That's right."

"Good work."

"In other news, we're firming up the theory that their brother Ahmed Rasheed actually survived the drone strike."

He shot her a look.

"I'm predicting fingerprint evidence from the gas can will confirm that he's the one who hitched a ride on that narco sub and then murdered Matt Palicek," she said.

"Damn, this news just keeps getting better and better. Next you're going to tell me bin Laden's back from the dead."

Derek cut across three lanes of traffic and exited the freeway. Elizabeth looked out the window as he maneuvered aggressively down Richmond Avenue, flying through intersections and running yellow lights. Finally, the sign came into view, and he turned into a lot.

Ed's Easy Pawn shared a pitted parking lot with a strip club and a brake shop. Burglar bars covered the store's windows, and a neon sign proclaimed WE BUY GOLD. Derek swung into a space out of view of the front door.

"Stay in the car," he said.

"Like hell."

"You're obviously a cop. He might not talk in front of you."

"Then why'd you bring me along?"

He smiled. "You look good in my truck."

She rolled her eyes and shoved open the door. He'd known full well she wouldn't stay behind. Whatever plan he had for this was bound to include her.

"I'll do the talking," he said, leading her to the door. "You have that picture on you?"

"Of Fatima? Yes, it's on my phone."

"We might need it. But keep quiet. Don't talk unless I give you the cue, all right?"

"Let's just see what we see."

He shot her a glare as he pulled open the door.

Elizabeth stepped inside and looked around. The shop was warm and musty. Guitars lined the wall to her right. The middle of the store was devoted to stereo speakers, amps, and other electronic equipment. Straight ahead was a jewelry counter, and to her left was a long glass display case filled with handguns.

Two men stood behind the gun counter, one with a buzz cut and the other with a shaved head and a full beard.

Derek approached them. "Vinnie! Wazzup, man?"

The shaved head snapped up. Derek reached across the counter and grabbed his hand in one of those cool guy handshakes. Vincent looked confused.

"Mendoza says hi." Derek held his grip. "We need to catch up, bro. Come on out back, take a break."

"But I—"

"Take a break."

His look of confusion morphed into a pained grimace. Derek was still gripping his hand. "Sure, fine." He darted a look at the heavyset woman eyeing them from the jewelry counter.

Derek let go, and Vincent led him through a door into the back. Elizabeth followed. As they made their way down the dingy hallway, she studied the suspect and tried to imagine him in uniform. She couldn't. Whatever shape this guy had been in by the end of boot camp was long gone.

He pushed through an exit door and into an alley, where he turned to face them. He dug a pack of cigarettes from his cargo pants and glared up at Derek.

"I been talking to your clients, Vinnie." Derek folded his arms over his chest. "Lot of unhappy customers around town, I gotta tell you. Mendoza says you ripped him off."

"Who the fuck do you think you are?"

"I'm a guy with some questions."

"Yeah? Well, fuck off."

Derek sighed and gave Vincent a look of disappointment. Then he exploded, jabbing him in the jaw and sweeping his legs out from under him. Elizabeth jumped back as the man landed on the concrete beside her.

"Shit!"

"On your feet," Derek ordered.

Vincent writhed on the pavement, clutching his mouth.

"On your feet!"

He rolled onto his side, then pushed himself to his feet, scowling. He shot a hostile look in Elizabeth's direction as he spit blood on the asphalt.

Derek stepped closer, backing him up against a Dumpster. "Matt Palicek. When was the last time you saw him?"

"I don't know."

Derek jammed his arm against his windpipe. "Listen up, Vinnie. I'm punching a clock today. Know what that means? Means I don't have time for some fat fuck like you giving me shit. When did you see him?"

Derek stepped back and waited.

Vincent darted another look at Elizabeth. She took out her phone and scrolled through her photos.

"Last week," Vincent finally said.

"When last week?"

"Tuesday."

"He alone?"

"What?"

"He come to see you *alone*, or did he have someone with him?"

"He had a girl with him."

Elizabeth eased closer. "Name?" she asked.

"How should I know?"

Derek motioned for her to hand him the phone. He showed Vincent the photo of the composite drawing. "This her?"

He shrugged. "Could be."

Derek eased closer.

"Yeah, fine. That looks like her. What the hell's this about, anyway?"

"What did Palicek buy?" Derek asked.

"Guns. What do you think?"

"What kind?"

"A couple nines and a shorty shotgun."

"What about an AR-15?"

"That was the time before." He looked at Elizabeth, obviously not liking the fact that she was a cop.

A cop who hadn't identified herself. A cop who was—for all intents and purposes—assaulting a suspect in an alley. She looked at Derek.

"What else?" Derek's voice was tight.

"What do you mean?"

"What *else* did you sell them? C-4? Det cord? Willie Pete?"

"No way."

Derek slammed him against the Dumpster. "Don't lie to me, you piece of shit." He shoved his arm against his throat and pressed until the guy's face turned red.

"Detonators," he choked out.

Derek backed off, and Vincent clutched his neck, wheezing.

"He wanted some detonators, okay? I sold him some."

"Where'd you get them?" Derek demanded.

"People I know. I'm a businessman."

Elizabeth's mind was reeling. She wanted to get out of there and call Gordon.

"What else? What'd you sell the woman?"

"An SR-25. Shit. Look, this isn't personal, all right? It's business."

"Business? It's called treason, motherfucker. It's called murdering innocent people."

Suddenly, Derek's arm snaked around her. He jerked the handcuffs from her waistband and slapped a bracelet on Vincent.

"Hey!"

A loud *clink* as Derek snapped the other bracelet to the bar on the front of the Dumpster. Then he was frisking the guy.

"Derek, what—"

"Hey, that's my phone!" Vincent yelped.

"It's mine now." He turned to Elizabeth. "Let's go."

"You can't just leave me here!"

He grabbed Elizabeth by the arm and propelled her down the alley and around the side of the building.

"Derek, what the hell are we doing? We can't leave him there like that!"

"He's a squirter." He tossed the cell phone at her, and she caught it one-handed.

"A what?"

"If we let him go, the second we leave he'll be out the back door, calling up everyone in his distribution chain. This way you guys can arrest him." He looked at her. "What? You should be thanking me."

He popped the locks on his truck and jumped behind the wheel. She slid inside. "Are you crazy?"

"No. But I'm a little pressed for time." He shoved the truck into gear and rocketed backward out of the space. "Check out that phone. See if there's anything from Rasheed or Ameen."

Elizabeth's heart hammered as she stared down at the phone.

This was bad. Everything about this was bad. And that didn't even take into account the extremely illegal "apprehension" they'd just made.

"Stop the truck."

He looked at her.

"Stop the truck! I need to think a second."

"No can do."

"But—what's an SR-25?"

He shot her a look. "You really don't know?"

"What is it?"

"A sniper rifle."

Chapter Twenty-three

She blinked at him across the truck. "A sniper rifle."

"That's right."

"But I thought he sold them bomb-making components?"

"He did."

Elizabeth clutched Vincent's phone in her hand. She dumped it into the cup holder and took out her own.

"Who are you calling?" he asked.

"Gordon."

It went straight to voice mail. She left him an urgent message and hung up.

"We have to figure out the target," she said.

"That would be useful right about now. My contact at the Delphi Center's been analyzing the comments on that home-improvement blog. He called me an hour ago and told me he thinks someone posted a launch code."

"Where are you going?"

"The hospital," he said. "Maybe the motel clerk knows something. Maybe she saw Fatima leaving for work, wearing some kind of uniform. Or maybe she chatted her up and she mentioned her job."

"She didn't." Elizabeth dialed Torres.

"Shit, where'd you go?" Torres demanded.

"I'll fill you in later. Listen, did you ever interview that maid from Happy Trails? The one who only spoke Spanish?"

"Just came from there. Talked to her for about twenty minutes. Dead end."

Elizabeth's heart sank. "She didn't have anything?"

"Nope."

"Did she see something in the room? Maybe a pay stub? Or maybe an apron like a waitress would wear or a bag of tips?" She was grasping at straws now. "What about a fast-food receipt that might be *near* wherever she works?"

"I asked all that. No leads. This maid never communicated with any of them face-to-face, just noticed them coming and going."

"So she saw three of them?"

"Two men and a woman," he confirmed. "And yes, the woman looks like our sketch. So that's something. But other than that, she couldn't tell me anything except she thought they were slobs, and they left food lying around and cigarette butts all over the place. I'm heading back now to write all this up. And where the hell are you? We could use a hand with this."

Elizabeth was staring out the window as billboards and shopping centers flew by. She thought about everything they knew and everything they *didn't* know about Fatima Rasheed. Elizabeth was now one-hundred-percent certain that Fatima was the face of the operation. She'd probably been here for weeks or even months making the contacts, doing the legwork, running the errands. An idea hit her.

"Elizabeth?"

"I have to call you back," she said, and hung up. Her heart pounded as she scrolled through her phone, looking for the photograph she'd taken at the ME's office of Rasheed's personal effects.

"What is it?"

She glanced at Derek, then looked around at the freeway sign. "Exit here, and pull a U-turn."

"Where are we going?"

"The Happy Trails Motel."

———

"Up here on the left," she said. "Just before the intersection."

"The gas station?"

"That's right."

Derek pulled into the parking lot and took a space near the door. Elizabeth rushed inside the store, with Derek close behind her.

It was the same cashier from the day before, the tall middle-aged woman who'd carded the teenager trying to buy beer. Elizabeth walked over and flashed her badge.

"I need to ask you a question," Elizabeth said.

The woman sighed and glanced at her line of customers.

"This will only take a moment."

"Right." But she came out from behind the counter and led them to the corner beside the beverage station.

"Have you ever seen this person?" Elizabeth held up her phone, showing the composite drawing of Fatima.

The woman glanced at it. "I don't know. We get a lot of people in here."

"Look closely. She's got a distinctive hairline. She was probably in and out a few times buying Marlboro Reds. She was staying at the Happy Trails Motel down the street."

Recognition flashed across her face. "Marlboro Reds. She had dyed hair."

"That's right." Elizabeth cast an excited glance at Derek.

"Yeah, she was in here. What about her?"

"You recall what she was wearing?" Derek asked, and the woman's attention settled on him for the first time. She looked struck by both his size and his intensity.

"I—I don't remember."

"She worked evenings," Elizabeth added. "Was she wearing a uniform that you recall? Maybe a hat or an apron or—"

"A hat, yeah. She had one of those blue ball caps."

"What did it say?" Derek asked.

"It didn't say anything, I don't think. It was just blue. Like her T-shirt."

"Did her T-shirt say anything?" Elizabeth asked.

The woman glanced down and paused, as if trying to pull the memory from the depths of her brain.

Elizabeth held her breath. Such a tiny detail, but it might make all the difference.

The woman looked up. "Minute Maid."

Elizabeth blinked at her. "You mean like the drink?"

"The park." She glanced at Derek. "She was wearing one of those uniforms, you know? Like she works at the baseball park."

———

Derek pulled out of the lot with a squeal of tires. Elizabeth dialed Gordon again and once again got his voice mail.

"Is there a game tonight?" Elizabeth asked.

"Not just *a* game. The All-Star Game."

"That's tonight?"

"Yes." Derek blew through a stop sign, earning a honk.

Elizabeth's phone rang, and she recognized Torres's number on the screen. "Where's Gordon?" she demanded. "I've left him two messages."

"That's why I'm calling," Torres said. "We need you at George Bush Intercontinental Airport, ASAP."

Dread filled her stomach. "What's going on?"

"A bomb just exploded outside Terminal D. The task force, the bomb squad, everyone's on their way over there."

She looked at Derek. "A bomb went off outside the airport."

"When? What kind?"

"Tell me about the explosive," Elizabeth said.

"I don't have a lot of details yet," Torres told her. "They're saying it was in a trash can outside the international terminal."

"Casualties?"

"A cabbie was injured. That's all I know."

She looked at Derek. "Looks like a trash-can bomb. A cabdriver was injured."

"A trash can? Sounds like a mindfuck. Put me on speakerphone."

She did. "Torres, you're on speaker now. I'm with Derek Vaughn."

"Any chemical burns?" Derek asked.

"Not that I'm hearing. The cabbie caught some shrapnel. He was pulling up to the curb when the bomb went off."

"Listen, Torres, a trash-can bomb is amateur hour. They're creating a distraction."

Pause. "A distraction from what?"

"We just got new intel," Elizabeth said. "A convenience-store clerk near the motel remembers Fatima wearing a blue uniform for employees at the baseball stadium. We think that might be the target of the main attack."

"The baseball park? The Midsummer Classic is tonight."

"We know," Derek said. "We're heading over there now."

"Shit, LeBlanc. You need to talk to Gordon. You've got orders to get your ass to the airport."

"I keep calling him, but he won't pick up."

"That's because he's already there. They're evacuating the airport and jamming all cell and radio communications in case there's another device on remote control."

"You need to get hold of him for me," Elizabeth said. "Tell him to call me on a landline." They hung up, and Elizabeth looked at Derek. "You think it's a diversion?"

"I know it is." Derek cut across traffic and gunned it onto the on-ramp of the freeway. It was rush hour, but he stayed on the shoulder, speeding past slow-moving cars and trucks. Her heart skittered as they raced past a motorcycle on the edge of the lane.

"Where'd you learn to drive like this?"

"Fallujah."

"Please be careful."

"Liz, listen to me. I believe the target's the stadium, but this attack at the airport is a definite. You ignore those orders, you could get fired."

She stared at him. "I can't believe you just said that to me."

"I have to put it out there. There's a chance I'm wrong."

"There's a chance *we're* wrong. I'm aware of that, but I don't think we are." She looked out the window and shuddered at how close they were to the concrete wall as he raced along the shoulder. She looked at him. "What does your gut tell you?"

"It's the baseball game." He didn't hesitate. "The crowd, the symbolism, everything fits."

"I know." She took out her phone and pulled up a search engine. That SR-25 was nagging at her.

Derek pulled out his phone, too, and she plucked it from his hand.

"You drive, I'll dial. Who do you need to reach?"

"Cole. He's there in my call history."

She put the phone on speaker in her lap as she juggled her cell. Cole answered after a few rings.

"Hey, it's Derek. You left town yet?"

"My brother's taking me to the airport."

"It's shut down," Derek said. "They're evacuating. The FBI's responding to a bomb there with one confirmed casualty."

"Seriously?"

"Seriously. Is there any chance you've got your new three hundred with you? The one with the Night-force scope?"

Elizabeth glanced over at him.

"Yeah, I'm checking it through. Why?"

"I could really use a hand over at the baseball park."

Silence.

"Cole?"

"This have to do with the thing at the airport?"

"Yes. But this is strictly off the books," Derek said. "If you're not up for it, I understand."

"Hey, I'm there, man. Tell me what you need."

Derek gave him instructions as Elizabeth scrolled through her phone, looking for anything in the news about VIPs attending the game.

She read a headline, and her blood ran cold. "Oh, God."

Derek glanced at her. "What is it?"

"I just found out who's throwing out the first pitch."

———

The name hit him like a punch.

"The former president? You're sure?"

"That's what it says here." She held up her phone. "I have to reach Gordon."

"You have to reach the Secret Service. Who do you know over there?"

"What? Nobody."

"Think, Liz." He spotted a hole in traffic and cut into it. "Law enforcement's a tight community. There's got to be someone."

"Lauren has a friend on the White House detail, but—"

"Call her up. Everyone on your task force is at the airport with a jammed cell phone."

She was already dialing, but no one picked up. "She's in a hospital room." She gave him an anxious look. "Her phone is probably dead or turned off. I'll try my team again."

Derek gritted his teeth as he maneuvered through traffic. There was no longer a shred of doubt that the stadium was the true target. Whatever was happening at the airport was a carefully planned diversion, and it seemed to be working perfectly.

"This is textbook AQ," he said. "Multiple, coordinated strikes. Maximum civilian body count. With all the cameras over there, it'll be a media splash, too." Derek pictured an American icon getting gunned down before a live television audience of millions. "They're going to assassinate the man right before our eyes, and then all hell will break loose. You watch. It'll be mass chaos, and that's when the bombs will go off."

Elizabeth was frantically calling people on her phone, without success. She left messages but couldn't get a live person.

"Call D.C.," Derek said. "Call someone. Hell, call HPD if you have to, but we've got to get word over there."

"I know!" She shot him a desperate look. "What time does the game start?"

He glanced at the clock. "Soon."

Orange traffic cones blocked the parking lot, marked AUTHORIZED PERSONNEL ONLY. Derek plowed right over them. He looped around a row of cars and sped up to a back entrance as Elizabeth sent a text message to Gordon.

"Gimme your badge," Derek ordered. "Just the shield, not the ID card."

A burly police officer rushed up to them, and Elizabeth hurried to pull out the leather folio. She removed her photo ID and handed the rest to Derek. He rolled down the window and flashed the badge.

"Special Agents Vaughn and LeBlanc."

Elizabeth held her breath.

The cop glanced at the shield and nodded. "You can't block this ramp, sir."

"Got it." Derek put the truck into reverse and backed out of the space. He drove over to an empty space beside a row of horse trailers with the HPD logo on the side. He handed back Elizabeth's badge and shoved open the door.

"Where are you going?" she asked.

"See if I can't find these tangos."

"Need my help getting in?"

"No, I'm good." He pulled the Sig out from under his jacket and checked the clip.

"Secret Service sees you running around with that, they'll think you're an assassin."

"They won't see me."

She checked her Glock and noticed that her hands were shaking. She was about to go up against a determined enemy with no moral boundaries and nothing to lose, the same enemy that had gunned down Lauren and Jamie only hours ago.

"You locked and loaded?" Derek asked.

"Yes."

His gaze settled on her, and she recognized the look in his eyes. She knew what he was going to say. *You should stay in the car, work your phone. You'll be more effective from here.*

"Be careful," he said instead.

She felt a warm rush of relief. He had no idea how much his vote of confidence meant to her, especially now, when she didn't know what fresh disaster the next few minutes would bring. She reached over and squeezed his hand. "You be careful, too."

She slid from the truck and set her sights on her objective: a security guard stationed beside a gate marked AUTHORIZED PERSONNEL. She strode over and held up her badge.

"I'm looking for the head of the Secret Service detail."

"Uh . . . I don't know exactly." He glanced over his shoulder. "Couple of their agents are stationed by the elevator."

"Show me."

———

Nicknamed the Juice Box, Houston's new baseball stadium was a blend of modern technology and classic architecture. Fans entered through a turn-of-the-century train station, but everything else about the park was modern, including the 292-foot-high retractable roof. Like most Houston ball fans, Derek loved the new park. He loved the open-air design, the Bermuda grass playing field, the view of the city skyline right behind left field. Having been to the stadium a bunch of times, he knew the layout well, although much of his knowledge centered around where to find the shortest beer line. He'd never really thought about the place from a tactical perspective.

Until now.

He sliced through the crowd, collecting details and making eye contact. Over the years, he'd honed his instincts for terrorists. He'd learned to spot their deadly intentions purely through body language, before they ever dropped an IED or tugged a trip wire or activated a remote-control detonator. He'd learned to read how they moved and how they stood and how they observed their surroundings just before they carried out an attack.

His phone buzzed, and he continued his visual reconnaissance as he answered.

"I've got problems," Elizabeth said quickly. "They're blowing me off until they verify my ID through headquarters."

"We're losing time. Raise a stink if you have to. You've got to talk to someone in charge."

"I'm trying, but I have to keep my cool here until my ID checks. If they think I'm some nutcase off the street, I'll be hauled off for questioning before I've had a chance to talk to anyone important. Now, the good news is I've got an agent on my side, and he tells me their bomb dogs just completed a thorough sweep of the executive level where Gray Wolf is sitting. Everything's clear."

"Gray Wolf?"

"That's the handle for the former POTUS. It's how the agents refer to him."

Derek eyed a woman carrying a bulky diaper bag with no kids in sight. Other than her auburn hair, she didn't look like Fatima.

"Executive level is low-probability," Derek said, "especially given the security. More likely they'd plant something on the concourse level, where they can maximize casualties. Fact, they'll probably put it on a ramp or near an exit, so when mayhem breaks out, people will be funneled right past it."

"Wait, there's more," she said. "I talked to a food-services manager, and he recognized the picture of Fatima. Said she works a snack bar on the concourse level. So that might give us something to look for. She could have smuggled in a gun or an explosive through the employee entrance. If she's planting a bomb, it could be in a beer cart or a food kiosk or maybe a cooler."

"Or a backpack or a trash can," Derek added. "She could put it anywhere. Liz, listen to me. The fact that we're having this conversation tells me they still aren't taking you seriously. If they were, they'd be evacuating by now, and they'd be jamming all cell-phone and radio communication in this place. That's SOP—standard operating procedure—for an ordnance-disposal team."

"Here comes my agent," she said. "I need to go."

She clicked off as another call came in. Cole.

"Where are you?" Derek asked, still scanning the crowd for suspects.

"About half a click northwest of the ballpark. I'm on the sixteenth floor of an office building staring right at home plate."

"You on the gun?"

"Yeah."

"Secret Service has shooters posted on some of the rooftops," Derek said. "Make sure they don't see you."

"I got it covered. What's your twenty?"

"Concourse level, right behind third base. Hey, we need to do this fast, in case they start jamming the comms. I want you to look at the layout and tell me how you'd play it if you were inside."

Cole was the team's best marksman and had a well-known talent for finding the perfect sniper hide. "If it was me, I'd go high," he said. "I'm talking up in the rafters, behind a bunch of metal, where I'd be hard to see and harder to hit. See that area behind the Budweiser sign? That'd be my first pick."

"Roger that. Call you back."

Derek looked up at the tangle of ductwork and lighting and support structures. He glanced around for an access route. The doors of a nearby service elevator slid open. A cart loaded with pizzas rolled out, pushed by a stadium staffer wearing a hair net.

Derek walked casually past the elevator, then turned and ducked inside as the doors slid shut.

———

"I need to see him *now*," Elizabeth insisted. "I don't care who he's on the phone with."

Her own phone vibrated. The screen said BUSH IAH, and she prayed Gordon had found a landline.

"What the hell's going on?" Gordon demanded.

"I've got intel about an imminent attack here at the baseball game." She rushed through a description of the evidence, hoping he could hear her over the sirens blaring in the background wherever he was.

"Secret Service is stonewalling me," she said. "I need you to—" Sirens screeched in her ear, and she jerked the phone away.

"What seems to be the problem?"

She turned to see a tall man in a dark suit striding up to her. The clear radio receiver affixed to his ear told her he was Secret Service.

"Elizabeth LeBlanc, FBI. Are you the lead here?"

"Rick Walker, special agent in charge."

"My task force just received credible information about an imminent bomb attack on these premises."

He frowned. "What information? I wasn't informed of any—"

"*I'm* informing you. That's what this is. Call up security so we can evacuate this stadium. And you need to get your guy out of here now."

———

"I can't reach the upper level," Derek told Cole over the phone. "Elevator doesn't go that high. What do you see?"

Although Derek was closer, Cole's high-powered scope would give him a superior view. Provided he could get the right angle. "Some movement to your north, but I think it's the lighting guys. Wait." He paused. "There's a shadow just east of you. Looks like—damn, I can't tell."

Derek squinted up at the suspended walkways.

"Shit, there's definitely someone back there," Cole said.

"Lighting techs?"

"I don't think so." His voice was tight. "I think I see . . ."

"What? What is it?"

"It's definitely a rifle barrel."

"Are you sure?"

"Affirmative."

"You have a shot?" Derek glanced at the field below, where performers were unfurling a huge American flag. "Cole, report."

"I don't have the shot, man. He shifted. I don't even have the gun barrel in my crosshairs now."

Derek sprinted past the maintenance elevator, which didn't access the upper level. He pushed through the next available door and felt a slap of relief. Stairwell. He raced upstairs and jerked open the door.

"Okay, I'm up," he told Cole. "What's the sitrep?"

"Behind first base, over toward the beer sign. I can't see the barrel anymore, but that's where it was."

Derek glanced around to get the layout. Steel catwalks criss-crossed the area, giving access to lights, speakers, and other equipment.

"Behind the spotlight?" Derek moved toward it.

"Affirmative."

"Okay, I'm going silent." He switched off his ringer and tucked away his phone.

He glanced down, pulse pounding. Stars and stripes blanketed the field. Derek took out his Sig, wishing like hell he had a suppressor. Any hint of gunfire up here would attract a swarm of Secret Service, and he was as good as dead.

There was only one way to do this. He had to take this guy down without a bullet.

The announcer's voice boomed from a nearby speaker. "Ladies and gentlemen, please rise for the National Anthem."

A hush fell over the crowd.

Derek spotted the catwalk leading to the sniper's hide. He ducked into a crouch and moved silently, scanning every shadow behind every light, speaker, and bulky piece of equipment.

Derek's pulse spiked as he spotted him.

Ahmed Rasheed knelt behind a spotlight, his rifle pointed down at the field. He wore the cobalt-blue uniform of the stadium staffers, including a blue ball cap, which reinforced Derek's suspicion that his plan today wasn't suicide. He had an exit strategy, and it probably involved blending into the crowd.

Derek crept closer, slowly, soundlessly. The familiar melody drifted up from the field as he neared the target.

A soft rasp as his boot scraped metal. Instantly, he knew that tiny sound was a monumental mistake.

The target glanced up.

Derek launched himself at him as the rifle swung around. They hit the deck in a tangle of limbs. Derek smashed his pistol against the man's face just as the rifle stock jerked up and caught him in the jaw. Derek clamped his free hand over the barrel and shoved it up against the man's windpipe, all the while landing blow after blow with the grip of his pistol. A fist connected with Derek's cheek. He ignored it, focusing every ounce of energy on the gun barrel clamped in his hand, pressing down on the tango's neck with all his might. Rasheed's face reddened. His eyes squeezed shut. With a low groan, he heaved himself up and managed to throw Derek off-balance and onto his side.

Derek's advantage vanished. Panic flooded him. He

rolled onto his back, and a sharp pain in his spine told him he was on top of the rifle.

Derek smashed his gun against the man's nose, and blood sprayed down on him. Teeth sank into his wrist. Derek fought to keep his grip on his pistol as Rasheed struggled to pry it free with fingers and teeth.

The rifle dug into his spine. Derek tried to shift the weight off him, tried to throw his leg around, but he was pinned. Pain shot up his arm as he felt his wrist being crushed and the muzzle of his Sig digging into his side.

I'll be damned if I'm going to die by my own hand.

Blood streamed down Rasheed's forehead, into his eyes. More flowed down from his ruined nose and dripped onto Derek's face, blinding him. He clenched his teeth and forced his wrist around, straining against the weight and the searing pain and the desperate fingers now clawing for the trigger.

———

Elizabeth struggled for composure as the agent frowned down at her skeptically.

"You expect me to—"

A gunshot echoed above them. All heads jerked up. There was an instant of stunned silence, and then an army of suits sprang into action, rushing for the exits, shouting into radios.

"Bravo, report!" Walker barked into his radio.

Elizabeth's heart lodged in her throat as she looked up at the rafters. A shriek from the field below, followed by another. Performers starting screaming and pointing up. Then panic set in. Like a herd of antelope scattering, everyone rushed off the field. People in the stands looked skyward and started moving en masse, pushing and shoving for the aisles.

"Bravo, report!" Walker said again. "Where's Gray Wolf?"

Whatever response he got was drowned out by the noise. Elizabeth elbowed her way through the crush of agents near the door and stumbled into a corridor. Someone grabbed her arm and spun her around. The agent who'd helped her before.

"Where's Walker?" he yelled above the din.

"He's—"

He shoved past her and grabbed his boss, who was standing in the doorway now. "Sir, the bomb dog just got a hit!"

"Where?"

"Concourse level, left-field exit! They've got a hot-dog cart down there packed with explosives."

Chapter Twenty-four

Derek raced down the corridor, trailing blood. Was it his? Rasheed's? He didn't know, and he didn't have time to care as he jerked open the door to the stairwell. Boots thundered up from below. He bounded down the steps, then yanked open the door and darted out of the stairwell just in time to avoid the coming cavalry. He found himself back on the executive-suites level, where people in suits were racing back and forth. Some were agents, and some were bigwigs who'd been enjoying thousand-dollar views until chaos erupted. Derek's eyes stung from blood and sweat, and he ducked through a door and into a service corridor, where he'd attract less attention. Although not crowded with fans, the passageway was filled with security people. It was only a matter of seconds before someone noticed him and tried to detain him.

An elevator slid open, expelling a scrum of Secret Service agents. Derek dropped into a crouch, pretending to tie his shoe as they hustled past him. He sprang to his feet and hopped into the empty car, then jabbed the button for the ground level as his phone vibrated in his pocket. It was Elizabeth.

"Thank God!" she said. "I thought you were dead."

"Nope, but Ahmed Rasheed is. He shot himself."

"*What?*"

"I'll explain later. What's happening there?"

"I need you on the main level. The bomb squad discovered a hot-dog cart packed with explosives by the left-field gate."

"Shit." He jabbed the button again. "They disarm it?"

"No, they didn't think they could do it fast enough. It was on a timer, so they rushed it into an armored vehicle and whisked it out of here."

The doors parted, and Derek found himself in another corridor, this one flooded with both civilians and stadium personnel. "They need to keep looking," Derek told her. "One is none, and two is one."

"What?"

He pushed his way through the crowd. "Demo guys like to back up their charges. They wouldn't rely on only one bomb. I guarantee you there's another one, probably on the opposite side of the stadium. We need to search the right-field gate."

"I'll tell them."

"And why aren't they jamming cell phones yet?"

"I have no idea."

"This is a train wreck, Liz. The next one could be remote-controlled—"

Sirens pierced the air as the emergency alarm went off. Red strobes started flashing, and a recorded voice came over the PA system: "Emergency evacuation is in effect. Proceed with caution to the nearest exit . . ."

Giving up on his phone, Derek plowed through a door into the main concourse. The surge of people hit him like a tidal wave, and he pushed his way toward the right-field exit, scanning the walls, the corners, the alcoves for any sign of another IED. He reached the ramp but didn't see anything suspicious. He turned and fought the tide back into the concession area, which had been abandoned by staffers.

He spotted it. Parked right beside a restroom, a lone hot-dog cart.

Derek pushed through the mob. He crouched beside the cart, which had three storage compartments, all secured shut with heavy-duty chain and padlocks. He peered underneath, sensing what he was going to see before he saw it.

Affixed to the base with a hunk of C-4 was a timer.

———

Elizabeth forced her way through the throng of people, searching frantically for Derek. She tried him again on her phone.

"Where are you?"

"Main concession area, behind right field. Send your bomb techs over here. I've got another one."

"Another IED?" She pushed through the crowd.

"It's on a timer," he said.

"How much longer?"

Silence.

"Derek? *Derek?*"

The call had dropped. Heart hammering, she

elbowed her way through the people, managing not to get swept into the riptide pouring through the ground-level exit. She spied Derek at the end of the corridor, kneeling beside a food cart. He had a pocket knife clenched in his teeth as he manipulated some wires.

She sprinted over. "How long?"

He glanced up at her and took the knife from his mouth. "Where's Gray Wolf?"

"They got him evacuated."

He glanced around. "We need to get this thing out of here."

"Any way to defuse it?"

"Not in four minutes."

"Four *minutes*?"

"That's right. And it looks to be rigged with a backup detonator that's locked inside."

"What can I do?"

He looked up at her, and for once, his eyes were easy to read. He wanted her to evacuate with the civilians, but he knew she wouldn't. "We have to get this thing to a contained area, preferably underground, but the elevators are down." He glanced around. "Go find a maintenance guy, a firefighter, whatever. Someone who can override the elevator switch."

"I'm on it."

———

Derek's phone vibrated again. He put it on speaker and tossed it onto the floor to keep his hands free.

"What's the status?" Cole asked.

"Tango's down."

"That's good."

"What's not good is I've got my hands around an IED. I'm looking at about eight pounds of C-4 and possibly a Willie Pete payload."

"Fuckin' A. Why aren't they jamming cell signals?"

"Beats me. Wouldn't help anyway—this thing's on a timer. She's a beaut, too. I don't think I can disarm it without setting off the backup charge."

"Want me to get down there?"

"No time," he said. "And I need your bird's-eye view up there. See if you can spot anything useful, like maybe a SWAT van or a hazmat truck near the stadium."

"Roger that."

"Also look for a maroon Nissan Sentra or a white SUV that seems suspicious." He glanced around, searching for Elizabeth. "We've got at least two tangos still at large."

"No armored vehicles," Cole reported, "but I see about a million white SUVs. That their getaway vehicle?"

"Maybe that or a car bomb."

"How much time you got on that thing?"

He checked the clock. "Two-fifty-two."

"Derek!"

He turned to see Elizabeth jogging up to him.

"I got us a freight elevator. In the back of this kitchen. Come on."

———

The doors slid open, and Elizabeth rushed out, with Derek close behind her pushing the cart. She was relieved to see fewer civilians down here, but there were still way too many people, including stadium staffers and emergency workers. A golf cart zoomed past with an ear-piercing beep.

"This isn't going to work," Derek said, looking around. He turned to the maintenance man who'd snagged them the elevator. "That door at the end of the ramp over there. Where's that go?"

Sweat streamed down the guy's flushed face. He looked stressed and rattled, especially now that he'd no doubt figured out what their cargo was.

"Uh . . . that goes to our underground garage. Storage for, you know, forklifts and heavy equipment and whatnot."

"Can you get me in there?"

"Uh, it depends."

"Yes or no, buddy. Come on."

"If my access code works, I can—"

"Try it," Derek ordered, then turned to Elizabeth. "I need a vehicle. Preferably an Abrams tank, but I'll settle for anything bulky. Even an ambulance or a squad car with bulletproof doors would be good."

She glanced at the hot-dog cart. Was he trying to get rid of her? She didn't have time to second-guess him.

"Tick-tock, Liz."

"I'll find something."

———

Derek glanced around, looking for a crowbar, a hammer, anything he could use to pry the metal garage door up if the maintenance guy couldn't get it open.

His phone vibrated with another call from Cole.

"Tell me something good, brother."

"No SWAT vehicles," Cole said, "but I spotted the maroon Sentra. It's parked in the driveway of the hotel right across the—"

A loud *squelch*, and Derek jerked the phone from his ear. The jamming equipment was up and running, evidently.

"Got it!" bellowed the maintenance guy.

Derek turned around to see the garage door sliding up. He started to push the cart through. An engine roared up behind him, and he turned to see Elizabeth behind the wheel of a black Suburban. She jumped out.

"It's part of the motorcade that got left behind!" she yelled. "Bulletproof glass, armored doors."

"Damn, that's brilliant. Where'd you get the key?"

"My Secret Service pal."

"Help me get this loaded."

———

"How much time?" she asked, racing to the back as he threw open the cargo doors.

"T-minus forty." Derek glanced around, probably looking for someone who could bench-press more than she could. "Your friend's bugging out. Damn, was it something I said?"

She turned to see the maintenance guy slinking away.

"Wait!" She sprinted over. "I need your access code to close it."

He darted his gaze at the Suburban as she

scrounged for a pen. She didn't have one, but he did, and she plucked it from his shirt pocket.

"Spit it out! Then you can go!"

He rattled off a five-digit number, and she wrote it on her hand. Then she ran back to Derek, who was folding down the Suburban's backseats.

"Gimme a hand with that end, okay? I'll take the weight."

"Be careful!"

Could they detonate the bomb by bumping it? She had no idea how fragile it was. Derek lifted it practically by himself, then maneuvered it into the back with a grunt, and she could tell it was heavy. He slammed the doors, making her nerves jump.

He rushed around to the front and hitched himself behind the wheel. "Listen up, Liz. In fifteen seconds, I want you to lower this door."

She looked at her watch. "But—"

"Fifteen seconds, whether I'm in or out."

Her heart squeezed. "I'll come with you."

"You stay here to close the door."

"But—"

"I need you to trust me." He cupped his hand around her face. "Okay?"

He'd trusted *her*. Over and over today, he'd allowed her to do her job, even though she knew he hated seeing her exposed to danger. She glanced at the tunnel, and her eyes filled.

"Fifteen seconds," she managed to say.

He yanked the door shut. With a squeal of tires, he took off into the tunnel. Another squeal as he rounded a bend. Elizabeth clutched her hand to her throat.

She checked her watch. Twelve seconds.

Her chest tightened. She looked at the chaos around her—people coming and going, firefighters, stadium workers, mothers and fathers and couples and *kids*.

Nine seconds.

She glanced at the keypad. She peered down the darkened tunnel and stepped inside. The air was cool and damp and smelled like diesel fuel. She strained to hear over all the noise, but she couldn't make out anything—not the distant grumble of an engine or the pounding of footsteps.

Six seconds.

Her stomach twisted. She walked back to the keypad and held her finger over the buttons. She read the numbers on the back of her hand.

Three seconds.

Come on, Derek.

Two seconds.

Tears stung her eyes.

One second.

She sucked in a breath. With a trembling finger, she keyed in the code. Her chest caved in as the door started to lower.

"Derek!" She peered into the dark void. The door slid lower. "*Derek!*" She rushed back to the keypad, clenched her hands into fists as the door slid closer and closer to the concrete.

Behind it, the slap of boots on concrete. Her heart lurched.

"Derek, *hurry!*" She reached for the keypad just as he rolled under the door, Indiana Jones–style.

"Oh, my God!" She grabbed his arm as he sprang to his feet.

"Come on!" He took her elbow and rushed her at full speed to the nearest exit.

"How much time—"

Her words were cut off by a deafening *boom*.

They dropped to the ground. Shock waves reverberated around them, and she was on her hands and knees on the concrete, stunned speechless.

Derek pulled her to her feet. "Come on, haul ass. They're at the hotel across the street."

"Who is?"

"The tangos. Cole spotted the Sentra."

He pushed her through the exit, and the summer heat hit her like a wall. Sirens and bullhorns filled the air as emergency workers corralled people into human rivers flowing away from the stadium. Parents carried crying children. Couples clutched each other as they trudged along. Elizabeth saw firetrucks everywhere but no fires or smoke. Yet.

"Did you get it contained?" she yelled at Derek.

"Let's hope. Look!"

She followed his gaze over the crowd-flooded street to a hotel. She spied the maroon Sentra parked in front. A man in the cobalt-blue uniform of a ballpark staffer was getting into the passenger's side.

She and Derek broke into a run, dodging around huddles of people, squeezing through barricades. A cop tried to stop her, but she shook him off and kept going.

Derek surged ahead, plowing through people like a running back. He neared the hotel just as the Sentra pulled into traffic.

The back window burst.

Elizabeth looked around, startled. Who was shooting?

The car lunged forward, and people scattered and yelled as it pulled into the traffic-clogged street. Derek was close behind, but his hands were empty. Who fired the shot?

The Sentra hung a left at an intersection, and another *crack* split the air. The car sagged with a flattened tire.

Derek turned and gestured for her to take the driver's side as the doors were flung open.

A woman jumped out. Blue uniform, long auburn hair streaming behind her as she fled down the street.

Elizabeth broke into a run. Her pulse pounded as she dodged around people and hurdled obstacles. She sprinted down the sidewalk. She was gaining, gaining, closing the gap. Fatima glanced back over her shoulder, losing a half-second advantage.

Elizabeth tackled her, and they skidded together over the pavement.

"FBI! You're under arrest!"

The woman kicked and flailed, and Elizabeth dug her knee into her back as she fumbled for her handcuffs. What the hell?

With a shot of panic, she remembered Derek swiping them from her back at the pawn shop. She glanced around desperately and spotted a cop on horseback clomping across the intersection.

"FBI! I need a hand here!"

He stared down at her from the saddle as Fatima struggled beneath her, squirming and yelling.

"Gimme some cuffs!"

He seemed to snap out of his stupor and produced a pair of handcuffs from his duty belt. He tossed them over, and Elizabeth snapped them onto Fatima's wrists.

The cop slid off his horse and walked over. Another officer jogged over from across the street, weapon in hand.

"What we got here?"

"This woman is in federal custody." Elizabeth held up her badge as the cop's gaze darted over her shoulder. His expression changed. Elizabeth whipped around.

She saw Derek across the street, kneeling beside a park bench.

Her heart jumped into her throat. She turned back to the officers.

"Guard this suspect! Do you understand? She's responsible for this attack."

They nodded briskly, and Elizabeth rushed across the street, clutching her gun. Derek was on one knee in the center of a park with his pistol aimed at Ameen.

Who had a young boy clutched in front of him like a shield and a gun pressed against the boy's head.

"Give it up, Zahid." Derek's voice was strained.

Ameen stepped back, dragging the terrified child with him. The boy was ten, maybe eleven. He had red hair and freckles, and Elizabeth guessed the sobbing woman behind Derek was the mother.

"*Now,* Zahid."

He continued to back up. Elizabeth spotted his objective: the taxi idling beside the curb. The cabdriver seemed to realize it, too, and jumped out of the car as Ameen stepped closer.

"Don't do it," Derek warned.

The boy sent his mother a panicked look as the terrorist tightened his grip and pulled him toward the cab.

Crack.

Ameen dropped to the pavement. The boy fell to his knees. Derek launched himself across the sidewalk and snatched up the kid. Elizabeth sprinted over to the terrorist, who was sprawled on the sidewalk with the contents of his skull splashed across the concrete.

Cops converged on the scene, shouting and barking orders as Elizabeth stared down at the corpse, dumbstruck.

She looked up at the skyline, scanning the windows and rooftops. Several black-clad Secret Service snipers caught her eye. So did the missing window on the office building across the street.

She looked at Derek.

"Cole?"

He nodded. "From up in the office building." He stepped over. "Fatima?"

"In custody."

"You okay?"

She looked up into his eyes. There were so many things she wanted to say, to tell him. But her throat felt swollen, and she couldn't get her mouth to work. She looked down at the dead terrorist, and a realization hit her. This was her case, her crime scene. She had to lock away her emotions and take charge here.

"Liz?"

She met Derek's gaze. "I'm good. Let's get this done."

———

It was three A.M. by the time Elizabeth made it back to the office, where the bullpen was packed with what looked like every agent in the state, plus reinforcements down from Washington. She wove her way through the crowd and found Gordon in a conference room talking on the phone, surrounded by legal pads and Styrofoam coffee cups. When she stepped into the doorway, he glanced over and wrapped up his call.

"The evidence response team's still at the ballpark," she informed him. "Hazmat's there, too. Decontamination is going to take a while."

"I heard. Shut the door, would you?"

She complied. But something in his look told her not to take a seat.

Gordon leaned back in his chair and watched her. His shirt was wrinkled, and for the first time since she'd met him he wasn't wearing a tie. "We're making progress with Fatima," he said.

"I thought she wasn't talking."

"She's not," he said. "She asked for an attorney almost immediately and hasn't said a word since."

Elizabeth could only imagine Derek's reaction to a terrorist using the Constitution of the country she'd just attacked to protect her from its legal system.

"We found her phone," Gordon continued. "The real one, not a burner. It was on the floor of the Sentra. Our techs are working on it now, analyzing every call she made from every location she made it, trying to get a handle on who else was involved in this."

"That's good news."

"Vincent Planter's also helping us on that front." Gordon raked a hand through his hair and sighed.

"Although the charges against *him* at this point are unclear." His gaze settled on her. "Given the unconventional nature of his arrest."

Elizabeth bit back a comment. "Where's Lieutenant Vaughn?" she asked. "I was told he and Petty Officer McDermott were back here for a debriefing."

"In custody."

It took her a moment to process the words. "They're—what?"

"They're being held at the Travis County jail until this gets sorted out."

"What's to sort out? They just risked their lives defending their country against a terrorist attack!"

"They also discharged firearms in a public place. We've got two bodies in the morgue and a lot of questions flying around."

She gaped at him. "That's outrageous."

"That's reality," he said. "And I'm working on it, but it might take some time."

She edged closer to the table and glared down at him, her current boss who outranked her by about fifty levels, and she didn't give a damn, because she was furious. "You have to fix this! You *caused* this. You lured Lieutenant Vaughn into this investigation using *me* as bait! You think I don't know what you did?"

"I didn't—"

"Those SEALs are involved because *you* involved them! They were your insurance policy in case we failed to do our jobs. Without them, we'd have mass casualties on our hands, and you let them go to jail?"

"I didn't *let* them go anywhere," he said. "Contrary to popular belief, I'm not actually in control of everything that happens in the Department of Homeland Security." He stood up, looking immeasurably tired, but she had no sympathy. "This is a complicated situation, LeBlanc."

"That doesn't—"

"Sit tight." He patted her on the shoulder and pulled open the door. "I'm working on it."

Fuming, she watched him walk away. Derek and Cole were in *jail*. Even if Gordon tried to fix the situation, the arrest put their careers in jeopardy.

Potter appeared at her elbow. She blinked at him, unable to believe he was still wearing a coat and tie at this hour.

"I heard about Vaughn," he said.

If he said anything about "extreme measures," she was going to slap him. Instead, he took out his wallet and tugged out a business card.

"Sounds like he could use a good lawyer." He handed her the card. "Just so happens I know one."

Chapter Twenty-five

Elizabeth stepped into her hotel room and leaned back against the door. Sunlight seeped through the gap in the curtains. She looked down at the bed she'd shared with Derek just last night.

Or the night before. Timing was a blur. Her brain felt like oatmeal. Her eyes stung from fatigue, and the entire right side of her body was covered in road burn from her struggle with Fatima.

She dug her phone from her pocket and dialed the lawyer Potter had recommended. The man was a nationally known criminal-defense attorney, but he was Washington-based, and his influence didn't extend to Houston, from what she could tell.

He answered, and she snapped to attention.

"Hi, it's—" She cleared her throat. "This is Elizabeth LeBlanc with the FBI. I'm calling to get an update on—"

"They've been released."

Relief swamped her. "Oh, my God, *thank you*."

"I wish I could take credit, but I had nothing to do with it. The jail supervisor told me they were picked up an hour ago."

A rap on the door behind her made her jump. She peered through the peephole.

"Thank you. So much. I have to go." She stuffed the phone into her pocket and jerked open the door.

"Hey," Derek said.

She threw her arms around him. He was warm and solid, and he smelled like fresh soap.

She pulled back and gazed up at him. "You're really out?"

"I'm really out. We both are." He glanced over his shoulder, and she noticed his truck parked across the lot. With Cole in the passenger's seat. And then she noticed his damp hair, his fresh T-shirt.

"You're leaving." The words tasted bitter in her mouth.

"I came to say good-bye."

She stared up at him and felt her throat close. She didn't trust herself to talk, so she just stood there. He was leaving. And all she wanted to do right now was drag him into the room with her and tackle him onto the bed. His eyes simmered.

"I can't," he said quietly, reading her mind.

She nodded. "When will you—" She caught herself. Why bother asking? It would only spark an argument. "I can't believe you were *arrested*," she said instead.

"I can. But they dropped everything when we agreed to the cover story. The Secret Service thwarted an assassination plot and took down the terrorists."

Her eyebrows tipped up.

"With help from the FBI," he added.

She glanced past him at Cole, and her stomach tensed. "So . . . will you make it back in time?"

"If we shotgun it."

She looked into his whiskey-brown eyes, searching for a reflection of all the emotion she was feeling. But he seemed so calm, so okay with everything, and meanwhile, she was on the verge of tears.

His gaze softened. "Come here," he said, pulling her into a hug, and she felt the tears spill over. She wrapped her arms around him and held him tight. He kissed the top of her head.

"I hate this." Her words were muffled against his shirt. "I never wanted to be the weepy girlfriend begging you not to go." She squeezed him tighter. "But I don't want you to leave."

He pulled back and looked down at her. "So that's it, then? You're my girlfriend?" He cupped her face in his hands and brushed her tears away with his thumbs. "Because I'm going to be gone for a while, and I want to make sure we're on the same page."

Her stomach flip-flopped. A long-distance relationship. She didn't know if she could stand it. She didn't know anything except, "I love you."

He smiled and kissed her.

She pulled back. "But Derek—"

"Always a but."

"This is going to be so hard."

"Hard is good," he said firmly. "Hard tests your commitment."

"But it's going to be *really* hard. Harder than before, and that was hard enough. I hated that. I—"

"You're right, it'll be hell. But we'll take it one day

at a time. That's the only way to do it." His look was intent, and she felt a flutter of hope. He wanted to do this. "There'll be times when I can't call you or write, but I need you to have faith. I need you to know I'm thinking about you."

And she'd be thinking about him, too. And all the anxiety came back and made her chest ache. She'd be thinking about him dodging bullets and bombs, and there would be so many sleepless nights. She was already miserable just knowing it, and her eyes filled up again.

His eyes filled, too, but he smiled down at her.

"Why do we do this to ourselves?" She swiped at her cheeks.

He kissed her. And his arms wrapped around her, warm and strong.

She melted into him and felt his kiss, and it filled her heart with so much love she thought it might burst. And she tried to savor it, tried to drink in enough emotion and courage and lust and friendship to sustain her while he was away.

He pulled back and looked down at her. "That's why."

———

Hailey sounded surprised to hear from him.

"Where are you?" she asked.

"Back on base." A Humvee zipped by, and he turned away from the noise.

"I didn't expect to hear from you," she said. "I figured the Audrey Hepburn movie marathon scared you off."

"Yeah, well. Nice try, but SEALs are tough to scare." He tried to keep it light. Maybe then she wouldn't realize it wasn't the classic movies that made him sneak out of her room at the crack of dawn but the fact that he was a complete and total coward.

"I thought you had leave," she said.

"We got called back early."

"Does that mean you're going somewhere?"

"I can't really say."

"Okay, well . . . when will you be back?"

He didn't respond.

"You can't say that, either?"

"I can't really—"

"It's all right. I get it. Anyway, I'm glad you called," she said. "I probably should have called *you* to tell you thanks for the referral you texted me. I'm starting a collection. Everyone I know is recommending a shrink."

Luke walked over to a chain-link fence. On the other side, his teammates were busy staging their gear. In only a few hours, they were spinning up on the mission.

Hailey's tone of voice had shifted, and maybe he should have done what he'd wanted to do and left town without making this awkward-as-shit phone call.

Sack up, Jones.

He cleared his throat. "I got that name from a buddy of mine who lost a leg a few years ago. He's been working with her ever since. I hear she's, you know, really good with veterans," he babbled on. "And she's one, too. She was in Iraq. So I thought maybe she'd get where you're coming from. More than that other guy."

She didn't respond, and he started to think she'd hung up.

"Hailey?"

"Thank you," she said. "I appreciate the referral."

It was a very careful response. She hadn't said she'd call the shrink, she'd merely said thank you. And Luke smiled, because he was a world-class bullshit artist, and that was just the kind of thing he'd say to get someone off his back.

So maybe she was annoyed with him, but he still hoped she'd make the call.

"Did you see the news out of Houston?" he asked, changing the subject.

"The assassination attempt? I saw it. Why?"

"You helped with that. I don't know all the details, but I know the intel you provided helped. I thought you should know."

"But even if you did know the details, you wouldn't tell me, right?"

"That's true." Damn it, he could not lie to this woman.

"Well . . . thanks for being honest, at least. It's actually very refreshing."

Luke turned and looked out at the surf. He felt a strange tightness in his chest. He wanted another night with her. He wanted to watch the ocean with her and talk with her and even sit through freaking *Breakfast at Tiffany's* with her if that was what she wanted.

And he suddenly knew he'd played this wrong, and he was an idiot. He should have left her thinking what she'd been thinking when he slunk out of her room at 0600.

"I have to go," he said, and she laughed at his abruptness.

"All right, well . . . thanks. For the shrink. And for talking."

"Yeah, no problem."

"If you're ever in Boston, you should give me a call."

"I will."

He got off the phone and stared out at the water. He'd finally done it. For the first time since he'd known her, he was pretty sure he'd managed to lie.

Chapter Twenty-six

Three months later

Derek was bone-tired and jetlagged, and the only thing keeping him going was the promise of tomorrow. After grabbing some food and a few hours' sleep, he planned to hit the road.

"Come on, one beer," Cole said, catching up to him in the parking lot on base.

"Can't do it. I've got an eighteen-hour drive tomorrow." It was going to be straight-up hell, but it would be worth it, because at the end of the road was Elizabeth.

"Come on, man. The whole team's there. *One* beer. It'll help you get to sleep."

Derek stopped in the parking lot. He didn't need help getting to sleep. But the team thing got to him. It had been a hard tour, and he should end on a good note, especially in light of what he planned to do.

Cole smiled, because he knew he had him. He jerked his head toward his truck. "I'm driving."

Derek climbed in for the short hop over to

O'Malley's. Cole found a parking spot at the end of a row of pickups.

Derek eyed the bar as he crossed the lot. It was loud and dirty. A young Marine sat on the curb outside, nursing a bloody lip. Not even ten, and already there'd been a fight. Some things never changed.

They reached the door, and Cole slapped him on the back. "It was a good tour, my friend."

Derek narrowed his gaze at him.

"See you next week." A smile spread across Cole's face as he looked out at the parking lot.

Derek turned around. And there was Elizabeth.

She walked over as he stood there, speechless. So many days and weeks he'd been craving her, and now she was right there in front of him, her eyes smiling, her hair blowing around her shoulders. She glanced past him and waved.

"Thanks, Cole."

"No problem. See you around."

She stopped in front of him. "Hi."

He pulled her against him and kissed her.

———

When he finally let her up for air, she was grinning. She couldn't help it. She'd had the same dumb grin on her face since she'd landed in San Diego.

"You're here."

She laughed. "Yep. And you sound as out of it as you look. Long flight?"

He scrubbed a hand over his face, then blinked down at her, still without words.

"Come on," she said. "I assume you want to go inside?"

"That's the dead-last place I want to go right now."

He wanted to go to bed, she could see it in his eyes. She wanted that, too, but not yet. "Let's walk on the beach." She took his hand. "I need to talk to you." He let her lead him across the street. At the edge of the sand, she stopped to take off her sandals. She was in jeans and a loose white blouse, and she could tell he liked it by the way he kept staring at her.

"Damn."

She smiled. "What?"

"I didn't expect to see you tonight." He pulled her in and kissed her again, longer this time, until her body started to throb. God, she'd missed him.

She pulled back and looked up into his eyes. Nerves fluttered inside her. "I have news," she said, and at his raised eyebrows, she stepped back. "Whoa. What's that look? I'm not pregnant or anything."

"That's not what the look was. Pregnant? I thought you were going to say you met someone." His brow furrowed. "Did you?"

"*No*. God. I got a job offer. In D.C." She looked up at him, trying to read his reaction. "It's with Gordon Moore's CT team. It's a promotion, and it puts me very close to Virginia. Only a stone's throw away." She swallowed. "Would you consider moving to Little Creek, Virginia?"

He looked surprised, then confused. He rubbed

the back of his neck. "You want . . . wait, start over. You're saying you want me to move across the country?"

"I was thinking if you joined the East Coast teams in Little Creek, we'd see much more of each other. We'd see each other every time you have leave and while you're stateside for training, too. And you'd still be a SEAL."

"I thought you didn't want me to be a SEAL."

"I want you to do what you love. I want you to be happy."

He didn't know that? How could he not know? Her heart chilled at the thought. They started walking down the beach, and she suddenly felt worlds apart from him. She'd spent so much time while he was gone considering everything, from every possible angle, and she'd thought she understood him better now. Maybe she'd been fooling herself. She watched him in the moonlight. The moon was full, just as it had been their last night together.

"You remember that night at the dam?" she asked. "When Lauren was in the hospital?"

"The night you attacked me in my truck?" The corner of his mouth curved. "I think I remember it."

"You told me that story about your first tour of duty, when Hill got hurt."

"Yeah?" He clearly had no idea where she was going with this.

"I didn't understand why you told me that. You'd always been so secretive about your missions, and I thought maybe, I don't know, you were trying to impress me or something so I'd sleep with you. But then later, I realized what you were trying to tell me."

She stopped and looked up at him. He towered over her, and she loved his height and his broad shoulders and the solid bulk of him. She loved the way he was looking at her, like she was a puzzle he wanted to figure out. She loved just being near him after so much time apart, and she dreaded the idea of him going back out there. But she'd accepted that if she loved him, it was something she needed to live with.

"Derek, I know there's no 'safe' for men like you. There's no guarantee. All you can count on for sure is your training and your brothers." She squeezed his hand. "You put your trust in them, and I need to put my trust in them, too."

He stared down at her, not talking, and she couldn't read his expression.

"So yes, I want you to be a SEAL. But I want to see you, too. I'm trying to figure out a way for us to do that."

He stood there for a moment, and then they started walking down the beach again. The sand was cool between her toes, and she tried to focus on that instead of her out-of-control nerves. His reaction wasn't at all what she'd expected. She'd thought he'd be happy.

He led her to a piece of driftwood and sat down, tugging her with him. He looked out at the water.

"See those rocks over there?"

She followed his gaze.

"I damn near killed myself on those." He shook his head. "Rock portage. Sean Harper and I almost drowned trying to get the boat out." He looked in the other direction. "I've run so many miles on this beach I can't even begin to count. Hundreds. Thousands."

His gaze settled on her. "The East Coast teams, they're not the same as here. They're not the same brothers."

Her throat tightened with disappointment. She didn't know what to say.

He picked up her hand. "I'm thinking of switching gears." He looked at her. "Gordon called me, too. He's recruiting me for HRT, the Bureau's hostage rescue team. I did a phone interview a few weeks ago, talked to the commander."

Her jaw dropped. She'd had no idea he was even thinking about leaving the Navy.

"I'd be in Washington," he said.

"I know."

"What do you think?"

"I think—" Her mind was racing with possibilities. "I think they'd be lucky to have you."

"But what do you think about it for *us*?"

"I think I'm blown away." She reached up to touch his cheek, his jaw. His stubble felt bristly under her fingertips, and she couldn't believe he was here and they were having this conversation. "You'd really go through so much . . . change to be with me?"

"Sometimes change is good." He looked at her. Then he looked out at the ocean and his face turned somber. "You know, ever since Sean died, I've been thinking a lot. I've been thinking about people and family and what matters." He lifted her hand and kissed her knuckles, and she felt a pinch in her heart at the tenderness of it. "You're the best thing in my life, Liz. There's not anything I wouldn't do for you."

He looked at her again, and the moon was so bright she could see the love in his eyes.

"But I'm worried, too," he said. "I have to be honest. Reentry is tough. And I've been away so long . . . I think I've forgotten how to be home."

She reached up and touched his cheek. "Let me show you," she whispered, and pulled him down to kiss her.

Hooked on Laura Griffin's Tracers?

Don't miss the next thrilling book
in the bestselling series . . .

Coming Fall 2015!

Chapter One

Evenings were the hardest, the time when everything unraveled. Catie's mind overflowed, her chest felt empty, and the craving dug into her with razor-sharp claws.

Catie's shoulders tensed as she pulled into the wooded park. All her life she'd been addicted to work and approval and success. Now, she was simply an addict.

Her high-performance tires glided over the ruts, absorbing the bumps as she eased along the drive. She turned into the gravel parking lot and swung into a space. *Forty-six days.*

Resting her head on the wheel, she squeezed her eyes shut. Her throat tightened and she fought the burn of tears.

"One day at a time," she whispered.

She sat up and gazed through the windshield. She'd

never thought she'd be one of those people who gave herself pep talks. She'd never thought she'd be a lot of things. Yet here she was.

Catie shoved open the door and popped the trunk. She tossed her purse inside, then rummaged through her gym bag, looking for her iPod. On second thought, no music. She slammed the trunk closed, locked the car, and tucked the key fob into the zipper pocket of her tracksuit. She leaned against a trail marker and stretched her quads. A few deep lunges and she was ready to go.

She set off at a brisk pace, quickly passing the dog walkers and bird enthusiasts who frequented the trail. Her muscles warmed. Her breathing steadied. She passed the first quarter-mile marker and felt the tension start to loosen.

The routine had become her lifeline. She registered the familiar scent of the loblolly pines, the spongy carpet of pine needles under her feet. She put her body through the paces, then her mind.

It was Wednesday. She was halfway through the week, another daunting chain of days that started with paralyzing mornings in which she had to drag herself out of bed and force herself to shower, dress, and stand in front of the mirror to conceal the evidence of a fitful night. Then she faced the endless cycle of conference calls and meetings and inane conversations as the secret yearning built and built, culminating in the dreaded hour when it was time to go. Time to pack it in and head home to her perfectly located, gorgeously decorated, soul-crushingly empty house.

But first, a run. Or a spin class. Or both. Anything to postpone the sight of that vacant driveway.

Almost anything.

Catie focused her attention on the narrow trail. Thirst stung her throat, but she tried not to think about it. She tried to clear her mind. She rounded a bend, noted the half-mile marker. She was making good time. Another curve in the path and she came upon a couple jogging in easy lockstep. Twentysomethings. At the end of the trail and still they had a bounce in their stride. The woman smiled as they passed, and Catie felt a sharp pang of jealousy that drew her up short.

She caught herself against a tree and bent over, gasping. Shame and regret formed a lump in her throat. She dug her nails into the bark and closed her eyes against the clammy onset of panic.

Don't think, Catie, Liam's voice echoed in her head. *Be in the moment.*

God, she missed him. Liam was way too smart and way too intense, and he didn't know how to turn it off. And she liked that about him. So different from Mark.

Liam never belittled her.

He knew evil lurked in the world and he faced it head-on, refusing to look away, even relishing the fight.

Snick.

Catie's head jerked up. She swung her gaze toward the darkening woods as awareness prickled to life inside her.

The forest had gone quiet.

No people, no dogs. Even the bird chatter had ceased. She glanced behind her and a chill swept over her skin.

Look, Catie. Feel what's around you.

She did feel it. Cold and predatory and watching her.

Mark would tell her she was paranoid. Delusional, even. But her senses were screaming.

She glanced around, trying to orient herself on the trail. She wasn't that far in yet. She could still go back. She turned around and walked briskly, keeping her chin high and her gaze alert. Strong. Confident. She tried to look powerful and think powerful thoughts, but fear squished around inside her stomach and she could feel it—something sinister moving with her through the forest, watching her from deep within the woods. She'd felt it before, and now it was back again, and her pulse quickened along with her strides.

I am not crazy. I am not crazy. I am not crazy.

But . . . what if Mark was right? And if he was right about this, could he be right about everything else, too?

A sound—directly left. Catie halted. Her heart

hammered. She peered into the gloom and sensed more than saw the shifting shadow.

Recognition flickered as the shape materialized. With a rush of relief, she stepped forward. "Hey, you—"

She noticed his hand.

Her stomach plummeted. Her mind emptied. All her self-doubt vanished, replaced by a single electrifying impulse.

Catie ran.

———

Special Agent Tara Rushing drove with the windows down, hoping the cold night air would snap her out of her funk. She felt wrung out. Like a dishrag that had been used to sop up filth, then squeezed and tossed aside.

Usually she loved the adrenaline rush. Kicking in a door, storming a room, taking down a bad guy—anyone who'd done it for real knew nothing compared to it. The high could last for hours, even through the paperwork, which was inevitably a lot.

Typically after a successful raid everyone was wired. The single agents would head out for a beer or three, sometimes going home together to burn off some of the energy. But tonight wasn't typical.

After so many weeks of work and planning,

she'd expected to feel euphoric. Or at the very least satisfied. Instead she felt . . . nothing, really. Her dominant thought as she sped toward home was that she needed a shower. Not just hot, volcanic. She'd stand under the spray and scrub her skin raw, and maybe get rid of some of the sickness clinging to her.

Tara slowed her Explorer as the redbrick apartment building came into view. Her second-floor unit looked dark and lonely beside her neighbor's, where a TV glowed in the window and swags of Christmas lights still decorated the balcony.

She rolled to a stop at the entrance and tapped the access code. As the gate slid open, her phone buzzed in the cup holder. Tara eyed the screen: US GOV. She'd forgotten to fill out some paperwork, or turn in a piece of gear, or maybe they needed her to view another video.

She felt the urge to throw her phone out the window. Instead she answered it.

"Rushing."

If she put enough hostility in her voice, maybe they wouldn't have the balls to call her back in.

"It's Dean Jacobs."

She didn't respond. Because of shock and because she couldn't think of a single intelligent thing to say.

"You make it home yet?" he asked.

"Almost. Sir."

Jacobs was her SAC. She'd had maybe four conversations with him in the three years since she'd joined the Houston field office.

"They were just filling me in on the raid," he said. "Good work tonight."

"Thank you, sir."

The gate slid shut again as she stared through the windshield.

"I understand you live north," he said.

"That's right."

"There's a matter I could use your help on."

Something stirred inside her. Curiosity. Or maybe ambition. Whatever it was, she'd take it. Anything was better than feeling numb.

"I need you to drive up to Cypress County. They've got a ten-fifty off of Fifty-nine."

His words surprised her even more than the midnight phone call. Tara knew all the ten-codes from her cop days, but dispatch had switched to plain language and nobody used them anymore. A 10-50 was a deceased person.

She cleared her throat. "Okay. Any particular reason—"

"Take Martinez with you. She's got the location and she's on her way to your house, ETA ten minutes."

Tara checked her sports watch.

"Stay off your phone," he added. "You understand? I need discretion on this."

"Yes, sir."

"And one more thing, Rushing."

She waited.

"Don't let the yokels jerk you around."

———

Emergency vehicles lined the side of the road—sheriff's units, an ambulance, a red pickup truck with CCFD painted on the door. A khaki-clad deputy in a ten-gallon hat waved them down.

Tara handed her ID through the window. "Special Agent Tara Rushing, FBI."

He examined her creds, then ducked his head down and peered into the window as M.J. held up her badge.

He hesitated before passing Tara's ID back. "Pull around to the right there. Watch the barricades."

Tara pulled around as instructed and parked beside a white crime scene van.

M.J. got out first, attracting immediate notice from the huddle of lawmen milling beside the red pickup. They looked her up and down, taking in her tailored gray slacks and crisp white button-down. Then again, maybe it was her curves they were noticing, or the lush dark hair that cascaded down her back.

Tara pushed open her door. Tall and willowy, she attracted stares, too, but for a different reason. She was still jocked up from the raid in tactical pants and Oakley assault boots, with handcuffs tucked into her waistband and her Glock snugged against her hip. Her curly brown hair was pulled back in a no-nonsense ponytail. She grabbed her FBI windbreaker from the backseat, and the men eyed her coolly as she zipped into it.

Another deputy hustled over.

"Who's in charge of this crime scene?" she asked, flashing her creds.

He looked her ID over. The man was short and stocky and smelled like vomit.

"That'd be Sheriff Ingram." He cast a glance behind him, where the light show continued deep in the woods.

"I'd like a word with him."

He looked at her.

"Please."

He darted a glance at M.J., then traipsed off down a narrow trail marked with yellow scene tape. The men continued to stare, but Tara ignored them and surveyed her surroundings. Someone had hooked a camping lantern to a nail on a nearby tree, illuminating a round clearing with a crude fire pit at the center. Old tires and tree stumps surrounded the pit, along with beer cans and cigarette butts. Someone had cordoned off the area with more yellow tape and placed evidence markers near the cans and butts.

Another khaki uniform approached her, no hat this time. "Who are you?" he demanded.

"Sheriff Ingram?"

A brisk nod.

"Special Agent Tara Rushing." She showed her ID again, but he didn't look. "And Special Agent Maria Jose Martinez."

If he was surprised the FBI had shown up at his crime scene, he didn't show it.

"We're here at the request of Judge Wyatt Mooring," M.J. added.

He glanced at her, then back at Tara.

With his brawny build and high-and-tight haircut, Sheriff Ingram looked like a Texas good old boy. But Tara didn't want to underestimate him. His eyes telegraphed intelligence, and he seemed to be carefully weighing his options. He stepped closer and rested his hands on his gun belt.

"I got a homicide." He nodded toward the woods. "Female victim. No ID, no clothes, no vehicle. Long story short, I don't have a lot."

His gaze settled on Tara, and her shoulders tensed. She could feel something coming.

"What I *do* have is an abandoned Lexus down at Silver Springs Park," he said. "Registered to Catalina Reyes."

"Catalina Reyes," Tara repeated.

"That's right. She was last seen there yesterday evening. Didn't show up for work today."

Tara glanced at M.J., communicating silently. *Holy crap.*

Catalina Reyes was a north Houston businesswoman who'd made a run for U.S. Congress in the last election. She'd been a lightning rod for controversy since the moment she announced her candidacy.

"She was getting death threats, wasn't she?" M.J. said.

"I think so."

Tara turned to look at the forest, where police had set up klieg lights around the inner crime scene. Workers in white Tyvek suits moved around, probably CSIs or ME assistants. Tara saw the strobe of a camera flash. She noted more deputies with flashlights combing a path deep within the woods. They must have assumed the killer accessed the site from the east, and Tara hoped to hell they were right, because whatever evidence might have been recovered from the route Tara had used had been obliterated by boots and tires.

The Cypress County Sheriff's Department didn't see many homicides and probably had little to no experience handling anything this big.

"Sheriff, the Bureau would like to help here," Tara said. "We can have an evidence response team on-site within an hour."

He folded his arms over his chest. "I think we got a handle on it."

Just what she'd thought he'd say.

"I'd like to see the crime scene," she told him.

He gave her a hard look that said, *No you wouldn't, little lady*. But Tara stubbornly held his gaze.

"Suit yourself," he said, setting off.

She followed him, with M.J. close behind. They moved through the trees along a path marked by LED traffic flares. The air smelled of damp pine, but as they neared the bright hive of activity everything was overtaken by the sickly smell of death. Ingram stepped aside, and Tara nearly tripped into a forensic photographer crouched on the ground aiming her camera at the body sprawled in the dirt.

Pale face, slack jaw. She looked almost peaceful . . . except for the horrific violence below her neck.

Tara's throat burned.

M.J. lurched back, bumping into a tree. She turned and threw up.

Think, Tara ordered herself. She forced herself to step closer and study the scene.

A five-foot radius around the body had been marked off with metal stakes connected by orange twine. Only an ME assistant in white coveralls operated within the inner perimeter. He knelt beside the victim, jotting notes on a clipboard.

Tara's heart pounded. Her mind whirled. She drew air into her lungs and forced herself to slow down. She felt Ingram's gaze on her and tried to block it out.

Think.

Rigor mortis had passed. Even with the cool weather, she'd been dead at least twelve hours. No obvious bruising on her arms or legs. Her feet were spread apart. Damp leaves clung to her calves. Toenail polish—dark pink. Tara looked at her arms. No visible abrasions, but the left hand was bent at a strange angle.

Tara walked around, careful not to get in the photographer's way as she looked at her face again. The right side was partly covered by a curtain of dark hair.

The photographer scrolled through her camera. "I have what I need here," she told the ME's people. "You guys are good to go."

The one holding the stretcher stepped carefully over the orange twine and crouched down beside the corpse. His partner unfurled a body bag.

Tara watched uneasily. They were taking away the body now, processing the scene, for better or for worse. Whatever chance Tara had had to involve the Bureau at this critical point in the investigation was gone. If that had been her boss's purpose in sending her here, then she'd already failed.

But she sensed there was more to it.

A knot of tension formed in her chest as she cast her gaze around the scene. The fire pit had been surrounded by evidence markers, but here, near the body, there were precious few.

Tara glanced at the deputy watching her sullenly from against the tree. She forced her attention back to the victim. An ME assistant tucked the hands into paper bags, and Tara felt a twinge of relief watching his skilled movements.

Tara checked her watch. Almost two. She turned her gaze toward the dense thicket and shivered, suddenly cold to her bones.

This case was a disaster, and they'd barely started. The circumstances could hardly be worse.

A flash of light above the treetops, followed by a low grumble. Tara tipped her gaze up to the sky.

It started to rain.